DROITS OF THE CROWN

A JOHN PEARCE ADVENTURE

DAVID DONACHIE

McBooks
Press

London • Essex, Connecticut

McBooks
Press

An imprint of Globe Pequot, the trade division of
The Rowman & Littlefield Publishing Group, Inc.
4501 Forbes Blvd., Ste. 200
Lanham, MD 20706
www.rowman.com

Distributed by NATIONAL BOOK NETWORK

British Library Cataloguing in Publication Information available

Library of Congress Cataloging-in-Publication Data
Names: Donachie, David, 1944– author.
Title: Droits of the crown: a John Pearce adventure / David Donachie.
Description: Essex, Connecticut: McBooks Press, [2023] | Series: John Pearce; 18
Identifiers: LCCN 2023005574 (print) | LCCN 2023005575 (ebook) | ISBN 9781493076833
    (hardcover: alk. paper) | ISBN 9781493076840 (epub)
Subjects: LCGFT: Action and adventure fiction. | Sea fiction. | War fiction. | Novels.
Classification: LCC PR6053.O483 D76 2023 (print) | LCC PR6053.O483 (ebook) | DDC
    823/.914—dc23/eng/20230206
LC record available at https://lccn.loc.gov/2023005574
LC ebook record available at https://lccn.loc.gov/2023005575

∞™ The paper used in this publication meets the minimum requirements of American National
Standard for Information Sciences—Permanence of Paper for Printed Library Materials, ANSI/
NISO Z39.48-1992.

CHAPTER ONE

DECEMBER 1796: WITH THE APPROACH OF A NEW YEAR, AT HOME IN England the name of John Pearce lay on the lips of a number of people: with one other it was thoughts, and these were filled with hate. Henry Dundas, Minister of War in the government of William Pitt, was the most commanding of the vocal participants, and he was talking to Samuel Oliphant, a confidential agent he had employed on more than one occasion.

They were discussing the high-value cargo of silver Pearce, in command of HMS *Hazard*, had taken when capturing a Spanish frigate, the *Santa Leocadia*, not that he'd done so alone. He'd been in the company of the frigate HMS *Lively*, under her aristocratic and well-connected captain, Lord Langholm, this just one of the factors complicating matters in what to do about it.

At the time of the action Spain had still, officially, been part of the coalition of European nations fighting the upheavals unleashed by Revolutionary France. John Pearce and Samuel Oliphant, both engaged in a secret mission on behalf of Dundas, had discovered incontrovertible proof of the Spanish intention to desert its allies and side with the French. The decision had already been taken in Madrid, enshrined in a binding, signed but secret treaty, action only awaiting the arrival of a cargo of silver coming from South America.

'The salts on the Board of Admiralty are in a bit of a bind thanks to Langholm,' Dundas admitted with a wry smile. 'They can't sanction Pearce and court martial him, which a majority are fixated on, without including Langholm in the process.'

'From what I hear, he's done his best to ditch Pearce while covering his own back.'

'He most certainly has, and I'm only able to speculate on the contents. But I'm sure if you were to read it carefully, it would hint at grounds for the Board of Admiralty to exonerate Pearce, no doubt composed with the aim of claiming, should it be forthcoming, half of any prize money. Our noble lord will have based his ability to escape censure on the grounds that, given I'd got an Admiralty pennant for him, Pearce had the power to ignore his orders . . .'

'A fact Langholm acknowledged.'

The look on Dundas's face told Oliphant his employer was unused to being interrupted but there was no verbal rebuke, more an explanation delivered in a weary tone.

'Such a pennant and the freedom it bestows are rarely granted, which even you must be aware of. Trouble is, certain people are now demanding to know why he was sailing under such a rare and unusual flag, indeed, why he had a ship at all.'

'Because of the silver?' Oliphant asked.

'Of course. I doubt Spain betraying its allies would have raised questions as to how the information was acquired. But your silver adds a whole new dimension to the affair.'

The following pensive silence was eloquent enough, foretelling difficulties not hitherto considered. At the demand of Dundas, the navy had reluctantly provided John Pearce with command of the fourteen-gun brig HMS *Hazard*. He and Oliphant had been sent to the French-Spanish border to find out what the Dons were up to since they had made peace, bringing to an end the so-called War of the Pyrenees, a border conflict in which the Spaniards had taken a drubbing.

Added to this was the aforesaid pennant, which allowed Pearce to ignore instructions from superiors, up to and including admirals; necessary, Dundas thought, given he would be sailing through the waters off Brittany. This was an area well policed by the Royal Navy seeking to keep watch on the movements of the French fleet and their main naval base of Brest. The pennant would prevent anyone interfering with the mission or demanding to know what orders they had, which would reveal

Dundas's involvement. Ordinarily nothing to be concerned about, the cargo of silver, valued in excess of two hundred thousand pounds, which the actions of the two naval officers had secured, changed the perception of the mission.

'Has a decision been made about the silver?'

Dundas shook his head. 'Not a decision, but certainly a lot of opinions are being aired about how it should be dealt with. One doing the asking is the Lord Chancellor, who is very unhappy at the notion of the *Santa Leocadia* being declared a prize. He is pushing to have it and its cargo declared droits of the Crown.'

'What does that mean?' asked Oliphant, adding, in response to a raised eyebrow, 'I have a stake in the prize money, not very much of one I'll grant you, but still a worthwhile sum.'

'For the crew, of which I'm assuming you were put down as being part of, it means nothing will come their way. Both ships' captains will get a reward, but it will be to the tune of a couple thousand guineas each, instead of the customary three eighths of the total value.'

'That's robbery.'

Dundas smiled wolfishly. 'Some say it's what we in government do.'

'Can you not stop it,' Oliphant protested.

'I would refrain from doing so on your behalf or, for that matter, Pearce's. You don't go lightly up against the government's top law officer. But I suspect some of my fellow cabinet members will use the case to try and wheedle out what you two were doing gadding about off the coast of our unreliable Spanish ally.'

Oliphant was not tempted to wonder at these kinds of enquiries. Dundas was, by a mile, the most devious politician in the Tory cabinet, a man who shared his secrets only with the prime minister, William Pitt, and even then there were some doubts he was fully open. He also carried the reputation of being the most unprincipled member of the government, using his position to promote his adherents.

Thanks to powers given to him by Pitt, he had the authority to grant sinecures to those who would support him, while employing his wiles to bring down or deny the same to his and the government's political opponents. Since no available post went without a number of competing interests—who would not want a job carrying a government stipend but no actual work or responsibility—he had no difficulty in making enemies. When it came to personal enrichment, of which he was regularly accused, this could rarely be done without someone else suffering deprivation, another reason for any number of people to hate and damn him. There was, Dundas claimed in his more reflective moments, a whole industry intent on bringing him down.

'Given the way Spain has behaved, could you not just tell them?'

Oliphant got a jaundiced look then, even if he had a valid point. Manuel Godoy, the treacherous first minister of Spain and no lover of Britannia, was responsible for the secret treaty with the French. But with matters not going well in Italy and on the Rhine, the loss of Spain and its navy was a serious blow, while its army was now free to attack and besiege Gibraltar, increasing pressure on an overstretched Royal Navy.

'Tell my colleagues I used money from the secret fund to spy on an ally?' Dundas mused. 'Would it not lead them to wonder how much I employed to spy on them?'

'Godoy gave you good grounds for suspicion.'

'You're right. I can justify being mistrustful of Spain, but what you do not see is the dangers of being frank in this. It's bound to set in motion enquiries into all the other places where I've used government funds to ensure the country is not at the mercy of unforeseen developments. To account for all the sums employed on clandestine business would be impossible.'

Or, Samuel Oliphant surmised, *money you might have used to bribe people, as well as all the places where you used the power you hold to shore up party advantage.* Perhaps it was the slightly smug expression these thoughts engendered that turned Dundas to another matter. It was one on which he had previously engaged Oliphant and, for the first time, John Pearce, sending them on a mission which eventually took them to the French capital.

'Which brings to my mind matters in France' was a point not raised with anything approaching satisfaction. 'Despite your glowing report of a lively opposition to the regicides of Paris, I discern, despite the sums expended, no active opposition to their tyranny, and, even worse, there's a chance emerging the French will poke their oar into matters in Ireland, which, I need hardly point out, are bad enough.'

Immediately on the back foot, Oliphant felt it best to look confused, as though he could not understand what Dundas was driving at. He and Pearce had been sent to find and encourage those who wished to reverse the overthrow of the Bourbon monarchy, but matters had not gone as desired, quite the reverse. Yet, arriving back in London before John Pearce, Oliphant, given his own desire for continued employment, had painted a glowing portrait of a strong counter-revolutionary movement just waiting to seize power. Pearce, even knowing it to be highly unlikely, had reluctantly agreed not to question this assessment, achieved more by silence than open collusion.

As to Ireland, trouble had been brewing there ever since the Americans sloughed off the British monarchy, only to seriously deepen after the French Revolution. It had gotten to the point where so-called patriotic leagues were openly parading in armed gatherings, while the more unruly elements were espousing an armed insurrection. Oliphant knew an excuse was required, and one was swiftly produced by a man who was a master of quick thinking, a trait honed by many years of covert activity.

'The French who support a restoration exist in a world of great personal danger, Mr Dundas. I would suggest they will not act, nor put their heads above the parapet, until they're sure they can succeed.'

'Well, they're taking a damn sight too long for my money.'

'Droits of the Crown?' Oliphant asked, desperate to bring matters back to the original nature of the discussion, the present one being very uncomfortable. 'Can the Lord Chancellor's opinion be ignored?'

'We will just have to wait and see,' was the enigmatic and unsatisfactory response.

The other place the name John Pearce was being discussed was in the offices of his prize agent, Alexander Davidson, the other person in the room being Emily Barclay, asked to call, given her very close connection to the man in question.

'I hesitated to bring this matter to your attention, Mrs Barclay, but I do have instructions from Lieutenant Pearce to consult you on any matters requiring a quick decision, one beyond his power to make due to time and distance. Also, in the event of him coming to any harm, you are named as his beneficiary.'

Emily knew what Davidson meant: it was a way of alluding to the possibility Pearce might be killed. She didn't know if she should be angry or grateful, given the trouble she'd gone to in ensuring her relationship with her lover, if not a completely watertight secret, was far from common knowledge and thus not the subject of gossip. As the widowed wife of the late Captain Ralph Barclay, Emily did not want it known she had left her husband many months before he was killed. This might draw people to the conclusion he was not the father of Adam, the son she had borne following her affair with the boy's real father.

Such scandalous behaviour would make her a social pariah and condemn the boy to excoriation through his life, as the product of an adulterous liaison as well as the charge of bastardy. A subject politely ignored in aristocratic circles—there was a whole raft of known illegitimate royal offspring, including half a dozen brats sired by the Duke of Clarence—it was heavily frowned upon in other segments of the populace.

Davidson, who also handled Emily Barclay's own considerable inheritance, would have had to be blind not to make the connection between them, but at least she could rely on his discretion. So she nodded and asked the purpose, then listened to the tale of the *Santa Leocadia*, some details of the battle which had ensued, and what it had carried in its hold. She also heard of the circumstances in which it had been taken, which rendered that taking questionable.

'I have irrefutable evidence a secret treaty of cooperation between France and Spain had already been signed at San Ildefonso.' This producing a look of ignorance, Davidson added, 'It's the Spanish Royal Palace outside Madrid.'

'Which,' Emily pointed out, 'does not explain your asking me to comment on it.'

'I have heard certain members of the government are inclined, given the silver was taken from a country still technically an ally, to claim the value as droits of the Crown.'

'I'm bound to ask how you know this?'

'Mrs Barclay, it is my job to know what is going on in certain quarters, so I can properly look after the interests of my clients.'

'Droits of the Crown you will have to explain.'

'It's a term used in law, which refers to certain customary perquisites, formerly belonging to the office of the Lord High Admiral of England.'

'I was unaware such an office existed.'

'It doesn't and hasn't for over a hundred years. The last holder was King James when he was Duke of York. Now income from such an office goes to the Crown and is paid into the Exchequer. The term "droits," better described in modern terms as "rights," covers a great deal of things such as salvage and flotsam, which are of no concern here. But it does apply to what can be termed treasure. In such a case as the one before us, the government could invoke the clause of a ship seized at sea in error. The question, and it's a pressing one, is should a campaign be launched to fight against such an action, given there are successful precedents.'

'On what grounds?'

'Spain negotiated in secret with the French. The treaty, as I said, was already signed, only awaiting the right circumstances for implementation. We are talking of a country more usually an enemy of Britannia than a friend and one for which the population of Britain has no affection, quite the reverse. To most of our fellow countrymen, the danger posed by the Armada could have been yesterday. It can therefore be posited we are dealing with Iberian treachery, thus the public mood could be raised to outrage, when and if it becomes known the men who held up this act of pure deceit are being denied fair reward.'

Ever practical, Emily asked. 'Would such a campaign be expensive?'

'It's too early to say, but once launched, such things can rapidly escalate out of control.'

'And how much are we talking of? I mean the silver.'

'Something in excess of two hundred thousand pounds. We are speculating, in the case of Lieutenant Pearce, since he was in company with another ship, of him receiving a three-eighth share of half the value, which would be something in the region of twenty-five thousand pounds.'

Emily Barclay could not be open and say why such a sum, truly a fortune, might be the answer to a great number of problems, for both her and the man she loved, but it left her in no doubt what John would want. Given his character, the fight would appeal to him more than the money. Yet to respond too quickly was unwise: she had to be seen to give the matter serious consideration, thus what followed was half a minute of deep reflection. It was resolved with a determined point of view.

'Then it must be co-founded, so you must tell me what steps you intend to take.'

Davidson, who would also gain substantially for a successful claim, likewise took time before answering. 'I propose to begin a public campaign on behalf of Lieutenant Pearce to be granted what is his due, while seeking cooperation with Lord Langholm's prize agents to cover a portion of the costs. Do I have your permission to use the funds I already hold on his account for the purpose?'

'This falls within your instructions?'

Davidson was firm in his reply. 'It does, and you may see them if you wish.'

'I don't see that as necessary, so proceed by all means. And should you require more, you may call upon me to help, discreetly of course.'

If you excluded the number of times he spent mumbling to himself, the third person was not talking about John Pearce. Yet there was rarely a day, and often an hour in the day, when his name did not enter the thinking of the smuggler Franklin Tolland, to produce curses rising to a stream of blasphemy at his present lot. HMS *Ardent*, the ship in which he was confined as a pressed seaman, was pounding up and down the North Sea, in the generally foul December weather. She was part of a blockading fleet tasked with containing the Dutch enemy in their Amsterdam harbour, while also being ready to give battle if the enemy ventured out.

Franklin had been made aware his elder brother, Jaleel, had deserted from HMS *Director* within a week of the event, the news coming through the usual grapevine of boat crews manning their captains' barges. These men bore their charges in an endless round of ship visiting, as commanding officers entertained each other to dinner or to a conference with their admiral.

Given there had been no report of Jaleel being had up, it seemed safe to assume he had got clean away, for which his younger brother felt relieved. Deserting the navy in wartime was a dangerous game, both in getting off the ship and staying free once ashore, there being a cash reward for return. Failure meant being brought back aboard the ship to be, as an example, flogged near to expiry in front of their shipmates. In some cases, where crimes had accompanied a deserter's attempt to escape, it was a rope from the yardarm, with the body left to dangle for days as a warning to the whole fleet.

Franklin Tolland's mind naturally became fixated on what steps Jaleel would take to get him free, for there was no way he would leave his younger sibling to moulder. They had a bond which transcended the mere fact of being kin; if anything, Jaleel had been as much a father as a brother, an easy role to occupy in the absence of a proper parent of either sex. Care had begun when Franklin was still a child and continued until he was old enough to participate in the smuggling by which the brothers had gone on to make a profitable living.

Successful in the business of running contraband over several years, this had all disappeared when they found themselves embroiled with a robbing navy bastard called John Pearce. He had stolen both the ship they owned and its valuable cargo, an act which left Jaleel Tolland consumed with the need for redress above all else. Every penny they possessed was tied up in what had gone missing, so he wanted nothing less than the thief's body, stripped of its flesh over hours of torture, left hanging from a tree.

Yet what was seen as righteous vengeance proved far from simple to bring about, Pearce proving to be a hard man to find and even harder to kill. Twice he had evaded their clutches. Worse, it was down to the same villain that both brothers, as well as the crew of their replacement ship, had ended up as so-called 'volunteers' in Admiral Duncan's North Sea fleet. Even more galling, Pearce had filched the second vessel and its cargo in the process, no doubt to once more sell and line his own pockets.

Not that they had accepted their fate. The original plan to get themselves free had centred on Jaleel's intention to make HMS *Bedford*, the ship into which Pearce had decanted the brothers and their men, so unmanageable and the crew so fractious, it would be forced to return to the River Thames. From there, the possibility existed of either getting ashore or communicating with their financial backer and secret partner in the trade.

A rich London businessman and a member of the Court of Alderman, he had bought them out of naval bondage once already and would do so again for the sake of his own profit. Should he demure, he would be reminded it would also save his own neck from the rope, keeping undisclosed certain bloody acts the Tolland brothers had carried out on his behalf.

To this end they, along with a group of two dozen hard-bargain smugglers, had set out to terrorise the crew of *Bedford*. The first act was to knife and chuck overboard a particularly mouthy bosun's mate, who had made the mistake of using a knotted rope starter on Jaleel, a man with a ferocious temper and no compunction about killing. While the act had to be concealed from authority, it also needed to be made known to their new shipmates so all would be made aware of the price of crossing these new arrivals.

The aim then was to work on the cowed or openly disgruntled lower deck tars, to magnify their grievances, of which they had many, even in a newly built vessel, HMS *Ardent* being no more than six months off the slipway. Discontent was many times more febrile in those in need of repair—ships which had been at sea for years, taking in water through overworked hulls to make winter life, already uncomfortable, a misery.

But the main complaints had no connection to weather or damp. Pay had not risen by as much as a penny farthing in near a hundred and fifty years. Poor victualling made for a disconsolate life, with beef and pork in the barrel often rotten and near inedible; this added, especially at the time of year, to a poor and intermittent supply of anything fresh in the way of greens.

Harsh discipline and excessive flogging by some hard-horse captains could be added to a heady mix of objections, like the need to pay, out of their poor wages, for the clothing necessary to ward off the cold. Then there was the near theft of false purser's weights, which gave fourteen ounces to the pound, not sixteen, on its own enough to render anyone mutinous, especially when it came to the measuring out of tobacco.

Another grievance, which extended to the majority of the seamen in the fleet, who were volunteers not pressed men, was the lack of shore leave. His Majesty's warships were now sheathed with coppered bottoms, so they no longer needed to be regularly brought into the dockyard to have their hulls scraped for barnacles. The concomitant of this was long periods spent at sea and no chance to maintain contact with kith and kin.

Jaleel, in counting all these, had reckoned it was possible, with a ship's company already unhappy, to so work on their gripes that they might be brought to the point where they might refuse to obey their officers. His aim had been thwarted by the *Bedford*'s captain, Sir Thomas Byard, a wily man with a nose for dissent and an even sharper gift when it came to indiscipline. He, with the blessing of Admiral Duncan, had arranged to disperse the Tolland gang throughout the fleet, with a particular aim to separate the brothers from not only their men but each other.

Not as murderous as the now departed Jaleel, Franklin was no slouch when it came to stirring up trouble. Since they'd been separated and sent to different ships, he had sought to carry forward the design of sowing dissension on the lower deck, of the kind to make *Ardent* just as ungovernable. Yet it was slow going, especially at sea, where the greatest concern right now was to stay warm and dry, not easy in a ship often shipping water through its hatches so it was ever damp below decks.

But he also reckoned it was far from wise to rely solely on either this or Jaleel, by some contrivance, getting him free, there being too many imponderables. Off his ship he might be, but did he have freedom of action, was he even still alive and well, had he made contact with Denby Carruthers in London? So Franklin had seen the need to contrive another plan, one based soundly on another's greed.

Where he and his half of the Tolland smuggling crew had come from was no secret, very little was in a battle fleet, so he had a set of tars wary of them as a group. He'd also gone to work on Posner, the ship's purser, sure in the knowledge there was not a purser born who could avoid the label of being an avaricious bastard. The move, at first gentle, played on him being known as no ordinary seaman. So, was it not to be expected, as a long-time and successful smuggler, that he might be the owner of substantial hidden assets? He then dropped a hint of being a fellow with many rich connections.

As a breed, pursers were always wont to claim they lived on the cusp of penury, while it was true they were engaged in chancy business. They provided for the needs of the crew, then indented a Navy Board for reimbursement and they were rarely swift to meet their bill. Thus, self-preservation was built into the system, the first job of a purser being to protect himself from bankruptcy. This he achieved by charging premium prices for everything, down to the provision of wood for stoves and candles for light, both essential at this time of year.

The peak of interest occurred when Franklin referred, without naming him, to his partner in smuggling being a City of London businessman, one who had the power to confer profitable positions on men he could trust. To the ears of Posner, a fellow ever worried about financial security, this was a bait to which he could not fail to respond. Thus Franklin, unlike most and over time, was made welcome in his quarters cum storeroom.

The provision of free tobacco was an inducement to be open about this city gent, but Franklin demurred, only obliging when he sensed rising impatience. Even then, what he revealed was drawn out as he described the activities of Alderman Denby Carruthers, or at least those of which he had some knowledge. He did not mention said alderman was also capable, if not of committing murder, of sanctioning it, as he had in the case of his unfaithful young wife.

Given it was the Tolland brothers who had done the deed on his behalf, they had on Carruthers more than just a common interest in profit. The connection and its possible benefits would have to be carefully employed, but it took no great wit to get Posner to compose a letter, one the purser would either send ashore on the almost daily postal packet or take himself when he went to the naval stores in Harwich to top up his stock.

In Posner's hand it was not subject to being read by an officer prior to delivery, and it was one which would surreptitiously alert Carruthers to his plight. Naturally, it was a missive in which Posner's own sagacity and fitness for advancement had to be emphasised. It suggested all means possible should be employed to get an unnamed Franklin Tolland free, which the purser saw as only fair.

Chapter Two

Lieutenant John Pearce was aware patience was not a virtue with which he was overly endowed and, as of this moment, it was being sorely tested. It seemed an age since he'd been told he was to face a court martial for his actions off Bastia, so to be stuck in an anteroom while other cases, regardless of how trivial, preceded his, amounted to a form of torment. He could only believe the commander-in-chief of the Mediterranean Fleet, who had set up the court and dictated the schedule, would be enjoying any discomfort caused to an officer he manifestly despised.

With him was his first lieutenant, Isaac Hallowell, whose logs, like those of his captain, were available to be examined by the court. One of the tasks of the premier in a ship of war was to keep a record of events so this could be set against that which the captain entered in his own. Under normal circumstances there should have been another lieutenant present, one who would act as an advocate for the defence, but a request from the court for one to step forward had met with a poor response. It was, in fact, no response at all; defending John Pearce was not a task, it seemed, which would stand as a positive mark on anyone's record.

More pressing was the problem facing the ships now at anchor off the Rock of Gibraltar, particularly, as far as John Pearce was concerned, HMS *Hazard*. She lay in too-close proximity to the much larger line-of-battle ships, and they were tugging at their anchor cables in what was fast approaching a severe gale. This regularly took him from his seat to a window of Admiralty House so he could satisfy himself none of these leviathans, if their anchors failed to hold, were likely to smash into what was a far smaller and flimsier vessel.

He had to hope the two subordinates still aboard, Lieutenants Worricker and Macklin, would have men standing by with axes to cut *Hazard*'s cable if the ship was seen to be in danger. With squalls of rain battering the glass, he could only observe, worrying in the fading daylight about weather which appeared to be deteriorating. The increase in the wind strength was made obvious by the various pennants and flags, whipping viciously to and fro from the upper masts of the fleet.

'This is absurd,' Pearce complained, glancing at his pocket watch, which told him the time was half past five. 'It's getting worse and it's getting dark. We should be aboard.'

'With respect sir,' was the soft response, 'we should be anywhere but here.'

Pearce favoured his premier with a smile, albeit an ironic one. He was wondering if Hallowell was more worried about the consequences for his own career over those of his captain, though he was not personally on trial: he had the protection of having acted under orders. But it was not unknown for a first lieutenant to suffer professional opprobrium alongside an arraigned superior, merely by association. This applied even if he had no part in the conception of the action about which they were going to be judged.

Such an attitude could not be held against him, it being nothing to do with loyalty or personal feelings. A successful naval career was a fragile construct, dependent on luck as much as ability and much affected by the amount of interest an officer could muster. With enough of that commodity, ability counted for nothing, which allowed for some very ripe specimens to achieve high rank. The nation, conscious of the peril this could cause, had the corrective of denying them employment.

All started as midshipman, then sat an examination to rise to the rank of lieutenant, from where they would then strive to rise to be 'made post,' which put them on the captain's list. Time would see a fellow rise towards the top and, partly aided by the Grim Reaper and personal good health, he could eventually raise his flag as an admiral. From there, if his luck held and decent postings came his way, lay the route to a possible fortune and a peerage. Entire families could rise to social prominence on the coat-tails of a successful flag officer.

Given the fickle nature of the element on which they plied their trade, to be in the right place at the right time was paramount. The greatest gift of all, one almost guaranteed to see promotions all round, was to be involved in a positive fleet and bloody action, but these were rare. More likely was a single-ship encounter, hopefully in a fight with a better-armed and larger enemy. This was just as uplifting, albeit riskier, though even a gallant loss could add lustre.

It was in a combination of the two which had taken Midshipman Pearce to his present rank, beyond which he reckoned there was little chance of progressing. John Pearce had been promoted by King George without sitting an examination, one designed to ensure candidates had the necessary competence required of a ship's officer who, often in his career, would have sole responsibility for the safety of the ship.

It was a level of skill John Pearce, even if he'd now been at sea for months not years, was far from sure he fully possessed. He had been elevated by an exercise of the royal prerogative, applied as a reward for conspicuous bravery. This had caused outrage throughout the service which, with some notable exceptions, had made his name stink. One person not an exception was Admiral Sir John Jervis, a first-class hater, who had convened this court martial and so arranged matters that now had Pearce twiddling his thumbs.

Jervis's disposition, naturally irascible in any case, was bound to have been made worse by recent events. He'd arrived in Gibraltar to find one of his inferior officers, Rear Admiral Mann, had, without orders, decided to take home himself and four line-of-battle ships, putting at risk Jervis's hope of facing and defeating a combined French and Spanish enemy on equal terms.

To compound his natural choler, a French squadron from Toulon under the command of Admiral Villeneuve had, just the day before this court martial, slipped through the Straits of Gibraltar. They'd taken advantage of a favourable wind, one which, in playing on a lee shore, had made it impossible for Jervis and the fleet he commanded to get out of Gibraltar Bay and mount a pursuit.

The C-in-C had chosen the officers who would make up the court and would have done so with one aim in mind: nothing less than the reversal of what the admiral saw as royal folly, added to unwarranted interference in naval procedures. He would be careful not to say so publicly of course; it would never do to accuse his sovereign of an error of judgement.

But if he could not kick John Pearce out of the service, he would settle for the next best thing: deny him any prospect of employment by so muddying his name he would become even more of a service pariah. Unbeknown to the man about to be tried, he'd already taken, in his letters home, all the steps he could to deny him any reward for the capture of a Spanish silver-carrying frigate.

Did he care about keeping his place was a question Pearce often asked himself. He'd not come into the navy as a volunteer hoping to progress but as an illegally pressed seaman. A stroke of good fortune had granted him his present rank and, much to the chagrin of his peers, this had continued on from the royal blessing. A run of singular circumstances had led him to the command of more than one vessel, to then subsequently see him promoted further to the courtesy rank and position he presently enjoyed: master and commander of HMS *Hazard*, a sleek and fast-sailing fourteen-gun brig.

Now he also had the prospect of serious wealth, but what was to happen as a result of the taking of the *Santa Leocadia* was not germane to this moment. He had long ago decided he would fight to keep his name, whatever baggage it carried, if only out of sheer stubbornness. He might give up the navy one day, but he would not have the choice to do so imposed on him by another.

Both he and Hallowell had been wondering on what was to come since leaving Corsica as Jervis and his line-of-battle ships made their escape from the Mediterranean. It had become a sea no longer safe for a fleet lacking a secure harbour, repair facilities, or guaranteed and regular supplies of fresh foodstuffs, while also being several hundreds of miles away from any prospect of rapid reinforcement. Troops shifted from the northern tip of Corsica, added to a small naval squadron, had been left to hold Elba, the last tenuous link to the struggling coalition forces on the Italian mainland, generally seen as a forlorn hope.

The French, under a rising star called Bonaparte, had the whole of Northern Italy under their thumb. The Austrians were now Britannia's last truly active allies, in what had once been a powerful alliance against the Revolution. They were hanging on by a thread, while Piedmont had already sued for peace and the Bourbon Kingdom of Naples was supine. Ferdinand, the feeble-minded king, had led his army north determined to trounce the French, flags flying and trumpets blaring. Such bravado had not survived contact; indeed the 'brave' sovereign had got home ahead of his shattered forces. Worst of all, perfidious Spain was now an enemy, which left Britain to fight on virtually alone.

The nation could not field the kind of land army to contain a rampant Revolutionary France. The only asset possessed by Britannia, apart from the money to subsidise its allies, lay in its wooden walls. Fleets and squadrons were spread, sometimes very thinly, around the globe to both protect vital trade and contain those determined to disrupt it. In those storm-battered hulls rested national security. Thus, the notion of losing any in quantity could presage disaster for the home islands.

'Lord, I don't know why I'm standing here. It won't do any good.'

Pearce opined this as, aboard the fleet, the great lanterns were being lit, providing more evidence, in their inconsistent and jagged movements, what the cables holding the ships at anchor were having to contend with.

'I would suggest studying your logs for justification, sir, if I did not suspect you have, like myself, been so employed since we left San Fiorenzo Bay.'

'And you would be right, Mr Hallowell. You know as well as I do this whole thing is a contrived farrago. I'm sorry you've been dragged into it.'

'I think, with my Uncle Ben confirmed as a member of the court, I can be more sanguine than you when it comes to judgement of my behaviour.'

'Both our fates might have been enhanced if you'd had the chance to speak with him.'

'I'm sure they would, sir,' Hallowell insisted. 'I trust he would have believed what I told him. And, be assured, I would not have had my concerns placed above those of yourself.'

This brought back how frustrating the voyage to Gibraltar had been, HMS *Hazard*'s orders obliging her to act a sort of back marker to the fleet. Pearce had been charged with keeping an eye out for any French vessels seeking to come up upon the rear of Jervis's lumbering vessels, sailing easy because it was wise to do so. His ships, especially the work-horse seventy-fours, had been many months, in some cases years, in the Mediterranean, so were thus sorely in need of repair.

Yet they were still formidable weapons of war, handled by well-worked-up crews, so the notion the enemy would come out from Toulon and seek to engage them was held to be unlikely. Every time they had done so these last two years, on the sight of a British pennant they'd put up their helms and run for safety, losing ships in the determined pursuits which followed.

Likewise, the Spanish. When the fast-sailing frigates investigated Port Mahon, their fleet base in Minorca, they found it bereft of capital ships. The vessels so recently berthed there had departed, some said fled, and at some time they must join with their confreres based at the Atlantic port of Cadiz. This should give them a numerical advantage if it came to a battle, one which was inevitable if Jervis decided to blockade the port, a commercial lifeline to Madrid.

Pearce had no doubt the idea of placing him behind the fleet was deliberate. It made impossible any contact with the few captains they might persuade to be sympathetic to their plight once the true facts were explained. It included men who might make representations on their behalf, like Hallowell's Uncle Ben. Also, Horatio Nelson, who'd never shown Pearce any hint of malevolence. There had been a hope he too would be part of the court, but this had proved not to be. Benjamin Hallowell, in command of HMS *Courageux*, was, but would he act to protect his nephew from suffering opprobrium and risk the ire of his admiral? There was no way of knowing.

It was scarce possible to stand and look at the scene before him and not let his mind wander to concerns which had nothing to do with the navy, moored ships, or the state of the weather. Not in any way confined, prior to this day, he'd been able to visit and talk, as well as drink and eat, with the governor of Gibraltar. Sir David Rose, despite being a very busy man, much concerned with the defence of the Rock, which he knew would be subject to siege at some time in the not-too-distant future, was very fond of both company and John Pearce.

Meeting with a man he esteemed, Pearce had been immediately appraised of the value of the silver he and Captain, Lord Langholm had taken out of the *Santa Leocadia*. Assessed at being in excess of two hundred thousand pounds, variable because of the assay value on the London exchange. Deemed to be prize money, half would belong to Pearce and his crew, with his personal share three eighths of the sum.

Still, as Sir David had stressed and Pearce knew, there was many a slip betwixt cup and lip. With the capture taking place before war was declared, it was moot if it would be so labelled. It could, in fact, lead to both he and Langholm being censured for acting prematurely and denied a penny. So, it was a prospect best not lingered upon, an attitude he had encouraged aboard ship; the notion to talk of it risked tempting providence.

Then there was his relationship with his lover, Emily Barclay, and what would happen in the future to both them and their infant son. The complications inherent in their differing views on what mattered in terms of appearances stood as a bar to a happy shared existence. Would it be changed by either events this day or what had happened with that cargo of silver?

Would Emily come to see his point of view, which was simply stated? John Pearce's upbringing had inured him against having any care about the opinions of others when it came to what was socially acceptable. In this he had imbibed the views of his radical orator father, Adam: that those who set the tone of society tended towards a high degree of hypocrisy. They evinced more interest in maintaining their comfort than any real concern for the fate of others, certainly when it came to their poorer brethren.

The service was full of people who reflected the views of the milieu from which they sprang. Officers of all ranks mouthed platitudes in matters of religion and proper behaviour while casually permitting egregious conduct in their own. When Pearce reflected on the probity of some of the people he'd been obliged to serve with, either alongside or as an inferior, it was impossible not to reflect, with a hint of inappropriate pride, that he was, perhaps, more honest than the majority.

Being in something of a reverie, it was some time before what was happening before his distracted gaze registered. The way one of those great ship's lanterns was now moving so far and so fast, it appeared the vessel which had them mounted had suffered what he had feared. Just as he was about to call Hallowell over to the window as witness, the door to the anteroom burst open to admit a harassed, dripping wet youngster in oilskins. On seeing Pearce, clearly a superior, he blurted out his message.

'*Courageux* has dragged her stern anchor, sir.'

'How do you know it's *Courageux*?' was posed by Hallowell as he shot to his feet.

'I was in charge of the captain's launch, sir. He ordered me to watch her and report to him if anything happened. Reckon he feared for her with the glass falling so fast and us short in the wardroom.'

'He was wise to do so,' Pearce replied, wondering at the meaning of the last part of the sentence.

'We must tell my uncle,' Hallowell insisted. 'He'll want to get aboard and see her safe.'

'And there's only one way to do it,' Pearce responded, striding towards the door to the chamber in which the court was sitting. 'Follow me, boy.'

Leaving a trail of rainwater on the polished floor, the midshipman did as he was asked, probably unaware the man who'd issued the command was about to break a cardinal rule and would include him in the transgression. There was no sense of discretion as Pearce pushed the door open, he quick enough with a hand to arrest the movement of a marine guard's musket seeking to prevent entry. It was then he realised he had no idea whom to address, never having met the man he had come to warn, so he just spoke to the entire room.

'Captain Hallowell, your ship is in grave danger.'

The scene before him was frozen like a tableau. The five senior officers in their best uniforms—only one of whom he recognised, a fellow called Truscott—sat at the green baize covered table, palpably shocked by the interruption. So were the advocates for and against those being examined, the clerks recording what was said, along with those sitting as spectators, which included, at the back of the room, Sir John Jervis.

It was Isaac Hallowell who pushed the midshipman into the room, no doubt aware the words from him could bear more weight than they would from a stranger. This and the use of his name brought the man required out of his chair, a tall and imposing fellow, slightly balding but with a steady gaze.

'Stern anchor's gone, sir,' the boy gasped, still out of breath from his running. 'Not sure the fore anchor will hold with the weather worse now.'

'You're sure, Mr Liversidge?'

'No doubt about it, sir.'

'Permission to look to the safety of my ship, sir.'

The evidence of his American upbringing, as well as his concern, was very evident in his voice, and there was no doubt as to whom the question was addressed.

'Denied,' Jervis growled. 'If you have a competent crew, they have no need of you to do what is required.'

'Thanks to a bout of serious oyster poisoning, I am short on officers to command them, sir, a fact I have communicated to you before today. Since they are being cared for ashore, I feel I must repeat the request.'

'And I must point out my response.' The Jervis gaze shifted from Hallowell to the figure part-filling the doorway. 'There is much pressing business to transact here today, and it cannot be set aside.'

'I—'

'Sit down, sir,' was an irritated bark. 'And those with no business in the room at present, get out at once. Especially you, Pearce, given you, yourself, are about to be brought before this very court.'

It was impossible not to take note of the reaction of the captains who would act as judges. Benjamin Hallowell was naturally furious and struggling to hide it. One at the far end of the table was nodding in agreement at Jervis's order, though not vigorously. Commodore Truscott sat in the centre fuming, hardly surprising given his regard for the man in the doorway being somewhere below that of the admiral. But it was the other two who drew the interest of John Pearce, demonstrating contrasting levels of disapproval, one brief and hurriedly covered up, no doubt from fear of crossing Jervis, the other more evident and sustained.

Jervis shouted once more for the interloper to get out, the marine moving to press his musket across the intruder's breast. Before he and the mid were ushered through the door, Pearce exchanged another glance with the officer the lad had come to warn, noticing how his anger had not abated and that he was doing little to disguise the fact. This got him an uncompromising response from Jervis, who chose to address the youngster.

'You have a boat, Mr . . . , I mean you, boy.'

'Liversidge, sir, senior midshipman.'

'Then let us get you back aboard so your premier will know he has to act as best he can.'

'He's been laid low, sir,' the boy replied. 'As is half the wardroom. Third had the deck when we left, but the premier has sent word from his quarters to say he would rise to the challenge if required.'

'The point I made, Admiral,' came from the ship's captain.

'Which I took on board, sir, and it does not change my opinion. Tell your third, boy, he must look to the needs of the ship, and he must do so, if necessary, as the senior officer.'

'I'll help you deliver the message, Mr Liversidge,' said Pearce as Benjamin Hallowell emitted an audible grunt.

'Permission to join you, sir?' asked *Hazard*'s first lieutenant. In response to the look this received, he added softly, 'Helping to secure my uncle's ship might sit well with the court. I'm sure it will with him.'

'Good thinking,' Pearce responded, aware his premier had arrived at the same conclusion as he, a somewhat disreputable one if properly examined, enough to slightly redden his cheeks. He grabbed his boat cloak and hat just ahead of Hallowell.

'Lead on, Mr Liversidge. Let's try to get aboard and see what assistance we can provide.'

'*Hazard*, sir,' was imparted as they hurried out of the room.

'There are two very good seamen aboard her, Mr Hallowell, and a competent crew. Worricker and Macklin might do a better job of salvation than me, but if you wish to return aboard . . .'

'I will stay with you, sir. Fate has proffered something which could be to advantage.'

Pearce nearly replied, *My thinking precisely*, but kept the thought to himself.

To exit Admiralty House was to kill all conversation. The wind was buffeting now, and with it came driving rain, so it was heads down and hands firmly on hats. Then there was the need for careful progress downhill on the wet cobbles, with only partial relief provided by the protection of an occasional building. Pearce, even if he knew the route to the quayside, let the midshipman lead the way, for he knew where lay his boat.

Conversation was difficult, but enough was possible to explain the stated shortage of officers, this due to the aforesaid meal of oysters which had decimated the wardroom and filled the onshore lazaretto. This included the ship's master, three of the ship's six lieutenants, as well as the doctor who'd been too ill to look after them. The premier, also struck down, had stayed aboard and claimed to have partially recovered, but Liversidge reckoned him far from fully as fit as he would need to be.

CHAPTER THREE

To come out and face the open sea was to feel the full force of wind and weather. They also found a boat crew sheltering in a warehouse doorway, with one poor soul left behind to make sure the painter holding the launch to the quay didn't part. Liversidge, with a degree of authority belying his age, ordered them back aboard. Pearce and Hallowell followed, subject to the odd less-than-friendly glance from his men. They were far from happy to be swapping the security of the shore for the surging waters of the bay while being saddled with the addition of two strange blue coats in the thwarts.

'You have a fix on *Courageux?*' the midshipman shouted to the fellow who had to be the coxswain.

'Can't miss her, Mr Liversidge, what with her lanterns dancing a jig.'

'Well haul away. For she will need every hand to make her safe.'

This conversation, taking part at high volume, was interrupted as Hallowell's mouth came close to Pearce's ear. 'What do you intend, sir?'

It took a like position to reply. 'To offer help, what else?'

'Which they may not appreciate.'

About to say whyever not, Pearce realised what Hallowell was driving at. While assistance was always welcome in such situations, this might not be extended to him. It was too late to do anything about it, but he was grateful to be reminded of what he had not thought of himself. This came with the added opinion that, once aboard, anyone who objected to his presence would just have to lump it.

Just getting alongside the seventy-four was hard enough, but it paled into insignificance given the difficulties of actually getting aboard. *Courageux* was not only being swung about on its one remaining anchor, but it was also subject to the rise and fall of significant rollers. These might be nothing like those which would be faced on open water, but they were still enough to make the deck lurch alarmingly. It was necessary to stand off until the wind took the bulk of the ship round, till they were in the lee of the hull, which eased the motion in the launch, allowing the coxswain to close with the still-rigged gangplank leading to the entry port.

It was fortuitous for Pearce and Hallowell they got on this when they did, for it was in the process of being hauled up, likewise the entry port, just about to be closed off. In doing so they left Liversidge in command of his boat, for there was no way to get it inboard given such conditions. This fact was made plain by a fellow on deck using a speaking trumpet, ordering the mid to stand off and get astern of the ship.

'Sir,' Pearce said once aboard, hat raised to a sodden fellow lieutenant, temporarily on a main deck, where the exterior noises were muted and the low light emphasised a very sallow complexion.

'It falls to me to inform you Captain Hallowell will not be able to assist in doing whatever is necessary to save his ship. Admiral Jervis has forbidden him to forgo his present duty on the court.'

'Damn the man, does he not know our situation?' was an outburst quickly covered for fear of it being reported. 'He is of course quite correct to do so. And you are, sir?'

'Lieutenant Pearce, HMS *Hazard,* and I am lucky to be accompanied by Captain Hallowell's nephew of the same name. We came to see if we can be of assistance.'

This got Isaac Hallowell a searching look, followed by, 'Grateful, sir, for we are damn short of officers.'

Anything he wanted to add was interrupted by a sergeant of marines coming to report, speaking as he did so, 'Spirit room secured, sir. I've put four men on it, and their weapons are loaded.'

'Quarterdeck, gentlemen,' was the reply as he moved swiftly away, 'for nothing will serve us here.'

'An introduction would help, sir,' Pearce called out in his wake.

'Burrows, premier,' was shouted over his shoulder as he hauled himself up the companionway.

This brought them back out to face the elements, with the driving rain now blowing right into their faces, causing all to pull forward their hats once more and lower their heads. Burrows turned to face Pearce and Hallowell, coming close to impart his message.

'We are seeking to get an anchor over the stern, Mr Pearce, a task requiring supervision. If you and Mr Hallowell could aid what is being overseen by a fairly green midshipman, I'd be grateful.'

'The anchor is ready?'

'Captain Hallowell had the foresight to order one fetched on deck afore he left the ship.'

'It may be easier in the lee of the stern.'

'For which I pray,' Burrows replied. 'But I fear for our bow anchor in this wind, even if we do succeed. I must risk getting some canvas ready, for without it we will be in dire straits if that fails to hold.'

Pearce was well aware of the risk so mentioned. The addition of any set sails, even with the yards swung right round to decrease the pressure, would increase the effect of wind and tide on the remaining anchor.

'Then see to your duty, sir, and we will seek to carry out what you require.'

Half turned away, Burrows turned back and asked. 'Pearce, you say?'

'The very same, Mr Burrows.'

There was little to discern from the look which followed, or the shrug with which it was accompanied. The man went forward calling for the main course to be loosed, an order which sent the topmen up the shrouds regardless of what dangers they faced. Pearce and Hallowell were off in the other direction, finding a party just about to haul on a whip to which was attached a spare anchor.

It would have been easy, indeed expected, to stand off and watch, but having served before the mast, John Pearce went to aid in the pulling without giving the act a second thought. This left Hallowell to explain to the young midshipman in charge, with cupped hands to his ear, what they were about. Once the anchor was clear of the bulwarks, the spar holding the line on a double block was spun out to sit over the waiting boat. This, as Pearce had observed and expected, was benefiting from being sheltered by the bulk of the hull.

If it eased the effect of the wind, it did nothing to settle the sea, which was surging by to create an eddy around the rudder, making it difficult to hold the cutter steady as a thick cable was paid out through the hawsehole. At the same time, the anchor was lowered till it could be gingerly laid across the thwarts, the rowers moving forward to compensate for the weight.

Liversidge had brought the launch astern to assist and there followed a most difficult task: to attach a thick cable to the ring by making an anchor hitch. So thick was the cable, this required, even on a stable deck and dry weather, the use of marlinspikes, mallets, and sheer brute muscle.

What followed, when this was achieved, was a seriously complicated manoeuvre which required careful timing, not helped by the news from Burrows, sent by a powder monkey, that two other seventy-fours had either dragged their anchors or cut their cables. It was suspected the latter had occurred on the one identified as HMS *Culloden*, her name known by the mere fact of her location. Having lain near *Courageux*, there seemed a possible danger of collision from a like-sized vessel, now possibly out of control.

The cutter pulled clear to take up a position off the stern, oars employed with great difficulty to keep the boat in a fixed spot and even more as the cable was paid out, which took the cutter back out into the heavily disturbed sea. Beneath their feet and amidships of the two Hazards, unseen men were preparing to work the capstan, to which was attached another cable controlling the bow anchor. This would be carefully, and by one pawl at a time, hauled in to give the new stern anchor a chance to bite.

Clearly Burrows trusted him and Hallowell to call out for the new stern anchor to be dropped overboard; either that or he was too busy or too weary to oversee the act. Pearce, having acquired a speaking trumpet, and at what he could only hope was enough distance, sent out the call to ship the article into the water. This was a far from easy task on a floating platform and one, badly executed, which could see the whole crew of the cutter tipped into the sea.

Whoever was coxing the boat knew his stuff, for he had it swung round to take the waves bow on. Then he waited till a roller ran under his keel to lift the prow before issuing an order to heave the anchor over-board. Not that any of this was audible: the wind was too strong for the voice to carry, while it was barely visible, even as the rain began to ease.

Word was sent to be ready to employ the capstan, so now the hope was simple: that one of the flukes off the stern, hauled along the seabed, would sink into the soft sand and take hold. This had all eyes on the cable to see if the sunken section would begin to lift itself clear. It groaned as it rubbed against the gammoning of the hawsehole but seemed not to rise, so it was as if time stood still for John Pearce. But soon Hallowell yelled, pointing to the way it was fractionally lifting from the water.

'Forward to Mr Burrows, lad,' Pearce called to the midshipman who'd been in charge until they appeared. 'Tell him we have purchase, but I would reckon not much. The seabed hereabouts is not the best.'

'He will need to go very easy on the bow anchor, sir,' Hallowell opined.

'Of which I do not doubt he's aware. Also, I sense the wind is not easing but growing stronger, which will not improve our situation. If I were a God-fearing man, I would pray it holds.'

'Would your man O'Hagan were present with us then.'

Pearce saw this for what it was; a jest and a welcome one, which was enough to produce a laugh as he contemplated the ways of his Irish friend. 'He would certainly issue enough supplications to cover us all.'

It was tense, watching as the cable slowly rose, to the point where it was at risk of being dragged by the minimal motion of the forward pull, the returned mid sent running once more to tell Burrows to desist, which he did and quickly. This left *Courageux* stationary, if you could use such a word when she was being severely rocked by the water running under her keel.

It was that which did for their efforts: not the myth of the seventh wave being the largest, but a truism. The impossible-to-account-for combination of wind, tide, and the seabed producing a mass of water greater than the average run of even a very disturbed sea. The higher wave thudded into the bows and lifted them, which put too much strain on the bow anchor, the result obvious to those watching anxiously; the fact, the sodden cable sinking into the water.

Burrows, being one of that number, was quick to react, calling, as the bows were pushed round by the wind, for the main course to be let loose and sheeted home; those orders issued as he came to take up his position on the quarterdeck. It was equally obvious to Pearce and Hallowell what had happened, the effect on a stern anchor cable lifting until it became taut before it too pulled itself free to become a drag on the ship.

Pearce didn't linger either as, with Hallowell on his heels, he went to join Burrows, standing by the men on the wheel, seeking to bring *Courageux* round so her canvas could take the wind. This was left flapping until the course was set, at which point he ordered the yards to be swung round and the main course to be sheeted home. At the same time a mass of men, unsupervised by any blue coat, were working to make effective the foresail and jib.

The effect was immediate as the seventy-four slowly began to move, every timber creaking as the hundreds of tons of wood, metal, humans, and stores began to gain a modicum of forward movement. This did nothing to ease the problems; if anything it multiplied them, for the ship was in the midst of a fleet, at serious risk of colliding with her compatriots. This had Burrows immediately reduce the area of drawing canvas so he could exert some control over her course.

Never sure of his own competence as a seaman, John Pearce was impressed by the calm way the man in command, clearly not fully recovered from his bout of food poisoning, went about his business in what was poor visibility. This took, as well, a crew in the hundreds, who rushed to carry out the necessary orders in what was an exhausting series of manoeuvres with an attitude born of long service.

In a series of panic-induced movements, Burrows reduced and increased sail as the situation demanded, sometimes spinning the rudder through its entire arc to gain a minuscule change of course. If it was hard to watch, it was ten times so for those required to carry out each act, with the odd tar dropping to the deck through sheer fatigue.

All Burrows had to begin with were the lights of the Rock itself, plus those on other decks to tell him what to avoid, gradually made easier as the rain stopped and the sky partially cleared. Wiser captains, apprehending danger and taking no chances on scraps of moonlight, began to send up blue lights which, even quickly blown away on the wind, provided a degree of certainty as to the required route to safety.

If disaster threatened, and it did, it was avoided, quite often by a whisker, being marginally aided by heavy fending off from the decks of *Courageux*, accompanied by the same from threatened vessels. Even a leviathan responded a fraction to such pressure on its hull, while luck at least ensured they came nowhere near the other vessels now drifting helplessly, according to what little could be seen.

Both John Pearce and Isaac Hallowell were fully employed, dashing, like everyone with authority aboard, to oversee the reefing and sheeting home of sails, as well as the opposite: the task of getting the right canvas in place to fit the immediate needs. Thus, HMS *Courageux* backed and filled its way out of the main anchorage, this taking two bells of creeping progress, not that such provided any security.

The next task was to run out the guns, for ahead of them and closing lay a long string of lantern lights illuminating the frontage of the Spanish port of Algeciras, as well as the flickering beacon fires of the bastions lining its shores. If the cannon sited there were themselves invisible, there was no doubting their presence or weight of shot, nor their readiness to fire now that Britannia was at war with Spain. Get too close to what would be forty-two-pounder, land-based cannon, and the result would make it near impossible to avoid sustaining serious damage, so it was necessary to stay out of range.

The wind had strengthened even more, cloud cover bowling in from time to time to obscure the moon, bringing with them more lashing rain. Little choice existed but to make for what could never be called open water, every man in the crew still working flat out, especially the topmen. They had to stay aloft throughout, hanging over the yards to set the topsails, their feet resting on a dripping wet underslung rope as the storm raged around them.

With these on the fore, main, and mizzen, it gave some scope to manoeuvre, allowing Burrows to come about before the range closed, which put the wind on his quarter, taking them out into the narrows of the Gibraltar strait. Movement at least allowed for the ship's boats to be lashed to the stern and the weary people manning them got aboard, not that they were excused from the need to help *Courageux* stay out of danger. They were put to work, young Liversidge included.

The risk of carrying too much canvas for such conditions was soon apparent. It put great strain on the masts, so sail was reduced as soon as they were clear. If it was a respite, it could only be temporary and, called to confer on the sheltered main deck, the man in command laid out their difficulties for officers and midshipmen alike, none of which were a mystery to the former.

Glancing at Hallowell, Pearce was wondering if he shared the same thoughts as his captain; they had volunteered themselves for a situation they had not anticipated. If being in the anchorage was far from safe, the waters into which the wind was raking them were hardly any better. He had to lean forward to hear Burrows, whose voice was far from strong enough to carry far.

'Although not certain of our present position, gentlemen, we are, by my calculations and before the change of watch, going to lack the luxury of sea room. So we will be required to come about into the wind for a short spell, an act which we will no doubt have to repeat several times as the hours go by. I fear we will be in peril until daylight allows us to properly assess our situation.'

If it was close to an admission of the obvious, there was no sneering at such a truism. All knew the Straits of Gibraltar were, at their narrowest point, no more than seven nautical miles wide. The bay from which they had just made their escape stood opposite the Moroccan shore, which was as unfriendly to a ship as anywhere in creation, even more so given it was under the imperial hand of Spain. Consulting his hunter, Pearce noted it was approaching eight of the clock, so the daylight on which Burrows was relying was a very long way off.

'I think you will have observed, as I have, the crew, the topmen in particular, are exhausted, and I do not exclude us either, myself included. Given the time we have been about saving the ship, in effect the whole day, everyone aboard has missed their dinner by several hours. So, it is my intention, in order to lift their spirits, to see the majority of the men fed. I have already sent orders to the cook to get his coppers going.'

About to say he thought it unwise, that a tot of rum might do just as well, Pearce held his tongue, for it was not up to him to decide what to do on a deck not his own. If it had taken every man to keep them safe till now, sending most of them below seemed a poor choice, especially when thick cloud cover had left them once more in darkness.

If they were in deep water, given the way they had jinked out of trouble, Burrows had more or less admitted he was guessing as to their actual position. Even with what now amounted to a handkerchief of canvas set, a glance over the side and the phosphorescence of the disturbed water would show they were still being driven forward, if not at any great pace, this underscored by it now being possible to cast the log.

'Permission to speak, Mr Burrows,' Hallowell asked, with a glance at his own captain, who merely nodded.

'You may,' was a reluctant response.

'Would it not be better to set a course due east with the aim of clearing the Straits?'

'Risking the open Atlantic' was delivered in a rasping whisper and not stated with anything approaching a welcome for the suggestion, driven home by what came next. 'I doubt it will be more comfortable than our present lot.'

'There would, for certain, be no lack of sea room, sir. And, in time, we could perhaps run before the wind without risking the ship.'

'Nor a lack of an enemy, Mr Hallowell. Can I remind you a French squadron sailed through those very waters just a day past; who knows where they are at present, likewise the Spanish fleet. Perhaps they are out there waiting for Admiral Jervis, it being obvious he will achieve nothing anchored off Gibraltar. What if we fall foul of them on our own? I doubt your uncle would thank me for granting them an opportunity to take his ship.'

The pause which followed was merely to make sure the point was understood.

'No, we will get most of the men fed and some of their clothing dried. Then we may consider coming up into the wind so we can seek to stay out in deep water. I anticipate some ten hours of toil and uncertainty, which will not be aided by a lack of vittles.'

This was followed by a direct look at the man who'd posed the question regarding their mood. 'I will readily admit to my own lack of vigour, which I am sure you have noted. I haven't eaten properly for three days and am far from sure, if I do so now, it will stay in my stomach.'

The pause preceded what Pearce was sure was coming.

'If you would take the deck for a spell, Mr Pearce, I would be most grateful, which will allow my officers and mids to likewise get some food down. The topsails are reefed, and I see no need as yet to change this. But you do, of course, have the authority, if you deem it necessary.'

About to decline, given it had not been his original intention, plus he did not want to be responsible for a vessel not his to command, especially one the size of *Courageux*, he was undermined by Isaac Hallowell.

'We will happily share the duty, sir. We did, after all, come to assist.'

This palpable truth being directed at Burrows left his captain with nowhere to go and, with Pearce's agreement being taken as read, the rest of the officers left the deck; he and his premier were, if you excluded the men on the wheel, close to alone on the quarterdeck.

'I wonder how the court martial is going' was said as a way of telling Hallowell he was far from happy.

Chapter Four

If it was eerie being on a near-deserted deck, it was something Pearce and Hallowell had experienced before. The ghostly light provided by the ship's lanterns and the binnacle showed the intermittent squalls, when pulses of sheeting rain were swept over the deck. There was no diminution in the strength of the wind; if anything it was increasing in power, which had the pair grateful the bulk of the poop at their rear afforded them some protection.

If there were supposed to be men available to aid them in any duty which suddenly arose, they were, and they could hardly be blamed for this, seeking a place which provided a similar degree of shelter from the elements. Lookouts had been posted further forward to keep an eye for danger, albeit they would be hampered by the lack of light in these conditions. Even listening for the sound of a storm-battered shore, a common precaution under the circumstances, was hard, given the screaming of the following wind whistling through the rigging.

When no squall rendered such uncomfortable, Pearce would occasionally go forward himself and stare over the side to seek any signs of danger, mainly an indication of waves beginning to break into surf on a shelving seabed. This too was close to futile, since not even a disturbed sea was visible for more than a few yards. Thus, what lay ahead was a mystery in which it was easy to conjure up any number of devils, enough to prompt a desire to act.

'It may be overcautious, Mr Hallowell, but I sense it's time to come about. An opinion?'

'A touch overdue I would suggest, sir.'

There was a dash of pique in the Pearce response. 'If you harbour such a feeling, I'd be obliged if you would speak up. We are in too much danger for reservations on rank.'

'Then can I suggest, sir,' replied a far from abashed Isaac Hallowell, 'it is time to call Mr Burrows on deck. It would be best if the decision came from him, would it not?'

'Quite right. See if you can find someone to take the message.'

'I can go, sir.'

'No, I think it best you and I stay where we are.'

If Hallowell wondered at the reason, John Pearce was not about to enlighten him. It was the very short exchange on coming aboard, when Burrows had name-checked him, and he recalled the look which had accompanied it. If he was unsure of its meaning, he had to consider Burrows would fall into the category of fellow officers to whom his name was anathema. In which case, any deviation from what had been requested was a potential source of further disparagement.

A gun captain sheltering in the lee of his cannon was found and sent below, the response coming not from him but from Midshipman Liversidge, a message to say the ship's officers were near to completing their dinner and all would be on deck shortly.

'I trust you were fully fed,' Pearce enquired, his tone full of irony. 'And no oysters.'

'All down bar the bread-and-butter pudding, sir, which I have been promised will be kept hot for me and, Mr Burrows added, for you and the captain's nephew. I have to say he seems somewhat recovered from his stomach ailment. He is eating his pudding heartily.'

Pearce burst out laughing, even if he felt what he was being told did not warrant such a response. For the premier and his subordinates to be indulging in such a dish under the circumstances bordered on the absurd. If they had to be fed, it should have been with whatever was going, this rapidly wolfed down so they could, in short order, be back on deck.

'I'm curious at what is funny about that, sir.'

The screeching cry of 'Land off the larboard bow' ensured Liversidge never found out. Both Hazards rushed forward, with Pearce ordering the midshipman to get all hands, officers included, on deck at once.

'Topmen first and aloft,' Hallowell added.

Soon, hard by the gammoning on the bowsprit, both noted the change in the sound. It was still hard to hear much, but on top of what existed already came the unmistakable roar of water crashing on to a yet-to-be-visible shore.

'We have to come about immediately,' Pearce yelled, rushing back to the quarterdeck with his premier on his heels.

There was no time to dally and think, there was too much to be done, the manoeuvre required to meet these circumstances being exceedingly tricky at the best of times. They were being blown towards a situation sailors dreaded: a lee shore, and by a wind of a strength to multiply the difficulties. Worse, in shelving waters, the effect of the sea on the hull would increase the speed of approach, adding an extra dimension of peril.

By the time they were back on the quarterdeck, Burrows was there, he and his limited subordinates shouting orders to the crew who, to Pearce, seemed somewhat sluggish in their response. Perhaps it was brought on by a combination of fatigue, being just fed, or too much of the small beer taken aboard at Gibraltar. He hoped it was not fear of certain perdition, the one sentiment almost guaranteed to bring on the drowning they dreaded.

At least the topmen, the youngest of the crew, were as nimble as ever, well on their way to the upper yards where they would, at the right moment, need to loosen the reefs in the topsails, an act which had to be well timed. *Courageux* would be required to come about into a near hurricane strength wind and seek to claw its way out into deeper water against a tidal flow seeking to drive the ship in the opposite direction.

'Mr Pearce, I would ask you and Mr Hallowell to oversee matters on the mizzen. I will ensure you have the right information to act in concert with the setting of the sails on the fore and main.'

If, in the light from the binnacle, Burrows appeared calm and well now, the very picture an officer should present in an emergency, this did not extend to his voice. It was tremulous and one on which Pearce was sure he could smell strong drink, possibly brandy, which prompted a question.

'The spirit room is still secured?'

'Checked it personally, Mr Pearce,' was the reply.

This led to a certain amount of speculation as to how close the check had been, but it was not an odd query at such a time. If the crew of a ship thought all was lost, most had only one desire before the sea took them: to die insensibly drunk. Hence the strong guard on the spirit room, the store for the rum which was the basis of their grog, the officer's wine, plus port and the surgeon's brandy. Should they gain access, they would plunder the stock and become a useless mob, incapable of carrying out the duties necessary to save not only themselves but also those with the faith or strength to resist temptation.

'Mr Liversidge, accompany Mr Pearce and act in support.'

'Aye, aye, sir.'

Greeted by worried glances as they reached the required station, the looks all three received did not inspire much in the way of cheer. This Pearce put down to their being strangers, while few mids like Liversidge were ever afforded much in the way of open respect. He wondered if an attempt at reassurance would help, only to put it aside. The men needed to do their duty, and it was his task to ensure it was carried out as required. This would not be aided by soft words.

In the situation which Burrows now found himself, it was necessary not to act precipitously. Yes, *Courageux* was in great danger, but the move required to get her to possible safety had to be perfect in its coordination. Better to close with the shore for a few more minutes than risk the failure of the required harmonisation.

'Christ,' came one growl from a sailor, barely audible given the surrounding noise. 'Badger's taking his time.'

'Silence there,' was the sharp response from John Pearce.

He needed to hear any order issued, and they came soon, Burrows—or Badger, as the hands clearly named him—using a speaking trumpet to ensure he could be heard. This coincided with the sky clearing to show stars and a quarter moon, the rain ceasing at the same time.

'Stand by to let fly the sheets.' Pearce and Hallowell both acknowledged, with no idea if it carried to the quarterdeck. 'Let fly.'

Out came the marlinspikes as the man on the rope tensed to hold it steady on one last cleat, this released as soon as Pearce was sure of the timing. Now the yards had to be hauled round, with the men aloft getting ready to increase the area of canvas at the moment it was required, while at the same time the rudder was spun fully to change course. *Courageux* very slowly came round side on, to ride what was now surf in a way that made keeping their feet hard for all.

'Sheet home!' followed from Burrows's speaking trumpet.

First, and hopefully, they could hold a course parallel to the shore, but within minutes the manoeuvre would have to be repeated in the hope of getting the bow facing out towards deeper water. Then, with topsails reset and the yards braced right round, the ship would have to claw its way into the wind, progress likely being measured in inches, but if held it should take them clear.

Unfortunately, on the second turn the ship missed stays, perhaps because the wind was too strong or the run of the current made it impossible. It mattered not, for the effect was fatal to any hope of getting clear. *Courageux* was side on to both the wind and the surf, which immediately drove her towards the shore, this closer even than John Pearce had reckoned. The keel soon struck underwater rocks, and this heeled her over on her beam ends so far that the mainmast went by the board in a mass of screaming topmen, flapping canvas, snapping cables, and groaning timber.

Rushing forward, Pearce found it had not fallen square onto the ship, but at an angle which took it over the quarterdeck. The mass of rigging, yards, and spars, all attached to the thick wooden mast, had torn out the decking and smashed into the wheel, while it was also obvious Burrows and God only knew who else were underneath it. There was no time to worry about how to get them out, this brought home by the regularity with which the heavy rollers were driving the seventy-four further into the rockbound shore, in a way which would soon smash the scantlings and begin to flood the lower decks.

Then came the reaction of the crew, many rushing below to do what: find a false sense of safety, retrieve their possessions, or try to get into the spirit room? It mattered not, for being off the deck was not going to aid their chances of survival, while Pearce was unsure he could summon up the authority to impose order. But too many of what remained were running around like headless chickens, yelling obscenities, which achieved nothing.

Courageux heaved over onto her beam end again, even further this time, which sent dozens tumbling into the scuppers. Also, one of the cannon snapped its breechings and came loose, thundering across the deck to take out and maim several poor souls before it smashed through the larboard bulwark. This immediately allowed a surge of the receding spume to wash across the deck.

'She'll be taking in water for sure,' Pearce yelled, hanging, like his premier, on to the hammock nettings as the ship partially righted itself.

'All we can do is get as many men off the ship as we can, sir.'

This was shouted by Hallowell and the words 'as many' were relevant: no ship ever had enough boats to provide succour to its entire crew, in the case of *Courageux* some six hundred souls. Some would always be left to the mercy of what became of their ship, and too often that was to drown. Pearce was frantically examining options, the only conclusion being he had to try to stay calm, not easy to maintain when Liversidge began tugging at his boat cloak, with enough strength to imply he was seeking to get him to pay attention.

'Leave me be, boy.'

'You must look, sir.'

'At what?'

'At the mainmast, sir. It has landed on the shore and provides a means of escape, a bridge of sorts.'

The sound of a pair of gunshots might be faint in the circumstances, but there was no mistaking what they were. It told Pearce the spirit room was under attack and would most certainly be broken into. Should he try to stop it? This was decided by another midshipman staggering towards him, the one who had charge of the anchor party they'd aided on coming aboard. Stopped by the mess of rigging, the lad stood aghast for a moment when he came upon the dislodged mast, as well as where it lay and what that implied. It took a hand shaking his shoulder to get him to speak.

'Marines have been done down, your honour. Some of the men have broken in and got to the rum and brandy. They're like a mob and set to be worse.'

'Then we must treat them as lost,' Pearce responded, manufacturing a coolness he certainly didn't feel. 'What's your name, young fellow?'

'Elliot, sir.'

'The mast, sir.'

Pearce and Hallowell followed Liversidge's pointing finger and saw the boy was right. The lower mast stretching out over the side was intact, and visible was the cap, from which the upper section, held by its gammoning, protruded. More important, at its extremity it was jammed between a jaggle of rocks washed by dying surf, which put whoever could cross it onto near dry land.

'Right, Elliot. You and Liversidge round up as many of the men as you can, the sober ones, and make sure you include the warrants and any of the sawbones patients. If any argue with you, ignore them, for I sense we are not gifted with time. Tell them we have a means of escape and it's their only chance of salvation, but it will only be so if they come here and behave in an orderly fashion. Mr Hallowell, I have no right to ask you to stay and assist in seeing such an evacuation, so if you wish to use the mast first, be my guest.'

'It depresses me, sir, that you think I would do so.'

'I intend no insult, merely you should be given the chance to survive.'

'Which I think you will not take.'

With this sobering thought now stated, the ship heaved on a pounding wave to grind against the immoveable stones, but this time it did not partially refloat, which had Pearce surmising she had taken in so much water it now never would. It also suggested many of the crew would already be trapped below, another factor it was necessary to ignore.

It was only a matter of time before the ship began to break up, which would make more perilous what was already deadly dangerous. But there was one positive: the mast, which had been grinding back and forth as *Courageux* had risen and fallen on the incoming waves, making it a less than wholly secure bridge, was now static.

If Pearce had ever wondered how youngsters, sometimes close to children, could be asked to perform as petty officers, the behaviour of Liversidge and Elliot would dispel it. With commendable coolness they did as they were asked, so the first bodies called to the side were soon arriving. Hallowell ensured no one rushed to save themselves but instead formed an orderly line, not easy on a sloping deck.

Pearce was there to help each onto the great round baulk of wood, watching as some, nimble topmen no doubt, skipped to safety, while others, older and more fearful, inched along with legs dangling over waters so disturbed they promised only a certain end. There was a calmness in John Pearce as he supervised this, with no thought to his own safety, and he assumed Hallowell felt likewise. If you were an officer, it was your duty, and to do otherwise was to invite disgrace.

Luckily *Courageux* had become partially wedged, which curtailed the effect the sea was having on her bulk, making easier the painfully slow task of getting the less fit onto their route of deliverance, in a line shrinking when it should have been growing. With no clear idea of the identity of those he aided, Pearce still knew there were several hundreds more who were either already gone, ignorant of the possibility, or were not even going to try. This came with the knowledge that nothing he could say or do would change matters.

There were hands seeking to get off all along the side, some standing on the hammock nettings, swaying as they sought what did not exist: a break in the chaos below which presented a hope of salvation. Eventually they would go over, yelling a plea to their mother or the Almighty, either of their own volition or because the push of the mass of hopefuls behind them was too great. There they would join those who'd gone ahead and, if by some fluke a few had survived being dashed on the rocks, the numbers now floating face down testified to the poor odds.

There would be even more, men Pearce couldn't see, waiting in the hope that by some miracle, the ship would provide a way to make the shore, the sort of flotsam to which they could cling. They would be matched by those who placed their faith in God to save them, mouthing futile prayers, for they were as prone to a drowning end as unbelievers.

Pearce was down to the last dozen hopefuls when the lower mast parted from the upper section, breaking at the very cap he had seen as holding them together. In doing so it dropped those already seeking to make their way along it into the raging surf, which was so fierce it rendered rescue impossible and survival unlikely. One or two managed to turn and crawl their way back on deck, aided by hands grabbing at their clothing and, in one case, a pigtail.

Only when this was achieved did the truth dawn; those left who'd failed to get ashore, including Pearce, Hallowell, and the two mids, were as trapped as anyone aboard, especially those who could now be heard carousing below. It was on the faces of the last of the line, from what he could see, men of more years than most of the crew, not old but possibly long serving. This had him realise they must have allowed anyone infirm or weak to get ahead of them in the queue.

Turning to relay to the youngsters, trying to find the words to say that probably all hope was gone, Pearce was dumfounded when there was no sight of the pair, boys he had intended would precede him if the mast had stayed intact.

'Well, Mr Hallowell,' he called, 'I'm not usually one to give way to despair, but I fear we are in the steep tub, and our two midshipmen seem to have realised it to be so.'

The cry, in an excited young voice, of 'Mr Pearce, sir,' was repeated three times as, using the ship's side to steady himself, Liversidge made his way to join them, gasping as he came close.

'The launch.' Greeted with incomprehension, he panted out a bit more. 'It's intact and where I last left it, lashed off on double lines astern.'

About to ask if he was certain, Pearce put that aside—he would not have spoken false—to look at what he had available in terms of hands, only to realise it was all he had and there was little he could do about it. A chance presented itself and must be taken.

'Lead the way, Mr Liversidge.'

He then ordered everyone else to follow, which became a staggering line edging along the deck of a ship breaking up under the pressure of the weight of water slamming into its timbers. Taken up onto the poop to join young Elliot, and eventually into the full force of the wind, Pearce looked over the taffrail to see the boat swinging to and fro on a pair of ropes.

By an unintended miracle, one was short enough to keep the boat with water under its keel and away from any rocks, the other of equal length stopping it from going too far in the other direction and dashing itself against the copper on the bottom of the doomed *Courageux*. The problem then became how to, from a position some forty feet in the air, get aboard.

CHAPTER FIVE

JOHN PEARCE WAS LOOKING AT WHAT HE RECKONED TO BE IMPOSSIBLE, with *Courageux* not far off being on its beam ends, the drop from the poop to sea level was too great, never mind the task of getting over the stretch of water between the launch and the ship's hull. He was aware that behind him, the others were waiting for him to tell them what to do; he was having trouble thinking of what to say, this not eased when he was joined by Isaac Hallowell. Yet the presence of his premier and the following conversation sharpened his thinking; he began to reel off a set of suggestions, some nonsense but others well received and, after very little thought, subject to being worth a try.

'It's not without risk, sir, but doing nothing is less attractive.'

Kept hidden from his premier now, as it had been then, was the thought Pearce had harboured when he became aware the mast had broken in two and what it meant: the fact that even if he was a strong swimmer, he had slim means of getting to the shore. He'd looked at the surging spume between the hull and the high-water mark, reasoning it was likely to be as fatal to him as it had been for others who had tried to save themselves.

He might be able to avoid drowning, even in what was a maelstrom, but the water was pounding a shore littered with rocks and boulders, and therein lay the real risk, for not even the strongest swimmer could stay clear of them. To act now, even in a desperate fashion, came as something of a relief as he issued instructions to Hallowell.

'I will go ahead, and you bring up the rear to chivvy people along. I would suggest the acquisition of some tools would be to advantage, also as many lengths of rope as we find. A marlinspike each and an axe might be handy.'

The marlinspike, even in the faint light, visibly raised a Hallowell eyebrow, to which Pearce responded with a growl.

'We will have to traverse the lower deck full of drunken tars, and I doubt the sight of an officer will be welcome. Before proceeding we must ensure everyone knows what we intend, as well as be aware, should they dally or demure, they will be left behind.'

On such a sloping deck, there was little choice to going back the way they came, which at least allowed them to acquire some of what they thought they might need. Once at the spot where the stump of the mainmast no longer offered a way off the ship, the tangled mass of cordage provided the means to get to the main companionway, which would take them down below. It also allowed them to see the foremast had gone by the board as well, taking with it even more of the rigging, its very top lying in the water.

'Get hold of anything you feel will be useful' was his shouted command, quickly obeyed. Before they moved on, everyone had at least a coiled rope over the shoulder and some kind of weapon. Axes they would easily find below, lashed to the beams above the ship's cannon. The sound of raucous singing, clearly audible at the top, rose to a higher lever as, with some difficulty, they descended the steps.

Pearce led the way with the two mids behind him, seeking, he saw as they were greeted by lantern light, to conceal their obvious doubts about where they were heading. Even on a happy ship—and there was no certainty *Courageux* was such an article—resentments festered, so these boys would be reprising those occasions in which they'd upset some of the tougher members of the crew. For Pearce and Hallowell, if trouble threatened, and since they were strangers, it would be a general dislike of officers.

The sound of the pounding waves on the hull was different down below, more like some muffled hammer regularly striking a wooden drum, the thuds sometimes so loud they overbore human vocals. Forced once more to the larboard side, they had to creep along, employing whatever came to hand to make progress towards the stern: mess tables, cannon, and the stored instruments used to work them. Their feet splashed through water already coming up through the planking, while they also had to step over the odd comatose body of a fellow so drunk he would lie in the encroaching sea until he drowned.

As they progressed, Pearce was alert to the looks being aimed in their direction by those few still perceptive enough to take notice of their passing, some seriously unfriendly, most too far gone to care. The wardroom door, when they finally made it, proved a difficult object to get to, Pearce reduced to crawling on hands and knees to reach the handle of the door, which released, opened so wide it crashed into the inner bulkhead.

One by one his party followed, his hands required to bring them over the last few feet and, once all were through the same door, took the strength of several to close. The next task was to use the furniture to bar entry to anyone else; indeed, Pearce was surprised to find it unoccupied, so everything moveable was jammed against it.

The room was lit by a few tallow sconces still showing a flame, as well as the moonlight streaming through the casement windows to rebound off the white enamelled walls, giving the wardroom an eerie quality. Hard to imagine, not long before, here was the place where the ship's officers and certain warrants had been scoffing bread-and-butter pudding. Yet the smell of food faintly lingered, reminding both Pearce and Hallowell of their own empty bellies.

At the rear of the cabin sat the painted cover hiding the head of the rudder which, once removed, would be central to what could loosely be called a plan. It might provide access to the water below in the space necessary for the rudder to work, and Hallowell was put to getting the cover off and assessing if its position would provide what they hoped.

But first Pearce needed, in the company of his mids, to move to the quarter gallery which, along with a row of tiny cabins, housed one much larger, if not anything like roomy. This was the first lieutenant's personal space, holding a desk and a tricked-up cot, these shared with a thirty-two-pounder cannon as well as the luxury of a casement window to provide natural light.

The wind was no help in opening this, even if the hinges were well oiled, but once achieved, the same helped force it fully ajar; indeed, it banged the frame flush to the scantlings, smashing the panes of glass. This exposed them to the full force of the tempest, but a look outside showed how much lower they were in relation to the launch.

This was still pitching up and down on the boiling surf, so hard it was a wonder the lines securing it to the ship held, but at least they were visible and not far off. Pearce reckoned it must also be taking on water as it swayed to and fro, to say nothing of the earlier rain, which would probably mean much serious bailing before it could take much in the way of human cargo.

'There will be a chamber pot in here somewhere; see if you can find it' was his order to the youngsters as he began to strip off his clothing. 'In fact, there will be one in every cabin. If I can get the boat alongside, they will be needed, as will you to employ them.'

The news from Hallowell came as they departed. 'Rudder is set for the last turn, sir, so well round it's right up against the sternpost.'

'Good. I need you to get a line attached to this cannon and one which will hold. If I signal the need, I will have to be hauled back in.'

It was hard for his premier to hide the thought of this being unlikely to succeed. 'You feel it is the only way?'

'I can see no other,' Pearce replied in a morbid tone, 'but if you can, I would welcome it being shared.'

Down to his smalls, barefoot and leaning out to look at what he faced, Pearce realised the first peril was his body being dashed against the hull. This had him call for help to get all the mattresses from the various cots, several of which were lashed together to provide a rough sort of fender, before being passed out to line the side and hopefully serve to keep him from serious injury. The last act was to lash the strong tie around his waist, with his premier voicing another concern.

'It will be near impossible to swim to the boat in such surf.'

'I don't have to. All I need is to get to one of the lines holding the launch and I can use it to drag myself to it.' There was a short pause before he added. 'Mr Hallowell, observe closely how I get on, for if I fail, it will perhaps aid the next person to try.'

There was no need to point out that if it would be a desperate throw, it was one which would have to be attempted; the option to do nothing did not exist. There was no doubt, from the amount of wood floating in the sea, *Courageux* was beginning to break up, and once any serious timber became dislodged, the rest would follow quickly.

'Perhaps someone else should go, sir.'

The laugh which accompanied the reply as Pearce put his hands on the frame of the missing casement was one manufactured to hide his true feelings. 'Not my method of leadership, as I think you know.'

It was a tight fit through the gap, one in which John Pearce risked losing the advantage of his height until he used the wind to stand upright, the pressure, added to one hand on the rim, holding him to the side. He needed to keep his eye on two things: the space between rollers and the nearest taut stretch of rope. If he hit the water as it was breaking, it would toss him about in the same manner as the flotsam being dashed against the hull, another danger he would have to avoid.

If the amount of light was not perfect, the creaming tops of the waves showed clearly, the distance between them condensed in the narrows of the channel between the Spanish and Moroccan shores. Given an alternative, John Pearce would have declined to jump, but it was a choice between what he risked now and the certainty of same within what might be imminent.

There was no time to think about what he would be leaving behind— Emily and his son, the rewards for the Spanish silver—and to do so would not aid his resolve. So it was with the conviction provided by absolute need, he jumped, the coiled line paying out behind him as he did so. The effect of hitting cold water could not be ignored, but he was required to strike out as best he could and immediately, which seemed pathetically ineffective. He dived below the surface, arms working furiously; praying the force of the surf would be reduced when he came back up could only be a wild guess that he would not be hit by the crest of a breaker or a lump of flotsam.

The idea of swimming in any normal fashion was quickly abandoned, so it was a wild kind of doggy paddle he employed, the fact he was not trying to swim into the waves but across them making some progress possible. It would have been impossible to do so anyway, because even seeking to cross the tidal flow kept taking him closer to the side of the crippled seventy-four.

Driven underwater several times, time having lost all meaning, swimming in such a rough sea and wondering if his strength would hold, it seemed a lifetime before he could get to one of the lines and secure himself with a firm grip. This had one added bonus: his pressure on the rope brought the boat towards him as he progressed hand over hand, until his chilled fingers got a grip on one of the tholes to which were lashed the oars. There he hung on for a long time, coughing up the seawater he'd ingested.

Breath somewhat restored, the next problem was to get in without it capsizing. There was no attempt to get over the side; it was hand over hand again till he was hanging on to the transom. Again, he had to use the sea by which he was so threatened as an aid, timing his heave to get his belly onto wood as the surf began to lift the stern, this while his weight held the boat on a nearly level keel.

His prophesy regarding the launch being waterlogged was correct, but thankfully, even with him aboard and the water close to the gunnels as it swayed, it floated, if sluggishly so. Moving carefully to the bow, he detached the line from his body, one which had been kept slack so as not to impede his movements. This he attached in the hope the boat could be hauled in towards the quarter gallery, with him paying out the original lines securing it in order to get it to where it was needed.

Could they see him, a soaked to the skin, pallid individual waving furiously toward the odd glimpse of a pale face in the small cabin, for yelling would do no good. It was only when the line he had attached went taut he knew they had, which set him another task on the original lines securing the boat.

It was a manoeuvre which had to be carefully managed, for to fail to show care would see the launch smashing against its mother ship. The tension on the trio of ropes had to be coordinated inch by inch until it was firmly alongside and secured, with a pair of wardroom mattresses between it and the hull. Now he and Hallowell were able to shout to each other, the first words a demand for chamber pots and the two midshipmen.

'They are lightweights, and anyone of bulk may sink her.'

For boys used to skylarking, what they had to do may have presented fewer fears to them than to a grown man. Edged out, feet planted on the hull, body rigid, they walked down on the ropes provided to join John Pearce with commendable aplomb. Soon all three were bailing, occasionally to no purpose, as the sea, in a sudden heavier body of water, replaced as much as they were chucking overboard. After a bout of furious activity, progress was made, enough for the man soaking and shivering to pronounce himself temporally satisfied.

Hallowell had not been idle while Pearce had been about his risky endeavours. Using the casements lining the stern, a line had been fed round from the one above the rudder to the open-to-the-elements quarter gallery. This was now used to gingerly get a more seaworthy launch round enough for the prow to get into the space between the rudder and the sternpost. This sat partially within the confines of the hull and offered a degree of protection, while the angle at which the ship had jammed to the seabed tended to divert the worst of the wave power.

Here, one of Pearce's ropes could then be fed up to the now open top of the housing. Another was employed to haul him up and into the wardroom. There an exhausted ship's captain ignored the praise of those who had been waiting, dropping to the deck and holding his head in his hands. He was quickly wrapped in towels, with hands working furiously to both dry and warm his shivering body.

They would wonder how hard the task he had set himself had been. But Pearce would never admit how close he had come to failure; he realised now, only the summoning of his last reserves of strength had saved him from giving himself up to the sea.

'Keep the boys bailing,' he gasped.

'One of our party found a flagon of brandy in one of the cabins, sir. I have allowed them a drop, and I suggest you take some too.'

Sat up, back to the rudder top housing, and recovering his breath, the fiery alcohol hitting his stomach acted as an aid to recovery. His uniform was fetched from the quarter gallery and laid by his side.

'A sail?' asked Hallowell when Pearce's breathing had returned to normal. 'In case the wind eases a fraction.'

'I doubt it would serve unless the wind seriously died away,' Pearce replied, voice low for what was something worth careful consideration. 'I reckon it would hamper more than aid us. Also, we would have to find a mast and canvas and then rig it, not artefacts normally found in a wardroom.'

'Which means going on deck, which might alert some of those drunks to the possibility of a way off the ship.'

'Something I had not considered, I must admit, but a telling point; it being a fight, given the numbers, we could not win. If we can get the launch away, we will be carrying as many as she can accommodate. No, I reckon it's oars or nothing. Now be so good as to help me to my feet. I must look through the cabins for some dry smalls.'

'All the sea chests have been opened and anything useful shared out. We found several boat cloaks, which must have belonged to those recovering ashore. I have passed to those wearing the fewest clothing.'

Pearce nodded as he was helped up. 'First we must sort out the best men to man the oars, which I fear will have to include you and I.'

'You need time to recover, sir.'

The banging on the bulkhead door, the sound of several fists, stopped any immediate reply, with neither Pearce nor Hallowell needing to state what must have occurred. The contents of the spirit room were probably exhausted, and those who could still stagger would be looking for more drink to consume. No doubt the captain's cabin and the sickbay had already been ransacked.

'Would that we had it,' Pearce gasped as he hurriedly began to put his uniform on over still-wet undergarments; this, as what sounded like the first axe hit the wood of the bulkhead. 'Start getting everyone into the launch. I doubt we risk less out at sea than we do here.'

The hastily made rope ladder was a godsend, as was the fact that the people who would employ it had not wasted any time. There was a sack of what food had been stored in the wardroom pantry and several bottles of wine in another. Pearce insisted on all the chamber pots being loaded, and not just for bailing.

'Never mind what they were used for before,' Pearce barked. 'If it rains, they can be used to gather water.'

Descending a rope ladder was far from easy, with both officers insisting on being the last aboard, placing themselves by the point at which the drunks were trying to create a gap in the wood through which they could gain entry: thankfully the precaution of piling everything at the door had made it secure.

'Time to go, Mr Hallowell,' Pearce said, 'and please, no objections.'

The order was obeyed, but it was only when he was on the means of escape himself that Pearce realised how little strength he had: his previous exertions had drained him too much. At one point he was hanging on the hemp, his head resting on the cold copper of the pintles holding the elm of the rudder to the oak of the stern post, wondering if he dare trust his weight to his aching arms.

The sound of shouting, an indication the men attacking the bulkhead might be close to getting through, gave him a shot of desperate energy, enough to get him down to where others could take his ankles, then his thighs, to ease him into the now-crowded launch. It took more hands to pass him along and into the thwarts, his protests he must help row the boat ignored. It was Hallowell who issued the command to cast off, just as a bunch of heads appeared above them, screaming obscenities.

The bottles thrown down missed them by inches and had to be ignored, for the problem now was not drunken tars but breaking, dangerous rollers seeking to drive them to certain perdition.

Chapter Six

THE MOMENT FOR MAXIMUM CONCENTRATION IN AN OPEN BOAT WHEN faced with heavy surf comes when the prow meets the water rising just ahead of the breaker. The top of such a powerful wave must be met head on and centre, for the slightest deviation will see the boat overset. It is necessary to ply the oars with maximum force as the prow begins to lift, to then ship them a fraction at the point of foaming spume. They then need to be once more employed, and quickly, for the boat must gain a bit of speed going into the trough so as to be prepared for the next white-topped threat, when the risks repeat themselves.

A still fatigued John Pearce, facing forward and helping with the tiller, clenched his stomach each time this occurred, relying, as did the oarsmen, with their backs to the threat, on the warnings of Isaac Hallowell. He had the task of alerting all to what was soon to be upon them. With the roar of the sea and the moaning of the headwind, this was far from easy, so elaborate hand gestures made as much impact as words.

Alongside a sailor acting as coxswain, Pearce was thankful, indeed lucky, to have before him men who had the requisite skills when it came to handling an oar. The combination managed to get them over the oncoming dangers a dozen times before the launch got out of the surf, to be faced with waves, still dangerous, but nothing as what they'd been through.

Easier to manage, it was possible to make a small degree of progress, using the North Star in a now clear sky as their navigational guide. The sound of the water having become muted allowed the pair in command to talk, the first point from Hallowell being that their course was far from certain.

'We risk a landing on the Iberian coast, sir.'

'We forgot to bring along a compass, Mr Hallowell.'

'How could we be so foolish,' came the reply, one larded with irony, so absurd it caused a relieved Pearce to laugh once more. 'Even more so, I appear to have lost my pocket watch and so have no idea how close we are to daylight.'

'Surely it can't be long. We must have been at our labours half the night.'

'The sky promises us a clear day, so we will have sight of the shore before we seek to land, hopefully off Gibraltar. Now I feel you and I must ply an oar, for those who got us out of danger must be past weary.'

To change rowers was a delicate task, the trim of the launch needing to be kept on an even keel. The two midshipmen, who'd spent the time since leaving the ship bailing, were put to an oar each, the task having previously been too much for such young bodies. Now, with a leavening of adults, their efforts on the sticks were enough to help keep the boat moving forward on the rolling sea, if at no great rate.

The wind was beginning to moderate, but this had little effect on the sea state, which, in terms of comfort and effort required, could be called kinder only because of what they'd just survived. It still demanded the conditions be respected, still had moments when the prow seemed to be seeking to get above their heads; if care was not exercised, the possibility of broaching still threatened.

Pearce had his back to the course now so, with the first hint of daylight in the eastern sky, it fell to the man still on the tiller to call out the sight of what he thought could be a topsail, not necessarily welcome in what were Spanish waters. The prospect of becoming a prisoner of that particular enemy was not something to savour, there being plenty of evidence from previous conflicts regarding the way they treated their wartime prisoners.

While the likes of Pearce, Hallowell, and, at a pinch, the two young midshipmen might, as officers, be exchanged, such did not apply to common sailors. For them it was held to be a life of miserable slavery—as bad as, if not worse than, being taken by Barbary pirates—unless Jervis had a large group of Spanish prisoners with which to trade.

North African corsairs would occasionally sell back their captives, the means provided by the charitable rescue funds which existed in most maritime nations. But not the Dons, smarting from so many defeats, especially at the hands of Albion. Tales abounded of numerous cruelties visited on British captives, never-ending toil accompanied by starvation added to an endless use of the lash. They faced the spectre of death on a whim in the hands of a race known for their cruelty, even to their own.

How many of the crew of *Courageux* had chosen to stay, get drunk, and go down with their ship rather than face such an existence, one which would surely greet those Pearce had helped make their way along that broken mast? Would they, in time, come to curse him for providing a helping hand? It was not a matter to dwell on, he had to decide.

It was as much a duty as a way to allow himself time to think that he ordered the distribution of the food and wine brought from the wardroom, though he counselled going easy on the latter. Not that he had much concern on such a score; the lower deck detested wine, while what passed for the object in the *Courageux* wardroom was not of a quality to invite overconsumption. But food and drink did help to revive the men aboard until he gave the order to head for possible deliverance.

'It will take a more than sharp eye to spot us in these conditions.'

Relieved of his rowing duties, Pearce could only peer forward with the naked eye, a telescope another artefact they had not had a chance to bring along. It took time, and he was not afforded much as the launch topped a wave, to try and pin the nature of the type of craft ahead, which likewise had to be on a crest. He eventually assumed it to be no warship, which had been his hope, perhaps a frigate sent out to look for *Courageux*, one which would find and rescue them. It flew a flag, but due to the wind, this was blowing square on and unidentifiable.

'Two-masted and I rate it too small to carry a threat' was his response when asked by Hallowell what he could see. 'A small trading vessel perhaps. I think we must seek to let him know of our presence, if for no other reason than to fix our position.'

Pearce had to consider that whatever it was, the likelihood of it being Spanish was higher than the hope of it being anything else. If it was some kind of trading vessel, this indicated a small crew, perhaps fewer men, if you included everyone, than he had in the launch. Given they must have survived much the same conditions, a boatload of survivors would not come as a surprise, even to men equally exhausted by their efforts.

'Messrs Hallowell, Elliot, and Liversidge,' Pearce ordered as he removed his uniform jacket, 'please be so good as to remove and hide your blue coats.'

This done, Pearce removed his shirt as well, waving it above his head at the top of the next crest, then waiting for the next before repeating the act. He was sure the rising sun would see it spotted, it being white enough to catch the morning glow.

'He's holding his course,' Pearce called. 'Damn the man.'

'Suspicious he will likely be,' came from the nearest oarsman.

There was no choice but to keep trying, aware the speed of the launch, added to the few times it could be said to be clearly visible, was a poor aid to discovery. Added to which, the course of the ship would take it across his bow, so it would soon be increasing the distance between them.

His efforts grew in frustration as the state of the light increased, so much so that in the rare moments when the ship was in plain sight, he took to cursing whoever had charge of her. He was mid-blaspheme when she slowly began to reduce sail and then start to alter course. The sluggishness of this helped convince Pearce it was a merchant vessel, for any ship of war would make such alterations at a lick.

'No one to speak but me, lads, and if you get a query aimed at you, look as if you don't understand it and respond like a Dutchman. Also, get any weapons you acquired last night out of sight but kept to hand.'

'Are we turning pirate, sir,' asked Hallowell as marlinspikes, axes, and the like were shifted.

'Only if it's necessary.'

The act of closing seemed to take forever, the launch constrained by the sea state, the ship by a rate of sailing which did not point to much in the way of competence. Assuming her being Spanish, this meant communicating in a language he did not have, and he soon found he was not alone. An enquiry to the men aboard producing blank looks, it was going to make what he had in mind difficult—impossible if the approaching captain took any precautions.

Why would he? The odds against it were promising. If the captain was, as suspected, in home waters, he was facing a boatload of distressed sailors after a serious storm, to which he had no doubt reacted by the law of the sea. This demanded a response to those in distress, the very best being done to effect a rescue. Surely, he would anticipate fellow merchant seamen, possibly of the same nationality, men he could carry to his destination port, so the notion of them being fighting sailors might never occur.

The approaching vessel had three gun ports, it had to be assumed on each side, but there was no sign of their lids being lifted, let alone cannon being run out. Why? A crew unaccustomed to firing them, a fear of the sea washing through in a vessel with a low freeboard? Sometimes on such vessels, they were more for show than use because they lacked the men, for reasons of expense, to both work them and sail the ship.

'Mr Elliot, how was the crew of *Courageux* when it came to boarding?'

'Hard to say, sir. We were in a hot action off Genoa, but never got close enough to the enemy to test our skills.'

Pearce called out, addressing everyone in the boat. 'Unless he's our fellow countryman, which I take leave to doubt, we are going to have to try to take possession of this fellow, and it can't be done by subterfuge. If they have cannon, they show no sign of employing them.'

'Might have muskets, your honour,' the fellow on the tiller suggested. 'An' within ten feet, it be hard to miss.'

'Which I set against being taken into a Spanish port.' There was no need to elaborate: the lengths they'd gone to in the last twelve hours to avoid such a fate was enough. 'If there are muskets, get prepared to grab the barrels or chuck an axe at someone's head.'

'We could throw the last of the wine bottles to put them off,' suggested Midshipman Elliot.

'Sound thinking, young man, get them out and distributed,' was said as a sop to the boy, a way of providing encouragement rather than the notion it would do much good. 'Everyone is to lie over your oars as we come alongside, looking as though you are totally exhausted.'

'Won't need much playacting, your honour,' was one response.

61

'Silence there,' called Liversidge, which was subject, in response, to a loud raspberry, though from an unknown source.

Seeing him about to react, Pearce intervened. 'I think our recent shared experience allows for a certain relaxation on discipline, Mr Liversidge. We have a difficult and uncertain task ahead so I, for one, can live with a little freedom for a man to speak his mind. Now, coxswain, put us below the catted anchor if you can, for that will be our aid to boarding the ship.'

The act of closing seemed interminably slow, but Pearce was much impressed with the way the men aboard took on the roles he had asked them to perform without a word from him. He knew tars loved playacting, a form of behaviour often visited upon officers, it being their way of asserting themselves while avoiding punishment for doing so, telling those in command they were not without spirit.

Most captains with sense accepted occasionally being gently guyed as part of the price of a happy and efficient vessel. Those who didn't were akin to tyrants, like the man who had pressed him and his friends into the navy. There was another point to wonder on, the power of his rank. Not once had those accompanying him questioned his right to make decisions, to which, the man thinking on it, was to repose faith where it was not wholly merited.

From a vessel higher in the water, and especially from anyone watching from the mainmast cap, the interior of the launch was plain to see. So at times, an oarsman would seemingly collapse, to be hauled off the stick while those free to do so sought to revive him, another taking the oar. Such games made slow progress glacial, but Pearce saw it as no hindrance, he with his own head bent for much of the time. This was leavened with less than energetic shirt waving, which allowed for a short and quick appreciation of what they might face.

The conclusion that they could not be facing much of a foe was made up of several small observations: the way the ship was sailing and the small number of faces appearing to cast an eye over the approaching boat before going back to their duties, which indicated a less than numerous crew. Also the gun ports stayed shut, with no sign of any other precautions being taken to account for potential trickery. Then there was the sea state, moderating now as the effect of the recent storm eased.

It was far from what could be called calm, but not so heavy as to prevent what he was now toying with, aware that the element of surprise, if positively executed, could compensate for any number of deficiencies he and the men who deferred to him might encounter. But before he could decide positively, he needed to run his idea past Isaac Hallowell, called from the prow to his side for a quiet word.

'I would say either course has risks, sir.'

'But are the men, or you and I for that matter, up to it?'

'Given what we have gone through and how far we've come, I would not fear to trust them.'

'Then quiet orders as you return to your place. And the more noise we can muster the better.'

It was ridiculously easy, Pearce waiting until the launch was less than ten feet from the side of the trading vessel. The reaction to his shout was immediate; seemingly dog-tired oarsmen suddenly turned into men of action as they dipped and hauled on the blades. The launch clattered into the side of the ship right under the catted anchor as required, the boat hook it carried immediately employed to get purchase and keep the launch stable.

As soon as the launch rose while the ship dipped, most of the crew, oars abandoned, leapt for the low bulwark, screaming a fate to the people aboard that required no translation. Those who'd been looking over the side, scruffy individuals, and this probably included the captain, disappeared immediately, none staying to contest the assault. So when John Pearce got on deck, it was to find he commanded the only occupants.

'Shall I cut down the flag, sir?' Hallowell asked, his face alight with either humour or excitement, probably both.

'I doubt it to be necessary. Likewise, I have good reason to believe there will be no sword to surrender.'

From the deck Pearce could see land both to the north and south, hazy shorelines with nothing particular to distinguish them, no Rock of Gibraltar to the north or Mons Abbas to the south; this as the two mids, sent to find the crew, returned on deck.

'Seems they've locked themselves in the captain's cabin, sir,' reported Liversidge. 'Door's barred and they don't respond.'

'Then best let me try and persuade them we mean no harm.'

'Do we not, sir?'

'If you can see a point in such, Mr Liversidge, I cannot. Meanwhile, Mr Elliot, if there's a telescope by the wheel, go aloft and see if you can catch sight of Gibraltar. We're still in the straits, so it can't be far off.'

'East or west, sir?'

'Both. Only the deities know how far we've drifted.'

Running nimbly up the ratlines, now with a telescope tucked in his waistband, Elliot yelled the good news seconds after his first sweep. Such a feature as the Rock was, if you followed the boy's finger to the north-west, there was no need look for charts or query the ship's captain.

It was pleasant to take station by the wheel and issue the orders which would take them there, the sails necessary to do so set with a speed which, had he come up on to the deck, would have shamed the man who'd had the command, as well as his slovenly crew. With the wind now in the same quadrant as the Rock, it was tack after tack to close with the bay, Pearce ordering the man on the wheel to make for a spot equidistant between Gibraltar and Algeciras. At which point he called everyone together.

'Time to take to the launch once more.'

The surprise was palpable: no ship once taken by the navy was ever handed back.

'The fellow skulking in his cabin, along with those he commands, acted to save us and, even if it is seen as the law of the sea, we have to reckon there are many who might have left us to our oars.'

'Saintly right enough' was the response from one tar, Pearce recognising it as the voice Liversidge had sought to silence.

'So it would not be that to deny the fellow his livelihood and perhaps condemn him and his crew to a life of captivity for what cannot be a prize of much value. Let him have his ship back, and he can sail it into Algeciras or not, as he pleases. We are close enough to boat back to the fleet, where we will have the sorry task of reporting the loss of the *Courageux*, quite possibly with all hands bar we few.'

One or two crossed themselves then, with Pearce thinking what seemed a lifetime from the point of coming aboard the seventy-four was, judging by the position of the sun, less than one whole day.

The amount of noise made getting back into the launch was not enough to tempt anyone out of their self-imposed confinement, so Pearce had it rowed past the stern windows, where he stood and waved, hoping it would be seen for what it was: gratitude. It was an act replicated by the rest of the men with him, and it worked. Before they'd gone far, the ship was crewed again and under way, heading, as Pearce had suspected they would, for the safety of the Spanish port.

'Did anyone get the name of the vessel?' Pearce enquired, realising he'd forgotten to note it, this to a zero response. 'Then we best hope Sir John Jervis doesn't ask where his eighth has gone.'

Chapter Seven

For Edward Druce to receive a letter from an unknown corre-
spondent was far from unusual. Since taking over the running of the
affairs of his late brother-in-law, he'd been in receipt of communications
from a number of Denby Carruthers's business contacts. Druce knew him
as a City of London alderman and a hugely successful businessman, but
even he was surprised by the extent of Denby's interests.

Calls came in regularly, requesting more funds for a speculative business while significant sums were remitted daily on past ventures. Also,
insurance profits from agents employed at the Royal Exchange were paid
out, while the landing of cargos from the East and West Indies massively
swelled the company coffers when sold. And this was before the offers of
new business opportunities available in the burgeoning city marketplace
came across his desk.

Having taken over the office in Devonshire Square while dividing his
time with this and his previous occupation as a partner in a firm of prize
agents, he now led a much busier life, though all was not plain sailing.
On Denby's violent and as yet unexplained death, Druce had expected
the extensive and valuable estate would be his to control, albeit the actual
beneficiary would be his wife. His brother-in-law, who clearly didn't trust
him, had ensured this would not be so.

He had, of course, left his fortune to his only living relative, but he
had also appointed an executor, a lawyer who would oversee its distribution, the payment of debts and any bequests, etc. But he'd thwarted
Druce by also empowering this fellow to ensure all decisions regarding
any ongoing business had to be approved by Denby's sister. In short,

Druce's wife, not her husband, controlled the activities, and this included what monies he could extract for his own services.

From being a rather meek and gullible spouse, to Druce's mind too forgiving of her bad-tempered and arrogant brother, she had become an inquisitive interrogator of his actions, demanding a full report on his daily activities. While she'd agreed to annul the loans her husband had taken to advance his career as a prize agent, quite substantial in truth, it was her habit now to constantly remind him she had done so. Thus, his marriage had gone from being a reasonably contented if far from exciting union to a daily grind, where missing dinner or a failure to report the day's business was seen as questionable.

The superscription on the newly arrived letter, one of several dozen which had come that morning, he read before breaking the seal; it told him this was from a fellow called Posner aboard HMS *Ardent* at sea. But there was no more until, skimming the contents, he read that the man was a ship's purser. Had Denby contracted deals with such people? It was entirely possible given he had fingers in so many pies. Studying further, he found the writer eager to pay his humble respects; before he read on, the words originally making no sense.

This stranger was requesting that Denby repeat an act previous employed, which had resulted in the release from naval confinement of persons he held to be deserving of assistance. Then he came to the telling paragraph, which mentioned a praiseworthy yet unnamed brother who surely, by now, had made contact, added to the fact he would know how to go about the necessary actions to achieve a similar result. The close of the letter was even more enigmatic:

If I can be of any assistance in this matter, please do not hesitate to engage my services, which I am more than willing to provide. I would also like, if I may, to bring to your attention my own qualifications as a successful and profitable purser. This is, as you will know, a difficult area in which to prosper, and the person on whose behalf I write has assured me I may be able to look to your good offices, should I choose to seek a change of vocation.

I am, with respect,
Cyril Posner

It had often been remarked by Francis Ommaney, though never within earshot, that his prize agent partner was not possessed of the quickest of brains, and in this case lay the proof. It took him an age—indeed much other work was undertaken and completed—before the connection was made by an inadvertent thought. A messenger was engaged to go to the Admiralty and acquire information on the present whereabouts of HMS *Ardent*. It was only when the fellow returned with the information that it was part of Admiral Duncan's North Sea fleet, that a possible and troubling solution presented itself.

Another messenger had to be sent out from Devonshire Square, this time the senior clerk, despatched to a tavern in Farringdon Road called the White Swan. He was to locate Walter Hodgson, who used the place as a sort of office, asking him to call upon Druce at his earliest convenience, on a most pressing matter.

The first reaction of the thief-taker was that Druce could go hang, which was a telling simile because, to him, it ranked as a fate he fully deserved. The fellow was not worthy of a response—a man who, to save his own skin, had been prepared to keep certain facts to himself which would see an innocent man hang. It mattered not that the person in question, to anyone who knew him, was deserving of no sympathy whatsoever, a complete rogue who'd probably committed enough crimes in his life to qualify for the rope.

There was only one problem: a lack of any villains to pursue and the consequent shortage of the steady income which came from such work, which left him eating into his saved funds. An occupation at which he had in the past done well was now at the point of drying up as a source of income.

Chasing those evading the law had ceased to be a task for individuals since Blind John Fielding, the Westminster magistrate, had set up the Bow Street Runners. Few cases were being passed from the courts to the likes of Walter Hodgson, and he was not alone. There were now too many thief-takers chasing too few commissions to make it the source of a good living, even for him, with his solid track record. So it was need, not inclination, which took him to Devonshire Square, the entry into the cul-de-sac bringing back memories of the bloody night Denby Carruthers had met his end.

It was impossible not to speculate once more on the mysterious events of that night, and to little purpose, for what had triggered the events remained a mystery. Jaleel Tolland had been one of a trio of victims, he dying of gunshot wounds out in the street, while inside the house-cum-office, Carruthers and his clerk had both expired from repeated knife wounds. It had been a seriously blood-soaked encounter, which had elevated to fabulous wealth the man he was about to see.

The greeting he received was odd; it was as if Druce was nervous. Hodgson didn't know the man was reconsidering, wondering if calling on his services for what was a supposition was unwise, given the trouble the association had brought down on him previously. Could he have found another person to act on his behalf? But then he'd reviewed the events of the last three years and come to an unhappy conclusion. It would have been impossible to explain to anyone else the complex train of events which had led to his present anxieties, as well as the dangers any exposure of certain truths would cause him personally.

'Mr Hodgson,' Druce said, not rising to greet his visitor.

When it came to quick thinking, the thief-taker was as sharp as a tack; he had to be to survive in what was often a dangerous occupation. Having dealt with Edward Druce on many occasions, the lack of courtesy in Druce's remaining seated told him a great deal. He felt himself in charge of the situation, unlike on those occasions when the prize agent had needed to be rescued from his own folly. Then it was 'Take a seat, Mr Hodgson, and can I fetch you a glass of claret?'

Instead, today it was 'I've had a most interesting communication from a ship at present with the North Sea Fleet.'

'Addressed to you?'

'Of course not' was the rather testy response. 'It was addressed to my late brother-in-law. It seemed to imply he was still alive, and it was a request, I think, to get someone free of the navy.'

'Which surely could only have come from one person.'

'It was sent to me by a ship's purser called Posner.'

'Dated?'

'Yes, three days ago.'

'So, since Jaleel Tolland is no more, on behalf of another person. May I be allowed to read it?'

The letter was passed over to be examined. Unlike Druce, the meaning was immediately obvious to Hodgson, and he said so. 'Franklin Tolland, even if he's not mentioned, is seeking assistance to get out of the navy. It implies this was a service provided before, one I know to be the case.'

'Yet not something on which you saw fit to enlighten me' carried a strong flavour of pique.

'The information was vouchsafed to me in confidence and was not germane to the business on which you engaged me.'

The response went past resentment; Druce was positively angry. 'Which leaves me to wonder how many other people were paying you a stipend when it was I who employed you to work for me.'

'Reflect on how you behaved, Mr Druce, then ask yourself if I did not owe service to a higher purpose.'

This left Druce trying and failing to look innocent. From the very beginning it had been a tangled affair, one in which Hodgson had originally been paid not to find a person on whom Denby Carruthers, the man who was footing the bill, wished to visit serious harm. Everything had gone through Edward Druce, which led to other areas of ignorance, for instance, the fact the prize agent was hand in glove with the person he was charged to find on some very questionable business. This left him trying to ride two unsteady horses at once. The second was to keep him, at his brother-in-law's expense, from being found.

Hodgson, at the outset, had no indication of this, but time revealed the truth, and it got worse. It was not the beating he had come to suppose but the permanent removal of a fellow, Carruthers's one-time clerk, a handsome cove called Cornelius Gherson, who had cuckolded the alderman by seducing his pretty and much younger wife.

If it had been complicated at the outset, it became increasingly so as time went by, with the man before the thief-taker at the centre of things, albeit he too had originally not known what was intended. This did not last: the scales had fallen from his eyes even before Catherine Carruthers was brutally murdered in the upstairs room of a Covent Garden bagnio, an act which might not have taken place without the passive assistance of Edward Druce.

Hodgson had, over time, managed to pin the act on two brothers, Jaleel and Franklin Tolland, first through descriptive drawings by which they could be identified then finally, when he was able to do so, by name. Much as Druce didn't wish to admit it, and he even continued to do so when the evidence was irrefutable, the man behind the foul deed of murder was none other than his late brother-in-law. The alderman, in a clever and cynical ploy, had so arranged matters that Gherson would stand trial for the crime and most certainly hang.

'A higher purpose which paid handsomely I should think, and I can guess who footed the bill. Given the amount of money Mrs Barclay extracted from Ommaney and Druce, she was well able to afford it.'

'Are we not talking of monies you, with the aid of Gherson, stole by manipulating the late Captain Barclay's funds? What a pity he told her the truth in order to save his neck. It would have been so much better if he'd just swung.'

The irony stung. Druce had no interest in continuing a conversation in which he could not emerge in an even close to virtuous light, which had him insist they turn to the matter at hand.

'Franklin probably doesn't know his brother is dead. Or your brother-in-law.'

'Is that not surprising?'

'Not if he's been at sea since it happened. They don't sell penny pamphlets to battle fleets on station; besides, Jaleel's name was never mentioned, so he's still a mystery, unless you recognise his face from one of my drawings.'

'Can he get free?'

'The prospect clearly worries you,' Hodgson opined.

'The answer to the question, if you please.'

'I believe it is possible, though rare, to buy a sailor out of the navy, either with a cash payment or by providing a competent replacement. I take it you're not planning to do either.'

'Of course not, but I do wonder at the involvement of this Posner fellow.'

'To which I would be unable to give you an answer,' Hodgson replied.

'Then that must be the first task, to find out about him.'

'Am I to take it that this is a task you wish me to undertake?'

'If I do,' Druce snapped, 'I require you act solely on my behalf. I do not want any muddied waters a second time.'

'And the terms?'

'The same as those on which I engaged you previously.'

'Which assumes, Mr Druce, I have no one else wishing to employ my services.'

'And do you?'

Hodgson nodded, smiling, not because it was true but because he enjoyed guying Druce. A period of silent contemplation followed before Druce added, 'I am prepared to increase your fee, and I will explain why.'

'You have no need to provide reasons. There are matters which you cannot afford to have see the light of day, the first being your late brother-in-law was an accessory to the murder of his own wife. Second, he also engaged in a conspiracy which would have seen an innocent man, albeit one of the vilest persons it's been my misfortune to meet, dangling at the end of a rope. I doubt it would be good for you or the highly profitable business you've inherited.'

Druce stopped himself from bleating that it was his wife's inheritance, not his.

'I would also add, should Franklin Tolland, by some miracle, get free of the navy, he would face justice for the murder of Catherine Carruthers, something I would make it my business to see carried through. But he would not go to the gallows without naming the man behind the deed, which would inevitably involve you. It will also emerge that your brother-in-law was a partner in a smuggling syndicate, in collusion with both Tolland brothers. Denby Carruthers's reputation would be trashed, and I would not be surprised if many of the people who dealt with him in the past would decline to do so in the future, or with the enterprise which bears his name.'

'I will double your fee,' Druce said, stony-faced.

'Treble it or find another to do your bidding, with a quarter of the annual sum in advance.'

'What!'

'I do not see you in a situation in which you're free to bargain, Mr Druce.'

Hodgson was bluffing, but it was a skill which he had been obliged to practise on many occasions, one necessary to extract information, to hint at threats which would unlock the memory of a witness, or to get a confession from a miscreant. He also knew he was not dealing with a sharp intelligence or a man who could respond in kind, proved by the speed of Druce's capitulation.

'Wait here.'

Druce stood and left the room, with Walter Hodgson realising he'd failed to use the time to tie up certain things in which he had an interest. What had happened to the ship John Pearce had taken off the Tollands and which Denby Carruthers, when it was put up for auction, had realised was one he already owned? Was there any more information on the strange events which had taken place in Devonshire Square, which had seen both Carruthers and Jaleel Tolland, supposed business partners, clearly intent on killing each other? What had caused the rift?

It had set the London rumour mill running at speed, with every Grub Street hack penning a penny to sixpenny pamphlet casting an opinion on the causes. These ranged from massive and unsatisfied debts to the previously seen as virtuous Catherine Carruthers, now portrayed as a promiscuous Jezebel. None of these satisfied the curiosity of the thief-taker, but it was not the first case he'd been engaged in which ended without complete answers.

'Thieves falling out, I suspect,' Hodgson said to himself in conclusion. 'Which is ever the case.'

In the cellar below, Edward Druce was standing over an open chest, looking at the leather bags of coin it contained, both silver and gold. It was a possession neither his wife nor her pesky lawyer knew anything about, so it was his to do with as he wished. It had only been discovered by him in the days following the murders, when he tested every key his brother-in-law had in his desk drawer, this itself locked and access taken from the waistcoat on his dead body before it was removed.

There was a lot less in the chest now than when first opened, for it was not correspondence which obliged him to use its contents, more the claims of visitors who hinted they had paid for contraband goods which had not been forthcoming. If there were books listing this to be the case, he had not found them, but not paying out risked what Denby had been up to becoming common knowledge. Hodgson had made a good point, but he probably didn't know just how much such information would damage what was now the family business.

Those who wanted to know the whereabouts of their prepaid brandy, tea, lace, silks, and Parisian perfumes were content to be reimbursed and stay silent thereafter. It would be foolish to brag about buying smuggled goods or even returned monies for same. But there was a substantial sum left, proving how profitable a trade it had been. It was a pity he had been unable to recover the last cargo and the ship Denby owned, which he knew to be stolen. But the risk was too great, so it had to be left for that naval villain John Pearce to profit from, by claiming it to be a French merchant vessel and thus a prize.

It was, however, a name to bear in mind, for if the possibility ever arose to do Pearce a disservice, Edward Druce would certainly take it. Reaching down, he opened one of the canvas bags and extracted twenty-four guineas, which as he saw as a payment for his own personal security. He had no idea of the real circumstances of Denby's death, only that it was murder and inflicted by a Tolland and there was another one of that breed still alive. He also suspected some of the money in the chest over which he was standing might belong to them: a dispute about it might have led to the bloody mayhem which had ensued and could do so again.

For a moment he imagined if it was possible to permanently dispose of Franklin Tolland and, in the kind of fantasy which he was too often prone, he conjured up a picture of a confrontation during which he would carry out the deed with cold-blooded efficiency. But in truth, he was motivated more by fear than illusory courage.

A smaller empty bag was used to hold Hodgson's fee, and he could only hope it was money well spent, while another few coins were slipped into his own waistcoat pocket. The prospect of going home at the end of the day—to the normal interrogation and a bed in which nothing occurred but sleep disturbed by snoring—was one becoming less attractive with the passing of time.

No one would see Druce as a hot-blooded individual, but the contents of the chest had provided the means to put aside his long years of dreaming but remaining abstinent in favour of a touch of carnal laxity. If it was small compensation for all he had lost, it was something he could look forward to.

He returned to find Hodgson rereading the letter, this put on the desk as Druce sat down.

'Well, what do you conclude?'

'Two choices, to reply or ignore it.' The quizzical raised eyebrows were an invitation to advise. 'Ignorance leaves you in doubt as to the true nature of the supposed supplicant, while whoever it is has given Posner this address.'

'Are you saying you doubt it's Tolland?'

'No, but it would be good to be absolutely certain, so I suggest a reply, but not from here. Let it be from the White Swan and me, using an alias. We need to know more of this purser.'

'Then?'

'I will seek a meeting with him.'

'To what end?'

'First we establish it is Franklin, then move to ensure he is kept where he is.'

It was obvious Druce wasn't keeping up, which Hodgson found frustrating, the man being so slow, obliging him to state what should have been obvious, so he tapped the letter on the desk.

'In this, he is clearly seeking something for himself, a position, which means he's not happy with his present lot, which is hardly a surprise. Lord only knows how many pursers go bankrupt every year.'

'You're not suggesting I employ him.'

'It would be cheaper to pay him to keep Tolland on board *Ardent* than have him working to get him free. If he's committed to such a course, he must be weaned off it.'

'And how much is that going to cost me?'

'No idea, and I will require some discretion when it's discussed. This is an arrangement which can only be secured face-to-face and ashore. But set it against your life, as well as the prosperity of your business, and it will be cheap.'

CHAPTER EIGHT

ALEXANDER DAVIDSON WAS OF THE OPINION A MODERN MAN HAD TO BE forward thinking. Therefore, when it came to disseminating the case for prize money being paid to John Pearce, he decided it was unwise, in the first instance, to mention either silver, its value, or the name of the officers involved in the taking of the *Santa Leocadia*.

The action would originally be hinted at, first through one of the many journals now published both on weekdays and Sundays. Following on, pamphleteers would be encouraged to take up the metaphorical cudgels regarding Spanish perfidy, especially when they had taken so much gold in subsidy from Britannia. They would then hopefully fire up a mob who would clamour for redress.

For him, the basis of the story was the treacherous defection of the Spanish monarchy in deciding to side with the regicides of Paris, men who had cold-bloodedly murdered their royal cousins. They were reputed to be weak personalities, entirely under the thumb of their devious chief minister, Manuel Godoy. Indeed, it was rumoured he even shared the marital bed with both: this, a common accusation aimed at monarchs, mattered less than betrayal.

To Davidson this was the avenue to pursue, which would, in time, be followed by certain revelations to keep the story alive, finally resulting in a release of the brave and timely actions of the officers involved. He would then seek to whip up a public demand they be properly recompensed. Only then would their names become public.

It was a proposition he outlined to the representatives of Lord Langholm, fellow prize agents Francis Ommaney and Edward Druce, to be slightly thrown by their lack of enthusiasm. He was obliged to enquire if their client wished to pursue his just reward. This was answered by Francis Ommaney, overweight, florid of countenance, and, as far as their visitor knew, the senior of the pair.

'But was it legal? Lord Langholm has reservations about making such a claim with the question unsettled.'

'And they are, these reservations?'

Druce took up the baton, not bothering to answer the question. 'You must understand, Mr Davidson, how highly Lord Langholm values his naval career.'

'Which I am sure he can satisfy by setting it against the sum of money he will gain from a successful outcome? It's enough to buy comfort and ease for himself, which, I gather, as a younger son of the family, he will not inherit.'

'If I can refer to our time in our shared profession, sir, I must point out to you, we may have experience in certain areas which you lack.'

The condescension from Ommaney, the intimation he was a tyro at the game compared to them, rankled. But the lawyer in Davidson, a career he had pursued originally, made him hold back from pointing this out, the lack of reaction obliging the perpetrator to continue.

'It will not surprise you to learn the noble lord has many connections and a high degree of interest in areas where such things matter. While he is not near the top of the list of post captains, Lord Langholm is in the upper half, while we are at present engaged in a war, one in which I can see no immediate prospect of peace. Added to this there will be a high degree of casualties, so it is therefore not beyond the bounds of possibility he can look forward to raising his flag as a rear-admiral before hostilities cease.'

'With the possibility of a plum posting to follow?'

Davidson asked this, not wishing to endure a lecture on the kind of sums which could accrue to an admiral on a profitable posting. To be part of a successful fleet action could set you up for life, but this paled beside a command in the furthest corners of the globe. The West Indies, given the American colonies, since they rebelled, were barred from trading with the Caribbean islands, could net the man in command sums in the hundreds of thousands. This came from an eighth share of the prize money earned from the interdiction of smuggling. The East Indies and the Spice Islands were just as lucrative, possibly even more so.

'Jam tomorrow, wouldn't you say?'

'We have our instructions,' Druce responded with a grave expression.

'Having said this is so,' Ommaney added, 'while we cannot combine with you in your putative campaign, I can assure you we will do nothing to impede it.'

And take any reward in commission which comes your way, Davidson thought as another occurred. If he could praise John Pearce for his boldness in the aforesaid capture, he could just as easily damn Langholm for his tardiness at the time, added to his timidity in the face of possible censure by the Admiralty. But this was not something to say, so he decided half a loaf was best, his silence indicating acceptance.

Given rumours were already circulating regarding the Spanish silver, placing stories in a newspaper was far from difficult, as long as he avoided papers which supported the government and were no doubt in receipt of funds to do so. Henry Dundas, William Pitt's right-hand man, was a past master at using cash payments to oil the presentation of the administration's position on matters contentious.

Yet he found he might, surprisingly, have an ally there, this vouchsafed to him by Samuel Oliphant, who, if he had not physically taken part in the battle off Vigo—the man was no warrior and even less a sailor—knew about it in great detail, having been aboard HMS *Hazard* at the time. Not least, he was conscious of the resentment felt by *Hazard*'s officers and crew at the way Langholm had behaved once the Spaniard struck its flag.

It had been John Pearce's ship which had taken the battle to the *Santa Leocadia*, both with cannon fire and boarding, to suffer damage and casualties as a consequence. The men from *Lively* had turned up when matters were all but concluded, to claim the victory and boast of it with not a drop of blood spilt, all this related to Davidson when Oliphant returned from Spain.

'There's a rumour,' Davidson, said, 'Dundas received a report from the governor of Gibraltar, in which he praised the actions taken by Pearce.'

'I left *Hazard* at Lisbon, so I have no knowledge of it.'

'You could ask Dundas for a copy.'

'Which I would be reluctant to do,' Oliphant hedged.

Davidson didn't ask him why, for the very sound reason that Oliphant would probably lie.

'I admit to thinking far ahead, but I do know from my contacts at the Admiralty that Langholm's report was, at the very least, equivocal. This hints at his primary aim being to protect himself from possible criticism. But the document will not be made available till there's a hearing in the Admiralty court, if indeed we get to such a stage, which I will seek to avoid. Such a despatch, together with one from such a source as Sir David Rose, could prove invaluable in defending both Pearce and the claim for prize money.'

'You see him as being in need of such?'

'If you knew anything about the navy and paying what is due, Mr Oliphant, you would be aware nothing is ever straightforward.'

'I have the impression Sir David Rose is fond of Pearce, so I daresay he will provide you with a copy of his despatch if asked.'

'There will still be powerful voices speaking against my client.'

'Including some of the cabinet,' Oliphant said. 'But it's Dundas they're after, not John Pearce.'

'Go on.'

'I'm not sure I should be so indiscreet.'

'It depends on what you want, like your share of any reward. I have calculated your share as a master's mate, in what is a vessel with a small crew, as in excess of four hundred pounds, enough to keep a man going for a year or two, if he's not too extravagant.'

Oliphant kept hidden his response to the figure mentioned, as much from habit as for any other reason. But it did resonate to a man who had worked as a spy and depended on Henry Dundas for employment, one who, if and when he eventually paid, was not overly generous. Oliphant was waiting to be rewarded for his recent efforts in Spain while worrying about the monies expended on the French business, the sum to which Dundas had alluded.

This had been expended to no purpose, there being a complete lack of effective resistance to the Revolution. All the contacts who claimed such a designation had first exaggerated their strength, to then be swept up and guillotined. What if he was called upon to account for it? Even worse, if the manoeuvres of Dundas came to light and were seen as wasteful, he might even be asked to repay it.

No exception to the norm, he ached for some stroke which would set him up so well, he could pick and choose his future work. His past employment had given him nothing but semi-decent reward for very high risk and poor recompense for anything else. Right now, he was without any work, and Dundas had held out no prospect of anything in the offing.

'It would be too dangerous for me to even enquire, Mr Davidson, but you have had a fellow in this very office who might be able—for a price, mind—to get the information you seek on Langholm.' The enquiring look from Davidson produced the name. 'You will recall Walter Hodgson.'

'Who is a thief-taker.'

'And so well versed in bribery, a very necessary tool in their armoury, especially when you might be chasing missing and fraudulent funds. I would not bet against him getting Langholm's despatch before it was needed.'

Davidson was pensive for quite a while, mulling over in his mind the positives, only to produce a negative. 'It would be impossible, and highly illegal, for me to instruct him.'

'But I could do so, as long as I have the funds.'

'Do you have an idea of cost?'

'I know how and where to find out. And if he is going to liaise through me—'

It was with a jaundiced expression Davidson interrupted. 'You too would require to be reimbursed.'

'Naturally.'

'Then it is just as well Lieutenant Pearce has been lucky in his captures.'

'Ah yes, the ship he took in the North Sea?'

'Auctioned for a tidy sum and, with cargo added, even more fruitful.'

'I do believe I'm due a portion there too.'

'Which you will receive when the settlement is paid out, something yet to occur.'

'Then I wonder if I may press you for an advance.'

Given Oliphant's services were required, there was no choice but to agree; it was, after all, his money.

'I need a figure on what your Hodgson will require, and it cannot be open-ended.'

'I think, in such a matter, it will have to be agreed in advance with the recipient.'

'And with me, Mr Oliphant,' Davidson insisted. 'And with me.'

When no response had come by return to the purser's letter, it left Franklin Tolland far from alone in disappointment. The man who had sent it on his behalf was no stranger to optimism and expectation. He, though it remained unspoken, had built up his hopes to the point which allowed his imagination free license, this now ebbing away. It was impossible not to note a falling off in the purser's optimism, given there was no more free tobacco, while the welcome to his storeroom, if granted, was given with much huffing and puffing about his travails.

Franklin had kept to himself the sending of the letter. He had not told the one-time members of the Tolland smuggling crew of his attempts to get clear of the navy, and for a very good reason: they were not included should it prove successful. But he still required them to help him keep up the pressure in playing on the grievances of their *Ardent* shipmates, and it seemed to be paying off. The mood on the lower deck was hardening, rendering them sullen when given orders.

The reaction of the captain, Richard Burges, was to bear down hard on any sign of dissent, which saw the grating rigged twice in one week, the miscreants getting their standard twelve for insolence. It was also plain the petty officers, those who faced the crew on a more regular basis than the blue coats, approved of this as a response, which saw complaints increase not decrease. Given the purser, albeit disliked, was a member of this group, he shared in the general approval.

'I was wondering about another letter,' Franklin suggested, having got him alone. 'What with you going ashore soon.'

'I scarce see the situation would be altered.'

'It must be worth a try, Mr Posner. For all we know, moves are already afoot to get the result we need. And what if something went awry with the post.'

The response was a rare display of real temper. 'Unlikely, given it goes to the Navy Board for distribution, and they are experienced at the task.'

'Recall we both have hopes in this.'

Posner was not in the least mollified. 'I recall being told there might be a prospect of advancement, which, given the lack of response, indicates to me I might have been deceived and deliberately so.'

'We must wait and hope' carried a note of desperation.

The look this received was not encouraging, which had Tolland suppressing his desire to fetch this pompous little arse a buffet round the ears. The time might come when he would allow himself the pleasure, but not yet; and if he paid at the grating, so be it.

'Matters never go as fast as one hopes, Mr Posner.'

This might be delivered like a supplicant, but it was the opposite of how he truly felt. There was no Christian charity in Posner, he being typical of the breed to which he belonged, which was hypocrisy of the highest order from a man who lacked even an ounce of such a commodity himself. But he resolved, if the situation did not improve, to make Posner pay a price not measured in pounds, shillings, and pence. He would find out the hard way the cost of failing to do what a Tolland wished.

Oliphant found the man he sought in his usual haunt and was more than willing to partake of the White Swan's excellent meat pies and a tankard of ale. While eating and drinking, he explained the way the case had come about and what was required, the involvement of Alexander Davidson not revealed. Also not mentioned was the fact that the man Oliphant was looking to employ had a prior task, on behalf of Edward Druce, and one for which he was being excessively rewarded. Hodgson, like his visitor, kept things close by habit.

'What's your interest in this?'

'I stand to gain a substantial sum of money, Walter, if it's decided to pay out prize money instead of the government claiming the silver as droits.'

'Not my normal beat' was the response; this before Hodgson, with a look of deep curiosity, enquired as to Oliphant's real identity.

When they'd first come across each other in Davidson's office weeks before, both, professionals in their own way, had managed to keep hidden the fact they had met in the past. This was even more the case on the thief-taker's part, given he had known the man now before him by a completely different identity. If he'd met John Pearce, he would have found a shared inquisitiveness. In Paris, Pearce had heard him confidently addressed by another name, and it bore no resemblance to the one Hodgson had known Oliphant by previously.

'I think I must ask you to stick to the one I'm using at present.'

'It makes no difference, except in the matter of trust; so, Oliphant, you may stay.'

'Not at risk in this commission. I am merely a conduit to the person picking up the bill and have no other role. But as I know you of old, shall we say, I'm also aware of some of your more public successes, though I'm sure not all. Not least the many stockjobbers and fleeing bankrupts you have managed to get arraigned before a court?'

'Easier to find thieves and fraudsters than murderers. They can't resist spending what they have stolen.' There was a significant pause before Hodgson added, 'But this is of another order.'

'You sense risk?'

'Slipping a few coins to an informer, for a tip on the movements of a villain, is not the same as seeking to suborn an Admiralty employee, which I will be obliged to do. I must be sure I'm not being drawn into some kind of trap. More importantly, how much time have I got?'

'Not a great deal.'

Asked why, Oliphant explained a coming campaign would soon have the public talking about a sum of prize money of which, at present, they were ignorant, with obvious consequences. The fortune hunters would come out of the woodwork in droves when it became known.

'Once that is out in the open, it will take no genius to connect what we seek with the level of reward which will accrue to the crew of *Hazard*. It renders the lottery rewards puny by comparison.'

'Not least its captain?'

In receipt of a nod, Hodgson was reflecting on this commission coming from someone other than Samuel Oliphant, not that he let on. This was not the first time he'd been engaged to work for a third but unidentified party, it being far from rare. Indeed, he would not have known about Denby Carruthers, never mentioned by Edward Druce, as the man seeking to find and harm Cornelius Gherson. It was the clerk who settled his bills who let slip who was paying for his services.

He also figured out the two tasks might dovetail in a fashion. Getting information on the purser Posner meant calling at Greenwich and the offices of the Navy Board, but he could hardly believe he would glean much about a fellow in a relatively low position. Oliphant's needs could only be satisfied at the Admiralty, and the risks there were manifest. Both must take precedence over the part he was reluctant to undertake on behalf of Druce. The ideas of travelling to Harwich, from which he suspected Admiral Duncan's fleet drew their supplies, in the middle of winter was not a prospect to relish but he feared would be necessary.

Yet he must establish beyond doubt it was the younger Tolland behind the letter and for reasons he would not divulge to Druce. Free, Franklin would likely go after John Pearce in the same manner as his late brother and for the same reason: to get back the value of his stolen ships or extract a blood price for their theft, not that he would be able to harm a man serving in the Mediterranean.

The vulnerable person was Emily Barclay, known to the Tollands as intimately connected to the man they were determined to harm. She had been at risk previously, he being in the process of acting to protect her on the very night of the bloody events in Devonshire Square. This had, thanks to his demise, spared her the threat from Jaleel Tolland but, with his little brother on the loose, she would be in danger once more.

'We must set up a method by which we can communicate with each other, Walter,' interrupted these worrying thoughts.

'If I am not in the White Swan, be sure they will know where to find me, Samuel.'

Chapter Nine

GIVEN THE CIRCUMSTANCES AND THE NEWS THEY HAD TO REPORT regarding *Courageux*, there was no choice but to make for HMS *Victory*, it being agreed to maintain silence regarding the Spaniard they had set free. So it was a shabby-looking pair who found themselves in front of Admiral Sir John Jervis, he reacting to the news of the loss of *Courageux*, as well as the majority of his six-hundred-man crew, with an air of grim inevitability: the sea was a dangerous element on which to serve, and losses, even in such numbers, had to be accepted as one of the perils of their profession.

Not Benjamin Hallowell, who, after close questioning of events leading up to the wrecking, still insisted he should have been with his ship—a remark to which Jervis made no comment, though it was easy to guess what the admiral was thinking. Either his less than fully recovered premier had made fatal errors or, even with his years and experience, Hallowell senior had avoided a similar fate. Yet, if either man did think the former, no words would ever surface to sully the name of Burrows.

Nor would those who had witnessed his actions, even if they were more than a touch questionable, facts ruminated on by Pearce in the open launch. There was no mention of bread-and-butter pudding, no questioning the wisdom of leaving two officers in charge who did not know the ship. The man had died in the execution of his duties; seeking to black his name would serve no purpose.

'*Courageux* was French built of course,' Jervis added. 'Never did like having captures like that under my command.'

Generally held to be lighter in construction than their British equivalents, and thus more vulnerable in foul weather, it was moot to John

Pearce if the origin of the *Courageux* had any bearing on its loss, and he said so.

'I doubt the nationality of the shipwrights had much bearing on the fate of the ship, sir.'

This remark, uncalled for, was on the receiving end of a basilisk stare from the admiral, this leavened by a kindly word from its one-time captain, though it came with a sharp look at his C-in-C.

'While I would like to thank you for your efforts.'

'Which they had no permission to undertake, Captain Hallowell. While I appreciate your need to proffer gratitude, I would also point out we only have the word of these two officers before us as to the true record of events.'

'I would take it as remiss, sir, if I thought you were calling into question the word of a member of my family.'

The abrupt reply, 'Of course not,' along with the contrite expression, left Pearce with the distinct impression Jervis had forgotten the connection to his premier, which left him with a chance to get in a dig. Nothing tickled his vanity more than bearding admirals.

'I think Sir John is referring to me, Captain Hallowell.'

'Since your accounts complement each other, I cannot see how.'

'Then,' Jervis barked, no doubt stung by his previous error, 'you are taking no account of the reputation of Lieutenant Pearce, whom, I have to say, is lucky to have such a reliable witness as your nephew to back up his tale.'

'The other survivors?' Benjamin Hallowell asked, leaving the impression it was not a subject on which he wanted to comment, so it fell to Pearce to reply.

'I asked, when we came aboard, they be fed and, if necessary, issued with new clothing. I'm afraid I laid a charge on you, Captain Hallowell, for the provision, but if I have exceeded your own inclinations, I will bear the expense myself.'

'Such nobility,' sneered Jervis. 'But I would remind you of what you must still face, Pearce, a reckoning for your folly off Bastia. The court martial will convene at four of the clock, when everyone has had their dinner. And since yours is the only case still to be heard, I expect we will be done with you before the sun goes down.'

'The composition of the court?'

'Remains as before.'

'Then, if you will forgive me, sir,' Ben Hallowell insisted, 'I must see to the needs of my men. With your permission I will arrange a service ashore tomorrow where we can pray for the souls of those we have lost.'

'Naturally' was the reply as Ben Hallowell departed, while Jervis continued to direct his ire at John Pearce. 'I might suggest you look to your own clothing. I doubt it will aid your defence if you appear before the court looking like a vagabond.'

'I have never been of the opinion clothing signalled virtue. In fact, the more braid, the less of that quality.'

'Get out,' Jervis growled, before softening his tone when addressing Isaac Hallowell. 'Forgive the tone, young man, which in no way applies to you.'

There is no explaining the speed of the gossip grapevine in a fleet. A little over an hour had passed since entering Jervis's cabin, yet it seemed everyone already knew of what had taken place with *Courageux*, the facts no doubt coming from the other survivors. Their reactions varied as the boat from *Victory*, in bright sunlight and a pleasant wind, took them through the fleet to HMS *Hazard*, not all being seen through the Jervis lens.

From a few quarterdecks came raised officer's hats, though most studiously ignored them. Others on the deck managed sad waves, while quite a few crossed themselves in the manner of Michael O'Hagan, which reminded Pearce that the fleet was manned by a high number of Catholic Irishmen. Here was a group who, if discontent manifested itself, were the most likely to demonstrate truculence.

The tale of their adventures had even carried to their own ship, where they found the side lined with many more men clinging to the shrouds to give them a cheer three times three. Given this was bound to echo across the anchorage, Pearce hoped it would penetrate the walls of the flagship and cause Jervis to grind his teeth.

Weary as he was, it was necessary for both Pearce and Hallowell to get a report from Worricker and Macklin as to how *Hazard* had fared during the storm, only to find out she'd come close to being driven under by the drifting HMS *Culloden*. A cable had required to be cut and a scrap of sail raised to get out of the way, and it had been nip and tuck.

Pearce then retired to his cabin for an hour of sleep, waking up partly refreshed. Once washed and shaved, he was ready to be waited on and served breakfast by his servant, Derwent. It didn't take long to find the tale had grown in the telling, and while he was enjoying this, he found out how his exploits had exceeded anything which had actually taken place. This included him having to single-handedly fight off not only the entire drunken crew of *Courageux* but also a whole mass of sea monsters as he swam to the launch.

His good friend Michael soon found an excuse to see him. Even after months in the job, Derwent still found the presence upsetting, mind there was no shortage of sufferers in that department. The Irishman was big and broad for a start, with a large and ruddy face topped by tight curls, a face usually wearing a sunny smile.

By nature benign, he was formidable when riled and well able, with his hamlike fists and outstanding physical strength, to take care of trouble. Lest he thought himself a paragon, John Pearce, along with two others aboard—all four pressed into the navy at the same time—had ample reason to remind Michael that, when drunk, he was a downright menace.

Pearce supposed poor Derwent, who was efficient if uninspiring, was feart of the opinion of the man who had preceded him in the role, given everything he did was subject to close examination. Michael, the most unlikely looking servitor in creation, had held the post for a long time and carried it out with surprising aplomb. Now, acting as master at arms, he was a presence sorely missed by John Pearce, being the only person aboard with whom he could be fully open.

'That miserable bastard did not run to even a cup of coffee, never mind a glass of wine.' This was imparted as soon as Derwent had gone back to his pantry, leaving ample coffee. 'And he's set my court appearance for four on this very day, with me not having slept for more than an hour.'

'Sure, you're a man to set going strong emotions, John-boy.'

This was accompanied by a wide grin, which was as good as saying it was as much his own fault as that of anyone else.

'Don't look so smug when you might have a new captain by six. The crew?'

For John Pearce this was Michael's most valuable asset. As master at arms, he went everywhere aboard and could keep his captain informed of the mood of the men he led. Even if they now seemed content, it had not always been so. On taking command of *Hazard*, the Admiralty had stripped out the existing crew, to then land him with a load of inexperienced Quota men. These were the dregs of the country's workhouses, chosen by their municipal masters to join the navy, usually to rid them from the public purse.

The voyage to the Mediterranean had been fraught with problems. He and the few men he had with any skills had to drive these Quota men to the tasks necessary to keep the ship safe, while at the same time trying to teach them some basic skills. By lucky chance this problem had been alleviated, a stroke of good fortune providing him with a band of highly experienced sailors. The two had seemed to meld over the following weeks, but the man in command still worried such might not hold.

'Did you not see them manning the shrouds to cheer you? Christ, they're proud of you, man.'

'Given what I've heard from Derwent, it's for things I haven't done.'

A knock at the door brought in Midshipman Maclehose, known to the crew as Jock the Sock. 'Boat approaching, sir, with a lieutenant aboard. I think it's from HMS *Captain*.'

'Why?'

'Can't be sure, sir, but I reckon it to be Mr Farmiloe.'

'If it is, he's a fellow I must welcome aboard personally.'

His coat, having been subjected to much steam and elbow grease, was nearly as good as it had been when he had worn it to his court martial, though his hat had suffered too much to be still the right shape. It brought home the fact of the need to go ashore for a replacement: he intended to look his best for Jervis.

By the time he was on deck, it was established Maclehose had the right of it; the officer approaching was indeed Dick Farmiloe, who came up the manropes with a broad smile and greeted, once he'd saluted the quarterdeck, with a warm handshake. Having served with Pearce before—indeed, he'd been a midshipman on HMS *Brilliant*, the ship onto which Pearce had been pressed, as well as subsequently on a mission to La Rochelle—they were warm friends.

'My cabin, Mr Farmiloe,' was imparted with the correct degree of respect when Pearce could be overheard. It was Dick as soon as they were alone with a decanter of wine, the immediate enquiry being, 'To what do I owe the honour?'

'Captain Nelson wishes to invite you to dinner, John.'

'Ah, an invitation I may have to decline?' A questioning look was followed by an explanation about the time of his court martial. 'Which does not leave much of a gap for the walnuts and port, never mind the taletelling.'

'What are you facing a court for?'

'Surely you know?'

'I doubt I'd pose such a question if I did.'

Pearce had to acknowledge how he could be in ignorance, given the way Jervis had made sure Pearce and his men had no contact with the other ships, and the old bastard was sly enough to keep a secret even in the fleet. The reason outlined saw Farmiloe's face go from amazement through disbelief to palpable anger, followed by the spitting out at the mention of a name.

'Toby Burns, that little turd.'

'Afraid so, and he has nothing less than our esteemed C-in-C in his corner.'

Farmiloe looked glum. 'I do know Jervis has a soft spot for him, the Lord only knows why, even gave him a ship. Tiddler, mind, but a command nonetheless.'

'On a duty which he was able to feed on his fear of risk. In employing it, he has been able to drop me in the steep tub.'

'Would it trouble you to tell me.'

'The long version or the short one?' Pearce asked as he refilled Farmiloe's glass.

'I fear it will have to be the latter, since I have my duties aboard *Captain.*'

The outline of what had taken place off Bastia was a simple enough tale in terms of fighting, less so with the background of both politics and possible insurrection. But there was no need to explain Toby Burns: Farmiloe knew only too well what he was like. Dick had even acted as a friend to the pipsqueak, advising Burns how to deal with the fallout from committing perjury on behalf of the late Captain Ralph Barclay.

'Needless to say, your turd played the coward, and I wrote a despatch saying so, while I have no idea what became of it. If this was ever shown to Jervis, he was told a different tale by Burns. It's one he has chosen to believe, for our dear admiral deplores my very existence. Did you know he sent me home from the Med once already? Nearly had apoplexy when I turned up again under an Admiralty pennant.'

'Which I do not see flying.'

'He took it away.'

'Which he's not at liberty to do.'

'To whom am I to complain? Perhaps when I get back to England. But out here he is the Almighty personified.'

'But surely, given what you've told me, your case is sound.'

'Not in a court where Jervis has chosen the judges.'

'I am no lawyer, but surely your representative can move to have the case delayed on those very grounds, the inability to get a fair hearing.'

'Would I had such a fellow, but I am confined to defending myself.'

The look this received was one of disbelief. 'You have not appointed someone to represent you, John? I know you to be capable of folly, but this qualifies as madness. I have an uncle who is a leading barrister, and he maintains it is never a good idea to make your own case.'

'A general message was sent out by the admiral's clerk, asking for a fellow of equal rank to be my advocate, but no one volunteered.' There was a slight note of pique in Pearce's tone as he added, 'Not even you, Dick.'

'When was this?'

'I was told two days past.'

'Well, it was never delivered to HMS *Captain*. If it went to Commodore Nelson, I'm sure he would have told all his officers.'

About to speak, Pearce was silenced by an upheld hand, with Farmiloe dropping his head to sit in deep contemplation, which lasted for several minutes.

'I smell intrigue here.' The pause was significant before Farmiloe added, 'Despite my duties, John, I think you must favour me with the long version. And I would welcome a quill, ink, and some paper.'

This was not a tale to be told without interruption, and there was much scratching of the nib as Farmiloe queried facts and notes were made. Dick was determined to get the details right, and so Pearce was forced to dig deep about matters to do with Bastia. There were, as well, events which had happened long before, in which Toby Burns had been a player. Finally, putting down his notes, he looked John Pearce in the eye.

'How did you intend to fight this?'

'By telling the truth. I saw my actions as justified and have confidence the court will see it so. And if I represent myself, I get the chance to question Burns, with an absolute certainty he will cringe when I do so.'

'I repeat, it's not a good idea to act for yourself, and you know it.'

'If I have no one else to do it, what choice do I have?' Farmiloe smiled and tilted his head to one side. 'You?'

'I will require permission from Nelson, but I have no doubt he will grant it.'

'So?'

'I will take pleasure in acting for you in front of the judges, but I have a couple of requests to make.'

'Which are?'

'First, your Pelicans appear in court.'

'In God's name why? I doubt they'll be allowed to give evidence.'

'Perhaps they won't have to' was the enigmatic reply. 'I would also like your marine lieutenant, Mr Moberly, to declare himself as a witness.'

'Dick, I will give to you the same advice I gave to him, for he was quick to offer. Have you considered what going against Admiral Jervis, which is how you appearing for me will look, might have an impact on your own prospects in the service?'

This produced a chuckle. 'If you'd ever served with Horatio Nelson, you wouldn't ask such a question. For the commodore, it's action which speaks, not opinions. And since he is soon to raise his flag, I'm happy he will offer me protection. From what you've told me, your case is heading for a miscarriage of justice, and I will do my best to stop it. Now I must go; there's much to do between now and four of the clock.'

The loose-leaf notes were rolled up and stuffed inside Farmiloe's jacket, his glass of wine lifted and drained. Pearce stood as well to see him off the ship.

The surprise in John Pearce's voice was genuine. 'How do you know all this?'

The question was aimed at the trio who, like him, called themselves the Pelicans, taken from the name of the tavern out of which they had been illegally pressed. He, a fugitive evading a writ for sedition; Michael O'Hagan, the prodigious Irish ditch digger; Charlie Taverner, sly and slippery, who could, he insisted, charm the birds out of the trees. Finally, Rufus Dommet, the not so young now ex-bonded apprentice—all, in most senses, ignorant of one another prior to the night Ralph Barclay's press gang had chosen to mount their raid.

Facing a hostile atmosphere aboard Barclay's frigate, HMS *Brilliant*, they had bonded for self-protection, thus earning the soubriquet of which they were now proud. There had been two others, one Abel Scrivens. He had been the wisest of the group, now long dead, paying with his life for the association. The other, Ben Walker, who had murdered his sweetheart and the man cuckolding him, was living out his penance in the bosom of Muslim Barbary.

Pearce had set out to explain the ramifications which had led to this farcical court martial, only to find it was unnecessary. The Pelicans knew already, and from the way they spoke, so did the whole ship's company, who were, it seemed, incensed at what was being done to their captain.

'Goes the wrong way, John-boy,' Michael said, only half joking, 'an' there might be a boarding party slipping over the side of *Victory* afore dawn.'

Chapter Ten

John Pearce and Isaac Hallowell, plus the other Pelicans, arrived at Admiralty House to find Farmiloe waiting, looking very professional, carrying a red leather folder marked with an elaborate coat of arms. Given others were gathering for proceedings, clerks as well as the curious, quite a few naval, he drew Pearce to one side for a quiet word, leaving the rest of his party in an isolated group.

Except for Michael O'Hagan, they sought to avoid eye contact with those entering and milling around. Typical of the Irishman, he was prepared to engage in a return stare with anyone who showed curiosity at their presence, regardless of rank, an inquisitiveness soon abating when his size and attitude registered.

'I put out an enquiry to a few of the other wardrooms,' Farmiloe said, 'regarding this notion of the court seeking you a friend. As far as I can see, no such request was sent out.'

'I think you need look no further than Jervis for such an underhand trick.'

'Which makes no sense.'

'What better way to drive home, in the King's Navy, the one thing I spectacularly lack, present company and a few others excepted? I did, however, expect the court would appoint someone. I would of course have paid him no heed.'

'You would have been right to sideline the fellow if the admiral had a hand in his choice.'

'Something now tells me any attempt to represent myself would have been disallowed by the court, who are his creatures. Jervis is determined to ditch me.'

'Well, we will humbug him as soon as proceedings begin.'

'In what way?'

The leather folder was waved. 'Trust me?'

Pearce beckoned to tell Hallowell he should join them, introductions following. Farmiloe ensured the premier had sought no contact with his uncle on the matter. Such an act, if made public, would result in Captain Hallowell having to stand down, which might be to Pearce's disadvantage. They were deep in discussion when a stirring in the room announced the arrival of Commodore Nelson, commonly the smallest man in the room, albeit with more presence than anyone of height. He made straight for their little gathering, to be immediately introduced to Isaac Hallowell, to then acknowledge how high he rated his uncle.

'Well, Pearce,' he piped in his high-toned voice. 'Another pickle.'

The temptation to lay the blame where it belonged had to be supressed. You don't go damning admirals, however perfidious, to a man within weeks of joining such an august group. Added to which, Pearce had learned on previous meetings, Nelson did not respond well to the denigration of senior officers. This had applied to William Hotham, Jervis's predecessor—generally held, for his lack of martial zeal, to have been a less than worthy commander. How much more so would it apply to John Jervis, against whom no such accusation could be levelled.

'It seems I cannot avoid trouble, sir.'

'Which matters not,' Nelson responded with a wry smile, 'as long as it's the right kind. From what Mr Farmiloe has told me, I would be inclined to say it is so in the case for which you are to be tried.'

From him, this was sailing close to his own personal wind, leaving Pearce to wonder if relations with Jervis were not as they should be. Both were aggressive when it came to action, though it had to be acknowledged that no one came within a mile of Nelson in such an attitude. Odds and difficulties never seemed to dent his desire to attack and destroy the enemy; it was common knowledge throughout the fleet that restraining him was quite a task.

'Still,' he continued, possibly aware of having gone too far, 'I am here to observe only and, while you have my good wishes, I cannot offer you more.'

'They are welcome and sufficient, sir.'

'Please take your places, gentlemen' was announced from the door of the temporary courtroom.

It was politic to let the others file in, to then come last. There before them was the table covered in green baize, though with none of the judges sitting behind it. But Jervis was there, in the same seat at the back of the room he had occupied before, not even deigning to favour Pearce and his group with a glare as they took their requisite places.

There was another officer who sat down at a smaller table, close to but slightly offset to the main table, where he began to shuffle certain papers, one who avoided eye contact: it could be assumed he would be there to prosecute. As soon as the room settled, the clerk asked that all rise, this followed by the entry of the officers making up the court. Truscott's sword was placed sideways on the table before him and they took their seats, at which point the clerk rose to read on the charges.

'That on the day named in the indictment, Lieutenant John Pearce, Master and Commander of HMS *Hazard*, serving in the waters off Corsica, did endanger the lives of his officers and crew, marines included, by mounting a rash assault on a vessel, carrying on its deck a large body of armed Corsican insurrectionists, aided by even more of the same ashore, the combination numerous enough to mark the attack as folly.'

There was a pause to let this sink in.

'By your action, a dereliction of your duty, you endangered the position of His Majesty King George on Corsica, as well as the naval and military forces there assembled on his behalf, this leading to the subsequent abandonment of the island. How do you plead?'

It was tempting not to laugh as he stood up: they'd be blaming him for Noah's Flood next.

'Not guilty.'

Farmiloe stood as soon as Pearce resumed his seat, to beg the indulgence of the court, wishing to be allowed to speak before the prosecution opened their case.

'If I may introduce myself. I am Lieutenant Richard Farmiloe, second on HMS *Captain*.' It was telling how many eyes swivelled towards Nelson, to which he did not respond. 'I am here to act as the accused's friend.'

This set up a buzz swiftly curtailed by Commodore Truscott's gavel.

'If it may please the court, I have a question to pose before we proceed to evidence.'

'Which is highly irregular.'

'Then I ask again for the court's indulgence.' Truscott was obliged to nod; to do otherwise was perhaps to expose immediately there was a malicious element to the proceedings. 'I have been told a general notice was sent out, with a request for any officer so inclined to come forward and fulfil the role I now occupy. Can I ask to whom the implementation of this responsibility fell?'

'I fail to see the point of the question,' Truscott huffed.

'My enquiries,' the red leather folder was held up in plain view so the gold-tooled royal coat of arms was visible, 'have established no such request was made. This would have left Lieutenant Pearce without representation when he is threatened with the loss of his career. Surely this constitutes a grave failure of the court's duty?'

Truscott made a point of calling forward the clerk to confer, which went on for several seconds until he said, 'It is an error for which the court apologises.'

If this was delivered with a calm demeanour, more interesting was the discomfort on the faces of the other four captains. One of them gave Truscott a startled look before rapidly composing his features.

'Which I must humbly accept, sir. But you will, I am sure, appreciate my problem. Having been appointed this very day, dealing with an officer suffering from the physical tribulations' attendant on the loss of HMS *Courageux*, I have been afforded little time to properly master by brief. I therefore ask for a delay of twenty-four hours so I can seek out witnesses to the events which took place off Bastia in the weeks preceding the action for which Lieutenant Pearce is being examined.'

'We are here,' Truscott insisted, 'to judge the matter outlined in the indictment.'

'While I will set out to establish, and am fully confident of my ability to do so, that events previous to the night in question have a bearing on the matter.'

'Most irregular,' a sort of mantra which was all Truscott seemed to be able to say.

'While I would point out to the court, to refuse to allow such evidence might prejudice any judgement delivered.' Pearce, glancing over his shoulder, took encouragement from the look of thunder on Jervis's face. 'Such a delay may allow me to present to the court a list of said witnesses, which in turn will provide an idea of how long this case should last.'

Farmiloe's tone of voice changed to one of friendly understanding. 'I have my duties to fulfil, and Lieutenant Pearce is still in command of HMS *Hazard*. He would acknowledge, as do I, your responsibilities far exceed ours, so time is a factor.'

'We will retire to confer,' Truscott murmured, standing and leading the others away.

Farmiloe sat down and smiled reassuringly at Pearce, though he cautioned silence. Whatever went on in the room behind the green baize table did not take long, but it was enough for Pearce to insist he would rather get the whole thing over with, this getting a sharp response delivered in a low hiss.

'Don't employ a dog and bark yourself. I have my reasons.'

'Which are?'

'I'll tell you when we're outside.'

'You're so sure we will be?'

'Certain. The last thing Jervis will want is a case which you can appeal to a civilian court, one with judges upon whom he would have no influence. There is also the possibility of it going so badly against the judgement, it would damage not only his reputation but that of all involved.'

Pearce glanced over his shoulder to see the Jervis chair unoccupied; clearly there was a back exit, for he had not passed by. 'I have to say, Dick, you sounded very professional. For reasons I won't enumerate, I have been in a court of law, and you sound just the thing.'

'I told you, I have an uncle in the Middle Temple. I used to go and watch him.'

'Then let's hope your professional tone alarms them.'

Looking at the faces filing back in to retake their places produced no clue as to what had been decided until Truscott spoke, agreeing to a delay.

'But you must be aware, Lieutenant Farmiloe, you are part of a fleet on active service, one which may weigh to do battle before long. Therefore, I cannot grant you a full twenty-four hours. The court will convene at ten of the clock tomorrow.'

The gavel brought an end to proceedings, Pearce surprised at the way Dick Farmiloe hustled he, Hallowell, and the Pelicans out of the building, bustling on, with them in his wake, to a side entrance, where he insisted they take station.

'Am I permitted to call you by your given names?' he asked to murmured agreement, which had him acknowledge Michael, Charlie, and Rufus, men he had served alongside as a midshipman on HMS *Faron*. 'Then, I suspect, out of yon gate opposite is going to emerge a certain Toby Burns. I want him to see you, no more. Don't speak, and try not give him the evil eye. Bland is best in expression, as long as he sees you.'

This got a trio of smiles; if there was a fellow they hated, it was Burns. Indeed, given the chance to show the sod how much, it would be a meeting he'd be lucky to survive.

'John, we best not be seen here. Once they've eyed Burns, I would suggest Mr Hallowell take your Pelicans back to the ship.'

This agreed, the pair set off down the steep sloping streets, taking them past bastions bristling with cannon to the lower town, where Pearce was led into the dingy interior of a tavern.

'The wine here is highly praised, no doubt smuggled in. Which does affect the price.'

'Then you best let me pay. Have you not heard, I'm a rich man.'

'I've heard you might be, so don't go into detail; otherwise I might suggest you employ the most expensive advocate plying his trade on the Rock. But there is another reason Jervis will not want an appeal. With the funds you will have, he will face the top legal minds in London.'

'I can't see him withdrawing.'

'Neither can I, but that's not the point.'

'What is?'

'You, or rather we, have to destroy Toby Burns.'

Even in the dim light, Farmiloe saw this went down badly. Whatever John Pearce felt about him, and he hated the little swine, he was Emily

Barclay's nephew. While she might say she shared his aversion, this might not last if he was seen being revengeful enough to destroy his career. This was, of course, something he could not say, but fortunately the expression on his face was misinterpreted.

'You're too soft, John, which is something I have thought for a long time. That's the reason I asked you to bring along Michael, Charlie, and Rufus. I want him to see he is not only up against you. The sight of them hints at the possibility that matters might go all the way back to Brittany.'

'Of which you know little.'

'I know more than you think. Remember I stayed aboard *Brilliant* when you and your friends departed. Do you really think anyone in the mids berth, indeed aboard the whole ship, could countenance the idea of Toby Burns as a hero? If I don't know the precise details of what happened ashore, I do know he's a coward and lacking in the brain for such enterprising actions as we were told took place.'

'I can't fault such guesswork, Dick.'

'Knowing you as I now do, I suspect he stole your thunder.'

'I got we Pelicans free in exchange, not that it lasted.'

There was bitterness in the last part of those words, given he had in his mind's eye an image of Burns handing them over to second impressment, this time a legal one.

'I also know, and you do too, he got his rank for helping Admiral Hotham and Ralph Barclay by perjuring himself.'

'Which doesn't explain Jervis.'

'I do agree the motives there are more difficult to fathom, but it is Burns we must play upon, perhaps to persuade the admiral he has chosen a poor horse on which to put his money.'

The delivered wine, a deep and enticing red, was indeed pleasant to the taste as Farmiloe outlined the notion of dealing with Burns. This must attack his wholly false heroic reputation, one which had, no doubt, protected him from being seen as a coward.

'It staggers me how he's got away with it, but we can call it into question with you, Michael, Charlie, and Rufus in the courtroom. It would take a stronger stomach than his to lie in the face of people well able to swear to the truth.'

Sitting sipping wine allowed Farmiloe to question Pearce closely, to extract from him the names of everyone who'd been involved in the attempts to stop Corsican insurrectionists coming onto the island from Italy and Elba. Proposing them as witnesses, Pearce declined the notion of plump and indolent Major Warburton, who had withdrawn with the fleet, as being of any assistance.

'Lieutenant Vickery, his second in command, would have been of help, he having taken part in the action. But he went back to Elba as part of the force under the command of General de Burgh.'

'Some of the men he commanded may have been retained for the defence of the Rock. I will put out enquiries. Then, there is of course Sir Gilbert Elliot.'

'According to Sir David Rose, he's gone on a tour of Italy to represent King George and try and prop up the Papal States. I dined with Rose last week.'

'You know the governor?'

Pearce's grin was so wide no dim lighting could hide it. 'We have crossed paths a couple of times.'

'And his opinion of what you face?'

'I know what you're asking, but he can't get involved. Relations between the Horse Guards and the Admiralty are bad enough as it is. It's navy business, and he's not likely to offend those on whom he depends for supplies, if and when he's besieged by the Dons.'

'I best be off; it's getting dark, which is no aid to finding a redcoat.' A couple of coins were dropped on the table. 'You stay and finish the flagon.'

'I told you I would pay for it.'

'Wait till you see my bill,' Farmiloe joked. 'I charge Middle Temple fees.'

It was fully dark when Pearce left the tavern, his way lit by a few flaring torches and the lantern light spilling out from windows. Far from drunk, he was pleasantly merry on a stomach which had gone without much in the last two days. Added to this was the feeling that, with Dick Farmiloe on his side, matters were looking a touch rosier than hitherto. Having slightly lost his way—you could not just proceed along the shoreline for the number of gun batteries and fortifications placed there—he made his way back the way he had come. The route to the harbour quay from Admiralty House was one he knew.

Soon he was traversing the same streets down which he'd been led by Midshipman Liversidge, cobbled and narrow, in which the lighting was nothing like the main thoroughfares unless he was by a tavern doorway, of which there were many. They were occupied by parties of sailors, all done up in their best shore-going rig, not one of them sober, even if the night was young.

Given what they would be about, either now or later, his mind wandered to Emily Barclay and the physical relationship they'd enjoyed before and would do so again. An inexperienced innocent when they'd first made love, she had quickly allowed him to draw her into the realms of carnal pleasure. These were the things he'd learned himself from the affairs he enjoyed in Paris. In a world where marriage was a fig leaf for pleasure, a young, tall, handsome and very willing John Pearce had taken full advantage. Would there be more children? He hoped so.

Lost in such a pleasant reverie, it was hardly surprising he heard nothing before the first blow was struck, one which only his already dented hat saved him from being really serious. But it was still enough to fell Pearce and so stun him that he was in no position to ward off the fists and boots which followed. He did hear the voice telling him this was to be a warning to back off, or next time his assailants would do for him proper. The sound of running feet he heard, and loud cries of anger also penetrated before he passed out.

'"Back off, mate, or next time we'll do for you proper." Which means, if they used such words, they had to be British.'

'How do I look?' Pearce asked.

'In no fit state to go a-wooing.'

'Lord, Dick, don't make me laugh,' he wheezed, showing on his face real pain. 'The court martial?'

'You can't appear in this state, black and blue for a start. I'll have to ask for another postponement. I'll get a note from our sawbones.'

'Who found me?'

'You were lucky a party of liberty men from *Captain* happened along. They chased off the swine who were intent on kicking you to perdition, then brought you to our sickbay in the tender.'

'Get a sight of them?' This got a shake of the head. 'No idea who then?'

'None. My young topmen were not in the best state, having been ashore for hours.'

'The court . . .'

Farmiloe put a gentle hand on his shoulder. 'I also have sent for the clerk of the court to stand witness to what has occurred. Not even Beelzebub himself would expect you to attend in such a state.'

'I need to get back to *Hazard*.'

'You need do no such thing. I've sent for O'Hagan, and he can tend to you till you're fit enough to appear.'

'Why just Michael?'

'He's the only person I know who can tell you what to do without argument.'

Pearce lay back, seeking to recall something, anything, which would provide a clue to his assailants, to then posit a notion. 'Do you see this as too much of a coincidence, Dick, happening when it did?'

'That way lies madness, but it is strange your purse was untouched. I suspect it was because your footpads were disturbed.'

Recalling the words just discussed, the man who then closed his eyes was far from convinced.

CHAPTER ELEVEN

JOHN PEARCE CAUSED ENOUGH OF A STIR BEFORE HE EVEN ENTERED THE courtroom, setting off a loud buzz of curiosity as to the condition of his face. The extra day's delay had allowed the dark blue bruises to begin to go yellow at the edges, while his stiff gait attested to other injuries covered by his clothing.

'People will reckon,' Farmiloe joked, 'I've had to go to extreme lengths to get the truth out of you.'

'Please, Dick, my ribs hurt like hell. Can I suggest we go straight in and take our seats.'

This agreed, the party trooped through the far door—the Pelicans and Hallowell to sit in the body of the room, Pearce and Farmiloe at the table set aside for the defendant. Having spent several hours the previous day discussing things, there was not much to say, but the eye was drawn to a noise at the rear when Jervis entered to take his place. Pearce looked hard to no effect; Sir John just ignored him.

One of the things talked about was the notion the admiral might be behind the beating Pearce had suffered. It was scoffed at by Dick Farmiloe, sure no man in his position would take such a risk, this on the receiving end of a Pearce glare. To him there were only three explanations as to the culprits: mistaken identity, Jervis, or the one not even he could accept, Toby Burns.

As the room filled up everyone made sure, trying and failing to make it look anything but obvious, to get a chance for a closer examination. No doubt once seated and talking to whomever was sat with them, it was the subject of many whispered exchanges. Within minutes the court was back in session and the indictment reread, with no enquiry as to whether the accused was fit enough to proceed. To sailors, bruised features were not unusual. Such harm came from tumbles on deck, falling down companionways, or the fights which took place below decks—contests to which, in the main, the ship's officers turned a blind eye.

The officer at the opposite side table stood and, having had a long and meaningful look around the room, addressed Truscott, though his words were solely for the fellow penning the transcript.

'For the record, sir, I introduce myself as Lieutenant Ivor Downson, presently on the muster of the Gibraltar station. I have been allotted the task of prosecuting the indictment on behalf of the admiral in command of the Mediterranean Fleet, a duty I will endeavour to carry out to the best of my ability.'

'Pompous sounding bugger,' whispered Pearce.

'Which does not render him inept,' Farmiloe responded.

They were too close to the green baize for even an exchanged whisper. Truscott banged his gavel and added a glare, this replicated in the expression on Downson's face, possible proof he too had heard Pearce.

'Nothing like getting the court on our side,' Farmiloe added, which was painfully humorous and left a look on Pearce's face which may well have coloured Downson's harsh tone.

'Lieutenant Pearce, would I be right in assuming the plan of action you undertook off Bastia was yours and yours alone?'

'It was.'

'So, you do not wish to have anyone else share the blame?'

'I object,' Farmiloe interjected. 'The word "blame" assumes there will be such a thing, which I think is, at the very least, presumption.'

Downson responded before Truscott had a chance to think. 'I withdraw the word, but I replace it with "responsibility."'

'I'm happy,' Pearce insisted, 'to take full responsibility for what took place. While I would happily have taken into consideration any objections of my officers, since there were none, it was something I was not called upon to do.'

'No objections at all?'

'None.'

'Such certainty is rare, Lieutenant Pearce.'

A nudge from Farmiloe was a signal not to respond. 'At what point did you realise the assumptions you'd made were wrong?' Pearce again not responding, Downson went on. 'I mean the point at which you realised your plan was based on false assumptions. I refer, of course, to the number of enemies you faced.'

This had been the nub of what he and Farmiloe had talked about because it was the epicentre of the case they were trying to bring against him, the answer worked out well in advance.

'If I may address the court rather than you, Mr Downson,' Pearce replied, his eyes ranging along the quintet sat behind the green baize. 'I think anyone who has seen a hot action would be well aware that, when planning such things, certain factors always remain in the realm of the unknown.'

Only Benjamin Hallowell responded with obvious agreement, but Farmiloe appeared to be satisfied with the others looking pensive; he nodded to Pearce to continue.

'It is also the case that the attack had several parts, charged to proceed on my firing of a blue light rocket from my boat. Those in command of the various elements were people with whom it would have been impossible to communicate, so once the signal was given, the only safe thing to do, for the security of all, was to proceed.'

'Regardless?'

'No, Mr Downson,' Pearce insisted, 'with due regard to the possibility of success.'

'Or glory?'

'Not something to which I aspire.'

'Yet one of your officers did not agree, so held back?'

'If you're referring to Mr Burns, he was not one of my officers.'

'But he was under your command?'

'No, Mr Downson, he put himself under my command. Had he objected to such a position, he merely had to say so and he would not have been included in the action.'

'And to what do you attribute such an attitude?'

Farmiloe cut in again. 'Surely, Lieutenant Downson, that is a question which should, properly, be put to Mr Burns. My client is many things, but he is no mind reader.'

'True. But when Mr Burns exercised a prerogative you admit he had, he was subjected by Lieutenant Pearce to both verbal and physical abuse.'

'Verbal yes, physical no,' Pearce asserted. 'By his action, or rather inaction, he endangered everyone else engaged in the assault.'

'I see, sir, while you are unable to read minds, you have no trouble with opinions.' A response was once more cut off by Farmiloe, so the prosecutor added, 'Are you willing now to acknowledge that Mr Burns's appreciation of the situation was wiser than your own?'

'No.'

'Yet you were forced to abandon your plan, were you not?'

'I dislike the word "abandon."'

'Please answer with a yes or no,' Truscott growled. 'This is a court, not a debating chamber.'

'Yes,' Pearce responded, adding to the fury of Truscott. 'But only when it became politic to do so and the end we were seeking had been achieved.'

'Really. Are you sure it was not when the fact of your being outnumbered left you no choice?' Downson insisted. Without waiting for an answer, he faced the judges. 'Gentlemen, you will find before you a copy of the report made by Lieutenant Burns to Admiral Jervis, in which he lays out the facts of the action, as observed by him.'

He made great play of picking up his copy and waving it, which, covered by a loud murmuring in the room, allowed Farmiloe to whisper, 'Man's a fool.'

'There,' Downson intoned, 'in plain English, is the truth to which the man who penned it wishes to add not a word. I hesitate to call Mr Burns for the very sound reason that to do so might subject him to scurrilous attempts to undermine his character, something to which no gallant officer should be exposed.'

There was a pause, but only for effect.

'Lieutenant Pearce has, in his testimony—'

'Objection,' Farmiloe called out, standing up. 'I fear Mr Downson's inexperience of the nature of a court martial is tempting him into a summing up of his case. It is not his place to do so before the testimony of Lieutenant Pearce and any witnesses he wishes to call has been heard.'

'The facts are plain and set here,' Downson responded, clearly stung by the accusation of inexperience.

'Are we to be denied a defence?' Farmiloe asked.

'The charge is indefensible.'

'Sit down, Mr Downson,' Truscott said, his face indicating he was being forced to say something he did not enjoy. 'Mr Farmiloe has the right of it.'

'If Mr Downson wishes to change his mind and call Mr Burns, I will not pose any objection.' This got a furious shake of the head, at which point Truscott nodded to Dick Farmiloe to proceed. 'Then, if it please the court, in defence of the actions of Lieutenant Pearce, I would like to call my first witness: Lieutenant Toby Burns.'

The noise this produced had the gavel working furiously and to no avail, so it was some time before the clerk could get ready to call the witness, this delayed when Downson objected.

'On what grounds?' Farmiloe asked.

'He's not your witness to call.'

'Commodore Truscott?'

Truscott was loathe to admit Farmiloe was within his rights, but as was the case previously, he knew the rules of procedure. If the defence wished to put a hostile witness on the stand when the prosecution had not, they had every right to do so.

'Clerk of the court, send for Lieutenant Burns.'

The wait was long enough to set some fingers drumming on the green baize. Eventually an embarrassed clerk returned to say said witness was not in the room set aside for his use, while a search of the building had not produced any sight of him.

'He was ordered to attend,' Truscott said, more to his fellow judges than anyone else; this before he faced Downson. 'Where is he, sir?'

'If he is not where he's supposed to be, sir, I have no idea' was the embarrassed reply. 'I can only suppose he has returned to his ship.'

'HMS *Teme?*' Truscott asked, to have this confirmed before he once more addressed the clerk. 'Send a file of marines to fetch him. He's to be confined also. The court will adjourn till tomorrow afternoon at four.'

Pearce, glancing at the back of the room, noted Jervis's chair was unoccupied, which left him to wonder at what point it had been vacated.

The orders arrived the following morning, not long after first light, while the decks were still being sanded and John Pearce, yet to be shaved, was still on his first cup of coffee. They led to a degree of bustle as he had instructions to go at once aboard HMS *Minerve*, to which Commodore Nelson had shifted his broad pennant, where he would receive further directions.

He was greeted by the premier of the frigate, Lieutenant Culverhouse, and immediately escorted to the great cabin. There he found Nelson breakfasting with Captain Cockburn and another captain, d'Arcy Preston of HMS *Blanche*, to whom he was introduced. Nothing on his face indicated any feelings on receipt of the Pearce name.

'No introductions required with Mr Cockburn, I fancy,' piped the commodore. 'Do come and join us, as I daresay you've yet to breakfast.'

Even seated, Nelson seemed dwarfed by the captain of *Minerve*, a tall Scotsman and an altogether more reserved character. Pearce had met him earlier in the year, in an action against Genoese privateers.

'We're off to sea,' Nelson announced gleefully. '*Hazard* too. Damn this sitting off the Rock and mouldering, Pearce.'

'I hate to allude to the fact I'm in the middle of a court martial, sir.'

'Postponed. Orders came for me last night, and Sir John was most obliging when I asked for you to accompany us.' Pearce nearly said *I bet he was*, when Nelson added with a guffaw, 'Mr Farmiloe will just have to wait for his great closing speech. Not pleased, not pleased at all.'

'Accompany you where, sir.'

'Back to where you came from, laddie,' Cockburn replied. 'You know the waters and the islands.'

'Which were in French hands the last time I looked, sir.'

Such a sarcastic response did not go down well, and Pearce was subjected to a frown. But it got another chuckle from the commodore as he corrected Cockburn.

'Elba is our destination. We're to get off the garrison we left to hold it. As well as that, we must pick up any waifs and strays, fellow countrymen, who are refugees from Italy. Leave them there much longer and they'll end up spending Christmas in the French oubliettes. How are your stores?'

'Well made up, sir, including water and wood.'

'Good, we weigh at midday.'

'Am I to abandon my court martial?'

'Why not?'

Pearce wanted to say what he'd been accused of was yet to be rebutted, and unchallenged, it would colour opinion. Then he remembered the general state of that commodity as far as he was concerned, so it was better to tuck into eggs, ham, kidneys, and mushrooms than dwell on it. He certainly was not going to exercise his right to refuse.

If Jervis thought getting rid of him would allow the matter to atrophy, Pearce had news for him. Before going back to *Hazard*, he would call upon Dick Farmiloe and ask him to submit a demand for another court martial be convened and one called by him, which was a right afforded to every naval officer.

'Can I ask, sir, when Sir John suggested *Hazard*?'

'Left it to me, Pearce,' Nelson replied. 'But he was happy with my choice. After all, we fought in those waters, in company before, have we not.'

They weighed at the time dictated by the commodore, passing on the way out of the bay the incoming mail packet from home. On deck and close enough to shout, it was possible for Pearce to hail the captain, Michael McGahan, a man he much esteemed. On a previous voyage, not long after Pearce's promotion, the Ulsterman had gone to great lengths to educate a true novice about the art of sailing and navigating a ship, general principles which applied to all vessels, regardless of size or function. He was a naturally kind fellow, but not without an Achilles heel.

'No duels this time, Michael,' floated across the divide. 'And have a care with the drink.'

'To the former, yes, John. But how can I avoid a tankard when I'm fresh ashore after two weeks at sea.'

It could not be a conversation of long duration with them passing each other, but it allowed Pearce to recall certain facts. McGahan was a strict temperance man at sea, for the very good reason it was safest to be so, and an intrepid imbiber ashore. In the latter state, he was a magnet to trouble, convinced no woman could resist his charms: they could, and their menfolk could also take serious umbrage at his salacious hints.

Intervening to prevent an army officer from a physical chastisement of a man pestering his wife, Pearce had inadvertently struck the fellow, which caused him to be in receipt of a challenge. Unable to decline saw him and his party atop the Rock at dawn and with pistols, at which point McGahan stepped forward to insist it was his fight, not Pearce's.

Finding arguments futile—he feared his man would be a poor shot—Pearce was forced to give way and let matters proceed, at which point he found out how wrong he had been. McGahan was no novice with a pistol, quite the opposite. At twenty paces he put a ball in his opponent's shoulder with consummate ease.

Watching his stern as the mail packet sailed on to land at Gibraltar, Pearce was thinking of the trouble he had subsequently faced because of that encounter. Had he still been ashore and able to meet and talk, would he have told McGahan of his later travails? Given it would mortify the man, probably not.

They were well out of sight when the mail was unloaded and taken to Admiralty House, where it was sorted ship by ship. The packet for HMS *Hazard*, several missives addressed to Lieutenant John Pearce, was placed, like those for *Minerve* and *Blanche*, in the storeroom for later collection. Naturally, by far the greatest number of communications had gone to Sir John Jervis, a mass of despatches along with numerous personal communications.

The one from the office of the Lord Chancellor raised a degree of curiosity, so the seal bearing his device was quickly broken, the contents, once read, bringing a smile to a face not often in the habit of wearing such an expression. By government decree, the claim of the *Santa Leocadia* being a prize was going to be denied. Even more pleasing, the silver had been officially declared as droits of the crown, so Pearce would whistle for his fortune. Pity about Langholm, but he was of good family and well connected in the service, so would prosper anyway.

This went some way to assuage his anger at the way the court martial had turned out. Burns had not acted properly when called as a witness but, in truth, even Jervis acknowledged he was not the most stalwart of naval officers. But it was the wiles of the man defending Pearce which really attracted his ire. To the Jervis mind, Pearce was so suffused with pride he would never have had the wit to call Burns as his witness, which is why steps had been taken to ensure he mounted his own defence.

But this Lieutenant Farmiloe had popped up seemingly from nowhere and, worse, with an understanding of what could and could not be done in a court, which lay well outside the abilities of the vast majority of naval officers. The sod had humbugged Jervis, so it would be a name he would never forget. Should any request come to advance his career, here was one admiral who would do all in his power to thwart it.

'Thank the Almighty Nelson asked for Pearce,' he murmured to himself, for it was obvious that seeking to proceed with the court martial would be a risky course.

There was still the matter of Toby Burns to deal with, but a man of his rank had little to fear from a fellow who had turned out to be so lacking in backbone, and one who had failed in the purpose Jervis had set him. When Burns hinted the despatch John Pearce had sent him to deliver to Jervis gilded what had been a near disaster, the admiral had allowed him to present his own, one in which Pearce was damned for excessive glory-hunting and Toby Burns vindicated for wise caution.

This suiting Sir John's purpose, the original having been set aside in favour of one with which it was possible, as Jervis saw it, to right a wrong, one readily taken only to fall foul of the person who had so obliged him. Burns would never say, but his presence with the fleet could lead to unwelcome gossip, so the best course was to send both him and HMS *Teme* home. He could carry the replies he would have to pen to the despatches now lying open on his desk, one warning of a possible French fleet putting to sea. The actual fact was itself questionable, as was the destination, but there was a serious worry the French might be heading for Ireland.

'Bridport's problem, not mine,' was his vocal conclusion.

Chapter Twelve

FIVE UNCOMFORTABLE DAYS AT SEA ENSUED FOR JOHN PEARCE AND HIS crew, with intermittent gale-driven squalls under cloudy skies and *Hazard*, by some distance, in the wake of *Minerve*, HMS *Blanche* well to the rear of both. The trio were covering many miles of open water, alert to both opportunity and danger, it now being clear the course Nelson had chosen to follow was going to take them mighty close to the Cartagena approaches. This was a significant Spanish fleet base, second in the Mediterranean only to Port Mahon, so it was thus necessary to keep a careful watch for enemy warships patrolling the intervening waters.

In the murky pre-dawn light, the sight of a glowing lantern high on a poop, nearly obscured by squally rain, had Cockburn immediately begin to close to hailing distance, no doubt to demand identification. Proximity and increasing daylight 'revealed not one warship but two, the second well astern and closer to *Blanche* than *Minerve*. Cockburn's question must have prompted a negative response, for the gold and red Spanish battle flags were immediately raised, a fact relayed to the quarterdeck by Worricker, set to observe from the mainmast cap. It wasn't long before other signals were raised.

'Our number, sir. Signal from *Minerve* reads, "Engage the enemy more closely and repeat."'

'Our flags aloft so *Blanche* can see the message, Mr Livingston, then acknowledge the commodore. And clear for action, Mr Hallowell?'

'Aye, aye, sir.'

These orders sent *Blanche* to intercept the second enemy frigate, while *Hazard*'s number once more, following swiftly, instructed her to stand towards Cockburn. When Worricker, from the tops, shouted down to identify the closest enemy as a three-decker frigate and report he could count the gunports, what he told Pearce indicated they were in for a warm afternoon.

'Forty guns, sir, so a match for *Minerve*.'

'Only superior by a couple of cannon, Mr Worricker,' was the Pearce response.

Looking astern showed HMS *Blanche* cracking on sail, so he knew d'Arcy Preston had the message. Before weighing, Nelson had outlined what he expected from this command, which was not the simple mantra of 'just go at 'em' for which he was renowned. As far as *Hazard* was concerned, she was an add-on only to what the larger vessels could achieve and her main role would be to come, this in the waters she sailed before. Pearce had been told, his command being so small, that if the trio ran into opposition, it was *Minerve* which would set the tone. If she attacked an enemy, so must they all. In the face of superior force, then the course to follow was obvious: they must run.

'If it's a fair contest, you have nuisance value, Mr Pearce, and I trust you and your judgement to make it count. But I value you whole, so choose what you do with that in mind.'

'I'll do my best, sir.'

'I expect nothing less.'

Since Cockburn was already closing with the larger Spaniard, Pearce did so too, though he had to avoid coming between any yardarm-to-yardarm slugging match. Instead, he would seek to get into a position to inflict damage while not endangering his ship. This, he hoped, would force the enemy captain to divert men and gunfire to drive him off, increasing the chances of success for *Minerve*.

Given such a grey day and infrequent squalls, it was at times far from easy to get a clear view of the three-decker Spaniard: *Blanche* and her opponent, so far off, were even less visible. But it was the Don who luffed up and chose to then open the cannonade. Glancing at his new watch, bought in Gibraltar, Pearce called out the time as seven forty, with an order to mark it on the slate, beyond which there was nothing he could do but observe.

Bow on as she closed, *Minerve's* sails suffered: Pearce could see where several were holed or shredded, which had no effect on Cockburn's intentions. His bow chasers fired several salvoes as aloft, his topmen, at serious risk to themselves, took the frigate down to fighting topsails, the course being held and punishment accepted until the ship could reply to the Spaniard in kind.

The rudder eventually brought *Minerve* round in a wide arc until she was beam on, at which point the flashes of fired cannon rippled down the side in a superbly disciplined broadside. Closer now, those on the deck of *Hazard* could see sections of the Spaniard's bulwarks disintegrate, while over the waves came the clanging sound of round shot hitting the muzzles of cannon.

It was easy to imagine the dead, dying, and mangled such damage would inflict, and it would get worse. What followed was a constant exchange, *Minerve* firing with a regularity the Dons could not match, their responses diminishing the longer it went on, which meant the result, lest some stroke of pure luck intervened, was inevitable.

First of the sticks to go was the Spaniard's foremast, soon to be followed by the mizzen, leaving her looking like a semi-hulk, but with a goodly number of her guns still firing. With manoeuvre constrained for the three-decker, it was time for John Pearce and his crew to enter the battle.

'Mr Williams,' Pearce called to the master, 'I wish to cross the enemy stern, but we must not get within the arc of her main armament. So as soon as we have stung her, we must back our sails, come round, and get clear.'

There was a tingling feeling in Pearce's limbs, one he knew would extend to a goodly portion of the crew. This was their purpose: to find, inflict damage, and, if possible, destroy Britannia's enemies. He also knew, from Michael O'Hagan, that he commanded a crew who took as a personal insult the lies of Toby Burns. They would thus be fired up to lay to rest any notion that, as a group, they were not doughty fighters.

Soon they would enter the great billowing clouds of smoke created by the battle before them, so in the nostrils and mouth would be the sharp taste of gunpowder. Looking around, Pearce could see everyone was at their allotted place, no one talking; as they approached the enemy stern, the air of anticipation was palpable.

'Cannon aimed high and double-shotted, Mr Hallowell; I wish to try and wound their poop and quarterdeck.'

Moberly and his marines, placed on the cap, were peppering the enemy taffrail with musket fire to drive away their Spanish opponents, men who suddenly disappeared as HMS *Hazard* came under their counter; they knew what was coming. Four-pounder balls would bounce off the thick oak scantlings, but against the thinner timbers of the stern deadlights and then up through the deck, they would kill and maim all in their path.

'Fire.'

The sound of shattering timbers was gratifying indeed, but Pearce, who had hoped to get off two salvoes, was acutely aware of approaching danger, which told him he needed to come about in short order and sooner than he wished. The present course, combined with the speed the brig was making through the water, would bring him into the rearmost arc of the heaviest Spanish cannon. He would then face weapons of a calibre, at close range, which had the weight of shot to blow *Hazard* to pieces.

He bellowed the orders to come about, which were immediately executed by a crew already primed and waiting to hear them. The just-fired cannon were quickly lashed off so every man jack was available to handle ropes and canvas as well as the movement of the yards. Backed sails brought forward progress to a crawl at the same time as the men on the wheel were spinning the rudder to bring the ship up into the wind.

This manoeuvre being carried out in close proximity to the Spaniard risked collision as, for what seemed an age, *Hazard* seemed to be drifting. But with the yards spun and the addition of the dropped main course, she drew away from the threat and retaliation. They got clear just as the Don's mainmast slowly went by the board, taking with it the usual mass of rigging and humanity.

Pearce was well out of harm's way and seeking, through the clouds of smoke and the continuing cannonade, an idea of what to do next. Suddenly the red and gold flag of Spain, now flying from the stump of the mizzen, fluttered down to the deck, the halyards having been cut away. The guns fell silent and a new sound replaced it: hearty cheering from the British decks. Pearce, having closed with *Minerve*, was able to see how much she too had suffered, but nothing like the Spaniard about to be boarded.

A telescope trained to the west showed HMS *Blanche* had enjoyed equal success, for her opponent had suffered even more; with the smoke of battle dispersing, it was apparent both foremast and mainmast were gone. She lay alongside her opponent and had raised the union flag to show the enemy was now a prize, with a boat on the way, no doubt to relay Captain d'Arcy Preston's request for instructions.

On *Minerve*, grappling irons were being thrown to grip what remained of the enemy bulwarks, hard pulling closing the gap. As soon as the ships were locked together, albeit grinding on the swell, a gangplank was laid between the upper decks, one which both Nelson and Cockburn could cross, there being no shortage of points of entry. The telescope revealed one sole individual preparing to greet them, sword in hand; closer examination showed a tall fellow of saturnine complexion, wearing a haughty expression which sat ill with what he was about to experience.

Nelson, towered over as usual, stood back to let George Cockburn accept the formal surrender and the sword, only fitting as he was *Minerve*'s captain, with Pearce wondering, as they spoke, what they were saying. Then the commodore was introduced to receive, in return, a formal bow before the man who executed it was escorted back to *Minerve*, where he would no doubt be treated as an honoured guest.

'He's on his own,' Pearce said.

'Sir?' asked Hallowell.

'The Spanish captain. He's gone aboard *Minerve* alone, so where are the rest of his officers?'

'Might I suggest, sir,' said Moberly, 'if you take a look from the cap, from where I have just come, you might see the shattered quarterdeck.'

It took a moment for the marine officer's words to make sense. 'Badly damaged?'

'Devastated, sir, and coated with gore. I daresay, if you were stood there and looked down, I reckon you would be able to see right through the wardroom accommodation to the water.'

There was every reason to suppose the cause of this had been the salvo from HMS *Hazard*, which produced an odd feeling of sadness. Only a beast, in Pearce's view, would rejoice in death and destruction once the heat of battle had faded.

The Spanish captain had been escorted through a vessel already busy with repairs, while to his rear Pearce watched as parties of British tars, now on the surrendered vessel, were busy cutting away the mainmast, axes swinging though stays and masses of ropes to release it into the water. Once floating, retaining lines would be employed to draw it into the hull, where it could be lashed off. No navy wasted timber: the lower part where it had been shot away may be useless, but the upper masts were intact.

'Signal from *Minerve*, sir. Captain to repair aboard.'

'Then bring us alongside, Mr Hallowell, while I change my coat. I have no notion to boat over and arrive soaked.'

As it was, such a drubbing could not be avoided, as yet another squall struck, which made Pearce glad he had on his boat cloak. Even on a busy deck, Culverhouse, who had greeted him, allowed him an inspection of the impairment, some obvious, as battens and frapping were being applied to the wounded mainmast.

'Every one is damaged, Mr Pearce, and our carpenter will be busy plugging gaps in the scantlings for a goodly time. It was a hot contest.'

'The bill?'

Being the premier, it was a figure he would have been quick to gather for his after-action report, so the answer came immediately. 'Eight killed, thirty-eight wounded, and four missing, no doubt blown overboard, which is light after near an hour of fierce exchange. The enemy has suffered many times more.'

'Do we have a name for the capture yet?' Pearce enquired.

'*Santa Sabina*.'

'I noted only the captain came aboard.'

'He would. Every one of his officers was killed, and only God saved him from a similar fate. I think he will be counting his casualties in three figures.' There was a pause before he added, slightly impatiently, 'I believe the commodore is waiting for you.'

Pearce entered the great cabin to find all three officers sitting and drinking wine and in receipt of an ebullient greeting from a clearly delighted Horatio Nelson. He immediately praised the actions *Hazard* had taken to aid the capture of the *Santa Sabina* as Cockburn's steward poured him a glass. As Nelson carried on, it was with a twinkle in his one good eye.

'And I suggest I have something to raise an eyebrow for you, Pearce. I have a memory of you having told me, like Captain Cockburn, you carry in your veins a tincture of Caledonian blood.'

It was clear Nelson was in a mood to be humoured, so Pearce obliged. 'More than a tincture, sir. I would guess it is wholly Scottish on both sides, paternal and maternal.'

'There you are, Cockburn; I told you he was one of your own.'

The response was guarded and not wholly approving. 'So you did, sir.'

Such reserve did nothing to dull Nelson's mood. 'Which makes three of a kind. May I introduce you, Mr Pearce, to the captain of the *Santa Sabina*, Don Jacobo Stuart. I'm sure you recognise the family name. His great grandsire was King James the Second and, as Duke of York, Lord High Admiral of Britain, so we should be humbled to have him as our guest.'

The fellow so named understood every word, and it was clear he did not share Nelson's jocular mien, not least being termed a guest.

'He bears a name to ring an alarm bell in Scotland, would you not say?'

'England too, sir,' Pearce pointed out. 'His forebearer gave most of the country south of Carlisle quite a fright.' The reply allowed Don Jacobo to produce a wisp of a smile, though Pearce's next words soon saw it off. 'Not that I'm a Jacobite sympathiser.'

'No one is these days, Pearce,' Cockburn growled, 'though I believe some have relatives who have sailed very close to that particular wind.'

Seeing the change in Pearce's mood at what was a clear reference to his father, who had carried the soubriquet of the Edinburgh Ranter for his radical speeches and writings excoriating privilege and hypocrisy, not least in monarchs, Nelson spoke to avoid a clash. He knew the son to be no respecter of rank.

'Who, I have been told by Mr Pearce, is dead, Captain Cockburn. A victim of the madmen in Paris and their infernal guillotine.'

The look this received hinted at 'serves him right,' but it soon disappeared, to instead produce the gruff vocal and standard, 'Then God rest his soul.'

Pearce, who had been about to pull Cockburn up short, nearly laughed. Old Adam would not have wanted anything to do with a deity any more than with a king. This would have applied by the ton to the member of the royal house of Stuart sitting ignoring his wine. But there was no chance to say anything, as a midshipman was brought in by another lieutenant, immediately addressing Nelson before handing him a written report.

'Captain Preston's compliments, sir; he wishes you to be informed of his intention to man the capture with a prize crew and render her fit to continue with us to Elba. He asks if this fits with your wishes?'

Nelson read what must have been hastily written to inform both Cockburn and Pearce the other capture was called *Ceres* of thirty-two guns. Don Jacobo, hitherto maintaining a haughty air, could not help but let his attitude slip as this was being discussed.

'It does, young fellow. We will do likewise once we have made *Santa Sabina* seaworthy, which we will have to do at a lick, given these are not safe waters in which to hang about. Captain Cockburn, it is up to you to appoint the officers you wish to man your capture, but I suggest that if they are not already aboard, they should shift.'

'I have to favour my premier, sir.'

'Naturally.'

Culverhouse would be in seventh heaven at such a prospect. Commanding a captured enemy frigate was not an automatic route to promotion, but it certainly added lustre. Nelson then addressed the lieutenant who'd brought in the midshipman from *Blanche*.

'You can second him, Hardy, if Captain Cockburn has no objection.'
Cockburn just nodded and Hardy said, 'Thank you, sir.'

'Make your confreres in *Captain* jealous, I should think,' which established Hardy as one of Nelson's own lieutenants.

'Mr Pearce, can you take this young messenger back to his ship and confirm to Captain d'Arcy Preston I wish *Ceres* to sail in company with the *Santa Sabina*, with Lieutenant Culverhouse in command. I leave it to him who he puts on her quarterdeck.'

He then addressed the Spaniard. 'Don Jacobo, you are of course my guest, but I hope it will not be too long until we can arrange for you to be exchanged.'

It only then took a look to dismiss those with duties to perform.

Pearce, towing the boats from *Blanche*, left a pair of frigates undergoing much hammering and fixing, all undertaken under still grey skies and with regular dousing from the frequent squalls. The captured crew were put to getting the intact parts of the mainmast up onto the deck where a derrick was being prepared to get it in place. A stump it might be, but once the men of *Minerve* had rigged and rove, then added some yards and spars, it would take a degree of canvas and thus be able to carry some sail.

It took little time to get to *Blanche* who, like her sister ship, was wallowing alongside the capture, with very much the same kind of work being carried out and in the same conditions to render her seaworthy, though *Ceres* had suffered a great deal less than the *Santa Sabina*. Hands from *Hazard* were sent over to speed up the repairs, and once she was declared fit to sail, a prize crew was left aboard with orders to stay in the wake of *Blanche*, while Pearce and his returned crew brought up the rear.

Having moved at no great pace, the trio was brought to more haste at the sound of distant gunfire and the blast of a misted orange glow caused by the latest squall. The passing of this latest burst of rainfall showed another Spanish frigate had appeared and, no doubt seeing the Union flag above that of Spain, had immediately opened fire. She was now being engaged by *Minerve*, d'Arcy Preston immediately signalling to *Hazard* she should shepherd *Ceres* while he went to the aid of Cockburn.

John Pearce was thus no more than a distant witness to a second hot action of the day, one which, in less than an hour, severely damaged both fighting ships. Whether it was that or the approach of *Blanche* which altered the Spanish captain's thinking, he bore away out of range of *Minerve*, with d'Arcy Preston asking permission to pursue; this denied.

Back aboard *Minerve*, Pearce was once more included in the discussion of what would come next. For Nelson, despite the severe damage to three of the ships, there was no choice but to proceed on the mission with which he'd been entrusted. This meant towing the *Santa Sabina*, on which repairs had been abandoned when the need to fight off a new enemy ensued.

Maximum effort, much of it carried out by lantern light, saw *Minerve* fit to proceed, and at first light, the great towing cable was hauled aboard the Spaniard to be raised from the water. Cockburn's frigate took the strain of the heavier vessel and soon the pair were under way, albeit at the pace of a snail.

At first there was no sign of the enemy frigate so recently engaged, but increasing daylight showed not only that she was in the offing but had been joined by two seventy-fours which, in terms of proximity, were too close for comfort and too large to engage. On his quarterdeck, John Pearce could see the danger this presented as well as anyone, with the two attached frigates wallowing along at no great speed while the enemy ships sighted were piling on sail.

'We've found hot water here, Mr Hallowell, and no mistake.'

'Am I admitted to point out, sir, we are undamaged.'

'You are, of course.'

His captain could see what the premier was driving at: the fact *Hazard* was whole, a fast-sailing vessel on what was a favourable wind, and so had the legs to outrun any seventy-four. But for Pearce there was another consideration: if they closed enough and sought to engage, what was he to do? Any help he could provide to his consorts would be ineffectual and for his ship, crew, and very likely himself, fatal.

The natural thing to do was to pack on sail and get well clear, but could he do so with a clear conscience? Or was the possibility of reputational damage to himself to be taken into consideration? There was no long consideration of this: he was not going to sacrifice the men he led to his fear of opprobrium. Just about to issue Midshipman Livingston an order to request instructions from Nelson, the cry came from the masthead.

'*Minerve*'s cast off the tow!'

This was quickly followed by a general order to make all sail, backed up by a gun, hardly necessary since Cockburn was piling on all the canvas *Minerve* could carry, *Blanche* likewise.

'The prize crews?' Hallowell enquired.

'We have no time to effect a rescue, and Nelson will have no wish to end up in a Spanish jail any more than I do. We have our orders; please see them obeyed.'

There were half-hearted waves from the decks of both the *Santa Sabina* and the *Ceres*, these from the officers and crews who would indeed see the inside of a Spanish jail. But no condemnation could be aimed at Nelson's decision: to save them he would have to fight, and to do so left the result in no doubt.

'Another signal from *Minerve*, sir. Our number and it reads, "Make all speed."' There was a gap as those flags were lowered and another raised to replace it, with the Mite reading it off: 'Take station ahead, sir.'

'Thank you, Mr Livingston. I daresay you can relax. I doubt we'll be receiving any more.'

If there was relief for Pearce in being ordered to save himself and his ship, there was still a residue of worry as to how it would be seen if both *Minerve* and *Blanche* were taken while he survived. Not that he would seek to disobey, and he had no requirement to be told what his subsequent duties entailed. If his consorts managed to outrun the Spaniards, he must stay ahead but in sight from the tops so he could apprise Nelson of any threats which appeared ahead. If they were taken, he would need to reverse course, avoid the Dons, and report the loss to Sir John Jervis so another pair of frigates could be despatched to Elba to carry out the evacuation.

Even if it was out of sight, he was sure the work of repair aboard *Minerve* was ongoing for, once on what he considered to be his allotted station, he monitored her speed by his own and it was plainly increasing;

marginally, but faster nevertheless. The other salient fact was he could get no view of the pursuit, which meant they were not closing the gap.

Pearce had known, almost from leaving Gibraltar, once he had seen where *Minerve's* course was taking them, that Nelson was taking a risk and may even have been disobeying his orders. He would do this to satisfy his desire to always carry the fight to the enemy. It had been the same, whichever admiral he served under. Circumstances always had him straining at the leash, either on his own or as part of a fleet approaching action.

Reluctant as he was to admit it, Jervis rightly esteemed Nelson for this, as had Lord Hood. Only the indecisive Hotham, who had held the command between those two, had gone to great lengths when it came to restraint, driving that particular inferior to distraction.

As the day wore on, Pearce became more and more convinced the chase had either fallen behind or given up, while over the prow nothing had been sighted to presage any danger. As night fell, he felt secure enough to light his stern lanterns so the commodore would know his position. He could also allow himself some sleep.

CHAPTER THIRTEEN

YOU DID NOT SEEK TO LAY ON AND SLUMBER IN YOUR HAMMOCK WHEN you heard the cry to 'show a leg,' especially when the man issuing it was Michael O'Hagan. To do so was to see the ties cut away from the beams and the occupant thrown to land painfully on the deck. He added to his duties as master at arms a physique which rendered protest at such treatment both futile and potentially dangerous. So it was something to remark upon that the most formidable member of the Pelicans was well liked.

Along with a sense of humour and the ability to appreciate a laugh, even at his own expense, all aboard knew he had a special connection to the captain. This was one which could be exploited to bring to his attention and get put right any of the petty niggles which would surface aboard any vessel. Not that the crew were always content; just like in every ship in the fleet, they moaned about lousy pay, food if it was of poor quality—and it too often was—wine to drink instead of small beer, purser's weights, and the like.

But it was accepted the man in command of HMS *Hazard* could do little to alleviate many of these while also one to avoid overzealous chastisement, he being no friend to the notion of lashing open a man's back. Only four people aboard knew the reason. Apart from an inbuilt aversion to a practice he saw as brutal, Pearce had been lashed to a grating himself when not long pressed, and if it had, in his case, turned out to be less than he had anticipated, the fear of what he had been about to face was something he'd never lost.

Punishments there were, like loss of grog and even, on two occasions, miscreants being stapled to the deck to exist for days on ship's biscuit and water. But these had been seen, given the transgressions, as fair, so no resentment was directed towards the great cabin. This left John Pearce, now up prior to first light, ready to sweep the horizon for potential danger, his guns run out and the crew ready to do battle, feeling he had the good opinion of the men he led.

From this point on the day would proceed with naval habit; with the guns secured, the decks would be sanded and holystoned by part of the crew, while the rest of *Hazard* was thoroughly cleaned with watered-down vinegar by others, leaving as healthy a space as could be achieved on a ship of war a long time at sea. The men would be piped to breakfast and, after being shaved by Shenton, Pearce could enjoy his own, with the luxury of solitude if he so chose or company if this appealed more. Prior to attending his duties in educating his midshipmen, he would receive the reports of his standing officers: the bosun, gunner, carpenter, and master.

All was recorded in the ship's log, along with stores consumed, including grog, the course decided upon, the sail plan, speed, and any punishments visited upon the crew. These would, in time, be first passed by an admiral's clerk before being sent on to the Navy Board for examination by eagle-eyed functionaries, men who delighted in seeking discrepancies to be chased up and charged to the man in command. Truly, as Pearce had often remarked, the navy ran on paper more than canvas.

This morning he chose to breakfast with his teenage midshipmen, all of Scottish parentage and beholden for their position to Henry Dundas. Maclehose, tall and confident, was as good as already an officer, unlike Tennant, a gloomy son of the Kirk. The youngest and no longer small enough to justify his soubriquet of the Mite, Livingston was now showing, in the eruptions on his forehead, the signs of progressing puberty.

Pearce made no attempt to teach them the subjects essential to their chosen profession, mathematics or navigation; this he left to the master, Mr Williams. But he did take them for fencing and fighting lessons or, like now, for education in the proper table manners every naval officer should acquire. For young men always hungry, it had to be driven home that eating like a pig at a trough was unacceptable, as was gulping your wine or, even worse, overindulging in same to the point of drunkenness. Pearce had explained many times that individuals each had a limit and that it was wise to get to know your own in short order, words which led his guests to wonder why this caused him to smile.

He could never say such things without conjuring up an image of Michael O'Hagan, an epic consumer of alcohol if given the chance, turning him into a menace. Gone would be the laughing, amenable Irishman, to be replaced with a man whose sole desire was to inflict as much damage as he could on his fellow humans. Indeed, the first experience Pearce ever had with him, in the Pelican Tavern, was the avoidance of a head-removing haymaker.

The proper way to pass the port decanter was important, as was the unacceptable notion of slipping any of the food you were served into your pocket for later consumption. Care should be taken not to be too loud in conversation, which had a double-edged meaning in naval terms when it came to dining in great cabins, be they admirals or captains.

Unlike John Pearce, too many senior officers only allowed their officers and midshipmen guests to talk when addressed or when they were invited to do so; therefore, conversation was never allowed to flow naturally. It was wise to consider your responses carefully in such situations, which were bound to arise eventually.

'And remember this. Keep your responses brief.'

The call of 'Sail Ho' was barely moderated by the glass of the skylight, nor was the following call, 'Hard off the starboard bow.'

All moved at once, with an invitation from their captain to take what was left on the table to their stations. He was handed his hat and a telescope by Derwent before following the youngsters onto the deck. From there nothing was visible so, in another departure from the norm, Pearce tucked his telescope into his breeches and went to climb the shrouds; not many captains were seen even in the mainmast cap, never mind up in the crow's nest.

Leg over an upper mast yard and secure in his position, Pearce opened his telescope to follow the finger of the sharp-eyed lookout, to espy what appeared to be a square-rigged two-masted brigantine which, at a distance, seemed about the same size as *Hazard*. He then counted four gunports on the larboard hull, which would be replicated on the other side.

'No flag when you first spotted her?'

'None, your honour.'

'Which marks her as unlikely to be navy, anyone's and certainly not our own. Yet she's properly armed.'

He also reckoned her, given her size, not to be British. The only national vessels this far into the Mediterranean tended to be merchantmen of some size, engaged in the Italian or Levant trade. Most sailed in convoy, but there were others in quick-sailing ships who chanced their arm alone, for the ocean was wide and the possibility of an encounter, even with a friendly vessel, limited.

This had been especially true with a British battle fleet to the north of Corsica, its frigates patrolling far and wide the routes such ships would follow. But did they know said fleet had departed San Fiorenzo Bay, while the few warships left were defending Elba. This alone could have turned these waters from a dangerous place to seek profit into a happy hunting ground for enemy vessels.

Pearce was fairly certain what he was observing, in a ship which would in time cross his bow, was either a French naval warship or a privateer, one with enough speed and firepower plus, no doubt, a crew in numbers to attack and take a Levanter. Such a vessel, on the way home to England, would be carrying cargo of a value to provide enough reward to keep a captain and crew happy for a year.

Turning his body, with his naked eye he could just see the upper sails of *Minerve* and *Blanche* well to his rear, so whatever was to happen was something in which they could take no part. It was, however, politic to inform the commodore of his intentions, for the very good reason he might forbid it. There was only one signal to send, in a book of flags very short on anything nuanced. He was also aware he might be wrong, but it required he close the distance to find out.

'Mr Livingston, signal to *Minerve*: "Enemy in sight." And hoist up, once I've confirmed it as acknowledged, I'm engaging.'

He spun back to see his potential quarry had raised a tricolour, which meant she was, given the following wind, unable to clearly see his union flag, one he ordered to be struck and replaced with another tricolour.

It wouldn't hold all the way, but it would get *Hazard* into a position to attack.

'Commodore's acknowledged, sir,' shouted Livingston, which saw Pearce take to a backstay and slide hand over hand back down to the deck.

'Clear below decks, Mr Hallowell, and make sure the guns are provided with powder and shot. We will wait to cast them loose.'

Once the banging below had ceased, with all the wedges knocked out and the bulkheads taken down, furniture taken below, the fact of what was common at sea surfaced: in short, time seemed to stand still. Pearce had deliberately not increased sail, which had been set to what was being made by *Minerve*, in order to render what was coming seem normal. Extra canvas would imply an overeagerness to get close.

The main activity now was the laying out of the artefacts necessary to board: grappling irons and hidden padded fenders so no damage came from any contact, which badly handled could harm the hull. There were the weapons needed also: axes, cutlasses, clubs, and nets which could be thrown over a clutch of opponents. Stood behind the wheel, he took from Michael O'Hagan his sword and pistols, then instructed Mr Williams to be ready to increase sail, using what was already rigged.

Pearce, given the amount of practice he had seen carried out under his instruction, knew to the second how long his men would need to get the guns loaded and run out, actions which could not be concealed when the captain of the vessel he was approaching could plainly see his deck. It was at such a point the tricolour would come down and the union flag raised once more.

With luck, his preparations would give him the advantage he needed to commit the Frenchman to a fight, for it should be too late to seek to avoid a contest. He had the slightly larger ship and probably the greater weight of shot, so there was a chance the fellow might strike rather than face a broadside. He could now, with his telescope, see the enemy deck, which meant *Hazard*'s would also be under observation, so the temptation to pace back and forth in order to quell his eagerness had to be avoided.

'Mr Hallowell?'

'Everyone is at their station, sir.'

'Any comments?'

'None, sir. If we can take her, it will be a fine present for the commodore.'

'If we do, she will be yours to command.'

His premier smiled. 'Then take her we must.'

Telescope back to his eye, Pearce was looking for the first sign of untoward activity, proof that it had occurred to his opposite number all was not as it had seemed. He would have a lookout in the tops, as did *Hazard*, and the time was fast approaching when the way her deck was manned, with gun crews crouching beside their cannon, could not be concealed.

Hallowell was stood to his rear, as was Williams the master and the Mite, with Pearce aware they would be trying to read his mind. Not his intention, which was obvious, but the thoughts on when to go from seemingly passive to fully active, to crack on sail and run out the guns.

What he was thinking would have surprised them: the possibility that in the past he had hoarded opportunities to himself, taken a role which in many cases he could have handed over to his premier. Reflecting, Pearce could conjure up sound reasons for doing so, but this did nothing to settle a troubling notion. Did his premier resent it? Would he if their positions were reversed?

'Her captain has already made his first error, wouldn't you say, Mr Hallowell?'

'Indeed, he has, sir. He should have turned away as soon as he sighted us, giving him the option to run.'

'The false flag does not concern you?'

'You've taught me the value of such a ploy.'

'Then,' Pearce said, passing Hallowell the telescope, 'I leave it to you to decide what we do next.'

'I'm conscious of the honour, sir,' came the embarrassed reply.

'I have, in the past, garnered to myself too many privileges. And given what will become of the capture, it's only fair you should have the choice of when to act. And if we do get a chance to board, I would ask you to lead it. It is I who will follow you, not the other way round.' The stiffening of the frame rendered words unnecessary as Pearce added, 'You have the deck.'

'I trust I'm free to request an opinion, sir.'

'You are.'

Pearce took a step back at the same time as Hallowell took one forward, which brought him hard up against his friend Michael, to get a whisper in his ear that he'd make a fine mother one day.

'I think our friend has sensed we might not be what we seem.'

Hallowell had the right of it, for the distance had closed enough for Pearce to see a sudden burst of activity on the brigantine. Given another telescope, he looked not at the deck but at the crow's nest, to see frantically waving hands.

'Mr Williams,' Hallowell added. 'More sail please.'

The second part of the sentence was unnecessary; slow Williams might be by comparison to others aboard, but he issued the required orders crisply; this as the premier ordered the guns run out.

'Might I suggest an alteration to the flags,' Pearce said softly, having waited for it to take place.

The response came without thanks, which pleased Pearce; Hallowell was behaving like the captain he may soon become. His next words were 'Mr Livingston, you know what is required.'

'Sir.'

If there had been activity on the enemy deck before the swap, there was real panic when it was complete, for there was now no way to avoid becoming engaged. HMS *Hazard* had all the advantages: enough speed through the water to close the gap to within range of its cannon, while the Frenchman needed to get his own run out. At the same time, he had to come about and seek to get clear, an act which would expose, albeit at quite long range, the most vulnerable part of his ship.

That he did so spoke of an efficient crew, for it was crisply done but not enough to render him safe. Hallowell, with admirable calmness, brought *Hazard* round so her larboard battery, under the command of Macklin, bore on the target, ordering aim to be carefully taken and each gun to fire individually, having sighted the fall of shot from its predecessor.

Two missed; one too high, though it shredded some sail; another creating a great plume of water, blown forward over the afterdeck. But two took his casements, on which no time had allowed for the rigging of deadlights. It took no great imagination to conjure up a vision of the shot going the whole length of the ship. What solid iron failed to mash would be taken care of by deadly splinters.

The order came to come back on course and close with a brigantine now seriously wounded and slow because of it. Hallowell, observing the crowded deck, typical of a privateer, issued another instruction, ordering Williams to hold the course and come alongside the enemy, the next command being for everyone to be ready to board.

This, as guns were lashed off and weapons taken up, had him take station by the starboard bulwarks, pistols at the ready and a cutlass in his sword belt, the crew, including the three midshipmen, crowding alongside him.

'Christ in heaven,' Michael said, crossing himself, as he always did when invoking the deity. 'Are we set to just watch?'

'Let Hallowell lead them. Once he's on the deck, we can join in.'

'Sure, you had me goin' there, John-boy.'

'Deny you a fight, Michael; that I will never do. A drink, yes.'

'Nought but cruelty, I say.'

The brigantine having slowed significantly, the time taken to come alongside was short. With a yell for King George and England, Hallowell was first on to the hammock netting and then the enemy deck, but not by much. The crew, no less loud in their screaming imprecations, were right by him.

'Would it please you, John-boy, to call out for Scotland while I bellow for Hibernia?'

'A good idea, Michael, and something tells me if we don't go now, we'll miss the action.'

Which they did, shouting for their countries, onto a deck where the brigantine's crew, even in their greater numbers, were already hard pressed with a mass of Hazards driving them back by sheer brio. Not that the press of bodies held up O'Hagan, who had spotted Charlie Taverner and Rufus Dommet fighting side by side.

The way he barrelled through created the space for Pearce to follow, which brought all four Pelicans into a line. If it did nothing to affect the effort, it for a second brought welcome smiles to their faces, the kind to signify men who trust one another. Michael hewed with his favourite weapon, an axe, one wont to cover everyone nearby with blood, this alone often enough to see their opponents shrink from combat.

With the other two, it was hacking with naval hangers; only John Pearce fought with anything approaching craft, able to thrust and parry any attempt to break their collective guard. Soon weapons were being dropped to the deck, those discarding them falling to their knees and begging for mercy. Not that the contest lasted long, for whoever was in command had the tricolour struck, which brought a halt to the battle as it fluttered down.

With a look at John Pearce, which got a nod in response, Isaac Hallowell stepped forward and accepted the surrender, to which his commander added.

'I give you joy, Captain Hallowell. Take possession.'

'The commodore?'

'How can he deny us what we wish, when he's just had to abandon two enemy frigates? Best signal him we have enjoyed success.'

The person mentioned, on receipt of said signal, sat down to write a letter to Admiral Juan Marino, the Spanish naval commandant at Cartagena, which would go to the port under white flag. In it, Nelson, in his most chivalrous style, assured the admiral he had made every effort to render comfortable the captivity of Don Jacobo Stuart and stated his trust in the generosity of his nation to make it reciprocal for British officers and men.

I consent, sir, that Don Jacobo may be exchanged, and at full liberty to serve his king, when Lieutenants Culverhouse and Hardy, plus the men they led aboard the Santa Sabina and Ceres, are delivered into the garrison at Gibraltar.

By the time *Minerve* had closed with Pearce and his capture, the letter was sanded and sealed.

Chapter Fourteen

Nelson was naturally delighted with the capture of the privateer, called *Marsouin*; this immediately translated to *Porpoise*. He agreed to give the command to Hallowell with a specific task in mind. Now they were well clear of any pursuit, he was to take on board Don Jacobo Stuart and return to Gibraltar, avoiding any contact with enemy vessels, where Nelson's exchange letter could be passed on to Cartagena by what was a regular cartel.

The command did however come with a proviso: such an act would require the approval of Sir John Jervis, who would have the decision to either take it into the navy or sell it as a prize, the value to those entitled the same. Being in sight of the action, albeit distant, this included Nelson, the officers and crew of *Minerve*, but not *Blanche*, she being too far off to the rear to bear witness.

Nelson also claimed it went some way to mitigate the loss of the two Spanish frigates, though Pearce doubted this to be true: the commodore was too much the warrior to be satisfied with a minnow when he'd had, in his hand the day before, a pair of substantial Spanish fish.

Continuing, foul winter weather apart, the flotilla sailed on without incident to raise a misty and wet Elba, anchoring off the harbour off Portoferraio.

They were in time to receive invitations to a Christmas ball, a pleasant diversion, added to a chance to meet the opposite sex, so much attention was paid in every wardroom to ensure they looked their best. The island was also a safe place to allow a certain amount of shore leave, the first for *Hazard's* one-time Quota men, given it was not a place from which it was easy to desert. But there was a need to be cautious elsewhere.

'I have to ask you, Mr Macklin, if you have faith in the men you fetched aboard to return to the ship, should they too be granted the liberty of Elba?'

'They won't run, Captain. There's another island of which I could not say the same, but there's nothing I can see to tempt them here.'

'Except women and drink,' Pearce replied, 'even for good sons of the Catholic church. Believe me, given Michael O'Hagan as an example, I know of what I speak.'

'True everywhere,' Macklin replied with a grin. 'Whatever size a man be.'

Which led Pearce to wonder once more about his acting lieutenant. He was an Englishman of common stock, married to a girl from an island off the southwest coast of Ireland, as were, it seemed, many of the Irishmen he led. There was so much he didn't know about Macklin, his real name included, for he'd stuck with the one first used when he came aboard, admitting it to be false, but refusing to open about his true identity or what he and his men had got up to before coming aboard *Hazard*.

There had been a strong hint that to do so might presage risk, which Pearce took to mean the crew members he had persuaded to volunteer had, like him, been engaged in some very questionable activities. An extremely competent seaman, he was such an asset it had been mooted he should sit the lieutenant's examination—one he would sail through—and so formalise his acting rank, but he'd not seemed overkeen.

'And you?' Pearce asked.

'Someone of rank must stay aboard, sir; let it be me, for I have nothing to seek at a Christmas ball full of fine ladies and gents.'

The next people Pearce had to see, and discretely, were Charlie Taverner and Rufus Dommet to tell them, and not for the first time, to try and keep Michael out of trouble.

'This station and our squadron are short on hands as it is. It won't help if Michael maims several more.'

Charlie spoke low to ensure no one could overhear the familiar way he addressed his captain. 'Happen you should come along with us, John, then you'd see asking and doing what you want ain't within a mile of the same thing.'

'No intention to be the one to suffer, John,' Rufus added in a near whisper, which only went to underline how hard O'Hagan was to control if his temper got the better of his normally jocose nature; in drink, not even his friends were spared.

'Well, do your best. Try to keep him in the right mood.'

Having seen the first party of liberty men away—all, if time permitted, would get a chance in rotation—he, his officers, and midshipmen, Macklin excepted, took the cutter, alighting on the quay. All were wrapped in boat cloaks, necessary to keep their uniforms dry on water and them warm on land, given the cold wind coming down from the Alps. They made their way to the governor's palace, an elaborate edifice built by the Medici family of Florence, waiting for the commodore and officers from the other vessels before entering, which gave Pearce time to issue a warning.

'Now you mids,' he admonished, 'behave yourselves. There will be Italian lads of your own age here, who will resent your presence and take even more umbrage if they think you have been overzealous with their female relatives. They're a touchy lot and quick to go for the knife if they feel their honour impugned. Let me down, and you'll be kissing the gunner's daughter come morning, with our master at arms wielding the cane.'

He did not add he had seen it before, quick-tempered youths full of bravado facing up to each other like fighting cocks, their mood not aided by the amount of drink they would be free to consume. That said, it was hard to hold back youngsters who had been starved of female company, which reminded him that this applied to both himself and his officers. He was saved from having to say so by the approach of Nelson, Cockburn, and half a dozen lieutenants.

The attendees, a healthy crowd, were a mixed bunch of all ages and several nationalities, the older folk deep in conversation while the younger guests saw it as an occasion for flirtation. This comprised a number of young English girls who'd been travelling with their parents in Italy. It also included several Italian *signorinas* who, like them, had fled from the advancing French, as well as coterie of young females of that benighted nation. The latter were the offspring of Royalist and anti-revolutionary parents, military and naval, transported to Elba after the fall of Toulon.

Trailing Nelson, the officers of his squadron entered the ballroom to loud applause, soon followed by the cheering sound of the orchestra playing 'See the Conquering Hero Come.' This was soon followed by 'Rule Britannia,' both of which brought the commodore to the blush. For John Pearce, thankfully slightly shielded from view by the height and bulk of George Cockburn, what he saw before him in those doing the clapping induced an emotion closer to shock.

In the crowd of those congratulating Nelson and King George's Navy was a face with which he was only too familiar, and it was one of telling beauty. The temptation to beat a retreat had to be resisted, but Pearce felt he'd rather face another Spanish frigate than what he knew was coming, given he could not avoid being recognised and engaged in conversation.

This did not occur immediately; indeed he'd fortified himself with two cups of a heady grappa-laden punch before the Contessa de Montenegro came close enough for a verbal exchange. In doing so, she wafted an odour of her faint lemon scent, one which stirred memories of their previous encounters, physically as well as emotionally uncomfortable.

'Lieutenant Pearce,' she said softly, this accompanied by a conspiratorial smile and a move to bring her closer.

'Contessa' was guarded as a response and seen as such, hardly surprising as the smile was not reciprocated.

The way she stiffened, both shoulders and neck, told Pearce he had caused offence, yet she was astute enough to retain her expression, which reminded him of her social aplomb. It was also a case of him suffering from a touch of déjà vu, for the present situation was so similar to last time they'd met, it was uncanny. A crowded ballroom, that time in Leghorn on the mainland, the feeling many eyes might be upon him, yet it was very different. Emily was far away in London, not in the same room and the object of speculation, she being recently widowed and in an advanced state of pregnancy. He was now a father of the child she was carrying and absolutely committed to both Adam and his mother in a way which it had been possible to question previously.

The first encounter with the delectable countess had been when he was in a relationship limbo, and had led to an escapade that had done nothing for his already dubious reputation. This had seen him flee her bedchamber in a flapping shirt, the rest of his clothing gathered in his arms, obliged to run from a jealous ex-lover who, along with several backers, was threatening to castrate him, leaving her behind and laughing at a situation she saw as absurd.

Yet he remembered her fondly as an amusing companion and an engaging and accomplished lover. He could not, and would not, tell the Contessa the reasons behind what had happened on their second assignation on the night in Leghorn, the fact he had unashamedly used her to deflect attention from the relationship between himself and Emily Barclay.

They, playing the part of a pair of acquaintances, were subject to the inquisitive interest of a group of English expatriate matrons; no wonder, given his concern for Emily and her condition must have appeared somewhat overzealous. Being women of a certain age and social position, this had them ever sniffing for any breech of convention, even more so for a scandal.

He, by the concern he'd shown for the widowed and heavily with child Mrs Barclay, had fed their suspicions, they clearly harbouring doubts about his claim to have promised her late husband he would care for his wife. It was also uncomfortable to recall how he, by his blundering determination not to be ignored, had so nearly exposed Emily to the shame she dreaded.

Following on from this, and in order to redirect the suspicious gaze of these matrons, he had made much of his attraction to the Contessa, dancing exclusively with her, eventually departing the ball with her on his arm. It had proved impossible, given the attention he had shown her—and in truth this included a lack of will to resist—to avoid another less hazardous visit to her bedchamber. Something he had subsequently been able to put to the back of his mind was now front and centre, and damned uncomfortable, given it reminded him of the scrub he was capable of being.

'I glad to see you got away safely from the French.'

It sounded feeble, but he had to say something. A wave of her fan in a room getting uncomfortably warm from the massed human presence, added to a loss of eye contact, seemed to indicate she saw it in the same light.

'For which I have to thank the British navy, especially your most brave and charming Captain Freemantle.'

It was impossible not to seek an extra level of meaning in what 'brave and charming' might imply. Never pretending to be virtuous—and why should she be, with a compliant Tuscan aristocrat for a husband—had the Contessa formed a liaison there? Was it one which would debar him from renewing the kind of relationship they'd previously enjoyed? This would come as a blessed relief for, as red-blooded as any man alive and a thousand miles away from home, he doubted his ability to avoid being drawn into temptation. It would require even more the strength of character required to resist if the situation was anything like what he had engineered before.

'I hope I'm not disturbing anything, sir.'

The sudden presence of Worricker came as a welcome diversion, and Pearce spun to provide a speedy introduction, immediately struck by the fact Worricker's eyes were not on him but firmly directed at his female companion. Introductions provided, his new premier was swift to take the Contessa's hand and plant on it a ghost of a kiss, an act which produced a look of appreciation, as attractive and welcoming as any which had ever been aimed at him. It also hinted at a level of dalliance Pearce never suspected.

The slight pang of anger, brought on by a touch of inappropriate jealousy, coincided with the sound of the musicians, who had been taking a break, beginning to warm up their instruments. This got both men a very flirtatious look from behind the fan, which reminded Pearce of why he'd found her such an interesting object of desire in the first place. She was no hypocrite, very clear in letting it be known she enjoyed dalliance and thrived on male attention, very much the kind of lady he'd known and learned so much from as a young buck in Paris.

The silence which followed was brief, with Worricker giving Pearce a quick sideways glance as the object of his interest flicked a look between the navy pair, as if wondering which one would first suggest she consent to dance. Since this was something Pearce wanted to avoid, Worricker had a clear field and was fairly quick to exploit it.

'If the Contessa would permit?' he asked, arm held out and with a very slight quaver in the tone.

Pearce got one more flick of those dark eyes in his direction before, with another alluring look at Hallowell, she replied, *'Avec plaisir, monsieur Vorricker.'*

The speed with which he led her away was almost indecent, no doubt brought on by the fear he might be denied what he sought by giving way to a superior. Had he bothered to look back, he would have seen his captain smiling like an indulgent parent. Yet, behind the smile, Pearce was indulging in a heartfelt wish. If only Emily could come to see the world like the Contessa, in not caring a fig what people thought of her. How much happier their life would be.

Approaching the commodore and the group around him, quite a few of them ladies, it was obvious he too had been at the punch. Famously lightweight in the article of drink, Nelson had got himself into several romantic scrapes in the Mediterranean, a place he had claimed more than once rendered 'every man a bachelor beyond Gibraltar.' The last ball at which he had seen Nelson, he'd behaved in a like manner, pawing away at a rather overweight opera singer.

It had appeared previously, and did so again now, that the job of his junior officers was to save him from committing an indiscretion, not that they reportedly had much success. This was especially necessary since his stepson, Josiah Nisbet, was one of his officers, albeit he was still aboard HMS *Captain* in Gibraltar.

Was Nisbet communicating such behaviour to his mother. The thought convinced Pearce, much as he liked human company and entertainments, given the presence for him of a possible indiscretion, it would be best if he absented himself. He knew the Contessa could be a determined person, so the safest place was for him to be aboard ship.

Called aboard *Minerve* the following morning, Pearce found the commodore in the company of Captain Cockburn and quite obviously suffering a bit from the previous evening's excess, not helped by the amount of banging and crashing as the work of repairing the much-damaged ship continued. But once Pearce was seated, he was still brisk in giving him a new set of orders.

'What do you know of the present situation on Corsica?'

'Very little, sir,' was the only possible answer, given he'd been on Elba less than twenty-four hours.

'It's not good, laddie,' interjected Cockburn.

Pearce was then treated to an outline of said situation. The French had reoccupied the fortresses of Calvi and Bastia but, as had happened before they were kicked out by the British, they were yet to make any progress in the interior. The Corsicans clinging to a hope of independence still held on to Corte, high in the mountainous interior and their chosen capital.

'From what I learned before, sir,' said Pearce, 'it's not an easy part of the island to control.'

'But control it they must, eventually,' Nelson pointed out, 'and it's sad to say they will have the aid of those locals who incline to France.'

'The very people I fought previously.'

If Nelson noticed the bitter tone, given it was this very fact which had prompted the attempt by Jervis and Toby Burns to bring Pearce down, he gave no sign.

'And how do you think such people will deal with fellow countrymen they see as traitors?'

'They might hand them over to the French.'

'Or, Pearce, they might just chop off their heads. And if they don't, the French probably will.'

'Am I to take it from this, sir, there are those in peril still on the island?'

This got raised eyebrows, but as a conclusion it was obvious. 'Perceptive and true. For the sake of our reputation and the future of a possible independent Corsica, we need to bring them off.'

Even if his exposure to the locals on the island was limited, he'd learned enough while there, not least from the viceroy's wife, how fractious the Corsicans could be. It seemed to Pearce they spent more time fighting each other than any external enemy, and this applied even when they had an outstanding and internationally recognised leader in Pasquale Paoli. The old liberator, now an infirm old man, had already been taken back to England.

'Are we in a position to communicate with them, sir?'

'Sharp again, Pearce, and the answer is yes, if imperfectly so.'

'HMS *Blanche* I will need to mask Genoa, and Captain Freemantle is at Naples, where he is waiting to collect Sir Gilbert Elliot after his tour of Italy and bring him back here to Elba. Not for long, I grant you. We hope to abandon the island almost as soon as he safely arrives.'

'I know Sir Gilbert well enough to be sure he will not wish to be evacuated. It took much persuasion to get him out of Bastia.'

'He's not alone, Pearce,' Cockburn growled. 'The damned bullocks are of the same mind.'

The sigh from Nelson was audible. 'General de Burgh won't budge without he has instructions from the Horse Guards, declining to take orders from me or, to be more precise, Admiral Jervis.'

'Orders that could take a month or more to arrive from London.'

'Exactly,' Nelson replied, 'and I cannot and will not hang about here until he has directions from London to load his troops aboard the transports and quit the island. Quite apart from it being a risk to do so, staying here achieves nothing. Our commanding admiral is shaping up to do battle with the Dons, not an encounter I'm inclined to miss.'

'We're hoping,' Cockburn added, 'de Burgh will be satisfied, if given instructions to evacuate from Sir Gilbert.'

'To that end he must be persuaded to issue orders to de Burgh,' Nelson insisted. 'Given the amount of repairs still needed on *Minerve*, I require you to undertake a task I otherwise would have given to Fremantle.'

This had Pearce sit a bit straighter in his chair, even if his mind did wander. The story of Thomas Fremantle's exploits along the Ligurian and Tuscan littoral, which had been related to him in detail on arrival, were deserving of renown. In the thirty-six-gun frigate HMS *Inconstant*, he had ranged up and down the North Italian coast, attacking shore installations, gun batteries, lines of supply, and even marching columns to slow the advance of the French army.

While he made life as difficult for the French as possible, it did demonstrate the limits of naval power. He'd not been able to stop their inexorable progress towards Livorno. It was the certain loss of this city, Leghorn to the British, which had prompted the abandonment of Corsica. As he followed the invaders down the coast, *Inconstant* had also rescued and taken on board a substantial number of his fellow countrymen and women—as well as other refugees, including locals like the Contessa de Montenegro—and had been doing so in Livorno harbour while the French were advancing on the main fortress. So close were they to the frigate, *Inconstant*'s cannon were being used to slow the invaders at the same time as the captain was still bringing off refugees.

'So, given my limited means,' Nelson continued, bringing his mind and attention back to matters at hand, 'you must take *Hazard* and effect a rescue of the members of the old government who supported Paoli. We need to get them off the island so we can claim they are the legitimate government.'

'Do we have a rendezvous, sir?'

'Not at present, but we await one.' He looked keenly at Pearce. 'Although this is your primary task, I have no desire to restrict you. Trusting the judgement of those under my command is a better way to ensure results than giving them too-constricting orders. When we have a place from where they can be collected, which I hope to have shortly, I will send a pinnace with the information you require. Until then, if you see a way to singe a beard or two, take it.'

If Nelson looked happy with such freedom, the same could not be said for Cockburn, who responded with a near imperceptible shake of the head. Of all the people he might have given their head, John Pearce sat way down the list.

'I will happily do as you ask, sir, but I feel the need to point out, having put a prize crew aboard *Porpoise*, I'm somewhat short-handed when it comes to devilry.'

'A situation which pertains to every ship in the fleet,' Cockburn growled.

'An extra squad of marines would be of benefit.'

'Soldiers, perhaps; marines, no, Pearce,' Nelson insisted. 'Those we must keep, for I can give them orders and expect to be obeyed.'

The mention of soldiers reminded Pearce of the bullocks from Bastia who'd been helpful previously. He had enough men to sail *Hazard*, but when it came to both fighting and having crew enough to tend to the canvas, they would be woefully short.

'I would welcome soldiers, sir, if they were of the right stripe.'

'The right stripe?' came with a piercing look. 'I think that requires you to tell me what you mean.'

'They need to be led by someone willing to cooperate.'

'De Burgh might be too embarrassed to refuse you twice, sir,' suggested Cockburn. 'It seems a reasonable request when his men are doing little.'

'Then we must find out if you are correct. Mr Pearce, I'll see what I can do, but please be so good as to get ready to weigh. Your written orders I will send over presently.'

CHAPTER FIFTEEN

ON A DAY OF WARM WINTER SUNLIGHT, AS JOHN PEARCE OVERSAW THE re-victualling of the ship, the hired transport vessel *William of Eastry*, sailing at a snail's pace through wind-driven sleet, finally drew alongside the jetty set aside for Haslar Naval Hospital. The substantial building lay in Gosport, across water from Portsmouth, the ship here to drop off the sick and wounded sailors she'd brought back from the Mediterranean.

As a sight, it did nothing to inspire the vessel's purser, Cornelius Gherson, well wrapped against the elements, who had come on deck early to get away from quarters far from immune to the all-pervading sounds and smells of bilge. Even worse were the long-occupied bunk beds and hammocks full of the sick and suffering. It was a noise and atmosphere he'd had to endure for weeks as his ship ploughed its way back home, through seas which seemed almost designed to see off many of the casualties on its lower deck.

Right now, he was impatient to get off the ship, even prepared to accept the discomfort of a boat. This would take him across the choppy waters to the defensive walls of Portsmouth and the Sally Port, to then taste the delights of a town he knew well. This accepted, it was impossible on a daily basis to avoid comparing what he called his 'present desperate plight' with the freedoms, comfort, and profits he'd enjoyed here when serving as clerk to Captain Ralph Barclay.

His late employer was a naval officer who typified the truth that, though competent in all matters to do with the sea, they could be absolute dunces when it came to prospering ashore. Because of this, he had originally given Gherson the task of seeing to his shipboard accounts. This included illegally disposing, on his captain's behalf and with a small amount deducted for himself, of a quantity of stores without the fact showing up in the log of Barclay's frigate, HMS *Brilliant*.

These logs would later be examined by the 'eager-to-find-a-discrepancy' functionaries at the Navy Board, so it took unusual skill to hide the frauds, this being one Gherson possessed. Having been on half pay for five years prior to the outbreak of war, Barclay had good cause to consider himself hard done by, so he saw such depredations as recompense for the failure of the Admiralty to give him a ship and the full pay which went with it. He had also recently acquired a young and beautiful wife, she such an added potential expense, he'd take her to sea aboard his frigate rather than face the added outlay of maintaining a household ashore.

To say his marriage had caused him no end of trouble was to understate the case: it had been an error of biblical proportions for a man like Barclay, humourless and an onboard martinet, to take a wife twenty years younger than he, a woman who turned out to be the very opposite of submissive. The endless ramifications of his marital troubles had rumbled on for two years, during which Barclay had even sunk to involving Gherson in acts of downright criminality, he obliged to take the risk in order to keep what had become a lucrative post.

Barclay had delegated to him the task of dealing with his firm of prize agents, Ommaney and Druce, and given he'd enjoyed a high degree of success in the matter of captures, Ralph Barclay had become a rich man, and so to them a valued client. Gherson, with his sharp brain and utter lack of scruples, found himself with access to a large investment fund.

Never one to pass up a chance of personal and underhand profit, behaviour which had caused him much trouble in the past, the clerk had entered into a private arrangement with one of the partners, Edward Druce. This saw the firm, aided by Gherson, engage in speculative ventures from which both he and Druce extracted hidden gains, the profits of which the man for whom they were supposedly acting was kept unaware.

The good life fell apart when Barclay, in command of a seventy-four-gun ship, had engaged in a battle he should, to the thinking of man like Gherson, have avoided like the plague. It was an act of glory hunting, typical of the modern naval officer, which cost him his head and his life, while Gherson and the whole ship's company, which included his recently kidnapped wife, lost their freedom as prisoners of war.

Matters had gone downhill from then on, with any number of vicissitudes on which to gnaw, but any such recollections could not but end with his coming to the nadir: the fact he'd very nearly been hanged for a murder he did not commit.

'Good to be home, Mr Gherson, is it not.'

These words were uttered by the ship's captain, a well-past-his-prime lieutenant called Junor. Over forty odd years in the navy and going nowhere, he was fit only to command a transport and, to his purser's mind, probably elevated above his abilities even then. The thought of the warm feeling of coming home did not surface, for Gherson felt himself to be a man who did not possess one—not even the cramped berth in which he had lived as the transport carried out the designated duty of supplying the Mediterranean Fleet on the outward voyage, bringing home its casualties on the return voyage.

'Indeed, it is, sir,' Gherson replied, given there was no way to tell the truth, just as there was no way to escape a reply.

As he heard the orders which would see dropped the ship's anchor, he wondered if the short-of-a-brain lieutenant would sense the real feelings behind the words: the desire to get away from the ship, the navy, and a wardroom life of boredom bordering on stupor, where making a dishonest penny was near to impossible.

'I advise a stout padlock, sir, if you're going ashore,' Junor added.

Gherson wanted to shout at him, to remind him how many times he had made this same remark since they sighted the Needles, but to do so would be a waste of time. Besides which he was half-tempted to leave his storeroom and cramped berth open so the crew, a bunch of leftovers like their captain, could filch everything within. Then he could indeed go ashore and just never come back.

'Mind,' Junor added, with grave seriousness, 'Mr Lowry will want to compare your final accounts for the ship's owners, as he will with mine, a bane we must both bear.'

'Thank you so much for reminding me' went right over Junor's head.

He was too dense to pick up either irony or sarcasm, but he was right about that bastard Lowry being a bane. In a vessel rented by the Navy Board—it was cheaper to do so than build transports—the owners always had representation aboard. So there were endless disputes about who should pay for what, and this extended to things supplied by the purser to the vessel and the crew.

Lowry was like a crow hovering over everything Gherson did, always demanding to examine his books to ensure his employers were not being charged for things which were the navy's responsibility. This meant there was no money to be made from wood or tallow, and when it came to tobacco, the small number of tars aboard a non-fighting vessel made the sums he could extract for his inaccurate weights hardly justify the effort. If he was going ashore, which he would do just to taste solidity under his feet, it was not with much in the way of riches.

'Have a care not to miss the returning tenders, sir, or you'll have to make your own way to London. We sail at first light.'

Since this was, once more, a statement Junor had made several times, it did not warrant a reply. He knew the said tender would depart the ship even before the wounded were taken off, so he intended to be at the gangway early in order to secure a place where he might find some protection from the spray thrown up by working oars and a choppy sea. If he was not well found in the article of coin, he had creamed off enough to purchase some very necessary carnal release and perhaps a wine better than the blackstrap provided by the navy.

Aboard the barge first, he took a place in the very bow, ignoring the glare of both crew and passengers, not one of whom he could call a friend. Those berthed off the wardroom—the master, a couple of lieutenants, and a surgeon—had long ago given up seeking his company, not prepared to be the butt of his biting sarcasm. Men from the lower deck had ample reason to despise him for his office, but to this was added Gherson's personality and penny-pinching habits, which added several extra layers of loathing.

First out of the barge—as he had cursed and jostled to be first in—as soon as he was through the Sally Port, he made haste to get away from those with whom he'd shared the journey. He headed for the Ship Inn on

Portsmouth Point, where what he sought existed in abundance. Nothing brought home to Gherson, still a strikingly handsome fellow, his diminished financial standing than the level of haggling he had to indulge in with a series of whores, and these were far from the cream of the crop. But once the price was agreed, it was a mere quarter of an hour before the necessary deed was done and he could repair to the tap room for a wet and some food.

Out of his foul weather outer layers, Gherson presented a much more imposing figure, for he was wearing underneath his oilskins the garments left over from his more prosperous past: clean, quality linen, including stock, under a cream silk waistcoat, and over that a green jacket of the very finest barathea. It was a blessing wigs were no longer the fashion, which allowed the showing of his blond, near to white hair, this carefully barbered after his bout with the whore.

There was limited pleasure in witnessing a scene he'd observed many times previously. Raucous tars and their female company, with their singing and forced jollity, were less entertaining than they supposed. He had also driven away from his table, with an icy glare, any stranger seeking to join him, people who approached wearing an insincere smile, no doubt with the aim of dunning him for money. Gherson was left once more with his less than comfortable reminisces of happier times, when his table would have been covered in empty bottles, while the chairs surrounding both it and him would have been occupied by the youngest, freshest-looking trollops in the area.

Catching the eye of a servitor, he asked to be allowed the latest journals, only to find a stack of the same dropped on his table with no civility whatsoever. Nevertheless, he set himself to read them, for this would not be his only port of call while ashore. He would, once he'd perused the papers, repair to The Blue Posts, a more salubrious establishment much patronised by ranking naval officers.

His purpose with the journals, and particularly with the *London Gazette*, was to bring himself up to date with the latest subject of concern and/or gossip and particularly any striking successes recently achieved by the King's Navy: single ship actions, cutting out expeditions, and the like. Fresh off the press, the reports described the wrecking of some vessel called *Courageux* and the loss of life this entailed, but of stunning nautical successes there were few mentions.

Courageux? It was not a name to register much, but he read about the incident with some interest and no sympathy. He absorbed the details of the loss and where it had occurred, which told him it had been anchored at Gibraltar, from where he'd just returned, fortunately before the storm which had brought on the loss. He'd had no contact with the warships berthed there, almost never going ashore, not even topping up his storeroom outside the very necessary wood, in a place where prices were higher than at home.

He flicked through the rest—the *Times*, which had the ear of the government, a gossipier Sunday newcomer called the *Observer*—taking in as much as he could in the time he had available, which was not a great deal. But it would be enough for him to engage in conversation with those who used and often stayed at The Blue Posts. Captains employed clerks to see to their paperwork, of which there was an almost over-whelming amount for a serving officer. Perhaps one would be in need of such services, a position for which he could bid and use the Barclay name as a reference.

It was a long shot of the highest order, for the job of a captain's clerk aboard a man-o'-war was a highly prized position, though serving under an admiral less so, for many of those employed several. This meant any new appointment was of the minion class, so it could be many years before a man, even one as clever as Gherson knew himself to be, rose to the top post. And there could be no playing fast and loose with monies at the lower level.

The well-thumbed and somewhat grubby two-penny pamphlet, dated many weeks before, caught between the *Observer* and the *Courier*, he would have ignored if the face sketched on the front had not caught his eye, it being one he vaguely thought he had seen before. It was quite obviously the visage and decorative accoutrements of a seagoing man: long, curled locks on hair sown with ribbons hanging from under his tricorne hat, a decent-sized ring in one ear.

It was not a pleasant face at which to stare, the whole hinting at a cruel and bloody nature, hardly surprising since the lettering above claimed him as an evil and violent murderer. Since the sketch came without a name, he was inclined to put it aside, until he realised there could be a story behind it which might provide a topic of conversation. Not all naval officers were addicted to the subject of their own profession.

Inside, a single folded page spoke of the death of three people in Devonshire Square in the City of London: one the fellow on the front, the second a lowly clerk. He was just ruminating on the fact he had worked for Denby Carruthers in said city square, a busy street of warehouses and a few dwellings, when the very same name leapt out at him as the third victim. Idle curiosity swiftly changed to deep concentration as he drank in the details of the story.

The nameless seafarer had died at the scene, his body, which had suffered from several pistol shots, found outdoors. Carruthers was discovered in his office with multiple knife wounds, his clerk also, though outside in a corridor, but who expired first was a mystery. The screed went on to speculate on motives, asking if Carruthers's murdered wife, hitherto seen as an innocent victim, was in fact a modern Messalina, making the cause of his death her unbridled lust?

A stunned Cornelius Gherson flipped the pamphlet closed to look again at the vicious face on the front, and because his ex-paramour was mentioned, it came back to him where he had seen the man before. It had been very briefly, in the company of another like-dressed companion, before he was clubbed unconscious in the upstairs room of a Covent Garden bagnio. He now realised he was looking at the face of the creature who had wielded the club, the villain who had gone on to rape and murder silly, besotted Catherine Carruthers. One or both had desecrated and mutilated her body, leaving her to be found with him by her side.

For all he saw himself as a fellow with a sharp mind, it took many minutes of silent staring before the truth dawned, although there was a period where he believed it had to be too good to be true. He was only on the *William of Eastry* to avoid the malicious intentions of Denby Carruthers, a man with a mind so twisted at being a cuckold near four years previously, he'd had Gherson thrown off London Bridge and into the raging Thames, where he was sure to drown.

Fate had played a hand to save him, which was why he'd ended up aboard HMS *Brilliant*, first as a pressed seaman before becoming Ralph Barclay's clerk. On finding him alive, the black-hearted and revengeful madman had gone as far as to arrange the murder of his own young wife in such a way that, through a vengeful law, Cornelius Gherson would share her fate, though at the end of a rope.

But if Carruthers was dead, the case was altered, the threat removed. Again, the unlikelihood of such good fortune had him doubting what he'd just read; his nervous fears could not be slowly eased. Anyone observing him at his table would have wondered at the look of stunned stillness on a face set like stone. But if the smile was slow, it did appear, to transform a fellow who had no time for his fellow humans into one beaming at everyone in the inn, even waving a hand in time with their latest singing.

There would be no Blue Posts now, for the need had gone, while his fantasy of leaving his storeroom to be plundered could be contemplated with equanimity; the bane Lowry could go to hell. Money, from which he had been constrained for too long, would no longer be a concern, and he knew precisely where to acquire the funds to live as he had when his late captain and employer had been alive.

He would indeed miss the returning tender, which would cast off before darkness fell, but the journey he would make would lack just as much if not more in discomfort, especially in winter. He was short of the means for an inside seat on the London coach, but he could reassure himself this would be the last time he would sit atop such a conveyance.

Fetching his foul weather gear, Gherson covered up his best garments and smiled his way out through the throng of customers, passing the pleading whores without treating them to his customary disdain when not in need of their services. Happiness, too long an emotion absent from his life, suffused his whole being as he made his way to the Hard, from where coaches came and went.

There was a moment, when he calculated how much the fare would lighten his purse, when the notion of sailing to London arose. But even if it was not so very far off, it would still take several days to make the commercial docks below the city, where the *William of Eastry* would take on the next load of supplies for Gibraltar and the fleet. With such a bright future on his personal horizon, these were days he knew he could not suffer.

He might have to forgo food, but this was acceptable to a person, man and boy, who had tasted poverty as many times as he'd been flush with stolen money. So he'd go hungry, as he had too many times in the past, but not for long.

CHAPTER SIXTEEN

ENTERING THE ROOM WHERE THE MEMBERS OF THE GOVERNMENT MET, Henry Dundas had reason to doubt where his good friend William Pitt stood on the subject of the Spanish silver because he had, this very morning, declined, when asked, to comment. Should it become a serious cause of contention within the cabinet, he was thus unsure of how far he could rely on his support. Pitt had one overriding principle: having been appointed the King's First Lord of the Treasury and the leader of the government, he had a position he was determined to hold on to.

This required constant attendance to shifting opinions, and not just among the public. If the Tories and others he led commanded a majority in the Houses of Parliament, it was not rock solid but dependant on shifting alliances, Dundas controlling one. The Scottish vote was his to deliver—not large in terms of numbers, but enough to threaten the defeat of the government if he so wished it.

He was not alone in heading a faction; Pitt's cabinet contained several Whigs and others who classed themselves as independent. When it came to positions taken, it equated to shifting sands, with no guarantee who would support whom. The only glue binding them was a collective responsibility which saw them present a united policy front when facing an opposition led by Charles James Fox, he against the war and clamouring for peace with France. Fox also challenged the cost of the war and the way it was close to bankrupting Britannia, which was a factor to worry supposed allies.

It did not worry Dundas; he was far from popular with his colleagues, and it was not just due to his endemic secrecy. He was also seen as the purveyor of high-handed behaviour, rampant interference in the work of other departments, added to an unscrupulous regard for matters which would benefit him and, to a lesser extent, his Caledonian cohort. There was also the recent debacle in trying to take St Domingue back from the French, who had sent the regicide Victor Hugues to reconquer the slave-ruled island. This had resulted in a slaughter even bloodier than the Terror at home.

Dundas had insisted an expedition be sent to take the island, the most profitable in the West Indies, deposing both Hugues and the slaves from whom he had taken over. This saw a fleet, as well as the limited home army, transported to the sugar islands, there to die in droves from yellow fever before utterly failing in their mission. The whole campaign, which was a fiasco, had been initiated and pushed forward by him, yet he'd survived any censure, shifting the blame for failure onto the naval and military leadership.

Quite apart from the cost in lives lost, so serious was this, it had hampered to the point of failure any efforts to contain France in the Low Countries. It had also drained the national coffers of close to a million pounds at a time when the exchequer was under great strain. The question raised by this failure was simple, if undiscoverable: how much had the powerful and avaricious sugar lobby, seeing fecund plantations going begging on the island of St Domingue, bribed him to advance it as a benefit to the nation?

Now, with increasing problems in Ireland, if any action was to be taken to contain it, the only troops available were the militia, part-time soldiers whose value was questionable. But it was a matter raised previously and one to beat the war minister with. William Pitt had defended Dundas throughout, for the sake of a close friendship as well as his personal support in difficult times, but there were consequences which could not be hidden.

Thanks to the war, trade was down, and with it the customs revenues on which the national finances depended. In the great scheme of things, a sum of around two hundred thousand pounds in Spanish silver barely rated a raised eyebrow; but in the present climate, where ways were being sought to increase taxation to pay for a war becoming increasingly unpopular, it took on a rare significance.

Since the matter of prize money was low on the agenda of this meeting—and it deserved to be, given the long debate on Ireland—Henry Dundas had ample time, in those moments when he was not engaged in discussion of another topic, to hone his responses for what he knew was bound to come. First was the situation in the Mediterranean, the loss of Corsica accepted, but this did little to calm the worries of those who feared for the fate of Jervis's fleet. Now they knew they were safe under the guns of the Rock of Gibraltar and planning the next move.

'Sir John assures me, in his most recent despatch, of his intention to give battle to the Spanish should their fleet emerge from Cadiz, and to this end he will take station off the port in a bid to lure them out.'

'You seem happy, Spencer. Not to mention from the same despatch his failure to intercept the French squadron who passed through the Straits under his very nose. Given the recent defection of Madrid, those French ships might well be planning to combine with Spain, which puts him at a serious numerical disadvantage. Matters were bad enough in that department to begin with.'

This observation to the First Lord of the Admiralty was posed by Lord Grenville of the Foreign Office, a man who insisted he had a network of information as good as anyone at the table. But he was rather under a cloud for his ambassador's failure to spot what Manuel Godoy was up to in signing secret treaties with the French, which tended to belie the claim.

'I daresay you will decline to mention the atrocious weather at the time' was Spencer's dry response. 'Please recall, we lost HMS *Courageux* with all hands.'

'The possibility of an excuse arises.'

'Not with Jervis surely,' Dundas opined.

'Should we not reinforce him?' Grenville asked. 'Send back Admiral Mann and his four of the line.'

Earl Spenser was not in agreement. 'Sir John would likely not have him, since he feels Mann deserted his fleet and we are short of other vessels to do as you ask. We must keep the French bottled up in Brest.'

'It's not up to Sir John who's in his command, surely.'

'No, Lord Grenville, it's up to me and the naval officers on my Board of Admiralty. And we have concluded that by the time we get another squadron ready for sea, always supposing we can fit out and man one, it would probably be too late to affect the outcome of the battle for which Sir John daily prays.'

This waspish response had Pitt declare it was for each minister to run his own department, as well as time to move on to more pressing business, namely the present fiscal difficulties, and here the cabinet splits were obvious. Those who wished to raise taxation in some way were evenly matched against those for whom this was anathema, which led to a lengthy discussion going nowhere. Dundas knew it was only a matter of time before someone referred to the actions of *Hazard* and *Lively*, and Alexander Wedderburn, Lord Loughborough, the serving Lord Chancellor, duly obliged.

'Am I alone,' he asked in a rather pedantic and heavy Scottish accent, 'in wondering at the means by which this farrago came about?'

He might be looking at another Scot when he raised this, but there was no fellow feeling in either his words or expression. He knew Dundas to be a fast and loose player with the concept of legality, and to him, a stickler in this regard, he saw a chance to trim Dundas's sails, as well as uncover some of the less salubrious things he got up to.

'Not a very serious matter, my Lord,' said Pitt, with a look towards his friend. 'Indeed it's further down the agenda, but only there at all because of your insistence.'

'Not something I feel the need to apologise for. I think I share with many of my colleagues a desire to be better informed of what the Minister for War indulges in, matters usually coated in mystery. Normally we know nothing of the aim, let alone the result, but here we have that rare thing, a visible outcome in the shape of the cargo of silver.'

Dundas looked round the table. 'You've had a full explanation of how this came about.'

'Not full, Dundas, for we have no idea what set the wheels of the action in motion, nor what you set out to achieve. I cannot believe it encompassed the interdiction of a Spanish frigate belonging to an ally.'

'An ever so tepid one, in the very act of switching sides.'

'This is a matter of some interest to me also,' Spenser added. 'I had no end of complaint from the salts about Lieutenant Pearce being given a ship, even more when he was granted a pennant, which allowed him to cock a snook at whosoever he wished.'

Pitt looked a bit miffed. The First Lord had promised to stay strictly above the fray in this matter; indeed he had gone some way to keep his 'salts' at bay when the news first arose of the action and its consequences. Now he was siding with Loughborough, who sat as an independent, while Spenser was a Whig. It was not a natural alliance, and those always set Pitt's nerves on edge.

'You will be aware, my Lords, not everything we do in war can be the subject of open discussion. This, I'm afraid, is one of those occasions.'

'Not good enough, Dundas,' Loughborough barked, ignoring Pitt's attempt at intervention. 'I dislike the notion of you operating in such a way. There's a risk you may put all sitting here at some risk of opprobrium for some escapade of which we are ignorant. I would suggest we form a committee to oversee your actions and give the things you engage in approval before they are initiated.'

'Then you might as well employ the town crier. What you suggest would oblige me to put at risk the lives of those who secretly support us, as well as the people I employ to maintain contact with them.'

'Excuses, Dundas. Name me one instance where this is the case.'

'I could name you several, but I won't.'

'Can we stick to why Pearce got a ship and his pennant?' demanded Spenser.

'To what end?'

Since it was Pitt who posed the question, this drove home the fact he felt let down. But Spenser was not to be put off.

'I have a board who want, indeed insist, they need an answer. When the facts of the affair become known—and they will, regardless of how we treat the matter of reward—they will be inundated with demands to explain why Pearce was so indulged from near every officer in the service.'

Dundas got a look: not a glare, but far from benign.

'He was clearly acting for you, Henry, since both were provided not at your request but at your insistence, which is another bone of contention, for it was not your place to do so. The Admiralty does not bow to the whims of the War Ministry. Also, I doubt I can convey the low opinion in which that particular officer is held within the service. Why choose him when you could have had your pick?'

'It does not occur to you,' Dundas replied smoothly, 'that being unpopular means he suits my needs perfectly.'

'And your needs were?' asked Loughborough.

The voice took on a hard edge. 'For someone who would carry out a mission without asking questions and keep his mouth sealed tight when in the company of his fellow officers. He is also, Earl Spencer, an individual who is, according to our sovereign, a hero, as well as one who has enjoyed the kind of success to which ninety percent of your blue coats can only aspire.'

'He's been lucky, I'll grant you.'

'The kind of luck you make, not the kind to fall into your lap.'

'Unless you have a Minister for War on your side' was the acid response.

'Well, I'll be damned if he's getting paid out for that silver, however brave you say he is.'

Dundas looked into the ruddy, determined face of the Lord Chancellor and asked, 'Is that to spite me or him?'

'It is, legally, the right and proper thing to do. He acted outside the law and so did Langholm, though he can be forgiven for acknowledging the fact and seeking to rein Pearce in.'

'An approach which might be a touch more difficult than you think.'

'I fail to see what you mean,' postulated the lawyer.

'Up till now, we have kept the news of the silver close to a secret, or at least we thought we had.'

Dundas pulled from his pocket a folded and crumpled journal and laid it on the table to a whole raft of enquiring looks from those who saw it to be a copy of the *Observer*. After a pause he picked it up and began to read the opening words, unwelcome to the men who constituted the government of the country.

'What is Billy Pitt trying to hide? Our old foe, the Papist Dons of Iberia, have behaved in the treacherous manner which is the key to their nature . . .'

'A partisan view,' opined Grenville, who was always trying to see two sides to every point. 'We are not immune to following our own interests when it suits us.'

'I look forward to you trying to explain in public why you take the side of the Spanish in anything, Grenville.'

'I don't take their side; I merely point out Madrid will not see it as treachery, even if we do.'

'But here's the nub,' Dundas added before continuing to relate certain details, not yet released. 'According to this rag, rumours abound regarding an action engaged in by two of our most gallant naval officers who, aware of the forthcoming defection of our long-time foe, took on and captured a Spanish frigate sailing from the Spanish Main to Vigo. For this action, the Admiralty is inclined to censure them, since they acted before war had yet to be formally declared by Madrid. We will make it our business to find the identity of these two heroes and to then campaign for their sterling service to be given the praise they deserve.'

'So, the matter is now public,' Pitt remarked gloomily.

'Not the silver,' Loughborough barked.

'For a lawyer, my Lord,' Dundas said, 'you are slow to see what lies ahead. If the fellow who wrote this knows of the actions of Pearce and Langholm, he will know of the result. So it's only a matter of time before everyone is made aware of what the capture was carrying.'

'You think I will be obliged to bow to the opinion of the mob?'

'No. But I do say you're going to have to deal with the fact none of your fellow countrymen agree with you. I have an inkling of how this story will play.'

'No doubt from vast experience of having carried out such manoeuvres yourself.'

It was Chatham, Billy Pitt's big brother and heir to their father's earldom, who made this remark, delivered with a wry smile, which removed any hint of malice.

'I don't deny I act for us all when it is necessary.'

'Without too often bothering to ask our opinion,' Loughborough complained.

'There's no time for discussion when you're seeking to kill off a rumour which could harm the government.'

'For which we,' Pitt reminded them, 'make funds available.'

'Another unaccounted-for purse,' Grenville pointed out.

The tone of the response from Dundas was hard. 'I account to the First Lord of the Treasury, my Lord, and will take as remiss any suggestion I fail to do so.'

'And I,' Pitt added, 'as the holder of that office, am perfectly satisfied the sums granted are put to good and proper use.'

This induced a degree of paper shuffling. William Pitt was known as being above corruption, taking not a penny from the treasury which was not his due. The fact he was firm friends with Dundas, who could be said to be the precise opposite, tended to mystify those who thought on it. The best opinion they could put on it was their leader was naive, for no one could call him stupid.

'I would reason whoever is pushing this is being paid to do so, and what we have here,' he tapped the journal, 'is the opening gambit in a sort of campaign. Next will come the names of the officers concerned, which will lead to a clamour that their efforts receive the gratitude they deserve. Finally, the nature of the cargo will be hinted at, alongside the fact that we, sitting here, are minded to deny them their just reward over a legal technicality. We will be caricatured as thieves.'

'They will get their just reward, Dundas, but it won't be in the nature of your damned prize money,' Loughborough insisted. 'To my mind the whole system should be discontinued and replaced by droits. Prize money leads to nothing but licensed piracy.'

'I'll take care,' Spenser joked, 'not to mention such a view in the Admiralty boardroom, with you as the author.'

Dundas added his view, addressing the whole room in a detached way. 'No prize money for our heroes who singed the Spanish beard, only droits of the Crown? At which point effigies of the estimable Lord Chancellor will be burned on every open green in the country and damned aboard every ship in the fleet.'

He spoke to Loughborough directly. 'I also hope you have stout shutters for your windows and some men with muskets to guard your front door.'

Dundas paused and looked round the table. 'We are dealing with Spain here, whom we have fought for close to three hundred years, a nation which has sought to invade us more than once. They signed a secret treaty with our sworn enemies and sat on the fact till it suited them to reveal it, while taking our subventions in scarce gold. This information disseminated on its own would be an incitement to riot. Add the notion of us cheating our heroic tars out of their rightful reward, and I would not care to have to control the result. It could be worse than the Gordon riots.'

'You exaggerate, but there is a principle at stake, and one I'm determined to abide by.'

'Then we must vote. It is up to you to compose a proposal, Lord Loughborough.'

This the Scottish lawyer did, droning it out in a dirge like voice, with Pitt asking if there were any counterproposals. When none came, hands were shown, most supporting the Lord Chancellor. Pitt and Dundas abstained.

'Why didn't you tell me about the story in the journal, Henry?' Pitt asked quietly on the way out of the room.

'I wanted a surprise, Billy.'

'And the story?'

'Whoever has set this in motion knows what he's doing.'

'It must be killed, Henry. I look to you to make it so.'

Alexander Davidson was at that moment in conversation with W. A. Bourne, the editor of the *Observer*, due out in three days' time, the man before him scribbling furiously as a further instalment of the tale was told, the cargo still a mystery.

'But I will have more for you next week, Mr Bourne, another piece of the jigsaw.'

Davidson's final act was to slip a leather purse over the table, a welcome gift to a man running a newspaper only six years old, struggling and failing to make enough money to stay afloat.

Chapter Seventeen

Having delivered the despatch from Sir John Jervis to the Admiralty, Toby Burns was at a loss as to what to do next. Duty said he should return to Portsmouth and his ship, but when it came to reluctance, this was top of the list. He'd never liked being aboard HMS *Teme*, with its cramped cabin and crowded lower deck, so close the occupants seemed to be almost in his lap. He had no regard for a crew whom he knew neither liked nor respected him, a feeling which was mutual; and if he could have brought himself to be brutally honest, he had no love for service in the King's Navy either.

The man to whom he had delivered the admiral's communication, clerk to the Second Secretary, had not even deigned to introduce himself, nor had he asked Burns for his name. He'd merely taken the official, sealed oilskin pouch containing the despatch, nodded, then looked at the deliverer as if to ask why he was still there.

Worse, Toby emerged to find the two-horse coach by which he had travelled had not waited for him. The Admiralty doorman informed him it had departed just after it had dropped him off, so he was left to face the freezing weather and snow-covered streets of London like an abandoned foundling. He was also strapped for cash, not having called at the pay office in Portsmouth before setting off for London.

He found a busy coffee house in which to avoid the cold and think, wasting much time in appearing to read the latest magazines and newspapers when he was really ruminating on his rumbling stomach and the circumstances which had brought him to this place. Back in Gibraltar, with a day to gnaw on what the trio of so-called Pelicans were doing standing outside the rear entrance to the court, he'd had even more to worry on when he heard they'd been inside as well, for they could only have one aim: to do him down. The advocate Downson's assurances that the bench would not call ordinary seamen to the court martial of an officer if they were not the complainants failed to fully set his mind at ease.

Having to face John Pearce was bad enough, but he'd seen in the silent stares of O'Hagan, Taverner, and Dommet the intention to visit upon him physical harm. This had prompted the assault on Pearce—a failure, despite what he'd been told by those he'd paid to undertake the beating. This had been proved merely by the fact of his turning up bruised and battered but walking. Burns had wanted him so badly hurt he could not attend.

Listening beyond the door to the court, he'd sighed with relief when Lieutenant Downson declined to call him as a witness: it had been arranged beforehand, but a nervous Burns had still worried it might not be so. The shock when Farmiloe did that very thing was total and he'd panicked, immediately running for the rear entrance. Naturally this had led to a tense interview with the admiral.

'Wandered off, Burns, bored indeed, so you went for a stroll? Can you imagine the position you put me in by such cavalier behaviour? We had to suspend proceedings.'

'I can only apologise, sir.'

Recalling this conversation now, he had to ask himself, did Jervis really believe what he was being told? Toby Burns could hardly trust it to be so, for he would not if the positions had been reversed. Perhaps his behaviour had more to do with the need to cover his own actions rather than that of the lieutenant he used, not that it much mattered now.

He could not even begin to go near the real reason he'd run away, to admit the fellow representing Pearce had been serving in HMS *Brilliant* on the fatal night John Pearce and his Pelicans had been illegally pressed. Dick Farmiloe knew precisely what to ask him as a witness, questions which would go on, eventually to entirely destroy his false reputation as hero.

There was a part of Toby Burns who might have welcomed such an outcome, for it had become something of a millstone around his neck. Such repute ensured when some dangerous mission was being mooted, his name was always first on the list to participate, when what he wanted was to be as far away from peril as was humanly possible. In the case of Hotham, he'd begun to suspect the admiral was putting him in harm's way to get rid of him, he having been witness to Hotham's part in rigging the trial of Ralph Barclay for illegal impressment—the aim to ensure he was acquitted.

But it was the Pearce trial which posed the more serious threat for, beyond the loss of reputation, there lay the possibility he might forfeit his life at the end of a rope. Browbeaten into committing perjury, taking the blame for what Barclay claimed was an error committed by his nephew, he could not face being questioned by a fellow to whom this was false testimony. Farmiloe knew that on the night in question, Toby Burns was aboard *Brilliant* and not out press-ganging with Barclay. And to make matters worse, a fellow whom he always considered well disposed towards him was acting on behalf of the man whose glory he had stolen. Anyone would have fled faced with such a combination of risks.

'Well,' Jervis had said, 'you'll be pleased to know you're going home.'

'Sir?' Burns had asked as the admiral pushed forward a sealed oilskin pouch.

'You're to take this personally to the Admiralty and demand it be put into the hands of Earl Spenser and no one else. It's not to leave your possession until it's signed for.'

This had left Toby wondering what it contained, for it was, even he knew, an abnormal errand: despatches normally went to the Admiralty Board, not to the First Lord. There was no point in asking so he merely nodded, the next words increasing his suspicion.

'And, if the risk of capture arises, chuck it overboard, d'ye hear?'

'The court martial, sir,' he'd asked, remembering now how he'd dreaded the response.

'Will have to wait,' Jervis had responded, 'and how long this will be, with you and Pearce not in the same place, I cannot say.'

'Will I be returning to Gibraltar, sir?'

'No. Once you've delivered my despatch, report to the admiral of the home fleet in Portsmouth.' Another less bulky sealed pouch had been passed over, with the comment, 'These are your orders and my recommendations.'

He's getting rid of me, thought Burns, not sure if that realization made him happy.

'You're to weigh at once and, for the love of God, don't go near Cadiz. Give it a wide berth.'

'Sir.'

'That will be all.'

Lost in these memories, he became aware he was being eyed by the proprietor of the coffee house as someone who'd extracted quite a bit of hospitality, and occupied a table, for one small pot of the brew. Fearing actual words might be spoken, there was no choice but to depart, having made up his mind to demand from the headquarters of the navy that they provide the means to get him back from whence he came.

'Think you'll find, young sir,' the gruff-voiced doorman responded, 'it falls to you to get yourself back to your ship.'

This came from the very same fellow who'd admitted him earlier, an ex-tar with the weather-beaten face and gnarled hands to prove it. But he declined to do so again, for missing was the vital document which had brought Burns to London. Thus, he now lacked the means of entry, while the response he received was given to him after a querulous demand for some form of transport.

'I am the personal messenger of the admiral in command of the Mediterranean Fleet and here on his business.'

'Happen that be so, Lieutenant, but I stand by what I say. It ain't in my gift to admit all and sundry who turn up seeking favours.'

'I'm seeking transport.'

'Charing Cross ain't five minutes off from where you is stood, more or less due east. If you make your way to there, you'll find coaches regular going to Pompey.'

'And who is to pay for the journey?' Toby demanded in what was, for him, a rare show of determination.

'Well, sir, if as you say you're on business for your admiral, I should ask him.'

'He's anchored off Gibraltar!'

The response was the sort of look to acknowledge this was a problem, while also letting him know the man he was addressing had no intention of providing a solution. Also, Burns, not the sharpest of men, failed to realise if he wanted assistance from an old seadog, it was best it came with a reward. A decent-sized coin slipped into the doorman's hand would have changed his attitude in a blink, but in its absence a finger was pointed east.

'Is there a pay office in the Admiralty?'

'You want the Navy Board at Greenwich for pay. Cross the river and a set of miles down the south bank, if you have your pay warrants.'

These were still aboard *Teme*, which had him snap, 'I'd be as quick going back to Portsmouth.'

'Charing Cross it is then, sir.'

Disconsolate and cold, Toby Burns followed the direction given, through alleyways which twisted this way and that, so much so a compass would have been necessary to keep him on the right lines. He did eventually find Charing Cross, the teeming hub for coaches going to every major destination in the country, with barkers shouting out routes and tariffs for their individual companies.

Movement was far from easy, and the obstacles were not just human. Nearly everyone had some kind of baggage with which to travel, from a mere bundle to sizeable trunks, while the general air of chaos was compounded with as many people arriving as those seeking to depart. Coaches were disgorging passengers before pulling away to find a change of horses and the men to control them.

Burns had to ask a couple of barkers before he found the fellow who sold seats on transport going to the south coast towns, only to be told the overnight coach from Portsmouth was due in, but late by an hour. He was also informed that since he'd missed the morning departure, there was no other for the route till late afternoon, which left him at a stand as to how he was to pass the intervening hours. His thoughts were broken by the rattle of iron hoops on cobbles as a large post chaise pulled into the square, the cries from his barker that it was from Portsmouth setting forth a surge of movement, people meeting those who'd travelled.

The interior passengers were disgorged first, so many you wondered where they all sat, with porters eager to offer their services to those who could clearly pay to have their luggage shifted. Then, one by one, those who'd travelled cheaply atop the post chaise were helped down the ladder, watched by a well-wrapped-up naval officer who was wondering if he could save some coin by making his way back to Portsmouth in a like manner.

The first down stood easing what had to be aching limbs before he turned to survey the scene. The muffler and hat pulled low had Burns wonder if he was imagining things, but the fellow stood still for some time, so the profile was constant. He also tipped back his hat and eased a muffler come loose in order to retie it, which exposed his whole face.

'Gherson.'

This was mouthed rather than spoken, with Toby slipping behind a travelling family group and their trunk so he could observe without being seen. He also wanted to make sure he was not mistaken, but he knew himself to be looking at a singular soul in terms of physical appearance: the near white, blond hair, the almost girlish handsome features, but most of all the arrogance of his posture.

Well aware the naval captain for whom Gherson had worked was dead, it was natural to wonder what he was about now and what he was doing here. Also, the fact he'd been obliged to travel in the open, which was not his style. The oilskins, his outer garment, looked to be the same as Toby's, so naval. But having elbowed his way to a glowing brazier, Gherson undid his outer layer to reveal the high-quality clothing underneath, which was more of what Burns reckoned to be in the nature of the man.

There was no temptation to approach, for he was observing a fellow he did not trust an inch and one—along with his uncle by marriage, Ralph Barclay, and Admiral Hotham—who had embroiled him in the legal case where he'd been coerced into committing the capital offence of perjury. There might be no point in allowing his hatred to surface, but it did so unbidden, for it was a trait in Toby Burns to lay all his misfortunes—and he could list many—at the door of others.

If Gherson did not rise as high in his pantheon of ogres, the peak of which was occupied by John Pearce, he was close enough for the youngster to hope his feelings were so strong they would smite the bastard where he stood. The sod, warmed by the coals of the brazier, was asking loudly for directions to the Oxford Road; Burns was sure he heard north as the reply. Then he posed a question more troubling in asking if the fellow, one of the barkers, had heard of a place called Fitzroy Square, only to acknowledge, in the face of ignorance of the location, he would find it.

'I have reason to believe it to be a new development.'

'Can't walk a foot in the Great Wen these days, your honour, without you step in sand and cement.'

'Nor horses' dung, fellow,' Gherson snapped as, having wrapped himself up inside his oilskins once more, he set off across a square much layered with this very substance.

After a brief question of what to do, Toby followed, though he was not quite sure why—perhaps natural nosiness or the fact he had a great deal of time to kill and moving was warmer than standing still. The ground underneath was mostly slush when it was not dung, this latter a factor of crossing every intersection, where Burns replicated Gherson in not tipping the young urchins acting as crossing sweepers.

For the man ahead, the fact the route took him towards Seven Dials prompted no fears, for this, London's most notorious area for thievery, had at one time been a place from which he'd operated as an occasional swindler. He'd already passed Long Acre, stopping for just enough time to note that Lady Barrington's bagnio, in truth run by an ex-whore called Daisy Bolton, was still operating and reflect it to be the place where Catherine Carruthers had been cruelly murdered.

Passing through Seven Dials, Gherson was tempted to undo his muffler so those idling about—not many, and pickpockets mainly—might recognise him and spread the word he was back. This brought on a smile: when the plan he was following came to fruition, he'd not need anything from the gangs or their members residing here.

Fifty paces behind him, his naval scraper a sure indication of his occupation, Toby Burns failed to cause a stir as he passed through the same area, with its seven roads leading off the central circle. The villains knew who to seek to rob and who were not worth the trouble: Gherson had the air of a fellow too fly to touch, while Toby, with no gilt on his hat, was firmly in the latter category, so both trudged on without causing a ripple.

By the time they made the Oxford Road, it had begun to snow, and here Gherson kept alert, for this route out of London was home to any number of footpads. No one travelled it by coach at night without they had armed themselves, often carrying a blunderbuss-bearing guard alongside the coachmen. The denizens who made their crust from such robbery were not gentle; they were armed and willing to employ their weapons.

Past the Oxford Road, on the long, straight route north, a log of it still market gardens, Gherson stopped frequently to question roadside costermongers, many of whom shook their heads, others scratching it before providing what looked like less than reliable information. This eventually brought him and his tail to a wide, muddy square with a row of fine houses along the lower side, all with a pair of bright lamps astride their porticoed doors. On the other three sides there was much banging and crashing as other houses, wrapped in scaffolding, were under construction.

Cornelius Gherson stood for a moment looking at one particular door, with Toby likewise still and curious as to what the man was about. After several minutes Gherson moved to approach the door and haul on the bell pull, the sound loud enough to reach Toby's ears. He moved to a point where he could see inside when the door opened.

A liveried footman answered, to exchange a few words with Gherson before closing the door, though Gherson didn't move, standing in the glow from the lights, arms behind his back, in a posture implying confidence. When the door opened again, Toby had no idea how Gherson reacted, but he gasped. There, framed in the doorway and wrapped in a shawl, looking far from pleased, stood his Aunt Emily. She was speaking, not that her nephew could hear what she was saying.

'By what effrontery do you turn up at my door and expect to be let in, calling yourself an old friend?'

Gherson shrugged, his tone jocular. 'I admit the last part to be an exaggeration—'

'It's more than an exaggeration, sir, it is a falsehood.'

'Nevertheless,' he replied in a less friendly tone, 'I would appreciate you let me enter, for it's cold and I'm sure you have a fire blazing in the grate. You must know I'm a creature who likes comfort.'

'No.'

'Then you will oblige me to shout out to your neighbours the true nature of the person they're living alongside. Not the sainted widow but a common—'

Emily interrupted him again. 'Am I never to be free of your malice?'

Gherson chuckled, but there was no humour in it. 'I can think of only one way that could come about, but since you have several times repulsed my advances, I cannot see it as a solution. Be assured, if you slam your door in my face, I will bellow enough to bring those unfinished houses down. And then I shall find a person to pen a penny pamphlet detailing your adultery.'

'You are a slug.'

'I've always admired your pluck, Mrs Barclay, which you practised successfully on your late husband, a man truly I despised.'

'A man you conspired to rob. And here I stand, having paid to save your miserable life, while you give me cause to regret it.'

'Let me pass or—'

Emily stood aside and Gherson passed through.

CHAPTER EIGHTEEN

NATURALLY IMPERIOUS WHEN HE FELT IN CONTROL, GHERSON STOOD, acting for all the world like he owned the place, and waited for the footman who'd opened the front door to remove his oilskins. The look he gave Emily Barclay as this was carried out had her seething but impotent. Nevertheless, she showed him into the downstairs reception room, where there was indeed a fire in the grate. Not wishing to spend any more time with him than necessary, she then went back out to the hallway, closing the door behind her, to give instructions to the footman who'd opened the door.

'Rouse out the others, Benjamin, and tell them to arm themselves with something, anything. Then I want you to go to Mr Lutyens's house in Harley Street and tell him what has happened. I would like him to pen a note to Mr Hodgson at the White Swan in Clerkenwell to inform him Gherson has surfaced and is acting in a threatening manner. I require his services as soon as it is convenient and would like him to call.'

She turned to re-enter the drawing room, then had a sudden thought. 'Rouse out Cook and ask her to prepare a meal, and a large one. If the swine is stuffing his face, I won't have to listen to him talking. Mind, he's such a pig he can probably do both.'

Standing by the door, holding the handle, Emily took a deep breath then turned the knob, knowing she might have to stay with Gherson to keep him from carrying out the threat he'd issued on her front doorstep.

'Arrangements in place?' he asked as she entered.

The smirk was infuriating and designed to be so.

'Listening at the door, were you?'

'No need to, Mrs Barclay. You seem to forget I have a brain, but then you always did underestimate me.'

'On the contrary, I have never been foolish enough to do that. I've always seen you for what you are.'

'What I am is naught but a product of my needs.'

'Which you are, no doubt, going to describe to me.'

'I doubt such is necessary if I say to you I am dissatisfied with my present position.'

'Which is?'

There was a sudden flash of anger, not the first time Emily had seen this on his face. That had been when, she newly married to Captain Barclay, he made improper and salacious suggestions, which she had rebuffed. Gherson had a very high opinion of himself in the seduction stakes, so was made livid by rejection, a response she'd been obliged to visit upon him on several other occasions.

'Don't pretend you don't know, madame. You may not have arranged it, but you are very well aware of what I was condemned to.'

Emily wanted to say, 'more than you deserve,' but irritating an already angry man was not wise. Yet the thought of mollifying him stuck in her craw, so the words which followed came out in a strangled fashion.

'I have ordered a meal to be prepared, which will be served to you here in this room.'

'And wine, Mrs Barclay, don't forget wine, and I hope you opt for quality.'

'I have other matters to attend to.'

'Like being mother to a bastard, no doubt.'

This broke the dam. 'Have a care with your tongue, sir, for even if it leads to my ruin, I will have you thrown back out into the street.'

'An empty threat.'

'Do not think I cannot guess what it is you are after. But it is a bad idea, if you only have one card to play, to throw it away, which you will do if you carry out your threat.'

Emily stormed out and slammed the door, just as the outside bell rang again. At another time the tableau she was presented with would have reduced her to helpless mirth, it looked so absurd. Two of her three footmen had taken up a position in the hallway, one with a long poker from the kitchen stove, the other holding one of the cook's meat cleavers, their faces set in the kind of determination designed to mask fear. The bell rang again.

'I shall answer it myself,' she declared.

Toby Burns, standing outside in the muddy street and getting colder by the second, had tried to process the notion of Cornelius Gherson visiting his aunt, something hard to make sense of. While he reasoned, to his recall, she loathed the man, she'd nevertheless let him in, so perhaps there was a connection of which he knew nothing. Toby was also aware he did not stand high in her regard; she had been present at her husband's court martial, where his aunt had witnessed him giving what she knew to be false evidence.

If he'd never been absolutely sure how he stood with her before that day, she'd left him in no doubt after Ralph Barclay was acquitted, albeit with a reprimand regarding his future actions when pressing hands. The words she employed were imprinted on his brain, as was her expression of disgust, a clear warning she wished to disown any family or personal connection. He'd feared she would write to them and expose him; that she had not, he'd seen as a positive. Now, cold and hungry, could she be so callous as to turn him away?

He'd approached the door more than once, only to get metaphorical cold feet to go with the real article, until he finally plucked up the courage to pull on the bell, his heart in his mouth, his hands trembling until it was opened. He was about to say what he'd practised to a footman—'Mr Toby Burns, calling on his Aunt Emily'—when he realised it was she before him, at which point his tongue seemed to become stuck to his palate. Wrapped as he was, she didn't recognise him and, in truth, he had changed somewhat in the last three years, a good bit taller and less puffy around the chops. It was the naval hat which drew her eye, and as he undid his scarf, he could see enlightenment in her eyes.

'Aunt Emily.'

'Toby?'

'None other.'

'What do you want?' was far from friendly.

It was a few seconds before he could summon up the words needed, for he'd decided any mention of his having just returned from the Mediterranean was bound to raise the name of John Pearce, which would lead to explanations he would rather avoid.

'Does a nephew in the second degree need an excuse to call upon a relative?'

Emily might have been more brusque if she did not have Gherson lounging less than thirty feet away while this, the advent of another surprise, seemed too much. Her eyes flashed as she responded.

'If you recall our last encounter, you most certainly do.'

It was hurt which made him say, in a weepy tone, 'So, you will entertain someone like Gherson but send me away, cold and hungry and near to stranded in London. One who shares your own blood?'

Not surprisingly, this induced a certain amount of confusion in a person not accustomed to exchanging words with people on her own doorstep. How did he know about Gherson? Were she to be asked afterwards why she relented, Emily would have manufactured the excuse that with two rogues in the house, one might cancel the other out. In truth, she did so for the mere fact of not seeing an alternative.

'For the sake of my dear sister alone,' she said, standing aside.

At least Burns had the decency to start to remove his own outer garments, with Emily wondering if it was more to do with the pair of armed footmen than good manners. She, as he did so, could not but examine the changes in the callow, timid youngster he had been, and not just in his height. Burns had filled out somewhat, to the point where what had been puppy fat was now the real article; his waistcoat strained at the buttons.

She was treated to a far from clear account of why he was in London and the difficulty he was going to have getting back to Portsmouth, since he lacked the means to pay for the journey—he meant inside the coach but didn't say so—because his pay warrants were aboard his ship and he could not redeem funds at Greenwich.

'Tell the cook food for two, Paul. You, come with me.'

The lack of the name was striking, telling Burns, if he'd not guessed it already, his aunt was far from pleased to see him. But if this was to be thought on, it paled when he was taken through the door to be presented with the sight of Gherson, in his silk and outer finery, lounging on a settle.

'I'm sure you recognise each other, so I won't bother with introductions but will leave you to amuse yourselves as you share tales of the people to whom you have lied.'

With that she was gone, heading up the stairs to where Adam would be waking from his late-morning nap. At least in the nursery, Emily could gather herself, calm down from these twin shocks, and contemplate how they could be dealt with, not that Toby Burns was a problem: he could just be evicted.

But Gherson? On past experience, he would be in pursuit of money, and on thinking about it, she knew with Denby Carruthers, the man who had tried to kill him, now dead, the threat which had kept him out of her life had evaporated. She could only hope Walter Hodgson, who had sorted the swine out before, could contrive a way to do so again.

'So, it was you dogging my footsteps from Charing Cross?' Seeing surprise, Gherson added, 'Do not take up trailing people as an occupation, Burns, for you will surely expire in pursuit of your quarry. I had you marked before we passed St Martin's Church.'

'You spotted me?' was the silly response.

'Half of London must have done so. And I must tell you, with some of the places through which we passed, had your presence troubled me, there were people I know who would have clapped a stopper on your little game, and not temporarily.'

It wasn't true, and even in his heyday as part of the underbelly of the city, he would have struggled to bring about such an outcome. It wasn't only sailors and the present reluctant hostess on whom he was imposing who hated Cornelius Gherson. A goodly portion of the criminal fraternity of London, if they thought of him at all, would have good cause to term him a snake and deserving of the knife. But there was pleasure to be had from threatening a creature like Burns, for there would never be a response to trouble him from such a coward.

'I had no idea we would end up here of all places, or that you were familiar with my Aunt Emily.'

'Familiar!' The word made him laugh out loud. 'We are mongoose and snake.'

'Which is which?' was a question only a naive dolt could ask, for it made no difference.

'Do I recall right, my impression you don't stand high in her estimation?'

'A situation I hoped to redress.'

'Then I wish you joy. I may loathe the woman, but she's not one to readily buckle.'

'If you loathe her, what are you doing here?'

'Seeking my just deserts.' He waved an arm to encompass something, perhaps the room, maybe the whole house, while snapping at Toby to sit down. 'None of this prosperity she enjoys would be hers if it were not for me.'

The lies tripped easily off the Gherson tongue; how, if Ralph Barclay had made a mint in prize money, it had been he, his ever so humble clerk, who had managed it and grown the fund to the point where his widow had inherited a fortune. He went on to tell how he'd discovered Captain Barclay's prize agents were not dealing fairly with their client so, when his employer had lost his life, he made it his task to see Toby's aunt received her full due, which did not come without difficulties.

He spoke with utter conviction, easy to do when he had convinced himself it was true, which meant Toby Burns swallowed this drivel whole, his eyes wide as he listened to how this genius with numbers had found his employer was being cheated by the seemingly respectable prize agents of Ommaney and Druce. On coming home, Gherson had bearded the guilty partners, forcing then to eat humble pie as they begged him not to expose their underhand dealings, not to condemn them to the Marshalsea as debtors, forcing them to make full restitution, his voice rising as he came to the end of this fantastical peroration.

'And what did I get as recompense for my efforts and honest endeavour? A position as purser of a damn transport ship.' The look with which he fixed Burns, added to the changed tone in his voice, was enough to make Burns sit back in his chair. 'But I'm here to correct matters and be granted my proper reward.'

'Will my aunt agree?' asked Burns, for the use of the word 'honest' from a man he knew to be the precise opposite had jarred enough to render the whole tale suspect.

'She damn well will, or—'The growl was killed off as the door opened and a trolley of food, plus a decanter of wine and two glasses, was brought in, to a cry of 'Splendid. God knows, I'm sharp set, and I daresay you are too.'

Heinrich Lutyens had to be dragged from treating a patient to respond to the message sent by Emily Barclay, though judging by the cries of pain emerging from his treatment room—sounds which died away as he came out into the hallway—whoever he was 'ministering' to would be grateful for his being distracted. The verbal message kept him out for some time as he scribbled a note to be taken to the White Swan, urging the footman to take a hack to Clerkenwell and back so Hodgson would know how serious things were. If he was not there, it was to be left with the proprietor.

His patient, who shortly afterwards hobbled to the front door, he despatched quickly. Then, taking up some of his surgical instruments and shoving them into his greatcoat pocket, he hurried round to Fitzroy Square, knocking discreetly rather than ringing the brass bell. The door was opened cautiously, but upon being recognised, for Lutyens was a frequent caller, he was admitted. Silently directed up the stairs to the nursery, he found a cheerful, gurgling Adam sat on his mother's lap. The looks exchanged between Lutyens and Emily made words regarding the situation unnecessary, given he was fully aware of everything that had happened in the last twelve months.

'And now I have my nephew Toby throwing himself on my charity. I have to find a way to get them both out of the house so I can make a plan to confound Gherson.'

'I'm sure the good Hodgson will think of a way,' Lutyens said as Adam slipped to the floor and began crawling around.

'I pray you're right, Heinrich. How I wish I were a man, for if I were, they'd both be lying bruised and in the mud outside, rather than eating and drinking in the comfort of my house.'

'Find them somewhere else to take their ease.'

'I won't part with a penny to such an ogre.'

'I fear you may have to, Emily.'

Seeing temper was about to make her argue, Lutyens spoke quickly, despite the fact the infant was now using his leg to raise himself upright, not comfortable to a man with a limited love of children, even one smiling at him.

'You must prevaricate, buy time. It is too much to expect Mr Hodgson to contrive a solution as easily as he did before. The threat which was his weapon is no longer in his hands.'

'What do you suggest?'

'Put him up in Brown's Hotel, where they know your name and station.'

'At my expense?'

'Even if I haven't talked to him as you have, Gherson will be sure he has the whip hand. I admit to not knowing him as well as you do, Emily, but you must use his certainty against him. Give him the impression of triumph, be meek—'

'He'll certainly smell a rat if I behave like a supplicant,' she insisted. 'I long to spit in his eye.'

'How ladylike.'

The remark brought forth a slightly pleased gurgle, which, if it was not a laugh, came as a sign of easing tension. Lutyens smiled at a woman he had once harboured hopes of ensnaring in his own life—beautiful, spirited and kind—who was now wholly committed to his friend John Pearce. There was no resentment now in this, such feelings and aspirations having subsided long past. He knew himself to be no match for her paramour, a man of action where he was not, tall and handsome where he was short, seen to be rather curious in his visage, which had often been remarked on as fishlike.

'True, so it is perhaps best left to me.'

'It is a great deal to ask.'

'Do you have any idea how offended I would be if you failed to do so. Pen a letter to Brown's and I will deal with Gherson. First a hack to take him there . . .'

'Which can drop my nephew at Charing Cross.'

A raised eyebrow suggested an explanation, which Emily declined to provide. 'It is too dull, Heinrich; just take my word it is the solution, though it will cost me a couple of guineas to be shot of the wretch, for he is short on funds.'

'It will be necessary to tell Brown's to indulge Gherson's needs.'

'So I'll be paying for his whores as well as his food and drink. The man is an absolute satyr.'

'Then let's hope his stay is short.'

'It's his life I want to be short, Heinrich. Anyone inclined to stretch his neck in future can do so without interference from me.'

Emily Barclay would have been surprised at his behaviour. Having freed himself from the company of tedious Toby Burns, off to rejoin his ship, Gherson, with the aid of the note, booked a room under her name and settled down to a good solitary dinner, with only one bottle of wine, albeit an expensive one. He was too exhausted to indulge in any revels, for sleep was not something much gifted to a fellow freezing cold while sat atop a post chaise.

He was soon alone in his bed, his mind firmly on two things: the differing comfort he was now enjoying compared to his on-board cot, and the life which would soon be his. It would be one of comfort and plenty, once he'd extracted what he was owed from both the people who'd done him down. His other mark he would confront on the morrow.

These thoughts didn't last long, for he was soon sound asleep.

Chapter Nineteen

Walter Hodgson, having spent most of a frustrating day in Greenwich seeking details on the purser Posner, was alerted to the fact he had two communications—one a letter, the other a note—when he got back to the White Swan. First was a reply to the response he'd sent Posner, the other the note sent by Lutyens. Prior to entering, he had been salivating over the notion of a good dinner, several jugs of porter, and a fire in the grate to sit by and overcome the January chill which had marked most of his day.

The response from Posner told him first how grateful he was for a reply and the offer of a visit to Harwich. Additional information told Hodgson the purser was coming ashore on a date, two days hence, to replenish his stores from the naval warehouse and was prepared to meet him to discuss how to advance matters. It named a tavern called the Tabard close by. Off his feet and warming himself, Hodgson then perused the second note with the added verbal message, which made him curious, given Lutyens was a man he barely knew.

Opened and read, the note with its enclosed name was inclined to ruin both his appetite and his thirst. Not that he was told much more than that a demanding Gherson had turned up at Fitzroy Square, with the implication of threatening behaviour. So, Emily Barclay once more required his services to deal with the scoundrel, which was immediately recognised as being easier said than done.

'And how am I to scare him away, now that a certain party is no longer a threat to his life?'

'Talking to yourself, Walter.'

He looked up to see Samuel Oliphant standing before him, a look of curiosity on what he could see of his face, not much since he was well wrapped up against the cold winter weather.

'Sometimes news you receive has such an effect.'

'May I join you?' This granted, Oliphant disrobed and took a seat, signalling for a tankard of ale. 'Anything pertaining to our business?'

'No.'

Oliphant looked amused. 'Do I take it from the brevity of your response, it's not something you wish to share with me?'

'Correct,' Hodgson replied, putting both letter and note in a waist-coat pocket. Oliphant's tankard arrived, he taking a long pull, allowing Hodgson to do the same.

'I'm bound to ask if any progress has been made there.'

The reply was so slow in coming, as the thief-taker sorted out in his mind what he could and could not say, it left time for Oliphant's smile to disappear, replaced by a brusque enquiry.

'Well?'

'I have feelers out among my own circles, asking for a name of anyone at the Admiralty who has known weaknesses. As yet nothing has come back.'

'People you trust, I hope, who're not going to enquire why you're asking?'

Known for his calm demeanour, Walter Hodgson now responded angrily. 'It may be trust is not to be expected in the games you play, but in mine it is. I need a name to approach, and I have two choices. One being to hang about in Whitehall and ask every Tom, Dick, or Harry if they are vulnerable or know of anyone who might be. The other is to put the word out in my own fraternity: people, I might say, I not only trust not to ask why, but believe will do their best to help.'

Slightly taken aback by the response, Oliphant adopted a more con-ciliatory tone. 'I'm naturally anxious, Walter, and as you have no doubt guessed, I'm not alone.'

'While I'm anxious not to take any unnecessary risks. Openly solic-iting information is a good way to raise the alarm with the very people I hope to bypass, and they are powerful enough to clap me in the Tower.'

'You say someone vulnerable?'

'Gambling debts, questionable carnal preferences, a bit of larceny in their background. I'm surprised you of all people have to ask.'

This was a reference to Oliphant's cloudy background, where even his name was suspect. There was no point in worrying about it: Oliphant was paying him, clearly on instructions from another, so what he chose to call himself was of no account.

'I do so because I have to answer when I'm asked, which I will be. Do you have any notion how long this is going to take?'

'None, but I don't anticipate it will be long. Thief-takers might compete, but it pays to do a favour when you are bound, at some time, to need one yourself.'

'A guess.'

'Day or two, no more.'

'And if no name is provided?'

'Then I'll have to think of another way.'

Taking another long drink allowed Hodgson to wonder if he'd taken on too much work already, so dealing with the needs of Emily Barclay was going to be difficult. He had to find a reason to oblige Gherson to back off, which he would do only if he felt threatened. Besides the difficulties there, he had to go to Harwich to meet Posner.

'I'm about to eat some dinner. Care to join me?'

'No, but thank you. I have another call to make.'

'Pity,' Hodgson replied, secretly pleased.

They sat for a short while, Oliphant silent, deep in thought, and seemingly much taken with sipping his ale, his eyes fixed on the flames bursting out from the burning logs. Hodgson was likewise contemplating how to juggle all the tasks in which he was engaged.

Drink finished, Oliphant began to dress for the outdoors.

'Anything turns up, Walter, keep me informed.'

'Of course.'

As he went through the outer door, Hodgson called over the girl serving drink. 'Send your pot boy out to order me a hack for half an hour hence. And ask the kitchen to hurry with my food.'

Sat in the back of the hack, bouncing along cobbled roads, Walter Hodgson was aware he'd eaten his suet pudding in too much haste, for he could feel it repeating on him, and he was still in some discomfort when he arrived in Fitzroy Square. Admitted and joining Emily and Lutyens in the same drawing room vacated by Gherson, he listened to what had happened, none of which came as much of a surprise, while he was aware his lack of an instant solution cast an air of gloom over things.

'Unlike before, Mrs Barclay, he will see himself in an unassailable position. It was fear of Denby Carruthers that got rid of him before, or the notion I would tell the alderman where he could be found. If he has turned up again, it must be because he knows the threat no longer exists.'

'I must keep my secret,' she insisted, as Lutyens nodded in support. 'Even if it comes at a cost.'

It was no secret to either of the men in the room: Lutyens knew both John Pearce and Emily too well, while Hodgson, too sharp to be fooled, had figured it out for himself.

'Which I would advise against,' Hodgson countered. 'Together we must find a way to put the fear of God into him, but as of this moment I cannot think of one.'

Seeing her distress, he knew he must provide reassurance, even if he had no idea how it could be contrived, but first he had to put his hand over his mouth to suppress a burp, then press a hand to his stomach to seek to alleviate his indigestion.

'Let me think on it. I will be in touch in a couple days, hopefully with a solution.'

'A couple days?' Emily remarked, clearly unhappy. 'Only the good Lord knows how much that will cost me.'

A hand had to go to Hodgson's mouth to cover the evidence of the acidity in his rumbling stomach once more, prior to him pointing out he had other matters with which to contend, the most pressing one taking him out of London.

'You seem in some discomfort, Mr Hodgson.'

'A rushed meal, Mrs Barclay.'

'Shall I get cook to boil a small pan of water? I have found it efficacious.'

'Please don't go to any trouble.' It was an answer he had good cause to regret.

Gherson was up with the lark, rested then breakfasted, prior to making his way to the city, a long walk but one in which he took pleasure. London was his locale, the place where he had plied his trade, sure there were enough dolts who could be persuaded to pay for the things he saw as necessities. In a life of much skulduggery and outlandish tale-telling, mixed with financial sleight of hand and downright theft, he had often tasted luxury.

He made his way with an air of superiority innate to his person when things were, as they would again be this day, on the up. Penury, to which he had been reduced many times, brought concomitant misery. There were very few people Cornelius Gherson did not hold in contempt, and those he did not, he hated. His father, who'd thrown his thieving son out of the family house. Emily Barclay, for her possession of an inheritance he had seen, given her adultery, as coming his way. Her lover, John Pearce, too.

To Gherson, Pearce was a sanctimonious do-gooder, a man Ralph Barclay had failed to properly flog when they were both aboard HMS *Brilliant*. He would have seen it done right, and the mental image of the swine at the grating, his back in bloody shreds, brought a smile to his face, one many a passer-by mistook for an outgoing gesture of bonhomie.

He had hated Denby Carruthers too, a blustering hard-horse and mean employer, which added piquancy to the cuckolding which had sent him near deranged and determined him on retribution. On him he would now take posthumous revenge, not as satisfying as doing so when he was alive, but certainly safer. Having worked for Carruthers in Devonshire Square, this too was pleasingly familiar: a dead-end avenue of warehouses, ended by a couple of elegant Queen Anne dwellings, one of which had been the home and office of his old employer.

The senior clerk who met Gherson at the door didn't recognise him, hardly surprising since there had been several since his day, while the last one had been skewered at the same time as Carruthers. Nor was the fellow much taken with his appearance, clad as Gherson was in his worn naval oilskins. But he had a job to do, which first and naturally led to enquiry about his reason for calling, to which came the query, in return, as to who was presently running the business.

'Mr Edward Druce, sir, but he's not with us today. He has other matters to attend to so comes here on alternate days.'

'In the Strand, perhaps.'

'Yes, sir. Do you know Mr Druce?'

'I do.'

'Then who should I say called?'

'An old client of his brother-in-law.'

'Mr Carruthers?' A nod. 'A sad affair, sir.'

'Quite' was the reply as Gherson turned away, silently castigating himself for not calling into the offices of Ommaney and Druce, which was on the way from Brown's. Should he wait another day or beard him now, for this seemed the best place to do it? It was impatience which brought on a decision: to put off for twenty-four hours the pleasure he'd been so looking forward to not being possible, it was a less content Gherson who retraced his steps to the Strand.

The reception at the prize agent's office was very different. There, the long-employed clerk recognised him immediately, and not with any sense of joy. He was adamant Mr Druce would not want to see him, which drew from Gherson a scathing rebuke about the fellow acting above his station.

'Do as I ask. And tell him every minute I'm kept waiting will add to the anger I will feel—also the price he will have to pay—when he finally consents to see me.'

Gherson would have been delighted, had he been witness to the reaction when the clerk told Edward Druce who was in the hallway. The blood drained from the man's face as he rushed for the sideboard and the chamber pot in the metal-lined cupboard, into which he was sick.

'I can't see him' came as a gasp from a burning throat. 'Tell him to go away.'

'I doubt he will do so, Mr Druce.'

'Then chuck him out, man.'

The clerk, tall, thin, and stooping, while not being in his first youth, replied firmly. 'It is not part of my duties, Mr Druce, to employ physical force to anyone calling. If he offers violence, I must step out of his way.'

'He won't; the swine is a coward.'

Which was a moot point coming from a man so terrified himself. In the end it was Gherson who decided the matter by just making his own entry, to then advise the clerk he could safely leave them alone, the only words he heard before he closed door coming from Gherson.

'I'm so glad, Mr Druce, to see you looking so prosperous.'

But the clerk could not help but notice the look on his employer's face. Having been sent to find Walter Hodgson on more than one occasion when it came to the activities of Cornelius Gherson, he took it upon himself to do so now, sure it would be what was required. When he failed—Hodgson was not at his usual haunt—he left a request that he contact Mr Druce at once before, with some trepidation, making his way back to the Strand.

The clerk was surprised to find Gherson was not only still with Druce, but there was no sound of dispute, when he put an ear to the door, in a meeting which had already gone on for quite some time. When Gherson did leave, it was with a smile on his face, added to a kindly word of farewell, utterly out of character, which rendered the fellow supremely curious when he entered to tell his employer what he'd done.

'I hope you will forgive the presumption, sir, but I felt it wise to ask Mr Hodgson to call at his earliest convenience.'

Druce looked pensive rather than pleased and took time to respond before finally saying, 'It can do no harm. Could you fetch for me the files on the business we conducted on behalf of Captain Barclay? I believe, since it has ceased to be for us an active account, they have been condemned to the basement.'

'The papers are incomplete, sir. Most of the files were sent over to Mr Davidson.'

'If my memory serves me right, we have retained the ones I now need.'

'And Mr Hodgson, sir?'

This again turned his employer meditative. 'Let it lie. I have to see him on another matter anyway.'

Walter Hodgson was in a hired post chaise being pulled by four horses, and he was the only passenger. The expense, one shilling and threepence per mile, was not a worry, given Edward Druce was paying for it, not that he would be aware until Hodgson sent in a bill for his services. With the new turnpike roads, such a conveyance could make eleven to twelve miles in any given hour, so with an early start, he could calculate a seven- to eight-hour journey to Harwich, with the return being made overnight.

If he was thinking about Gherson, it was not on behalf of the man paying for his travel, but on that of Mrs Barclay, and the ingratitude of the sod who would still blackmail her even if she had helped save his miserable life by paying the fees of Garrow, the lawyer who'd pled his case. The low opinion Hodgson had of Gherson had surfaced within minutes of meeting him, on behalf of Druce, in Newgate prison while he was awaiting trial for the murder of Catherine Carruthers. Having encountered and apprehended villains of every stripe over a long career, Hodgson had quickly concluded he was in the presence of the lowest of a breed whose morals were those of the unwashed privy.

How many crimes had the sod committed in his life? Dozens, no doubt, but he'd somehow escaped paying a price for his felony. This he achieved by always dunning people in such a way they could not complain to a magistrate. Blackmailed, Emily Barclay would not, for to do so would oblige her to state the reason she was under threat.

Likewise, Denby Carruthers, who could have sent Gherson to rot in Botany Bay if he'd been prepared to admit the one-time clerk who'd robbed him had also seduced his young and smitten wife, a fact which must remain hidden.

Edward Druce had conspired with him to fiddle monies from Ralph Barclay's account, so to say a word about Gherson's part would see both in Newgate awaiting the gibbet, his reputation in ruins. If Gherson was a snake, he was a supremely cunning one.

'I must find a way to get him had up,' he muttered to himself, the words addressed to the velvet of the empty seats opposite.

Now they'd left behind the endless noise of the London streets and were out in the quiet of the country road, he closed his eyes, seeking to get some sleep after a night in which his stomach had kept him awake.

Henry Dundas was not content to leave all his work to others and, in this case, he would not have entrusted it to anyone else. His disappointment at the decision to claim the Spanish silver as droits of the Crown had to be accepted; his job now was to ensure neither he nor the government suffered damage from what was clearly a campaign being mounted by persons unknown to do just that. They were trying to stir up a mob in favour of Pearce and, to a lesser extent, Langholm. Once active, this was a situation which could easily get out of hand, with unknown consequences for him personally.

The printer's workplace was dingy and quiet, which was hardly surprising early in the week for a newspaper only distributed on Sundays. He found the owner-cum-publisher sat behind a desk composing copy, so engrossed in doing so that it was some time, and it took the tapping on the floor of a tall walking stick, for him to realise he had a visitor, one he recognised with a tone of uncertainty.

'Mr Dundas?'

'The very same, Mr Bourne. It will not surprise you to know I have a deep interest in the publication of journals such as yours, so I have come to see how you are faring.'

'Tolerably well, sir. But I cannot but be surprised you find time to call. Surely the needs of the nation are of more importance?'

'The needs, as you call them, will take care of themselves for an hour or two. Does "tolerably well" mean you're profitable?' Dundas removed his hat and sat down in a very deliberate fashion, coming level eye to eye with Bourne, both hands resting on the top of his stick. 'One issue a week must make it difficult.'

'There are many weekly journals, Mr Dundas, and we, sir, are filling a gap. Being the sabbath does not preclude a desire to know what is happening in our troubled world.'

'You claim the world?'

'We go where there are matters of interest.'

There was just a hint of a tremble in the proprietor's voice, a hint that he found the presence of the Minister for War uncomfortable, and why not: many other people did. The next words were delivered with no attempt at anything dramatic.

'Like rumours of Spanish silver perhaps?' Dundas smiled, as if amused by the reaction, Bourne looking as if he had no idea of what he was talking about. 'Come, Mr Bourne, it is easy enough to follow your hints these last two issues. I wonder what you have for us on this coming Sunday.'

'I generally advise people to wait and see, sir.'

'While I wonder if you will gain repute by spreading tales being printed on scurrilous penny pamphlets?'

'We choose our sources with care. And we publish items which often expose truths other people want to keep hidden.'

'Like being so seriously in debt. Your Sunday *Observer* is in dire need of investment.'

'I fear you are misinformed, sir.'

'There are many things people can say of me, Mr Bourne, but misinformed is rarely one of them.' The next statement carried with it a tone of deep irony. 'So, if I posit you are near to having to close down your estimable publication, I suggest I may have the right of it, would you not agree?'

The nervousness evident when Dundas first entered had not abated, quite the reverse. The hand which had held the quill throughout was now slightly but visibly shaking. But Bourne was determined to bluff it out, even if he could not quite manage to sound convincing.

'The business is sound, sir.'

'So, if you were offered a lifeline . . .' Seeing Bourne once more about to object, Dundas paused, seeking to look contrite, before continuing. 'I refer to the fact, of which you must be aware, it is sometimes in the interests of the government to financially reward those who support our policies—in short to hew to the proper line on contentious topics.'

'A far from ethical manner of behaviour.'

'I wonder if you understand the concept of the necessity of survival, Mr Bourne, which applies to parliamentary majorities just as it does to struggling journals. I see my task as ensuring the former, with no like duty to preserve the latter. Indeed, if they were to be seen to be printing stories harmful to my party interests, why would I not seek to ensure they fail?'

'Do I sense a threat, Minister?'

Dundas smiled as he stood to replace his hat. 'Is that not a rather crude allusion, sir, lacking in delicacy?'

'Surely the sole point is this: is it real?'

'Which indicates you're somewhat unsure. Perhaps, in reflecting on our conversation, you will come to a more definite conclusion which, I venture to suggest, will not be aided by my continuing presence. So, I will wish you good day.'

The tall walking stick tapped several times on the way out, sounding like mockery to Bourne. This took him from his composing of a piece on the latest French successes in Italy—unbeknown to the editor, already well out of date—to consider the ledger on his desk. This, opened and studied, told him just how deep was the hole in the newspaper's finances.

All attempts to fill it had fallen on stony ground, and it was plain that Henry Dundas knew it to be so. To go up against such an adversary, well known for his lack of even the most basic principles, could likely ensure that his project—one he'd been sure would make him rich—would instead fail. Defiance was attractive; he aspired to be seen as a crusader in pursuit of truth. Tempting, but was it wise?

He'd taken money off Alexander Davidson: not enough to support his paper but sums which helped keep at bay his most pressing creditors. A man getting more desperate by the week could delude himself that it was only right and proper, with the excuse that, in an imperfect world, sometimes such lapses in the high standards he professed to uphold were required. It was a problem he gnawed on long after Dundas had gone but, in the end, he knew there was no choice, so the requisite letter was penned. It simply said, appraised of what the government required in the way of support, he would provide, if they'd be so good as to keep him informed.

There was no need to ask for support in the form of cash injections. These would follow, discreetly but regularly, and if they failed to make him rich, they would ensure the *Observer* survived.

Alexander Davidson received, as arranged, his copy of the *Observer* mid-afternoon prior to the day of publication, searching eagerly for the story agreed with Bourne, the tone of which was to ask why the government was hiding certain facts. It was now public that Spain had, over months, negotiated in secret with Paris, but this was to be repeated, with the story of how a valuable cargo of silver, needed to facilitate this betrayal, had been intercepted by two enterprising naval officers. But he searched in vain, nor was there any mention of the government's intention to deprive these two unnamed heroes of their just reward by claiming the cargo as droits of the Crown.

Instead, there was an article questioning the whole provision of prize money paid to naval officers for what was surely licenced piracy. Certainly, they should be rewarded for the capture of an enemy warship, which involved both a fight and a risk to their person. But to pay them money for taking merchant vessels surely led them into a temptation to ignore their proper duty in the pursuit of personal profit. And no such monies should be forthcoming on those occasions—of which there were too many—where there were questions regarding the legitimacy of the seizure.

There was no need to read between the lines, for it was a stark rebuttal of the very point Davidson had set out to establish, which meant, quite simply, Bourne, whom he knew to be struggling financially, had flipped. This could only have come about because, in the cause of John Pearce, he had been outbid. Not that Davidson was inclined to back off: he would launch a legal challenge as soon as the government announced any decision to invoke the right to impose droits of the Crown on the *Santa Leocadia* cargo.

But experience told him that such a case, brought in the Admiralty court against the whole force of the office of the Lord Chancellor, would take years and come with a serious risk of defeat. He had two letters to write: the first to John Pearce, a second to Mrs Barclay to tell her what had happened.

Chapter Twenty

HMS *Hazard* was taking on fresh water, this the last of the articles needed to get to sea and undertake the task given to John Pearce by Horatio Nelson, not that he had any clear idea of how to go about it. It seemed inconceivable he could emulate the exploits of Captain Thomas Fremantle, which is what the commodore had hinted he sought. It seemed not a day went by when he and his crew were not engaging someone somewhere and inflicting demoralising damage in a series of striking raids of the kind to appeal to Pearce.

The first constraint on emulation was the size of HMS *Hazard*, and not just in tonnage and weight of shot. She was seriously lacking in the kind of manpower which would facilitate operations against an Italian coast now on high alert for such attacks. This accepted, her captain was not one to be disinclined to try, but he would need to show more care than Fremantle in picking his targets. And he also had the constraint of the need to make a regular rendezvous with a pinnace bringing news from Elba about the timing of taking off the threatened members of the Corsican government.

He needed to know both their chosen location and some idea of numbers, the only indication as of now that it would be somewhere on the east coast. This was no doubt determined by the difficulties inherent on getting from the capital, Corte, deep in the mountainous interior, to where they could be lifted off. From what Pearce could discern from Nelson's words, this meant any escape had to be clandestine and included the fact that their political opponents might try to stop them.

In the midst of taking his breakfast, with a map of the Tuscan and Ligurian coast to hand and mulling on possibilities, he was informed of two cutters approaching across the choppy waters of the harbour, full of men in red uniforms. On deck, once Pearce cast an eye over them, he was fairly sure he could give a name to the officer who sat in the thwarts, so before the soldiers came alongside, he called loudly over the side.

'Mr Vickery, I hope I find you well. I do remark, however, your uniforms are not the ones I recall you wearing on our last encounter.'

The smile in response was for Vickery to remember, while serving on Corsica the previous year, the Mediterranean summer had reduced their red coats to a wan pink. And this was before they suffered the effects of wear and tear in a landscape full of tough, spiky undergrowth, almost designed by nature to ruin clothing of any kind. But if they had been less than prepossessing specimens on first sight, they had proved highly capable in contact with the enemy.

'We intend to dazzle you, Mr Pearce.'

'Do I also observe you have been subject to a promotion?'

'A temporary one, sir, to the rank of acting captain, which means more responsibility without the proper pay to go with it.'

The boats came alongside carefully, this because they were being closely observed by the *Hazard*'s crew, who were unforgiving of anyone who scraped paint from the hull, and included a third vessel, a barge carrying the soldiers' packs and weapons. Vickery came aboard first to raise his hat to the quarterdeck and accept the salute of the ship's marines before ceremony was abandoned and the greetings became general and friendly.

Those aboard fondly recalled the service Vickery and his men had rendered, aiding them to interdict the incursion of French-supporting Corsicans boating over from Italy, not least in the final action, which had caused Pearce so much trouble with Jervis. While this formed the opening of the conversation in Pearce's cabin, it was short in duration, for the soldier wanted to know the purpose of his being seconded to this duty, assuming there was a specific aim. It was a notion of which he was quickly disabused, as Pearce recounted his orders and the freedom this provided.

'I'm hoping to cause general discomfort to our enemies.'

'Where?'

Pearce would never reveal the notion which came to him at that moment, as tempting as it was sudden, and, like so many of such ideas, seeming to arrive fully formed.

'I thought we should start with Bastia.'

This received a quizzical look from the soldier, it having been the site of his previous posting, and a damned uncomfortable one for the army before the island was abandoned.

'I have in mind to pay back in kind those who caused us so much trouble. And the best of it is, those very same people have shown us the way to do it.'

This required no explanation and obviously appealed to a man who'd been run ragged by the Corsican insurgents for a lot longer than John Pearce.

'And when would you propose to undertake this?'

'You will have noticed crossing the harbour, we have a wind, which is a Levanter, though not one of full strength. But it will certainly take us to where we want to go within an easy day's sailing.'

'Will the defences not be alarmed at the sight of your sails?'

'That's all they'll see, and they'll need to be sharp to identify them. I won't approach the shore till after dark, and then it's take to the boats and see what mischief we can commit. I take it you are free to act as you see fit?'

'My sole orders are to cooperate with the navy. The staff quartermaster was glad to get me and my men off the rations muster. Better the navy feed us than the Elba establishment. Being cavalry, he cares more about fodder for his horses than rations for infantry.'

'Then we shall seek to feed you properly while you're aboard.'

The head of young Livingston appeared. 'Mr Worricker's compliments, sir, and we are ready to weigh.'

'Return them and say I'll be on deck presently.'

'I best see my men settled,' Vickery said.

'And then perhaps a conference to see how we might go about paying back some of the Corsicans for the trouble they caused.'

The gathering was convened not long after they cleared Portoferraio harbour; the first point established in any incursion should be of short duration, which on its own settled the location of where they should touch land. They would use the trapped waters of the Etang de Biguglia, as had their previous opponents, this an efficient way to move the things the Corsicans planning an uprising had to carry: muskets, barrels of powder, and ingots of lead.

'We should be able to move with more freedom,' Vickery pointed out, it not being necessary to add they would have with them only the arms they needed to be effective.

Pearce had his doubts. 'I would be inclined to take along a couple of small barrels of powder in case we venture upon a tempting target or require a distraction to ward off any reaction.'

'Are you planning an assault on the citadel?' the soldier joked, everyone aware it had required an invasion force under Lord Hood to achieve anything against such a formidable fortress.

'Quite the opposite, Mr Vickery. I should like to avoid going near the place.'

'They will surely have patrols out, sir,' Macklin suggested. 'From what I recall, not all the locals were enamoured of the return of the French. They'd not be Corsicans if they were failing to cause trouble.'

'That or at least the threat,' added Worricker.

'Then let's hope we don't stumble across any' was Vickery's gloomy thought. 'We'll end up harming the wrong people.'

'Would you have done anything differently before?' asked Pearce.

If he'd made a gloomy remark, the recollection of what he and his men had been through made this a condition. Vickery had had as a superior an extremely indolent major called Warburton, who never left the citadel but insisted on his inferior undertaking regular and risky patrols in the very area they were proposing to land.

'I did suggest we sometimes use boats to extend our area of operations.'

'I need hardly say it was sound thinking, but you didn't mention it before, for I would have been happy to transport you.'

'I have no reason,' Vickery replied, 'to doubt the navy is the same as the army. When a superior officer declines your proposal, it's a bad idea to press matters.'

You would need to be an insensitive soul not to notice the reaction of the majority present. Mr Williams, the rather staid master, taking no part in the tactical discussions, looked askance, while Worricker and Macklin were amused. John Pearce tried and failed to look innocent, to the point where Vickery asked what he had missed.

'It may be as a service we are a mite less hidebound,' Pearce said. 'And, of course, being at sea, we are very often required to act independently.'

This got a smile from the soldier. 'Or it could mean that I'm in the presence of a fellow not much given to obeying orders.'

Which turned it into smiles all round, Williams excepted.

'There's a matter I may raise with you when we have worked out what we intend, Mr Vickery.' Seeing him about to enquire, Pearce added, 'in private.'

This, and the possible embarrassment it might cause, took them back to full concentration on the prospects of the coming night's operation, with Pearce opining they would only get one chance for outright surprise.

'Which indicates a desire for more forays,' Vickery responded, his doubts obvious.

'More than one perhaps,' Pearce said, 'with many a gap in between, but not continuing when it is seen to be risky.'

'At least it will be cool, unlike when we patrolled in the middle of summer.'

'Which brings me to a thought I had,' Pearce said. 'I recall being surprised, for all the state of your uniforms, Mr Vickery, you still went out at night with your webbing fully blancoed, which could not help but pick up the light and reveal you to those you were seeking on a night with a moon.'

'We were required to be properly dressed' was the response, an order that obviously came from the same indolent and stupid source. 'Do you not recall the inspection we were subjected to before departing the citadel?'

Indeed, Pearce did. Men lined up in an unshaded part of the parade ground, with the sun beating down on them and their faded coats, their plump and lazy major emerging for minutes only, his own coat strikingly red, before he made the shade and a cool interior again. Pearce and

Michael O'Hagan had gone out with Vickery and his men to sweat and near expire from the trapped heat of the stunted forest until they parted company and found the sea breeze.

'Which brings me to my point,' Pearce continued. 'Given the different conditions, I was about to suggest your men would be better off and less visible in their greatcoats. I will most certainly insist on dark clothing and use burnt cork on the faces of my men.'

Vickery smiled. 'You have no idea, Mr Pearce, how pleasant it is not having to answer to anyone but myself.'

'And your men will be up for it.'

'Most are the same fellows who patrolled this very coast and got sick to the back teeth of the way the Corsicans outwitted them. They are thus seeking revenge.'

Given the time *Hazard* had been at sea, her topsails were a long way from the unblemished cream colour they'd been when she set out from the Thames. So, as he turned for the coast of Corsica, having sailed to and fro until the sun went down, John Pearce had no worries his canvas would alert anyone to his presence. The binnacle light was heavily shaded, while Mr Williams, being given the rate of sailing by the man casting the log, could calculate at what point it would be best to take to the boats.

There was enough moon to show the outline of the interior mountains, and the silhouetted peak to aim from had been identified in daylight. Pearce, in the cutter—coxed by Michael O'Hagan and the other two Pelicans along, for they hated to be separated—had Vickery and half his soldiers aboard, near invisible in grey and they too with blackened faces.

The other two boats going in had mixed contingents, but it mattered little since they were all aiming for the same landing point, part of the sandbar enclosing the Etang de Biguglia. Much as they'd discussed what to do once ashore, it had been accepted much was down to chance. But there was little concern about landing, the surf being noisy enough to cover human movement. If there was no reaction at this point, they could proceed.

The first necessary act was to get a boat into the inland waterway, transporting it over the sandbar at the run, something sailors were able to accomplish through experience. It was something the previous years' enemies could not do, having come from Italy in a vessel carrying cargo. Pearce's first act had been to find and destroy any boats they had hidden away, forcing them to use a longer route.

Once this was accomplished and the two small powder barrels had been transferred, the party could advance on both sides of the Etang, to then look out for opportunities. Having patrolled here for weeks on end, and even in the dark, Vickery had a knowledge of the terrain which naturally inclined him to the inland shore. He also had a very clear idea of where he had posted his packets of men along the route back to the Bastia citadel. So it was he who first signalled to John Pearce in the accompanying boat that he had picked up the sound of a human presence.

'Close with the shore, Michael,' Pearce whispered, which he knew to be the case when the prow ran into the soft sand. Clambering out, with O'Hagan as ever by his side, Charlie Taverner and Rufus Dommet right behind, it was easy to move soundlessly over the aforesaid sand to join with Vickery in a whispered conversation.

'I reckon there's a party in the spot where I used to leave the furthest out of my men, and it seems the French are using the same spot. They're making little attempt at staying silent, so clearly they don't anticipate trouble.'

'Would that mean there might be more, further up the Etang?' asked Pearce.

'Possibly. It's what we did, if you recall.'

'I take it you feel capable of taking care of this lot?'

The soldier's teeth showed in the moonlight, which was enough of an answer. 'Then I'll take my party north.'

'If they're like our friends here, you'll have no trouble in placing them.'

'No noise, Mr Vickery, and I hope you'll forgive me for saying it.'

'It never hurts to be reminded of one's duty, Mr Pearce.'

Pearce had his men follow the waterway in single file, the boat left for Vickery in case he required a quick departure. If the soldiers he had attacked put up a fight, there was no evidence of it, for no sound came; and it was Michael who put a hand on Pearce to stop him, then indicate the faint sounds up ahead. A bit closer they saw, flickering through the trees, the sight of a small fire on what was not truly a cold night.

'Breaking on the wheel for this lot,' whispered Michael.

'You, Charlie, and Rufus into the trees. See if you can get close to their rear, and no noise.'

The three ghostly shapes were gone almost before he finished hissing his orders, while he moved forward himself with the rest of his crew behind him. Taking them was ridiculously easy for perceiving themselves safe, they sat around, muskets leaning against the trees—four blue-coated soldiers too busy seeing to their comfort to put up any resistance.

Instead, they were manhandled into a group where Pearce could question them, his pistol produced and put to a forehead at the first sign of reluctance to answer his questions. No, there were no more men stationed further up the Etang. Yes, their officer would come before sunup to lead them back to their barracks; and yes, a patrol came out every night. No, it was not always the same men on duty. The notion which came to Pearce then was of the same kind which had brought him to this shore in the first place, a pleasure to contemplate and complete in its outlines.

'Right, tie their hands, then back to Mr Vickery to see how he's done. Any one of them makes a sound, club him hard.'

There was no need to employ subterfuge most of the way, and it turned out none when they finally caught up with him. His corporal, jabbing gently his four unhurt and trussed charges with a bayonet—men of the same stripe as Pearce had taken—had them too terrified to think of taking any action to get free. Pearce ordered them to be put in the boat and went after Vickery.

If he'd succeeded in taking the last section of the patrol, it had not been without bloodshed. One of their number, having going further into the maquis to relieve himself, had come back to find his comrades with their hands in the air and being threatened with both muskets and bayonets.

'You have to admire the sod, Pearce; he tried to take us all on and save his mates. I just thank the Lord he was despatched without the use of a musket.'

Pearce looked down at the body, lying still, which was hardly a surprise, since Vickery said he'd been seen to, in regulation training ground fashion, by a couple of bayonets, striking twice each.

'So, we got a dozen in total, eleven alive and able to walk. This one will have to be carried.'

'Carried?'

'Yes, let's get them into the boat and transferred to the ship. We have plenty of darkness left and so enough time.'

'You want to take them on board?'

'I do. And I want the places they occupied to show no sign we were ever here, and that includes the blood from the man you've killed.'

It was Pearce's turn to produce a smile so wide it bared his teeth. 'They have an officer coming along before sunup to fetch them in, and I intend we should take him too. Imagine what will go through the mind of his superiors when there's no sign nor a trace of any of his men.'

Vickery burst out laughing, which was infectious.

'And the powder barrels?' the soldier asked.

'Another night,' Pearce replied. 'Let them worry about deserters and perhaps even demons.'

Pearce got the majority of his men and his French prisoners away while it was still dark, then had the small jolly boat pulled across the spit of sand and hauled up till it was partially hidden, the cutter having been sent away. He was waiting for the first grey light of dawn to clean up the blood staining the ground of the first piquet post, using seawater and sand, of which there was already plenty blown into the undergrowth by successive winds.

The man—in truth a boy—they were waiting for turned out to be a young *sous lieutenant* whose approach was noisy enough to give plenty of notice; nor did he offer any resistance when John Pearce stepped out, a pistol in his hand. By the time the Pelicans and a couple of other oarsmen had gotten the jolly boat back into the sea, the lad was in tears, which earned him a gentle pat on the back from Michael O'Hagan.

Chapter Twenty-One

Walter Hodgson had no fear of using his own name, as he had done in his letter to Posner, admitting he was acting on behalf of a principal who did not wish to enter into direct negotiations. He had done this without any assurance it was necessary, for he had no idea what the purser had been told about Denby Carruthers. But the possibility did exist the man had been made aware of the alderman's less honest activities, so the inclination to discretion would seem wise.

It is impossible not to form some kind of visual idea of a person's appearance even if you've never met them and, for the thief-taker it was a game he enjoyed and one in which, almost for necessity, he'd often indulged in his career. So there was some pleasure in seeing in Posner very much the kind of fellow he'd expected to meet, for he'd had him down as small of stature and likely to be the type to indulge in false confidence. This was borne out when he was shown to the table where Hodgson was enjoying a dish consisting of several varieties of the day's catch.

'Your guest, sir,' pronounced the fellow who owned Tabard Inn, advised beforehand to expect one.

Being fixed with a cold and unfriendly look had little effect. Hodgson rose to greet his visitor and invite him to sit, noting his lack of height and his clenched fists, thumb within his fingers and rigid by his body. This was a sure sign he was seeking to control himself, added to a lack of confidence. There was also a tightness in his voice which belied the attempt at inconsequence. But sit he did, so at least his hands were hidden.

'Will you join me in partaking of some fish, Mr Posner; the mullet in particular is very fine.' In truth it was in no way superior to the others on the serving dish, but the comment served to divert the purser from his aim of appearing firm in his resolve. 'I'm also drinking the local ale, but there's wine I can order, if you prefer.'

Posner did his best not to be disarmed or distracted, but the tone of voice in which these options were offered, another part of Hodgson's armoury when dealing with strangers, made it difficult not to respond in a like manner, though he did try.

'Is our business going to occupy so much time, sir, as to allow for indulgence?'

'I reckon we both hope for a harmonious outcome, and I can't see such a thing being hampered by a good meal, can you?'

Posing it as a question obliged Posner to answer and, as suspected, he was engaged in a performance, which he struggled to hold to in the face of such bonhomie.

'Can I take it I have the name of your principal?'

Hodgson smiled, seeking to convey understanding. 'At this stage, I think it best to assume nothing, sir.'

'You will find me a hard man to dupe, sir,' was blurted out.

Hodgson took it for what it was, the complete opposite of the truth, but made no gesture to refute it, keeping his tone of voice even and friendly. 'I feel I have the right to certain information before I can respond to such a query. You are clearly acting on behalf of another, and I need to know that name before I can think of divulging any like information to you.'

'Are you seeking to imply you're prepared to risk this meeting coming to nothing?'

The look this got was close to sympathetic. 'I am, Mr Posner. Are you? Now how about I order you some food?'

The sharp nod told Hodgson he had what he wanted, control of what was to follow, but he didn't press. Instead, once he'd ordered the food and drink, he produced a raft of seemingly innocent questions about the state of the fleet of which Posner was part, his duties aboard HMS *Ardent*, as well as the difficulties inherent in his occupation.

The latter was the key, for even if he had tried to dissemble, his host had taken him on to his favourite topic. His gripes about being a purser in general and his own difficulties in particular: impecunious officers,

tight-fisted warrants, common seamen who had nothing but their promised but as yet unforthcoming pay with which to keep going his ability
to show a tiny margin of profit, added to a late-settling Navy Board. To
this was added the indifference of authority to the way such business was
handled.

Hodgson was content, with the odd nudge of a query, for Posner to
keep talking for, at home on his turf, he relaxed somewhat. Also, what he
was saying revealed to be correct his questioner's instinct about his own
needs being the driver of the original correspondence. If he was helping
a Tolland, he would only do so if there was personal advantage. It also
established he knew nothing of the events in Devonshire Square or of
the fate of Jaleel Tolland, which established this also applied to Tolland's
younger brother.

'What you say about the life of a purser is intriguing,' Hodgson lied;
he couldn't care less. 'But I wonder if you can comprehend, in your efforts
to aid a no doubt deserving case, you may unwittingly be exposing others
to risk.'

The startled reaction to 'deserving case,' much as Posner tried to mask
it, was nearly enough to cause Hodgson to laugh, which almost made the
next words superfluous.

'It pains me to insist, but I do need the name of the person on whose
behalf you're acting before we can proceed.'

'And if I decline to be open first.'

'Then we must bring the meeting to an end. I have a post chaise
waiting to take me back to London, and it matters not if I depart now
instead of at a later hour.'

'A post chaise?' Hodgson nodded. 'The regular postal carrier, surely?'

'No, I've engaged it privately.'

Posner was stunned: even if he could never afford such a thing, he
knew, if not to the penny, how much such a conveyance cost.

'Let me say, Mr Posner, before you commit to silence, I do have the
authority to see if my principal can do anything to relieve your own bur-
dens. It may be he cannot meet your original request for reasons of his
own, but that is no reason you should not be rewarded for your charity.'

Posner was left staring silently at the fish bones on his plate, as well as the shell of a dressed crab. Now fed, watered, and listened to, any defences he had were beyond their limit., Before meeting Walter Hodgson, he would have had hopes of his dream being fulfilled—that his pitch for a place with a good and steady stipend, in which he could employ what skills he possessed and, more importantly, on dry land—had a good chance of being met. He was now being told it was not the case.

'So your principal has no desire to see Franklin Tolland free of the navy?'

'A sharp piece of deduction, Mr Posner,' the thief-taker replied, wondering why it had taken him so long to conclude the obvious. 'But have you seen the concomitant requirement?'

This left hanging, Hodgson changed the subject. 'He's brother to Jaleel Tolland.'

'A deserter. He ran months past.'

'Indeed.'

The query allowed Posner to wander off into another area to which his host was indifferent, to relate that if Franklin Tolland was a dangerous fellow, his elder brother had been ten times worse and had committed murder when on the loose.

'Got clean away, mind, which has led Franklin to suspect help from your principal, whom I assume to be Mr Denby Carruthers.'

'Not so, Mr Posner. A go-between at one time, yes, but the principal, no.' Faced with incredulity, Hodgson added, 'It is common in certain types to think they know it all when, in truth, they are only permitted to know as much as they need to keep them active. When you talk of Denby Carruthers, you speak of someone who is no longer with us and has not been for some time. The letter you sent arrived at an address where he no longer resides and was passed on to where it could be acted upon.'

'To you?'

'Eventually, and it has brought me here as an agent for another.'

It took him a while to process this till he asked, 'And Jaleel Tolland?'

The shrug was to say *I have no idea.* 'But I doubt if I'm required to point out to you how dangerous the world is for a run sailor in wartime, especially one who has committed murder. He could be anywhere, even aboard another King's ship. If he was taken up by the press, he would hardly admit his name, his crimes, or his having run from whatever vessel he was in.'

'True.'

'Mr Posner, I must ask, did you show Franklin Tolland the contents of the letter which brought you here today?'

'I did not. I wished to see what was on offer before doing anything.'

'On offer for you?'

Posner, in his pinched face, had enough conscience to blush and was quick to seek justification. 'While I'm the type to aid a fellow in need, I'm not inclined to do so, at some risk to my position I might add, for no reward.'

'I can see I'm dealing with a shrewd mind, Mr Posner,' said Hodgson, lying once more.

The purser had not stood very high in his estimation to begin with, but this admission, much as he hated the idea of Franklin Tolland being free, did nothing to enhance it. The fellow was a grubby little opportunist at best and likely to be inclined towards larceny in his chosen occupation.

'I've come all this way, Mr Posner, and at some expense, to ensure no harm comes to the reputation of my principal.'

'While I'm wondering, Mr Hodgson—if that is your real name— whether you are in fact acting on your own behalf.'

The actor in Hodgson allowed him to produce a fleeting appearance of being alarmed, enough to convince the plodder with whom he was dealing that he had the right of it, before he replied to continued disbelief.

'Given the wealth of my principal, I wish it were so.'

'You hinted at an offer.'

'One available to you if you understand what is required.'

'It can only be you have no desire to see Franklin Tolland free of the navy?'

'Another clever deduction, sir. For him to be kept aboard HMS *Ardent* would have certain advantages.'

'And the recompense for such an assurance?'

'Four guineas per quarter, Mr Posner, deposited wherever you choose to keep your funds.'

'I was in search of something more.' A quizzical raised eyebrow got a response. 'A position ashore?'

Hodgson pretended to be confused and also to give an erroneous impression the leading voice in this conversation had shifted, that it was he on the defensive. 'I'm at a loss to know where this would be, sir.'

'It was what Tolland promised.'

'Then he exceeded both his worth and his knowledge.'

A penny which should have dropped previously finally did so. 'If there's no Denby Carruthers, there's no alderman, no rich businessman, and no partner in smuggling.'

'An inventive soul our Franklin but, apart for him being a smuggler, he's sold you a pup.'

The face closed up, the voice bitter. 'I knew I shouldn't trust him.'

'He's fully deserving of your justified anger, Mr Posner, but he must be a convincing liar.'

'Which makes it sound as if you don't know him' was sharply delivered.

Hodgson had made a mistake, but he was quick, he thought, to cover it. 'He's never lied to me, sir, so I have no experience of it.'

'Six guineas a quarter,' Posner demanded.

Hodgson smiled to imply it was too steep. 'On which a man can live in reasonable comfort.'

The look was not returned; if anything, there was bitterness in the tone. 'Comfort for me is in not being had up for bills I cannot meet.'

'Anything else?'

'The first instalment before I depart this table and a signed commitment to guarantee future payments, witnessed before a notary. I take it, as a man with the means to hire a post chaise, such a request will not trouble you?'

Hodgson looked to be thinking long and hard, but in truth he couldn't care less: it wasn't his money. 'Do you have a notary in mind?'

'No.'

The thief-taker kept him hanging by his silence, until he said, 'Then we must ask the man who owns the Tabard. I'm sure he can find us one who will call here and oblige.'

'It must be done at once. I sail back to HMS *Ardent* on the morning tide.'

'Of course.'

Posner must have realised he was being too brusque, at risk of offending the man who would provide a windfall, one which would ensure he need no longer worry about his present precarious position. So he sought to sound emollient and make amends.

'You must forgive me, sir, for sounding so insistent. It is a matter of some importance to me, and if I have spoken as if there's no trust between us, please forgive me.'

'But we only just met, Mr Posner. You would be a singular fellow indeed if you repose complete trust in me on such short acquaintance. Please, be assured, I take no offence.'

'Then I am much relieved.'

'And just so I can establish this is so,' Hodgson said, producing a weighty leather purse, 'I will pay out the first instalment even before we send for a notary public.'

'Which hints at necessity.'

Hodgson just smiled and called a servitor to fetch the owner. Once asked after, it wasn't long before said official arrived, a string bean of a fellow with straggly hair, in black clothing which had seen better days. He carried an inkwell and quills, plus the paper on which to compose the agreement.

It was written down as a stipend to be paid for services rendered, now and in the future, aboard HMS *Ardent*, to be terminated should either side fail to meet their obligations. This would be set out in a separate document, to be provided by Hodgson and agreed to in writing by Posner, with monies to be paid quarterly to the purser's account with the Navy Board.

It had long been dark when the whole was concluded. Having got rid of a now over-solicitous Posner, Hodgson was soon back in the coach and on his way home, thinking once more of how he was going to deal with the other problem he would have to face come morning: Cornelius Gherson and his threats to Emily Barclay.

When it came to milking people, Gherson was determined to learn a lesson, much mulled upon atop the coach journey from Portsmouth; the first being it was dangerous to be too greedy, which could result in potentially fatal consequences. Looking back over the previous four years, Gherson reckoned himself lucky to have survived, shuddering as he recalled being thrown off London Bridge. He had also been clubbed unconscious in Covent Garden, come close to being hanged at Newgate, and all for a dalliance with a hysterical ex-lover for whom he cared little.

Those he intended to prey upon would look for ways to stop him, so who was the most dangerous as against the most vulnerable: Emily Barclay or Edward Druce? He lacked complete conviction that she, a woman of spirit even if he despised her, would not at some point damn him to do his worst and report him to a magistrate, even if it cost her the reputation she'd so carefully cultivated.

He would still put pressure on Emily Barclay, but it would be of a gentler hue, enough to keep her pliant without raising to a level where her malice towards him would spill over into action. There was no need to rush; he had both his quarry where he wanted them, so haste, or really impatience, which he had been guilty of in the past, should be avoided.

Compared to her, he could mark Druce as a milksop, as well as the person who could least afford exposure, given they'd been locked in a larcenous alliance—both having dipped into the well of Ralph Barclay's prize monies. But the risk of exposure applied equally to him, so a way had to be found to mitigate such yet still leave a way to prosperity, and it was these conclusions which had coloured his approach to the prize agent.

'Do calm yourself, Mr Druce, I beg,' he had said in a sympathetic tone. 'And forgive the shouting I indulged in outside your door. I fear your clerk was being obtuse.'

When an ashen Druce failed to reply, he'd added, 'You would not begrudge me a glass of wine, I'm sure, and since you seem somewhat shaken, I will help myself and pour you one too.'

This he'd done, placing both filled glasses on Druce's deck before disrobing to reveal his quality garments. Sat cross-legged and outwardly relaxed, he'd taken to sipping his wine and eyeing his quarry like a cat stalking a bird.

'Do you fear me?'

'What do you want?' had emerged as a gasp before the wine glass was grabbed and emptied.

'I would hardly expect you to agree if I said I'm in search of my due, and I find you well placed to ensure I get it.'

'Your due?'

Gherson had made a point of looking around what was a very finely appointed room, good, highly polished furniture and scenes of naval battles on the silk-covered walls.

'To think, this is only one part of the source of your wealth, now you've inherited the Carruthers business, which in profits dwarfs what you collect from here.'

'I didn't inherit it,' Druce had objected immediately. 'My wife did.'

Gherson had laughed. 'A trifling point when it comes to control of the funds.'

The mood of Druce had changed, his face going from fearful to an odd expression of triumph, so quickly it had surprised Gherson. What came out had emerged at a rush, nothing less than the way Denby had humbugged him with details of how it had been brought about, with him having to report to his wife like a lowly factotum. Then came a final expression of suppressed detestation for the man who'd done the deed, soon followed by self-pity.

'A man I did so much for and he clearly despised me. So, if you've come looking for money . . .'

'You'll be telling me you have none.'

Druce had then burst out laughing, which had been more convincing than any amount of pleading a want of funds. It had done nothing for Gherson's aim that he thought such an opinion warranted, but it did change the nature of what he had come to propose, namely that Druce should finance an enterprise in which they would share the profit. Life growing up in streets full of threat meant a mind of lightning reflexes, and this emerged now.

'Then I have come,' he'd said, 'as an answer to your prayers, Mr Druce. More wine?'

Walter Hodgson was not long back in the White Swan when he was informed of something he should have guessed would arise. Gherson would not confine himself to pressuring Emily Barclay when Edward Druce was such a tempting prospect. Being in for a busy time was all very well, but it still left him with no idea how to stop Gherson, short of putting a ball in his brain.

Chapter Twenty-Two

JOHN PEARCE WAS NOT ENJOYING HIMSELF. FOLLOWING ON FROM HIS raid of the defences of Bastia and the mystery he left behind, he had dropped his prisoners off on Elba, where the British army put the soldiers to digging trenches around the more exposed bays and inlets. Vickery was baffled by this, since the approaching abandonment of Elba was now common knowledge, leading to an exodus of Tuscan refugees heading for Naples or the Papal States. Worricker was moping for the absence of the beautiful Contessa, to the point where his captain, in a fine example of hypocrisy, had to pull him up short.

Back at sea and off that very coast, either because of what Fremantle had achieved or because of much more effective precautions, there were very few opportunities for raiding. The major harbours were out of the question for HMS *Hazard*, while the smaller ports, of which there were dozens, offered very little in the way of worthwhile targets, and he was not in the business of ruining the lives of fishermen and their families. At the same time, he needed to keep a weather eye out for larger warships: with Jervis gone, the French were free to exit Toulon when they pleased; indeed, there was some surprise they'd left Elba alone.

Vickery, sharing Pearce's cabin, was simply more content to be at sea than ashore, free from any duties apart from a daily inspection, the only time he was obliged to be in full uniform. He was vocal in not missing, for one second, being the duty officer when it came to mounting guard, which he'd had to do too often at the fortifications overlooking Porto-ferraio. Both had privately and frequently discussed the court martial initiated by Sir John Jervis, Vickery, if possible, angrier than Pearce at the duplicity of Toby Burns.

'But, in reality,' Pearce opined, 'he's more a tool of Jervis's malice than his own. I can hardly blame him for not cherishing me, given I once as good as threatened to kill him. I fear I would be unable to carry out such a threat, even if he would stand up to fight.'

'Not much chance of that from what I've seen,' Vickery responded, well on the way to emptying a bowl of nuts. 'Beats me how he's kept his blue coat.'

'You're not alone. He seems to have the knack of charming admirals.'

'Not, I've heard, a trait you share.'

'My officers talk too much' was the waspish response.

'Not just your officers, Pearce. They wonder at it, while others praise you to the heavens.'

There was no doubting the source of that remark. Vickery had got to know his Pelicans, and if they talked too much of John Pearce, it was with pride: never mind his rank, he was still one of them. So the soldier knew chapter and verse of his illegal impressment, and how Burns, no doubt on orders from Ralph Barclay, had doubled the sin. The tale he was told took Pearce's story all the way from his remarkable promotion to his taking command of HMS *Hazard*, bearding superiors along the way, and with such regularity, it was surely exaggeration. This led to an abrupt change of subject.

'I was wondering if a court will accept your written testimony when it is sworn before an Italian lawyer? I can only hope I'll still have Dick Farmiloe as my advocate, for they'll be chary of challenging him.'

'I'll do it again in front of a British notary as soon as chance permits.'

Maclehose, now acting third lieutenant, knocked and entered, to then tell Pearce there was a pinnace approaching bearing a commodore's pennant, which meant it was from Nelson, this taking Pearce onto the quarterdeck. The orders were soon in his hands, quite simply telling him to return to Portoferraio. When shared with Vickery, the soldier was far from cheered, given it probably signalled the end of his pleasant cruise.

Elba being no great distance off, they raised the snow-capped mountains at dawn the following day, Pearce going straight aboard *Minerve* even before they'd dropped anchor, to be greeted by the commodore.

He was in the presence of Captains Cockburn and Fremantle, the latter newly returned from Naples.

'I take it Sir Gilbert is with us too?'

'With us and also against us,' growled Cockburn. 'He's worse than that bonehead de Burgh.'

'Sir Gilbert won't budge from here either without orders from London,' Nelson sighed.

'Damned inconvenient,' opined Fremantle, a stocky fellow who looked every inch the fighter he was reputed to be.

'There are a number of things which could be said to be damned inconvenient, Fremantle,' Nelson grumbled, in a way which surprised Pearce. He was addressing an officer of whom he was said to be inordinately fond. Fremantle was not in any way cowed; his reply was openly defiant.

'I think you are aware of my reasons, sir.'

Nelson touched the eye damaged at the siege of Bastia. 'I would require to be blind not to.'

There was clearly something amiss, but given it was not anything Pearce was privy to, he was left to wonder. With *Inconstant* returned, Fremantle was sent north to fetch back *Blanche*, currently on a station which would give early warning of a Toulon fleet getting to sea. She would be required to help the evacuation of both the military and civilians.

'The duty I spoke of before—of how I might deploy *Hazard*—will now definitely have to be undertaken by you. The information we have indicates the members of the old Paoli government, led by Signor Pozzo di Borgo, need to depart the island. The latest information we have received, a very short note, tells us they're heading to Porto Vecchio, which is down the east coast.'

'I know it, sir. Large bay, narrower entrance, and a shoreline backed by high hills. There is deep water and, as far as I know, good holding ground.'

'Is it a place you would feel safe to anchor and, if necessary, wait?'

'Would I be required to?'

Nelson looked at Cockburn, who took up the explanations. 'I fear you might, Pearce. The information we have is these people are not travelling without those who oppose them seeking to prevent their departure. It is my impression they would require to be certain of being taken off before they would approach the actual coast, which means they would need to see a waiting vessel, and one clearly British.'

'Could I then request, sir, I retain the services of those soldiers I already have aboard. Failing their continued assistance, I would require crew members, namely marines, from other vessels on station to make up the numbers. I see this as vital if I'm to operate effectively ashore, as well as at anchor, when I may need to get to sea in a rush.'

The reaction was to be expected: both Cockburn and Fremantle visibly stiffened. No captain liked the idea of lending crew or marines to another vessel at the best of times, and this, with everyone short on their complement, was far from such a situation. Nelson could order it, but nothing in his demeanour suggested he was willing to do so.

'I will speak to General de Burgh again,' Nelson said after a significant pause. 'Captain Fremantle, I take there are no restrictions on your relieving *Blanche?*'

'I cannot imagine what they could be, sir,' was not the expected answer, smacking as it did of the relationship being less warm than had been reported.

'Your new wife finds being aboard congenial, then?' had a sly quality, not in the commodore's normal nature.

'It would be more accurate, sir, to say we both do.' Fremantle stood up, his posture close to defiant. 'Now, since you wish me to brook no delay, I will weigh forthwith.'

'You will oblige me by doing so' was brusque.

With Fremantle gone, Nelson threw a look at Cockburn, one which implied the burden of command, before he turned back to Pearce.

'Captain Cockburn will go through the correspondence we've had from Corte so you understand fully what the requirements are, but on this occasion I must press you not to be distracted from this duty, which Captain Cockburn will include in your written orders. Get di Borgo and whoever is with him safely to Elba with as much speed as you can muster. I have to see both Sir Gilbert Elliot and de Burgh this very morning to try and browbeat them into agreeing to get themselves aboard the transports, which is the other pressing requirement. We simply cannot remain here, and it is becoming more pressing every day that we depart.'

'Tell 'em you'll leave them behind if they don't, sir,' growled the taciturn Cockburn.

'You have no idea,' Nelson sighed as he stood to depart, 'how I wish I had such authority.'

Cockburn followed Nelson out of the cabin, adding an indication that Pearce should wait until he had seen the commodore off HMS *Minerve* with the ceremony such a departure always entailed. After the sound of stamping boots and bosun's whistles, he was soon back to produce a file of correspondence from Pozzo di Borgo, the man who'd run the Corsican government prior to the British exodus.

Pearce went through it slowly: several letters some months old, all formal communications; others more recent, detailing increasing concern; and finally a series of shorter missives displaying a greater sense of urgency. The last did nothing more than name a window in the next week, and the intention to make for Porto Vecchio.

'An odd choice, sir, given there are places on the west coast which must be easier to get to from the interior.'

'Which leads us to suspect they need to fool some of their opponents about the fact of their departure. The natural place for di Borgo to make for is Ajaccio. It's not only closer, I'm told he was born there and still has estates.'

'He doesn't say in this correspondence they're actually in any danger.'

'Read between the lines, Pearce. I would say, on Corsica, it's best to assume such and be relieved it doesn't arise. You know, from your previous duty here, there are any number of factions and clan feuds. If the government is quitting the Corsican capital, it has to be because, now the French are back on the island, albeit not in great numbers, it's unsafe to remain. Di Borgo and those who support him would be a prize to hand over to their new masters. And the Jacobin regicides are far from safe people to be surrendered to.'

Having spent time with the wife of Sir Gilbert Elliot, Pearce needed no telling of the nature of Corsican politics, for she had been a sound source on both the island's history and present state. Originally Genoese, they'd found the place and its fractious inhabitants too hard to control, forever seeking independence. The Genoese tried to suppress this but failed, finally losing in battle to national hero Pasquale Paoli, at which point it had been ceded to France.

Paoli and his forces had subsequently been defeated by the much stronger forces of Louis XVI, with Paoli fleeing to London, where he was lionised as a hero. When present war broke out, following on from the Revolution of '89, he had returned to the island, with a British fleet and several regiments of redcoats, to once more become the leader of the government.

But his situation had never been stable. There were too many factions vying for power, seeking to advance their particular cause, disputes as viciously bloody as they were passionate, leading to him becoming an exile for a second time. A few powerful clan chiefs hankered after a resurgence of Genoese rule, under whom they had prospered. For others it was the French who held out a better prospect, especially following on from a polity promising liberty and equality. What di Borgo represented would be anathema to them both.

'I have always thought, sir,' Pearce said, having read through the file, 'if you scratch someone who espouses a love of Corsica, you'll find a person more concerned for the weight of their purse.'

The response from Cockburn was larded with deep irony. 'Not dissimilar to Scotland then.'

If he didn't necessarily disagree, John Pearce had no intention of being drawn into a discussion on the politics of his place of birth, unsure as he was of Cockburn's opinion. If he had, he would have been obliged to say how different were the Highlands from the Lowlands, and this took no account of the particular desires of the folk on the Western Isles. It would have been a discussion in which his father, Adam, would have happily engaged, but he'd have extended it to the whole of the country north and south of the border, to point out poverty did not discriminate: it was universal and nothing short of a crime when set against those who clung like limpets to their excessive wealth.

'Have you formulated a plan?' Cockburn asked.

Pearce waved part of the correspondence. 'It has been made for me. Those I am required to take aboard are vague about a precise rendezvous time and who it will consist of, for di Borgo names no others. So I must respond to meet his needs as and when they are made plain. Beyond that, I have little room for manoeuvre.'

'From what I've heard of you, Pearce, you'll find a way.'

Unsure of the nature of the remark—was it a compliment or a condemnation—Pearce was left none the wiser when an unsmiling Cockburn let it be known he wanted his cabin back. But a curious fellow wanted an answer to a question, even if he risked a rebuke, given the general attitude of the man he was asking.

'Before I go, sir, I wondered at the relationship between the commodore and Captain Fremantle. I understood it to be warm.'

Cockburn didn't bite his head off; indeed, he was quite pleasant. 'It was, when he was a bachelor. Got himself married in Naples to the eldest Wynne daughter, Betsy. You may have met the rest of the family at the ball. He's sailing with her aboard, and it seems Nelson does not approve. Pretty creature, quite flighty and just eighteen. Can't help wondering how she'll take to witnessing a flogging. I'll send your orders over shortly.'

Pearce very nearly replied he could guess about watching a flogging, especially if this new bride was anything like Emily Barclay. She had recoiled in horror.

The nature of the bay into which he would be obliged to sail occupied Pearce as he returned to his own ship, the deck busy as, once more, stores were loaded—extensive given he would have an unknown quantity of passengers to feed. Nelson was again successful in his request to General de Burgh, so by the time a happy Vickery rejoined his men, Pearce had certain notions of what would be required to ensure his own safety and that of his ship. These he put ahead of those he was supposed to rescue, which led to a request, quickly squashed.

'De Burgh won't release any field guns, Pearce, they're too valuable,' Vickery insisted. 'But there's some old ordnance belonging to those who held the island before that he might give up, they being old.'

'Old is fine, but would de Burgh be prepared to lose them?' Responding to the look, Pearce clarified his meaning. 'If I'm obliged to depart in haste—and I might be—they'll be left behind.'

'They'd be left here when we go, so I can't see it as a concern.'

'Then I require you to ask.'

Vickery pulled a face. 'Have you ever met General de Burgh?' Pearce shook his head. 'Lucky you.'

Recalling the conversation in the cabin of *Minerve*, Pearce offered up, 'Some of our naval officers think him a bonehead.'

'I can't imagine why they seek to flatter him,' Vickery responded with a wry look.

'Will you ask?'

It was a less than enthusiastic soldier who nodded.

The reaction of Mr Low, the gunner, when the two old and somewhat archaic pieces came aboard, along with a quantity of unchipped round shot, was to enquire if the Hazards were set to seek assistance from the likes of Drake and Hawkins. This was less than fair, given the guns were not that ancient, but they ran to no such luxury as flints; it was slow match to the touchhole.

'They'll do for what I have in mind.'

'Wouldn't stand too close when they go off, your honour. If'n they don't take your leg off when they recoil, they're like to burst, given we'll be loading decent powder.'

'If you continue to carp, guess who'll be given the duty?'

'Pity,' Low responded, he being a man who liked to exercise his wit. 'Decent barky would have some real hard bargain defaulters it would do well to be rid of. Be gone in a flash they would, saving hemp and strain on the yardarm.'

'Cartridges, Mr Low, if you please,' Pearce insisted, and on turning to face the quarterdeck observed his officers and midshipmen were amused, not that it lasted in the face of his manufactured glare. 'I hope we're ready to weigh, Mr Worricker.'

'Aye, aye, sir.'

'Then let us get under way.'

Under a grey sky, with occasional bursts of rain sweeping west to east, HMS *Hazard* stood off the large bight which had at its base Porto Vecchio, not a town so much as a large parish. John Pearce could recall only too clearly his last visit and how close the ship's company, of which he was then a part, had so nearly come a complete cropper.

They had been completely humbugged by the French, incurring casualties, the major loss being his then-captain. Reassurances from the Corte letters that it was a safe place to meet did not incline him to take any chances, so the cutter was brought in under oars, Pearce using a telescope to carefully study the narrows which formed the entrance.

To call them such was a misnomer: even at their most constricting point, they were close to three-quarters of a mile wide, so it was only in comparison to the whole, which widened out substantially into a main bay with another smaller bight to the north. What took most of his attention were the significant heights of the southern arm, this being where, if a risk to his position existed, it could easily manifest itself.

Rowing on, he made no attempt to close with the shore, for the bay was, by reputation, malarial and, like much of the Corsican coast, bordered with extensive shallows. There was a dilapidated fortress on a hill behind a port full of fishing boats, flying no flag, which hinted at its being unoccupied, as well as a large church which looked, even at a distance, to have seen better days. Natural curiosity had knots of locals gathering to stare, but with no sign of anything to hint at danger, he left them to wonder, carrying on round the shoreline to check for other threats, relieved to observe there were none. This was passed on when he was back on board.

'My first aim is to ensure that when we enter the bay, we will not be at any risk of being trapped. Mr Vickery, I am going to ask you to take your men ashore and set up a base near the shoreline below Monte Fiori.' A finger on the map identified this as the high ground which had occupied so much of his attention. 'I leave it to you to tell me if the cannon you've brought aboard will serve to render the northern arm of the bay uninhabitable to an enemy.'

'No doubt, using my two old cannon.'

'They have the range.' Pearce added, 'You have fetched aboard round shot, and Mr Low will provide you with grape.'

'Can I suggest a lookout atop the mountain,' Vickery suggested, 'with perhaps the ability to send signals if danger comes from any other quarter. This would require a midshipman and a couple of hands, plus the rigging of a signal mast.'

'Good thinking,' Pearce acknowledged.

'I would like to fully survey the bay, sir,' said the master. 'Reminds me a bit of the Carrick Roads, so we might be looking at a fine fleet anchorage.'

'I do hope, Mr Williams,' his captain replied, his tone serious, 'we will not be here long enough for you to complete the task. Now let us test the waters by taking up a central position, anchoring and seeing if my impressions are correct.'

Chapter Twenty-Three

THE FOLLOWING MORNING SAW CYRIL POSNER ON HA'PENNY PIER, SEE-
ing to the loading of his purchases aboard the fleet tender and on the
receiving end of hidden glares from those doing the portering. To them
he was an old worrywart, known as a man who had not an ounce of trust,
who weighed his tobacco just before it was loaded to ensure he had the
right quantity, thus depriving those who worked at the naval storehouse
a chance to fiddle a few ounces.

On a cold but sunny day, once they'd cleared the mouth of the twin
rivers feeding the anchorage, a well-wrapped-up purser did not, as normal, retire below. Instead, he stayed on deck contemplating several things,
the first how he was going to employ his new source of income. As long
as it continued, it would relieve him of dependency on his too-meagre
purser's profits.

How he wished it could be employed to get him out of the trade,
harbouring as he did a vision of some kind of enterprise ashore and one
more rewarding than that in which he was presently engaged, with perhaps a wife and a hearth and home to call his own. But even with this
quarterly windfall, he was stuck aboard *Ardent*: even if it was ten times
the amount, the money would only flow while Franklin Tolland was
confined aboard the ship.

All he could do was save and hope the war lasted and that Tolland
never got a chance to run or fall victim to the numerous ways in which
a common seaman could expire. In time he might be able to build up a
tidy sum so when peace came and dozens of ships would be laid up in
ordinary, he would be free to do as he wished. So could Tolland, of course,
but where he went then, Posner could neither care about nor control.

He was glad he'd not shown the ex-smuggler the letter he'd received, one which had failed to raise his hopes the original premise would be forthcoming. Carefully composed, it had admitted his principal request was difficult to meet, while stressing he was in a position to do the sender a service, one which could not be settled by correspondence. How long had he sat in his quarters trying to work out what it meant? The sole conclusion to reach: there was only one way to find out.

Now he knew he'd have to work out how to handle Tolland, for if the rogue ever suspected Posner was double-dealing, he would be seriously at risk. Too friendly and it might lead to suspicion, while too standoffish might provoke a reaction. He'd have to find a middle way.

The equanimity with which Druce received Hodgson's report on his dealings with Posner came as something of a surprise. The prize agent always gave the impression that to part with money, which must apply even more to a regular and significant stipend, was like a knife to his heart, Druce convinced, unlike the thief-taker, he had one.

'It seems the matter has come to a satisfactory conclusion, Mr Hodgson,' was the response when he completed his tale. 'Please see my clerk about settling your final account when it is drawn up. This will, of course, be once we have set up the method of payment.'

The thief-taker was a hard man to shock, but he came close now, so much so it showed in his voice. 'I was given to understand you required my services in another matter, and with a degree of urgency.'

The smug look accompanying the response came over as even more curious than the words. 'I take you to mean the reappearance of Gherson?'

'Who else?'

'Are we finished with Posner?' was a question designed to avoid the subject, but it did demand a reply.

'There's no rush there, as payments are quarterly, so you have time to finalise the details. Unless you have anyone you can implicitly trust, I have, as a friend, a very discreet solicitor, who I would suggest you employ.'

'What you have arranged seems simple enough. Does it require the involvement of a lawyer?'

'Your choice, but I would recommend it. I would also suggest it be someone with no previous connection to you or your business in the city or here in the Strand.' Getting no reply, Hodgson added, 'What you are agreeing to provide, while not illegal, is highly questionable.'

'Would security not come from the agreement applying to both parties, myself and your man?' Druce asked.

'A properly worded contract will tie Posner down. You must ensure he can neither risk the matter becoming public nor plead for greater reward. Please recall he is dealing with Franklin Tolland and what harm he can bring down on you, both commercially and personally. He will not be in ignorance of his brother's fate forever, or that of Denby Carruthers. And neither can we be sure circumstances won't change in such a way as to render the agreement void and the danger once more manifest.'

The mention of the name Tolland broke the air of passivity, possibly reminding Druce he was dealing with one of the pair who'd murdered his sister-in-law and would not hesitate to do the same to him if the need arose. The change in his demeanour was reflected in the less certain tone of his next question, carrying as it did a hint of uncertainty.

'With the generous sum you've agreed, it would surely seal his lips?'

'Unless you include human nature, especially in the kind of man who agrees to what has been proposed and who, by the way, originally demanded a much higher sum for his cooperation. What starts off as enough soon comes to be seen as merely fair, while that, in time, is judged to be a bare minimum for the service rendered.'

Hodgson adopted a serious tone and look to drive home the validity of what he was saying.

'This could happen when Posner becomes accustomed to the increase in his income and what it buys. At which point, it is a short journey to considering the sum less than adequate. Having met the man, I would guess he could, at some time in the future, look for an increase. This makes it essential to tie him to a binding agreement from the very beginning, one which will cease as soon as he is at any risk of being unable to keep his side of the bargain.'

'This solicitor. . . . ?'

'A fellow who is discretion itself. If you feel it better, I will deal with him so all which will be required is a letter from you to me giving me permission to act on your behalf.' Sensing acceptance, Hodgson added, because he was dying of curiosity, 'Gherson?'

'He came to see me.'

'So I gather' was imparted with a hint of impatience. 'No doubt he had certain demands.'

'None that he specifically mentioned.'

'I find it hard to believe, Mr Druce, he did not demand anything of you. It flies in the face of his nature.'

'There was nothing specific,' the prize agent replied in a way to make Walter Hodgson wonder why he was being evasive. So, in his response, he made no attempt to avoid sounding exasperated.

'Then oblige me by being open. What did he want generally.'

Druce's hands flopped uselessly, as if he was seeking a word, which eventually led to the admission that Gherson, patently an invention, had talked of past events and how things had been allowed to slip out of control, which was to be regretted, not a word of it believed.

'So, he didn't demand money?'

'He asked for only enough to meet his current needs, which I felt the need to provide.'

Hodgson tried and failed to imagine Gherson asking, so the impression of Druce being disingenuous was reinforced, which begged another question.

'Yet you sought to involve me in your dealings with him?'

'My clerk did so without asking, brought on by alarm at what a man like Gherson might do. As it turned out, such a reaction was unnecessary, though I have commended him for his concern. As it is, I see no need to involve you.'

'You see no need to call upon my services?'

'Once this Posner business is out of the way, no. Now, if you will forgive me, this is one of my days to oversee matters in Devonshire Square, and I'm already late.'

'I'll see myself out,' came the reply, larded with irony, for Druce was dismissing a seriously concerned man.

A Gherson behaving out of character was somehow more troubling than one acting as he had in the past, because this new iteration was unpredictable. The man could do with Edward Druce whatever he liked—they deserved each other—but Hodgson still felt a strong need to protect Emily Barclay. He had decided, before he got back to the White Swan, whatever the slug was up to, Gherson would not be turning an honest penny, so a way had to be found to discover what he was doing, given it was unlikely to be obvious.

He'd also come to the conclusion, with he being so well known to Gherson, his options for finding out were severely limited. A point must come where he would need to challenge the man face-to-face, but beyond that, his ability to investigate what Gherson was up to could prove impossible, while he was sure he needed to know. The man was prone to overconfidence, which in turn led to mistakes, errors which could be exploited to provide the kind of threat to put him beyond being a threat.

'In short, Mrs Barclay, I feel I will require help for the reasons I have just outlined.'

'I have no choice but to ask you to act as you see fit, though, rack my brains as I have, I can see no way to get Gherson out of my concerns.'

'If I know my man, he will provide.'

'And so will I, Mr Hodgson.'

Once the thief-taker had departed, Emily went back to the letter from Davidson telling her the case to deny John Pearce his due—declaring the Spanish silver droits of the Crown—was being pursued by the Lord Chancellor on behalf of the government, while his hopes of raising a storm of support looked to be harder than previously thought. He also laid out the difficulties of bringing a case in the Admiralty court, which would involve at some future date the instruction of a barrister. The cost of this would, he was sure, have to be borne by his client, no help coming from Lord Langholm's prize agents, Ommaney and Druce.

This had Emily lift her head and curse the name, thinking it typical. It had been they who, with the active assistance of his clerk, had cheated her late husband out of large sums of money. The price of the evidence which saw her recompensed in full had been to pay the cleverest lawyer in London to defend Gherson against the charge of murder. Then she went back to the letter.

Feeling as he did, and given the time it would take to come to court, Davidson concluded that this was beyond either his or, he suggested, her decision to make. The choice to proceed or drop the action would have to be made by John Pearce himself, and Davidson would write to him, though this did not preclude her doing likewise.

Calling, as arranged, at Devonshire Square late morning, Cornelius Gherson was admitted to the inner sanctum, which had once been the lair of Denby Carruthers. His first thought was how little it had changed in the intervening time, if you excepted the man behind the desk was now Edward Druce. There was another alteration, and that was in mood, the atmosphere being tranquil in place of the bustle and the bad-tempered behaviour of the previous occupant. He was invited to sit, and coffee was provided before Druce asked, in a calm voice, what his visitor proposed.

'As you describe it to me, the constraints placed upon you in the will make it near impossible for you to take full advantage of the position you hold.'

Druce tried hard not to sound impatient. But he struggled in the face of the fact Gherson was stating the obvious about a situation which had made him fume at the time the will was read and still rendered him apoplectic every time he thought on it.

'Yet you are in control of substantial sums . . .'

'Yes, yes, yes' was a plea to get to the point.

'I'm sure, if you've not seen the possibilities up till now, this has changed. You're very much in the same boat as you were with Captain Barclay,' a slight smile, 'if you'll forgive the pun.'

'There are dangers for me in adopting a like strategy, which I would have thought I'd made obvious.'

'But I would posit you have reached the same conclusion as I. Collectively, we made sure the trades in which we indulged were never divulged to Barclay. The same can be applied to your wife and this annoying executor, as long as you do not appear to be a participant. As before, I will act as proxy to conceal your involvement.'

'I am reluctant to mention certain facts which would make me hesitate,' Druce said. 'In order to be above suspicion, any actions will require to be undertaken and fully so by you.'

'Requiring trust.'

'Naturally.'

'Then you must ask yourself, Mr Druce, why would I cheat you now when I did not as Captain Barclay's clerk.'

'You did not have control, so you could not. That rested with Francis and me.'

'Mr Ommaney would have no part in what I'm proposing, and no monies from your prize agency should be employed. But the accounting of any off balance has to be kept away from the eyes of your brother-in-law's executor, so the funds cannot be part of those to which he and your wife have access.'

'We could employ the same methods,' Druce responded, with just a hint of greed in his demeanour.

There was no need to answer. The 'method,' as Druce termed it, was fairly straightforward and had been used to make money with the Barclay fund. Find an investment which looks promising and buy a few shares, then slowly but surely garner more, in a way to carefully raise their value to a point at which it would be seen as an exciting stock market prospect. This would lift the value way beyond what they were truly worth and signal the time to pull out: the moment when the share price had peaked. The holdings would be sold to eager buyers, while the projector—in this case Gherson and Druce—could walk off with a handsome profit.

'I hid the true nature of the transactions for Captain Barclay, which was not difficult, but it takes time and application. I'm sure, Mr Druce, I can do the same for us.' Noting the word 'us' led to a changed expression, Gherson added, 'And you will find you're being rewarded with profits you have no need to report upon to anyone.'

'While I carry on the business of Mrs Carruthers as normal.'

'Naturally. I can foresee a time when you may be able to rid yourself of such a responsibility.'

The reply was bitter in tone as he waved to encompass the office. 'I won't relinquish this, Gherson, but I may demand I fully control it and so cease to feel like a lackey.'

Gherson was satisfied. He had every intention of ruining the man before him, first for personal satisfaction for the way he'd acted when Gherson had been threatened with the rope. Druce may think the notion he was prepared to let Gherson hang was a secret, but it was not. It was Emily Barclay who had saved him, not Druce, albeit for her own reasons. But second to this was the determination to take posthumous revenge on the man who'd tried so hard to kill him. Denby Carruthers had bequeathed a thriving concern. By the time his one-time clerk was finished—and he wouldn't be until he'd secured his own future—the firm would be nothing but a cauldron of unpayable debt.

'I want him followed. I need to know where he goes and who he sees, which is a job I can't do myself. He knows me too well.'

The three men Hodgson was addressing were all in the same trade as he, all lacking work in the way they had in the past, so eager to oblige a man with whom they were often in competition.

'No tailing him two days on the trot—'

This led to a swift interruption from Chester Tom, so named for his place of birth. 'Trust us not to be stupid, Walter. We know the game as well as you.'

Hodgson held up a hand to acknowledge his blunder. 'He'll be stealing from someone, for he's a man who can't abide not to. So, Brown's Hotel it is in the morning, where I will confront him in the lobby, which you can occupy without attracting attention. This will allow you to mark his face and manner. I leave it to you who dogs him first.'

The eager look Cyril Posner received, not long after he came back aboard HMS *Ardent* and got his purchases put away, had brought him face-to-face with the problem on which he'd been cogitating on the way back to the fleet. Franklin Tolland soon contrived to catch him alone, and it was no look now, but a direct verbal enquiry.

'Odd you should ask' was delivered with a frosty look, 'and I would struggle to explain why I did it, but I penned and posted a second letter to the same address while I was in Harwich. We must wait to see if there's any response.'

'For which I can but thank you' came through gritted teeth.

Posner wagged a precautionary finger. 'But I fear, Tolland, if we again get no response, you will have to find your own way to freedom.'

'Was there any word of my brother in the town?'

'None.'

Sat at his mess table later, he was once again relating the tale of how his and Jaleel's ship had been stolen from under their nose, he unaware that having heard it a hundred times, his listeners were scarcely paying attention. But that altered when he turned to the way they'd ended up where they were now. Franklin Tolland wasn't alone in wanting to roundly curse the name and villainy of John Pearce.

Chapter Twenty-Four

HMS *Hazard* entered the narrows of Porto Vecchio bay with her guns run out, everyone aboard silent and alert. John Pearce was ready to react swiftly to any threat and come about, prior to a hurried exit, even if the option did not exist to both remain out at sea and properly fulfil his mission. It would lead to complications when it came to dealing with those he was supposed to rescue, people who may have to be lifted off with some alacrity. Whatever it comprised in terms of bodies, they would not be sailors, while he could not be sure, for several reasons, the communications necessary for a smooth transfer from shore to ship would exist.

Barring a full easterly gale, he would enjoy calm water inside the bay, this not guaranteed offshore, which might make difficult getting inexperienced civilians aboard from boats. Also, at this time of year, there was always the possibility of weather so foul he would be forced to seek sea room, always a concern, the need to do so driven home by the fate of HMS *Courageux*.

The silence persisted until they were fully through and he was reasonably sure there was nothing about which he need worry. Pearce anchored central to the shoreline, with the canvas necessary to quickly get under way left loose, requiring only to be sheeted home. As a final precaution before nightfall, he gave the order to rig boarding nets and lanterns to avoid any surprises.

The following morning, the weather crisp and cold and with nothing in sight to trouble *Hazard*, Pearce had a long swim in the sea. Refreshed and breakfasted, he sent Midshipman Livingston ashore with a party and the equipment necessary to rig a signal mast on Mont Fiori. He was to carry the limited number of flags he would need for the signals he would be required to employ, which was in essence a red one to warn of danger. He had to keep watch on the seaward approaches for, at the first sign of a sail in the offing, *Hazard* would need to be cleared for action in case it proved to be an enemy.

'You'll need to take supplies of food, small beer, and kindling, Mr Livingston,' Pearce had said when he gave him his orders. 'Plus a small container of grog for the men who will be left with you. There you must ensure the distribution is per the daily ration and not a drop more. Is that clear?'

'Aye-aye, sir.'

'I will relieve you in two days if the folk we are here for have not shown up.'

If the Mite was concerned about being on such a lonely duty, in command for the first time, with no superior to appeal to, he hid it well. This pleased his captain, the lad being one for whom Pearce had always had a soft spot. He would send Macklin up later to ensure there were no problems, but with clear instructions, if all was as it should be, he should treat Livingston as having authority.

Getting Vickery ashore was a more complex operation, hauling his old cannon plus their carriages out of the hold and transferring them to boats, which involved much rigging of blocks and pulleys, many yards of rope, and the working of the capstan in lowering them into boats. Vickery had also taken on board quantities of sand, cement, and ringbolts, which would be used to create fixed and sunken points by which the weapons could be restrained on recoil. The blocks and tackle needed to run them up to a firing position also required fixed points.

He needed bodies over and above his soldiers to fill the sandbags needed to raise the kind of revetting behind which both the cannon and the gunners could be afforded some protection. Boats plied to and fro with all the things the soldiers needed, but Pearce declined to go ashore until he could see the mast going up atop Mont Fiori, pleased when Livingston raised the blue pennant to indicate no threats were visible.

Arriving at the base of the massif after noon, he found Vickery stripped to the waist and toiling alongside his men, well on the way to completing the tasks he had set himself, which included rigging tents in which he and his men could shelter plus the digging of a latrine. Luckily, he'd found a spring to provide fresh water.

'I will test the guns tomorrow, once the cement in the pits has set. Let's hope it holds.'

'At which point I can cease to worry,' Pearce acknowledged.

The sailors who'd come ashore with their captain were set to rigging the blocks, pulleys, and ropes which would provide a way for the cannon to be run up to the newly constructed sandbagged embrasures. The tackle included the stout restraining cables which would hold the guns once fired.

Of the many points discussed on the way, it had been a certainty the old cannon had to be tested, if for no other reason than to ensure the barrels would not burst. Then the range had to be worked on for the twin tasks they would be required to perform. One was the ability to do serious damage to any vessel entering the narrows; second, and more importantly, to ensure it could not be rendered too dangerous to exit if anyone occupied the opposite bank.

The potential for this had been the main topic of casual speculation, and the more it was aired, the less sanguine became the notion of a simple and risk-free evacuation. The letters from Corte, which Pearce had brought along, shared with Vickery and his own officers, did little to provide comfort. The more they were studied, the more it seemed di Borgo wasn't departing, he was fleeing; this a firm opinion of the marine Moberly.

It was raised again when Vickery stood down his men so they could rig their tripods, light their fires, and begin to cook their food, which they were happy to share with Pearce's boat crew. The soldier had brought fresh supplies of his own from Elba, one of his redcoats acting as his batman, so he invited Pearce to his tent and, for a sailor, a late dinner. In this the fellow proved to be a daft hand with a beef stew and winter vegetables, while ample Elban wine had been fetched along to wash it down.

'Am I at liberty to make a suggestion?' Pearce asked when both had eaten.

'It's in my instructions, you're free to issue me orders,' Vickery replied, smiling to ensure his words were not misinterpreted.

'Only aboard ship. But once you have fired off the cannon, I think it advisable to send a patrol—your men plus Moberly's marines—to the main town to see the lie of the land.'

Porto Vecchio had a long line of buildings fronting its part of the bay, but every inlet in the large bay—and Pearce had noted dozens—had small fishing boats drawn up on the nearest beach. There were also usually one or two rickety dwellings to house the men and their families.

'They need to see redcoats and to also know we pose no threat. The fisherfolk didn't go out this morning, did they?'

'Because of our presence,' Vickery responded, to which Pearce nodded.

'Given we have no idea how long we will be here, it may be they will fear to do so until we're gone. Would it not be better to reassure them it is safe?' Pearce grinned and followed it with a sudden thought. 'I wonder what they'll make of cannon going off?'

'The noise might give them a fright,' Vickery replied, 'which will be nothing to how my men and I will feel when we light the touchholes.'

'Till morning,' said Pearce, standing up. 'After my swim.'

Vickery shuddered for, like *Hazard*'s crew, he rated throwing yourself into the sea to be madness. 'Thank God we found that spring and can wash like proper humans.'

Conscious of the words Vickery had used the previous night, Pearce fetched ashore a spool of slow match to fire the cannon, which would allow both to stand well back when they went off. With him came the powder required, as well as both grape and round shot, the former to be discharged first as putting less strain on the barrels. Fairly sure the recoil would be halted by what had been rigged, Pearce and Vickery would set the slow match alight, though stood well away from the wheeled carriages.

'I almost feel,' Vickery joked, 'we should have a salute to perform, given the nobility of our ordnance.'

'Make it mine,' Pearce retorted. 'Two cannon is just about what the navy would allot me as a mark of respect.'

'Ready?'

When Pearce nodded, the soldier put a torch to the slow match, taking an extra step back as it began to fizz, which, given it was aptly named, took over a minute to reach the guns. Even having been measured as equal, they did not go off together, there being a split second between the discharge. Out of the muzzles, as well as hundreds of small metal balls, came a huge cloud of black smoke which, given the wind was in the northeast, blew back over the pair, obscuring any chance of seeing where the grape had struck.

The cannon shot backwards on the recoil, which had both officers jump sideways, glad to observe this was unnecessary when the guns were brought up on their cemented ring bolts and the sailor-rigged blocks, while the cannon seemed to have survived the experience. Next it was round shot to be fired, with all the worming, swabbing, and ramming home of powder and wads this entailed, more slow match jammed into the touchholes.

'I would suggest,' Vickery said, 'we stay further back this time. If they're going to burst it will be now, and splinters of metal could go anywhere.'

'I'm going to get out of the smoke,' Pearce replied. 'I want to see where the balls land.'

'If they fall short, you must keelhaul your gunner. He measured out the charges.'

'Better still, if that happens, I'll put him to firing a salvo and on shorter slow match.'

'I'm surprised you didn't fetch him along.'

'You wouldn't be if you'd heard what he said about your cannon. Ready?'

They were well clear of the discharge, both able to see the balls as they arced across the narrows to land on the southern headland, throwing up great founts of earth on the forward part of the hill.

'Perfect,' Vickery said. 'I reckon we owe Mr Low a tot of rum.'

Porto Vecchio was the obvious place to first set foot ashore, while common sense said it had to be accomplished with proper precautions, given the unknown nature and affiliations of the inhabitants. So Vickery stood off amongst the bobbing fishing boats, the red coats of his men as obvious as the glistening bayonets on the end of their muskets. As the cutter approached the strand, Pearce stood up so he could be clearly seen, his sword remaining in its scabbard. Michael O'Hagan, normally his coxswain, was at his back, two pistols loaded and cocked.

Home to several hundred people by the look of it, there was no sign of any of them on a foreshore devoid of humanity, only the boats they used to fish, drawn up out of the water. Able to step out onto the sand once his cutter beached, Pearce took a few steps, allowing Moberly and his half dozen marines, bearing muskets but without bayonets, to follow and line up alongside. Moberly's sword, like his captain's, remained sheathed but, needless to say, Michael was still at his back, using Pearce's body to hide the fact he was armed.

Seeking to overcome a slight feeling of disquiet, Pearce said, 'Well, I didn't expect bunting or a band, but this is unwelcoming in the extreme.'

He turned and signalled to Vickery, who brought the section he'd fetched along ashore, where both stood to examine what lay before them. It consisted of a number of decent-sized, rough-built, local stone buildings interspersed with wooden constructs and a couple of boatyards. The whole frontage was cut by narrow alleys leading into a town backed by a steep, densely forested hill, the church spire prominent.

'I should have a care to go down those alleys,' Pearce said, 'without I know I could get out again.'

'We have to assume,' Vickery responded, 'as Corsicans, they will be armed, though possibly not with muskets.'

'I see no choice, Mr Vickery. If they will not come to us, we must go to them. I wonder what the local argot is for "We come in peace." Oblige me by waiting here. Mr Moberly, with me.'

He stepped forward onto what was hard-packed earth, right before him a stone archway and one of those aforesaid alleys, dark within where limited light penetrated, the sound of boots echoing off the walls. Looking up the sides of the buildings, the upper storeys of which seemed to overhang his head, Pearce could just see slatted shutters concealing openings, but again no sign of any locals.

The stronger light at the end told him, before he came to it, the alley opened out into what would be called a public square, but again there was no one to occupy it. It too was surrounded by rough stone and shuttered buildings, with a low wall enclosing a space by the church, which looked to be a cemetery, as well as a fairly central fountain.

'Would that be a tavern, sir?' Moberly asked, directing Pearce's gaze to a sloping roof of leaves and grasses, with a couple of tables and chairs underneath.

'Well spotted. Let's you and I see if they have any refreshments for a thirsty traveller.'

Moberly did not respond to the jocular tone, being too tense. 'My men, sir?'

Pearce had a good look round before he replied. 'They can rest on yonder wall, and please be assured, if we find anything, it will be sent out to them. They are to look relaxed but be ready to get behind the wall and defend it till Mr Vickery can bring up his men to get us out.'

It went without saying, if trouble did manifest itself, their chances of getting out were slim, for there were several ways to access the square and only one route back to the beach. Since nothing was said, Pearce assumed Moberly accepted the risk, just as he did, and he knew from experience that if it came to a desperate fight, the marine was a good man to have at his side.

'You still with me, Michael?' Pearce asked without turning round as Moberly issued orders to his men.

'Sure, I'd not be trusting you to be out alone, would I.' The 'sir' was fractionally late for the marine officer, who frowned, though if he didn't know how close they were by now, he was the only one aboard ship.

'Pistols ready?'

'They are.'

Nodding and stepping out, seeking to look confident, Pearce made for the cover of the lean-to roof. Both he and Moberly took one of the chairs leaning on the wall, sitting down by a table with the air of everyday customers, hats removed and laid aside, legs crossed and out to show they were relaxed.

'Doors open, your honour,' Michael said softly. 'I have a mind to see inside.'

'Slip me one of the pistols, then do so.'

The butt put in his hand was hot from Michael's but kept as much as possible out of sight, with the Irishman, who'd jammed the second into his belt as his back was turned, disappearing into the dark interior but not for long. He was soon back out, holding a stone flagon with a cork jammed in the top.

'I'm glad to see you resisted temptation' was the wry comment. 'Any idea what it is?'

Michael's teeth were employed to remove the cork, his nose to sniff the contents, followed by, 'Strong spirit of some kind.'

'Did you find anything to drink it out of?'

Michael disappeared again to re-emerge with a couple of stone cups, which, on the command to pour, he obliged. The contents when consumed had both men pull faces, to then gasp slightly as it slipped down their throats.

'Do you get the feeling, Mr Moberly, we are being watched?'

'I have it at this very moment, sir.'

Pearce pulled himself upright, using a leg to hide the pistol, and pulled out his purse from a coat pocket. Opening it, he slowly emptied a few coins onto the table, the sound as they struck each other seeming to set up and echo, then indicated to O'Hagan to provide a refill.

'Find something which can be used to give our marines a wet, and yourself of course Michael, but go easy.'

'And you do not believe there is a God.'

'This is one occasion when I hope you're right and I am wrong.'

Pearce raised his cup to Moberly. 'A toast, sir, to a successful mission.'

Cups clinked, they both drank, to then watch Michael walk round each of the marines, proffering a frequently filled cup from which they could drink, they too reacting like their officers—a slight gasp when the rough spirit hit their throats.

'Now let us see if that brings out the mice.'

The sound was faint—whoever was making it moving with care—which had Pearce tighten his grip on the pistol, prepared to whip it up and shoot. The sound had been picked up by Moberly's men, who'd visibly stiffened, as had the hold they had on their muskets. The sound was repeated several times until a goat revealed itself, slowly entering the square to stop and look at the humans it contained as if they were intruders.

Pearce burst out laughing, remarking to Moberly that if Vickery saw it, he'd shoot the creature and have it for his dinner, a jest to raise no more than a wan smile on the marine's face. But it disappeared as he saw his men pull themselves to attention and move their muskets to a ready-to-fire position, which they held as the space slowly began to fill with men, all armed and not one of them looking friendly.

'Stand your men easy, Mr Moberly, while I seek to exercise my skills at diplomacy.' He looked for Michael, but there was no sign; the only conclusion he could come to was the Irishman had gotten behind the low stone wall. 'I'm leaving the pistol I have on the chair.'

'Sir,' Moberly replied without taking his eyes off the group of locals, 'they don't look welcoming, quite the opposite. I would say they are dangerous.'

'In which case, once you've identified the leader of this lot, make sure he doesn't outlive me.'

Chapter Twenty-Five

John Pearce managed a remarkable number of feelings and impressions in the thirty or so paces he took to get from the table to the front of what was a sizeable cluster of unsmiling men with sun-darkened skin, a high number of straggly moustaches, and the odd beard. Their hair was black or greying under a variety of headgear, nothing of a quality in their coats, breeches, and footwear to single out an individual as important.

He was trying to work out who, if anyone, was the leader, the person to whom he must talk. In dress and physical attributes, they were very like the people he'd seen in the streets of Bastia, dressed in breeches and animal-skin boots, with dun-coloured shirts and a variety of outerwear and headgear. Several were armed with slung muskets, others carrying every possible kind of weapon from clubs to knives, but none of them overtly threatening.

Their silent stares and collective unity made identifying the man to talk to problematic, but that was only one problem. He had to decide what language to use to whomever he addressed, which boiled down to English or French. He knew little Italian apart from a few words and expressions learned from the Contessa, and no Corsican, if indeed such an all-island language existed. More likely it would be a local argot particular to the area around Porto Vecchio. The chance of anyone speaking English was remote, while using French on an island where they were seen as invaders to a large proportion of the population carried its own risks.

The only thing he could truly control was his features, and even this created uncertainties. A broad and friendly smile might be seen as false, too rigid an expression of superiority as hauteur. So, in the end, he adopted a look of curiosity, which he wondered might be interpreted as 'What the hell are you doing here?' This forced him to suppress a chuckle: it was no doubt what they would want to ask him.

'Good morning' came out loud enough to echo slightly off the walls, so the tone had to be softened before he added his name, ship, and rank, immediately translated into French when faced with a sea of incomprehension. This, at least, raised a flicker of interest on one or two faces, but more telling was the way some of the men before him looked to a stocky, central individual. He was one of those with a musket and, now he was close enough to see, a pistol in his belt as well as the protruding haft of a large knife.

His eyes shifted, a quick glance over Pearce's shoulder, which had him wonder what Moberly and his marines were doing—hopefully nothing threatening, given his precarious situation. But when they returned to examining this blue-coated officer, it was head to toe, finally coming to rest on the hand holding the decorated hilt of the sword. This he pointed to with a gesture that it should be produced, which brought it slowly out of its scabbard, to be handed over.

'As long as you don't run me through,' Pearce said, finally smiling; this not returned.

Able to take in the features as the fellow examined the blade, Pearce had the impression that if he was not high born, neither was he a peasant, for he had a self-assurance which spoke of authority. Also, the features had a cast about them which, while far from refined, appeared well fed. The eyes were black, but this was commonplace, the cheeks full and not marred with either scars or any sign of smallpox, while the lips were full. He was holding Pearce's dress sword flat, running his fingers over the lettering, which Emily had asked to be added when she'd bought it for him as a present.

'*Questo sei tu?*'

It took no genius to realise the nature of the question, so Pearce nodded to say it was indeed him, at which point the man put a finger to his chest and stated, 'Battisti.'

'*Ammaliata.*'

It was one of the words Pearce had learned from the Contessa, the Italian for 'charmed.' She'd advised him it was a catch-all to use upon being introduced to a stranger, so it was pronounced with confidence. That it produced a burst of laughter from this group of villainous Corsicans, added to many pointing fingers, confused him, while Battisti raised a quizzical eyebrow and said, quite firmly, '*Ammaliato!*'

After a few seconds, Pearce's knowledge of French helped him identify his mistake: he'd used the feminine case instead of the masculine, and all he could do was hold out his hands in a futile gesture to denote he was confused. Battisti's shoulders began to shake in evident amusement before he uttered a stream of incomprehensible words which had the whole group laughing. The sword was returned, this followed by a gesture to lead him back to the taverna.

Pearce turned to see Moberly sitting half forward, his eyes fixed on Battisti, and he knew, even if he couldn't see it, the pistol was cocked and ready for use. Likewise, the marines, weapons at the ready, looked up for a fight, though they would have struggled to get their bayonets fixed before these Corsicans got amongst them. And naturally the muskets, fresh from the boat, were not loaded.

'Stand your men down, Mr Moberly,' he called as he made his way back to the table. 'They might see me as a fool, but I don't think they see me as a threat.'

Unbeknownst to him, though he could hear the movement of many feet, only Battisti and a couple of men were following, the rest either melting away or taking up positions to lounge against the walls of the buildings. What he could see was Michael O'Hagan reappearing, still holding the stone flagon, a sharp Pearce eye ensuring the cork was in the top: his Irish friend drunk was the last thing he needed.

Moberly got to his feet as the smaller group approached, so there followed introductions, which were just as useless as what had gone before. Michael joined them to put the flask on the table, at which point, after a sharp word, one of Battisti's companions slipped through the tavern door to reappear with more cups. Their leader indicated to the Irishman they should be filled, including those of the two officers. Michael did not miss out on his own, even if he was not invited, as were all the others, to sit down on more fetched chairs.

'*Saluti*,' Battisti said, raising his cup, this responded to by Pearce's 'Good health,' and the cups were drained, the rough throat-burning spirit appearing to have no effect on the Corsicans.

'Michael,' Pearce said, his eyes still on Battisti, 'a word to Mr Vickery, if you please, to say I reckon it safe for him to come and join us, but I'd leave his men on the beach for now. Mr Moberly, I think it wise to tell your men to rest easy.'

Then he turned back to Battisti, knowing he was in for a trying time. How to explain why he was here and who was coming, what was intended—with a strong possibility he might be dealing with people who were no lovers of Paoli or di Borgo—so they might be more interested in hindering rather than helping the party coming from Corte?

The coins Pearce had emptied out were still on the table and, after a glance at Pearce, Battisti picked up a couple of Dutch florins, testing them with his teeth before slipping them into a waistcoat pocket with a wicked smile. He then added a gesture to indicate it was the price of the flagon. Pearce, as a precaution, swept up the rest and put them in his pocket.

As soon as Vickery joined, following more introductions and another toast, Pearce mentioned di Borgo in a way which invited acknowledgement, this forthcoming as Battisti nodded to agree he knew the name, but with no sign of an opinion. Lacking a map, Pearce began to draw on the table, using a finger dipped in the rough spirit, to say 'Corte' and show it in the middle of the board, which got another nod. Also 'government,' which, if it was a wild guess Battisti would understand, seemed enough of a good one.

He next, very roughly, drew a circle on the table edge to represent the bay of Porto Vecchio, with an extravagant wave towards the sea and his ship. He then used his walking fingers to denote people travelling from the interior, all the while looking to Battisti to ensure he was making some kind of sense. Finally, he repeated 'di Borgo' and 'government,' holding up his fingers to denote numbers, adding a gesture with spread hands and a look of doubt to imply it was unknown.

'*Quando?*'

Guessing from the facial expression that went with the word, which he took to mean 'when,' all Pearce could do was shrug and use his fingers once more to tick off imagined days, accompanied by more signs of ignorance. Battisti was silent for a while, several times looking at the drawings drying on the table, while Pearce wondered how to explain the risk hinted at—that there might be people trying to stop them from leaving the island—which took time and both his hands.

He named di Borgo again by tapping his right while, with a gap between them and moving slowly, he tapped his left and said '*Francais*' with some force. He then jammed his fists together a couple of times, thumb on thumb. It was clear Battisti hadn't got it, which meant more hand miming till the point dawned; this when the Corsican forcefully clapped his knuckles together, adding a fierce-looking expression.

A relieved Pearce nodded vigorously, then touched his eye before using a finger to make a large circle which indicated the surrounding hills. He then went back to wetting the table, seeking to convey a need— one he had just seen as a good idea—for a watch to be kept outside the town for the approach of di Borgo.

'I've asked him to help us by keeping an eye out for them before they get to the beach,' he said to Vickery and Moberly, having realised they might be wondering what he was about. 'Which will save us no end of trouble.'

'It will if you trust him, sir,' Moberly replied, his doubts obvious.

'Not sure we have much choice. Just like putting a watch up on Mont Fiori, I believe it best to do so here to avoid surprises, like the fact of the possible pursuit being close behind. It's either that or we have to do it ourselves, which means a daily stint on duty in the hills and another way to send signals.'

'Is the sight of the ship in the bay, flying a union flag, not enough?'

'I wish I could be sure it would be.'

'The road from Corte, sir,' Vickery asked, 'do we know where it is and where a watch could be kept?'

Pearce had to suppress a groan, which might not sit well with Battisti, who had watched this exchange with deep interest. 'Sadly, it's up to me to find out.'

So it was back to the tabletop, drawing a fresh route from Corte to Porto Vecchio, the original having dried up, with first a finger pointing at the line of damp, then at Pearce's own eye, finally a stab at his chest to indicate he wanted to be shown where the road from Corte came into the town. Battisti made a gesture of agreement then stood to indicate they should follow him. Moberly, in calling for his men to come as well, got an expressive shrug of indifference from the Corsican, who headed out of the square, the men from HMS *Hazard* following in his wake.

This very quickly had them walking up a steep hill which, even on a day when the weather was clement and now not much above warm, was tiring work. Worse, for those who'd been drinking the rough spirit, it induced a serious thirst, this alleviated by the marines, who'd filled their water flasks at the well. It was no road, more a rutted and rough cart track, one in which many a stone had embedded itself, a surface which would turn to mud when it was subjected to heavy rain. Finally, they reached an elevation where they could see it wend its way up into even higher hills, a dusty track often obscured by trees and the dense maquis.

Pearce pronounced himself satisfied, stamped a foot on the ground, and said, 'They won't be coming by coach on this.'

'Donkeys or on foot more like,' suggested Vickery. 'I take it you're still worried they might have problems?'

It was Moberly who replied, addressing Pearce. 'That's my reading, sir.'

'Perhaps a pessimistic one.'

'Would you advise any other?'

'No. But the question is, if there is a pursuit, what can we do about it? We have limited means and no idea of the numbers we would face in seeking to protect those we're expecting.'

'But you have in mind, I suspect,' Vickery said, 'to ask your Corsican to help.'

Pearce nodded. 'I'll wager he and his men would know what's going on in their bailiwick long before anyone comes in sight of this place.'

'It goes back to my question, sir. Do you trust him?'

Pearce looked first at Moberly, then to where Battisti and his two companions were stood, a short distance ahead, to wonder what they were talking about. For him, his thinking was sound, the paramount concern being for the safety of the ship. If Nelson had sent a frigate, it would have had a crew sufficient in numbers for the task: he did not, especially with Vickery's men committed to manning the cannon covering the narrows.

'It would solve more than one problem if we could,' he said finally. 'Battisti, judging by the men in the square, has the numbers we lack. So regardless of what dangers there are, he can warn us of any attempt to stop di Borgo. He might even be able to get them to the shore and signal to *Hazard* to come and pick them up, while discouraging anyone seeking to stop them. It simplifies the whole business of getting them aboard.'

'They're a rough-looking crew,' Vickery pointed out, 'so he probably has the means to deal with it.'

'Precisely. The notion of our setting up a post to do the same, Mr Moberly, would fall mainly to your marines. I have serious reservations about it being as effective, not least because of the men needed to man it and no knowledge of what they might face. I would be obliged to denude *Hazard* of a goodly proportion of the crew to ensure you weren't overrun, but also to abandon you all if the sight of an armed enemy vessel forced me out of the bay. No, let us see if we can bargain and get the locals to do what is needed, which will only require an occasional visit to ensure they are meeting their end of the bargain.'

'I look forward to watching you explaining it to him,' Vickery added with a grin.

'It doesn't occur to you he's got there already? Whatever else he is, I would say Signor Battisti is no fool and is working out how much money he can extract from us.'

Which he found out to be true when, back in the Porto Vecchio taverna, having sent away everyone but Michael O'Hagan and his boat crew, Pearce got down to the task of securing Battisti's aid. This took place over a meal of roasted wild boar, fresh vegetables, and copious amounts of the local spirit, brought out from one of the houses off the square by a couple of women. Both made sure they didn't catch a strange male eye before scurrying back from whence they came, while a couple of Battisti's men were sent to the beach with food for the boat crew.

When it came to communication by gestures, the Corsican could match and even outdo John Pearce, so the deal was struck over a couple of hours, with much arm waving, finger pointing, wet map drawing, and endless facial expressions, to then be sealed with a final drink. This was the last of many, following on from an agreed sum in payment, to be presented aboard ship the next day. For a fee in guineas, Battisti would keep an armed watch from the hilltop from which they'd just returned. If the party were in danger, they would try to discourage the pursuit and see them safely to the beach.

Like every vessel in the Royal Navy, HMS *Hazard* carried a certain amount of British guineas, the metal being a currency which, by its weight and quality, had a realisable value anywhere in the world. This allowed a captain to purchase fresh victuals or cordage and canvas, so Pearce could satisfy the man's desire to be rewarded for the services of him and his men.

It was moot if the document he would be asked to append his mark to the next day would pass muster with the Navy Board, but this was a problem to be taken care of in the future. Really it was one for Nelson to account for, he being the man who'd sent *Hazard* on the mission, essentially with instructions to act as the needs of the moment dictated.

Vickery saw what had been agreed as wise, given their numbers, but it was obvious, even if he kept it to himself in terms of verbal reservations, Moberly was far from sure. It was necessary for Pearce, once back on board, to point out he bore the responsibility while outlining, once more, the reasons the same could not be provided by the ship's company. Then, having consumed too much of whatever the locals brewed and put in their stone flagons, Pearce retired to his cot to sleep it off.

It was telling, when he had a swim in the morning, that he was surrounded by a number of small boats fishing in the bay. According to Macklin, officer of the morning watch, the larger vessels which Pearce had seen drawn up on the Porto Vecchio beach the previous day had headed out into deeper water before sunrise. Both were seen as a positive: the locals no longer feared their presence.

Battisti arrived halfway through the forenoon watch, to be welcomed aboard and taken to Pearce's cabin, where on the desk lay twenty guineas, the agreed sum. The document outlining what he was being paid to do, already drawn up, was presented to a fellow who had no idea what it said, which meant going through the whole rigmarole of explanation for a second time.

Eventually a quill was presented to Battisti, with a finger pointing to where he should put his mark, which turned out to be a quite elaborate device, this before Pearce appended his own signature. Determined to make it look official, he affixed a ribbon by pressing his naval seal onto the paper. Then and only then, knowing he was with a serious imbiber, did Pearce ask Derwent to fetch a bottle of wine so the agreement could be finalised with a toast.

Pearce was ashore early in the first dog watch, he and Michael heading up the cart track to check on the arrangements, pleased to find at the point they'd stopped the day before a quartet of Battisti's men already in position, armed with muskets. Grunting, one led them into the trees where they'd set up a rough encampment, the already-lit fire evidence they were there for the night.

'What do you think, Michael?' Pearce asked on the way back to Porto Vecchio, the object having been explained on the way up.

'Sure, John-boy, it looks sound, but a word or two exchanged would not go amiss. Hard to feel all is right when you can't understand them and they you, not knowing a word of anything outside their heathen tongue.' There was a pause before he added, 'Will you be minding if I have a minute or two in the church?'

'If you find a priest, don't confess, Michael, or we'll be here half the night.'

Pearce took a seat on the wall outside to wait, sure Michael would want to see the inside of the confessional, only to be slightly surprised by the speed with which he reappeared, even more so by the look on his face, a hint of hurt and anger, which prompted an enquiry as to the presence of the expected divine.

'Sure, I've never had it happen before, John-boy, to be knocked back when looking to confess. The sod refused. Shook his head when I pointed to the confessional and shooed me away in his heathen tongue.'

'Maybe he didn't understand you.'

It was still light enough to see the look this got, and the words were bitter. 'The man has to be an unbeliever to refuse. Never have I been turned away when asking for absolution.'

There was not a lot Pearce could say, when he thought the whole thing questionable.

Chapter Twenty-Six

THE NEXT TWO DAYS WERE SPENT ON MOSTLY NORMAL TASKS: REPACK-ing the holds to make better the trim of the ship, hauling out and airing canvas, blacking cannon, and chipping shot, with a run ashore for Wor-ricker and Macklin to spend time at the post Battisti had set up, able to reassure Pearce all was as it should be. Vickery and his bullocks were ashore improving their position, creating, with the addition of earth-works, a more impressive bastion, also cutting and lining the exterior with foliage to disguise its presence. Dour Midshipman Tennant was sent to replace Livingston at the signal post atop Mont Fiori.

For the wardroom, great cabin, and gunroom, being so close to Porto Vecchio provided a greater variety in their diet than normal, especially in the articles of fish, chicken, and pork. John Pearce, with little to occupy him, could enjoy regular dips in the sea then get down to the task of get-ting his logs in proper order. He also spent time on deck, merely taking the air, where he could not help but look to what he could see of the high mountains of the interior and wonder where the bodies he was expecting had got to.

At night, with HMS *Hazard* well illuminated, the weather being reasonable and only an anchor watch set, many of the crew could gather on the deck to smoke their pipes, sing songs, dance the odd hornpipe to a scraping fiddle, and swap tall tales. Their superiors, with very few duties to perform, enjoyed a relaxed time in which things left undone by being fully occupied were completed, not the least repairs to things like stockings and breeches.

Mr Williams was out every daylight hour in the jolly boat with his two master's mates, casting lead weights greased with sand, taking soundings for an up-to-date chart. In the evenings, using the rough sketches he'd made afloat, he'd turn them into accurate drawings of the contours of the hills surrounding the bay. In time, these would be submitted to the Admiralty so new charts showing physical characteristics—if any differences were identified—could be produced for the future.

When the ship settled down for the night, Pearce could allow himself some longer periods of reading—there was rarely time normally—settled on the casement cushions with a book in his lap, in this case Thomas Paine's *Age of Reason*, which had lain in his sea chest too long. Here was a fellow traveller and kindred spirit of his own father, a man who'd been a friend to Adam senior and a fellow victim of the duplicitous government. He did wonder if the mere fact of owning such a radical treatise was grounds for a court martial, for a serving naval officer.

The arrangement for the next day, suggested by Vickery, was that a group of the officers, along with some tars to act as beaters, should go hunting. He was sure that not far off there would be woods full of game, and for a moment Pearce's thoughts turned to the prospect, a speculation that evaporated when Macklin, the officer keeping watch, knocked and entered.

'There's a man off our quarter in some sort of wherry, and he's called out several times.'

'Odd hour to be trying to sell us something?'

'He's not, sir, he's asking for you, and he's doing it, quiet like, in English.'

Tom Paine was quickly put aside as Pearce swung onto his feet, following Macklin to the quarterdeck to peer out to larboard where, just on the edge of the glim thrown by the lantern lights, he could see the faint shape of said boat.

'Was it by name?' he asked.

'No,' Macklin said softly, 'just rank.'

The voice that floated to Pearce's ear confirmed what he was being told, but it was far from a shout. It came as a call so quiet it barely carried, which could surely be no threat, and it asked to talk to the captain.

'Ahoy there,' Pearce called, his voice level matching the one he just heard, having noted the fellow's spoken English seemed to come with a pronounced accent. 'I am the captain. Come where I can see you.'

'Who speaks?'

'The man you want to see.'

The shape took on greater definition, but not by much, so Pearce stepped closer to one of the hanging lanterns where he would be clearly visible.

'What do you want?'

'To talk only.'

The request to Macklin for a pair of his armed marines had the man move, quickly but quietly, though showing no sign of undue haste, pleasing his captain, for it showed a sharp mind.

'To talk of what,' Pearce called.

'Why you here.'

The speed with which the marines appeared surprised Pearce. Macklin came alongside, using the starboard side to stay out of sight, likewise the lobsters, again impressive in his thinking. As soon as they were still, the marines began to load their muskets, silently removing bayonets to do so.

'I pulled them off guard duty, sir,' Macklin whispered as he rejoined his captain. 'Seemed quickest.'

'The rest of the ship?'

'Quiet as the grave, except for snoring.'

Pearce called over the side again. 'You can only talk to me if you come aboard.'

'Corsicans there?' carried a note of alarm.

'None. Only British sailors. Come alongside.'

Now Pearce could see the oars dip as the small rowboat came into sight, but the man rowing had his back to *Hazard*, so the only thing visible was a dark coat and a sort of pulled-down hat. The action of the oars seemed uneven, which tended to denote a man unaccustomed to them. But he took great care not to make noisy contact with the side, Pearce leaning over to direct him to the larboard battens and a spot where the boarding nets overlapped. There he began to untie the lines holding two together, which created a gap.

'Mr Macklin, a line for his boat, please.'

On a deck with a mass of ropes, this was quickly produced, one end dropped over the side. Once it had been looped and knotted through a ring on the prow, the visitor hauled his craft in slowly till it was touching the scantlings, at which point Pearce secured it.

'Before you come aboard, sir, I need to know who you are.'

'Messenger I am.'

'From whom?'

The hesitation was obvious, and it was several seconds before he replied, this time in a strong voice. 'His Excellency, Signor di Borgo.'

'Make your way up the side, but be warned the battens are slippery.' Pearce turned to Macklin to impart in a low tone, 'I take leave to doubt he's a sailor.'

The ascent, slow and laboured, went a long way to confirm this, so it was some time before his head appeared above the empty hammock nettings to reveal a lined and pale countenance in the ghostly lantern light. Unbeknown to Pearce, a bosun's mate had come on deck to ring the quarterdeck bell, which he did four times, the very first clang producing a look of alarm and a half movement backwards, as if the man was leaving. The continuing sounds, probably aided by the lack of apprehension of the faces of the pair waiting to help him onto the deck, seemed to deal with his obvious fears.

'Captain Pearce of His Britannic Majesty's vessel HMS *Hazard*.'

The hat came off at speed, to show a full head of tight grey curls over the face of a fellow not in his first youth, but one suddenly very erect. '*Commendatore* Perreti of the Presidential Guard, your service at.'

The rank had Pearce pull himself upright, at which point he realised the dark coat to be some kind of uniform, though it seemed to be missing any of the usual military fripperies which went with the stated rank. He introduced Macklin before saying, 'If you will accompany me to my cabin, *Commendatore*?'

The eyes took in the near empty deck before he nodded, following Pearce, who asked Macklin to place the two marines outside his door and to rouse out Derwent. It was impossible not to note the man's gait was that of one either too old or too tired for a steady bearing, and while the motion of the ship was so slight as to be unnoticeable to a sailor, it seemed to affect this visitor.

Offered a seat as soon as they were inside, the *commendatore* sank into it gratefully, Pearce immediately enquiring if he needed food, to be answered that a glass of wine would serve. Derwent, who would not have retired until he knew the man he served was abed, was on hand to quickly provide this, the goblet emptied swiftly, followed by a sigh.

'You say you wish to talk to me, *signor*, but I'm happy to wait until you feel fully recovered from what must have been quite an effort.' Seeing a look of slight incomprehension, Pearce added, 'I mean rowing the boat. It's no short distance to shore.'

'May I beg you slowly speak,' Perreti replied. 'English difficult. Used not for many years.'

Derwent had also supplied Pearce with wine, so he nodded and took a sip, his mind coming to some rapid conclusions, among them how this should not be happening. If this *commendatore* was from di Borgo, why the surreptitious approach, especially his enquiry as to the presence aboard of his fellow countrymen. And the way the older man was now looking at him, a bit wary, was far from right, so he spoke, albeit slowly and carefully, to get a reaction.

'It's rare for anyone from the island to speak English. Can I ask how you learned yours.'

'In London I was, with Paoli. Of His Excellency you know?'

'Of course. A great hero.'

There was a certain amount of exaggeration in this; he had been a child and travelling the length and breadth of Britain with his father when the 'hero' was being lionised in the capital, mainly on the grounds that anyone who was an enemy of France was a friend to Britannia, so the name then hardly registered.

'I was expecting a party from Corte, travelling by road.'

The crestfallen look told Pearce this was not as it should be, watching as his visitor seemed to gather himself to tell a tale, one to which he listened with increasing disquiet. Yes, they had come from Corte, heading east for Porto Vecchio, while those who would stop them—and had tried—expected his president to make for the west coast and the much closer port of Ajaccio, which was his home. This diversionary tactic would only work for so long, the *commendatore* fearing the enemy had uncovered the truth and were now not far behind.

'So close we dare not a fire light for fear. They seek His Excellency prisoner to take and hand him to French.'

'How many are in the party?'

'Four and twenty, including wives and children.'

It was hard not to look slightly surprised at the numbers and composition. Further enquiry established they were, as had been suspected, using donkeys or walking, seeking to avoid contact with villagers unless in need of food and water. They were well aware that the silence of such people, poor and easy to threaten or bribe, could not be guaranteed. Thus, their route, and soon their destination, would cease to be a mystery.

'And where are they now?'

'Two leagues Porto Vecchio about.'

Pearce smiled. 'Then you may tell them it's safe to come on, *signor*. I have arranged with a local chief to see you safely to the shore.'

The look Pearce got then was of the kind he'd seen before: it made him think of Jervis.

'Battisti' was spat out with a venom which seemed to overcome his weariness.

'You know him?' was not asked with comfort.

'Pig and traitor' had the same rancour as the name.

'I've paid him.'

Pearce said this with no great confidence before calling, to cover what he suspected was going to be embarrassing, to Derwent to fetch more wine. The laugh, more a cackle, did nothing to raise the feeling.

'Catch di Borgo, kill he will, or to French sell.' He used a hand to denote a slit throat. 'Others, God have mercy.'

'*Commendatore*,' Pearce said slowly. 'I need you to tell me everything.'

It would not have been a pretty tale in perfect English but, being in the same broken tongue, it somehow seemed worse as he described Battisti and his less than sterling background. It was one to set in motion a sinking feeling in Pearce's stomach, which did not improve the more the older man spoke.

Treason was moot, given the politics of Corsica, but the father of the man Pearce had eaten and drunk with had betrayed Pasquale Paoli, both as a fighter for freedom and as head of the army which lost to the French. *Commendatore* Perreti was sure the father had betrayed the plans and troop dispositions of the great hero, contributing to his defeat and flight, which naturally included, as a very young officer, the man telling the tale.

The son was no better. Inheriting his father's position, Battisti ruled locally like a tyrant, he and the men he led—the dregs of his clan—terrorising the people of the region. They lived off what could be extracted from their meagre incomes from fishing and hardscrabble farming, added to outright banditry. Worse, di Borgo and his party, even though they had no idea how close were those pursuing them, never moved without scouting the road ahead, with an obvious conclusion.

'He knows, somehow, we come' put the final nail in Pearce's discomfort. 'Wait he does to take, catch, and kill. I come for help.'

'Which I will most certainly provide' was the reply from a naval officer who was wishing the deck would swallow him up. 'But I will need to know exactly where your party are, and there is nothing which can be done now and in the dark.'

A weary nod accepted this as a fact, which had Pearce call for Derwent to have a cot made up in the side cabin in which their visitor could get some sleep.

'And care for the gentleman's clothing and any other needs he may have. You may raid my sea chest for a clean shirt.' Looking at the grey stubble on the older man's chin, he added, 'And of course he may have use of my shaving kit.'

It was uncomfortable sitting opposite him now, with no idea what to say and no intention of relating how he'd been humbugged. Then he reflected on that word, which was feeble in the extreme, given he comprehensively had been made a fool of. He needed to think about how to remedy matters, and to do so without the watery eyes of the older man looking at him for salvation.

'You will forgive me if I have duties to perform,' he said.

This didn't sound convincing to him, so he wondered how it lay with his visitor. Thankfully he got a nod from a fellow who felt the need to run a hand over his brow—part worry, part exhaustion. This earned him a pat on the shoulder, one designed to bring comfort to the giver not the receiver.

Out on deck, Pearce was subject to a raft of thoughts, not least how he was going to explain this to his own officers. Moberly, for obvious reasons, would be the most difficult person with whom to exchange even a glance, but no one could possibly fail to think he had been too optimistic. Perhaps they would wonder if the drink he'd consumed had clouded his judgement, but Pearce knew it was his over-eager desire for what seemed a simple solution which had allowed him to follow the chosen course.

Pacing to and fro on the windward side of the quarterdeck, he sought an excuse in the fact that the whole thing had been too nebulous for firm actions—no fixed date, no idea of numbers, and no exact assurance di Borgo and those with him would even turn up—but it would not hold. He now had to think the reason matters were so unstructured was because of the threats the man faced in Corte, including people who would do anything to stop him leaving the island.

The face of Battisti swam before him often, it now being seen not as passive but as deeply calculating. And, given what he'd just been told about his way of operating, it explained why Porto Vecchio had seemed deserted when he landed. Likewise, the women who served the food he ate: they weren't, as he'd supposed, too fearful of censure for exchanging a look with a male stranger. They were terrified of the local clan chieftain.

Matters had to be put right, but he was damned if he could think of how. There was no way he was going to return to Elba and admit he failed, for he'd have to explain the how and why, and whatever excuses he conjured up now would not wash.

'Including women and children. Well, that's just dandy.'

'Sir?' asked Maclehose, who'd replaced Macklin.

The word 'hunting' popped into his mind, the idea they would do so the following day. Would it serve as an excuse to get those taking part in the rescue ashore without causing suspicion? He had to see for himself what the problems were, to try and work out if there was a way to get past Battisti's men without them knowing so that he could lift the others off.

Should he keep the aim to himself or share it with Vickery and his officers? The notion of saying nothing didn't bear examination, and if he'd acted on his own instincts previously, it wouldn't be an idea to do so now. He would have to call his officers together, admit the bind he'd created for them all, and use their collective minds to seek out a way to proceed.

Back in his cabin Derwent assured him the *commendatore* was properly settled, with the added information that he'd felt it necessary to gift the old man a brandy to help him get to sleep.

'Then you'd best fetch me a bumper, Derwent; I'm damn sure I'm going to need it.'

Once more, on the quarterdeck the bell tolled the timing of the watch. To the ship's captain, being helped out of his uniform coat, it sounded too like the knell of doom.

Chapter Twenty-Seven

THE PRESENCE OF THE *COMMENDATORE* AND WHO HE REPRESENTED WAS, thanks to Macklin, common knowledge long before John Pearce called his officers to confer. There was a slight delay until the boat, sent early to pick up Vickery, had returned, he arriving attired in a short green jacket and breeches, armed and dressed for the proposed hunt. In the meantime, Pearce's thoughts continued to be consumed with the various approaches he could employ and the possible reactions, only to conclude it mattered little in the former, while there was only one with the latter.

Finally called to his cabin, they filed in, their attention naturally taken by the somewhat restored Corsican officer, who had benefited from a good night's sleep, while Derwent had done some work on his uniform. Already sat at their captain's desk, he was speedily introduced with his rank and position added, as well as the fact that if he spoke English, it was with some difficulty, to which he nodded forcefully.

The weariness had gone, so his whole manner spoke of an eagerness to tell his tale. This was not what Pearce wished, thinking anything imparted by him would sound worse than his own explanation, so he made a point of ensuring his guest knew who would be doing the talking.

'Gentlemen, I fear I have to tell you matters and steps I have taken ashore are not as I hoped and expected. They are in fact the very reverse, which has put the mission we're here to carry out in jeopardy, rather than providing a means to achieve it.'

The cough from Moberly was enough to halt the flow, but he had the good grace to apologise and blush slightly.

'The positive news is the party we are expecting are within striking distance of Porto Vecchio, not much more than a league distant.' Ignoring the nods, he continued. 'But those we were expecting to see them safely to the shore are, according to the gentleman beside me, more likely to hinder their progress than to aid it, to the point of posing a danger to their lives. I must also add, he tells me there are good grounds to believe they are also being pursued by elements opposed to the government we helped put in place, and it is feared they are not far off.'

'How not far off?' asked Vickery.

'Impossible to tell, but what it means is we must act as if they are in imminent danger and do something to not only alleviate it but get them to the shore and on board the ship in very short order.'

'Would it be right to assume, sir,' asked Moberly, 'this could well be opposed by the fellow Battisti?'

'*Bastarda!*' came from the *commendatore* at the mention of the name. He had been following the conversation closely, but confining himself to nodding. The word required no translation.

Pearce looked at him before replying. 'I'm afraid so, Mr Moberly, and I must apologise to you for not taking your obvious concerns more seriously.'

'Am I allowed to say, sir, they stemmed from it all being too opportune for the man in question.'

'Indeed, but it's an embarrassing fact that the folly in believing what he said is mine.'

A general mummer, implying what he was saying was nonsense, was brought on, Pearce thought, as more of an automatic reaction to ease his mood rather than a genuine sentiment. He was saved from further abasement by Vickery, who addressed the whole gathering.

'I don't recall him saying very much, but going over old ground will get us nowhere, gentlemen. We either act on what we now know or abandon the mission.'

'Which we will not do, Mr Vickery, I do assure you.'

'I never supposed we would, so let's put our mind to how we might go about it.' He looked at the Corsican. 'Does our guest have any ideas?'

'We've had a brief discussion and have come to the conclusion, which I rate as obvious, getting them into and out of Porto Vecchio will be difficult, if not impossible. Their mode of transport, as we surmised, is donkeys, while the party consists of twenty-four souls, including four women and six children.'

'So, another route must be found,' Worricker suggested.

'Obviously,' Pearce acknowledged, 'but can it be both found and negotiated without it becoming known?'

He then asked his nocturnal guest to explain the position and reputation of Battisti, which the *commendatore* did with great relish. This included his murderous tendencies, iron control of the locality, several references to his questionable parentage, many rude gestures, and a couple of fists thumped on Pearce's desk. The tirade was brought to a conclusion by the owner placing a hand on his shoulder and speaking firmly enough to stem the flow.

'A thoroughly nasty piece of work, then,' Worricker concluded.

'And, if what we're being told is true, it might be impossible to move in his backyard without it coming to his attention.'

Pearce felt it necessary to go over some of the conclusions he'd reached the night before: the lack of people both on the beach, also outside the church, which must be a focal point of gathering in such a pious Catholic country. Then what had happened with Michael and how the priest had reacted to him seeking absolution. All pointed to the people of Porto Vecchio being terrified of Battisti.

'If everyone is in such a place, even the clergy, then we can't look to them for help or even the turning of a blind eye. We obviously can't use the main cart track, which would mean coming into contact with Battisti and his men and having to get into a firefight. It also means avoiding anything smacking of a well-used footpath and getting them to a place with a beach—one we can seal off and, if necessary, defend.'

'Not easy,' opined Vickery, before explaining to the sailors about the undergrowth he'd experienced around Bastia. 'It's thick and sometimes impassable.'

'Which I can attest to,' added Pearce, referring to the morning rides he'd taken with the viceroy's wife during the summer. 'I found it's even hard when mounted.'

'Donkeys are tougher beasts,' insisted Worricker.

'Are you suggesting, sir,' asked Moberly, 'we might have to cut our way through to get to their location?'

'Can be done!' the *commendatore* asserted, proving he understood the nub of the conversation. 'Must be done.'

'Does the party have food?' Pearce demanded. 'And if so, how much?'

'One day,' the old man replied, adding a doubtful shrug, which put the whole claim into question. 'Maybe two.'

Pearce explained about his ideas of masking any plan by using, as cover, the hunting party. 'But I fear we must say what we're about.'

'You mean ask permission?' said Moberly.

'It very much comes down to that. I won't claim the scales have fallen from my eyes, and I suspect I'm twenty guineas lighter for my credulity, but I now have Battisti, in my mind, as bound to be suspicious of anything we might do. If we are seen going ashore and armed without his knowledge, what will he do?'

'Seek to find out what we are about.'

'My thinking too, Mr Vickery. He must be brought to the conviction—one he might already hold—that I'm a gullible fool, so I won't ask. But I will say it's our intention, and the sooner that is done the better.' He turned to address the master. 'Mr Williams, in your survey of the bay, would you be able to point us to a location which will suit out purpose?'

Hitherto silent and possibly wondering why he had been called to join this meeting, Williams now got an inkling but, being the man he was, there was no swift answer. A hand was put to the chin so he could think, which had Pearce having to hide his impatience, not alleviated by the slow delivery that followed.

'The only one I think might suit is a long strand on the west bank of the upper bay, which has the advantage of being out of sight from Porto Vecchio itself. It has a stretch of flat country between it and a set of quite steep and heavily wooded hills, which might be hard to traverse. My opinion of how easy it would be to defend the beach compares poorly with yours or that of the other officers present, sir.'

'No others?' Pearce said.

'None, without you have to make your way inland to cross a river, for it splits into two estuaries before entering the bay. Also, being on the eastern shore and so visible to the head of the main bay, it may be you could be spotted if there was much activity.'

'Prepare me a rough map, Mr Williams, if you please.'

The response was grumpy and offended. 'I'll do you a proper map, sir, or not put quill to paper.'

'For which I will be grateful,' Pearce replied, seeking to be vocally emollient. It did nothing to fool his officers, who took the mood from his voice. 'Gentlemen, and those joining us, I wish you to search your sea chests for your oldest working garments, for we cannot go a'hunting in our best blue and red uniforms. I don't know about Battisti, but it would make me wonder if we did. Mr Worricker, you will remain in command of the ship. For now, I'd like the cutter manned, if you please, as I must go and beard our devil.'

'And act a part, I reckon.'

'Very true, Mr Vickery, and I have him down as not an easy fellow to deceive.'

'How many of my men do you think you'll require?'

'Half should suffice. I don't want your cannon left unmanned. I suggest extra powder and shot for those who come with us, and perhaps one day of cold rations.'

He found Battisti at what he now knew to be his tavern, hailing him like an old friend and seemingly happy to partake of more of the ardent spirit he so enjoyed, as well as pay for it. The problem of communication still existed, though Pearce now wondered if he was as ignorant of French as he claimed. But if it was a performance, it was a good one and something he had to match, with many a gesture to denote game and the shooting of same. Also, and this was a problem when dealing with a man who had all day to linger, there was the matter of time, with a possible eight miles to cover.

When Battisti indicated the hills behind Porto Vecchio, using a whole range of hand gestures to imply good hunting, Pearce had to think quickly. It was a suggestion not anticipated and one he had to react to as though pleased, his true feeling the polar opposite. This, over a couple more cups of spirits, he countered, in a flight of imagination which surprised even him, by pointing out it would lead to gunshots close to where the lookouts had been placed. How would the approaching party from Corte react if they heard them: would they not be frightened and decline to come on?

It almost amused Pearce the way Battisti reacted, for he was now much more acute in examining his expressions, and he saw, when what he was driving at appeared to hit home, playacting which was certainly a match for his own. The pretence that it didn't matter, then a slow air of growing doubt with added nods, mingled with apparent deep thinking. Pearce then indicated it would be best to be on the outer reaches of the bay, which had Battisti smiling and nodding in agreement.

The feeling of impending success was soon marred. Battisti signalled to a couple of his men, to whom he issued a stream of commands, then indicating they would accompany Pearce on his hunt. Gesticulations that this was unnecessary were waved away, with sign language to imply it was a gift from one good friend to another. There was nothing to do but smile and show gratitude, to then enquire after their names and invite them to join him in the cutter.

It was almost as if Michael O'Hagan had overseen the whole animated conversation, for he was quick to pick up much of what had just happened, he having been afforded a hurried explanation of what had taken place since the previous night, as well as what was intended.

'Holy Mary,' he grinned, 'it's to be hoped you've got a way to see this sorted.'

'Don't just leave it to me' came with a slightly bitter tone. 'Put your mind to finding a solution.'

If Michael did so on the way across the bay, he didn't divulge it, but when he shouted the required '*Hazard*' to the deck of the ship, he had the sense to add, in case they hadn't seen, 'and a pair of local scullies.'

There was no need to ask if it had been understood as a message to keep the *commendatore* out of sight. Once they were back on board, O'Hagan proved he had indulged in some deep thinking when he asked to be allowed access to the spirit store. He then indicated his intention to entertain the pair, all quietly imparted to his friend.

'Not many can sink much neat rum, John-boy. Give me a couple of bells with this pair, and they'll not be wanting to go anywhere.'

'Are you planning to join them?'

'Never fear, now. If you're going ashore, would I be after trusting you to care for yourself, so sober I'll stay.'

Battisti's men going below was not seen as odd by them or the crew, and Pearce did not witness what Michael got up to. But whatever it was, it kept them occupied while everyone going ashore made ready to depart. This would be in every boat HMS *Hazard* possessed, plus the one Perreti had arrived in the previous night. It would be with as few bodies to row them as possible, which had the officers and Moberly's marines doing much of the work. Perreti was the only passenger, his hat pulled well down to hide his features, around his feet freshly sharpened swords, axes, and unlit lanterns.

Down below, organised by Michael, the rest of the crew were taking turns to share and press rum on the men Pearce had fetched aboard, enjoying more grog than their normal ration and failing to tell their 'guests' what they were relishing had not been cut with water and lemon, so was full strength.

And the man who'd organised it was right: in two bells they were disinclined to go anywhere and in no fit state to do so anyway. The only downside was the livid reaction of the purser, Mr Porlock, who demanded to know who was going to pay for it. But the message it was safe to go was passed to the necessary cabins, and there was Michael acting as coxswain and, as he'd promised, stone cold sober. Likewise, the two other Pelicans, Charlie and Rufus, would be going ashore.

The beach Mr Williams had chosen was a soft sand strand of about a quarter mile long, backed by less than dense woods through which it would be easy to make progress, something they assumed would not last once they got to the hills. There the forest was likely to be much thicker, as would be the undergrowth.

Moberly's job, with the rest of *Hazard*'s officers, was to hold the beach with his marines, they being taken into the trees where their presence, on a cloudy day, would meld with the background, their task to form some kind of defendable position. Once Pearce was satisfied, he indicated to the *commendatore* he should lead the way, which was more of a courtesy than a necessity: as of this moment, Perreti had as little idea as anyone of the route to take.

Pearce used the south-easterly sun and his compass to give him an indication of where he was heading, and if the hills they had to traverse made progress harder when they reached them, they provided an occasional vantage point from which the group could place their location. It also allowed them to look out for dwellings and the smoke from hamlet chimneys: if it wasn't winter for the men from *Hazard*, it was to the locals; besides, it was the only way to cook food.

Making progress was not always easy, but the use of axes and the thick-bladed naval swords helped to hack a way through when the undergrowth was too thick, Michael O'Hagan at the fore and swinging mightily. Pearce had a musket discharged on occasions, which would reverberate across the bay; if Battisti was listening, he would assume it to be aimed at game.

This had to cease when it was thought they were getting close to the heights above Porto Vecchio, and here the older man became a positive asset. He'd been here the day before so had a good visual recollection of the point from which he'd headed for the shore, a clearing which gave a panoramic view of the bay, to eventually take to the water. When Pearce remembered to ask him how he acquired a boat and oars, he sheepishly admitted that he'd stolen them, to then regret making a poor man poorer, which was not the action of an officer and gentleman.

'It may be you can return it,' Pearce said to cheer him up.

Prior to this point he had marked the trees he passed with a deep knife cut so he would be able to recognise his route of return. This, added to the fact they were in a less than dense forest, speeded up progress till they reached a point where the *commendatore* suggested he go on alone. He feared what would happen if his party suddenly saw a group of armed men approaching.

'Rations,' Vickery called to his men, 'but keep enough for the return.'

Given there was no way to light fires, this was fresh bread, baked in Porto Vecchio and brought out to the ship early each morning, sustenance enough to get them through the day; the same for the sailors they'd brought along. Pearce, Macklin, and Maclehose had some cold chicken from the previous day's wardroom dinner, in both cases washed down with fresh water. It would have surprised anyone coming across them to see the group sat around the clearing, their backs to a tree. But they were alert enough to be on their feet and ready when they heard an approach.

Perreti entered the clearing with another man, wrapped in a good-quality cloak and having about him an air of being important, to face a line of muskets, bayonets pointing out from behind various trees, which had them stop and stare. John Pearce came from behind a tree, putting away his pistol as he approached the pair.

'*Capitaine* Pearce. Allow me to you present His Excellency Signor Carlo-Andrea, Pozzo di Borgo, president of the Legislative Council of Corsica.'

'Honoured, captain,' di Borgo said, in near accent-free English.

'Likewise, sir. I hope the rest of your party are safe and behind you.'

'This is not possible. It has been explained to me what you wish us to do, which does not take account of the make-up of our group. The women especially would find it impossible.'

'Then, sir,' Pearce said in a frosty tone, 'you must consider leaving them behind.'

'*Impossiblie*! You are speaking of members of my family.'

'I am speaking of them staying alive, *signor*, for the *commendatore* assures me they will not if they fall into the hands of Battisti. Also, it is my duty to preserve the lives of my men, as well as the safety of His Britannic Majesty's ship *Hazard*, which I have the honour to command.'

That di Borgo was furious was obvious, and his features—heavy lowered eyebrows over coal black eyes—showed the feeling of a man not accustomed to being checked. But Pearce was prepared to be adamant. Having hacked his way this far, he was not going to back down.

'I leave it to you, Your Excellency,' he added, pulling out his hunter and flipping it open to look at the time. 'And we must go immediately if we are to make my boats before dark.'

The standoff didn't last long, and the commander of his guard, in a burst of Italian, must have said something to change his mind. Turning away and taking up the pose of a man for whom such matters were beneath his dignity, he stared into the trees. The *commendatore* sped off the way he had come, which left everyone else waiting until, after some twenty precious minutes, he led a rather bedraggled group into the clearing, even the children subdued.

If his women had set out in finery, it wasn't that now—silk and a seat on a donkey did not mix—but at least the animals sped their progress, and the route back was made easier by being already cut. Charlie Taverner and Rufus Dommet brought up the rear, chivvying along the weary menfolk, even carrying some of the smaller children. It was close to dark, which came quickly in these parts, when they rejoined Moberly, the animals released to wander, including the pair used to carry trunks. Pearce insisted on leaving those behind to be collected in the morning.

'If they are stolen overnight, sir,' he barked at a pleading di Borgo, 'you will just have to shift without the contents.'

In the end he had to allow two small caskets, one of which he suspected held money and valuables, the other personal items of the women. They set off in their now-overcrowded boats, the unnaturally quiet children, all seeming to be under about ten, perched on adult laps. By the time they reached *Hazard*, lit like a beacon in the middle of the bay, Worricker was calling to Pearce through a speaking trumpet.

'Mr Tennant, sir. He's been flying a red flag from Mont Fiori since noon. He sent one of his men down to say there are two enemy warships beating up from the south.'

Chapter Twenty-Eight

As soon as Pearce got everyone aboard, he had all the lanterns dowsed and shaded the binnacle before ordering the boarding nets to be reset, with a watch to be kept for any attempt to mount a cutting-out raid. Creating a space for the passengers, especially the women, was far from easy, but it had to be done, despite the grumbles of men obliged to sling their hammocks closer together. Di Borgo had to be accommodated in Pearce's side cabin, with the *commendatore* shifted to the doctor's quarters, Mr Cullen gracious about his being cramped. Finally, Pearce knew he had to talk to the man who'd taken his berth, who had been silent since they left the beach.

'I have to tell you, sir, we may be about to engage in battle.' Pearce held up a hand to stop him responding. 'There are two warships off the coast, and I have no idea if they will sail on over the course of the night, seek to enter the bay, or take station offshore. But if they do either of the latter, it has to be because they know we are here; and if it is happenstance, the fact will be plain to them in the morning. I need to consult with my officers, and I would be obliged if you would go into my side cabin and stay there.'

'It will be my pleasure, lieutenant, to report your discourtesy to someone of higher rank.'

'Report what you like, sir, but if you do not do as I ask, I'll have your bed shifted to the lower deck, where you can join the ladies.'

In truth, there was not much Pearce could do till daylight but be ready, and whatever he faced would be quickly known. Vickery must get to his cannon to either employ them or spike them if the danger passed, something he doubted would be the case. Pearce had no intention of sailing out to do battle with vessels of which he had no knowledge, and unless Tennant had exaggerated, he must seek to draw them into the narrows, where the old ordnance might be able to inflict enough damage to reduce the odds.

In the end, it was in the wardroom he issued his instructions to everyone. For reasons he could not explain, he did not want di Borgo overhearing what he had in mind, being sure the man would have an opinion—and a useless one—which would not stop him from airing it. Having repeated the possibilities he'd outlined to di Borgo, he shared with them his thinking.

'I cannot see anyone with sense risking the narrows in the dark, so we will find out at dawn what we face. Regardless, Mr Vickery is to be boated ashore as soon as the sky shows the first hint of light, the same crew to fetch back aboard Tennant and his men. Let's hope that once he was sure you had his signal, he struck the red flag. Mr Vickery, if I'm to face two armed enemy vessels—and I intend to draw them in—I require you to disable at least one of them. Do you see this as possible?'

'I'll make it so.'

'Mr Worricker, if we have enemies to face, we will clear for action as normal but stay at stations, the men on the cannon to forbear loading and to be fed by the guns.'

'And if they stay out of the bay, sir,' asked Macklin, 'will it not force you to fight both in the open?'

'They won't stand off, Mr Macklin. Not when I'm bombarding Porto Vecchio.'

Given the ship was roused out before dawn on any given day, the only people disturbed were the passengers. Just in case they were alarmed, di Borgo, roused out when the cabin bulkheads were taken down, was sent to tell his people what to expect. First the sound of whistles and shouts, then the thunder-like sound of running out the guns, and later, possible cannon fire. They were to stay where they were unless called to move by a naval officer and to ignore instructions from anyone else, a point which got His Excellency's thick black eyebrows twitching.

Pearce was in the tops with a telescope as the light grew stronger, to see his worst fears realised: first the red warning flag still flying atop Mont Fiori and second, the vessels which had caused it to be raised. A pair of square-rigged brigs, they were beating to and fro off the narrows and flying tricolours. They appeared to be at least a match in each hull, one showing half a dozen gunports a side, the other eight. They too would now be cleared for action but prepared to wait for *Hazard* to try to exit, which would give them a huge advantage with an easterly wind, manoeuvring being impossible till he was in open water. Even then they would have the weather gage.

He called down and gave the orders to raise the anchor, taking a long look at the men on the deck, those not so employed ready for battle, less pleased to see di Borgo had come from below to stand by Worricker. Pearce could tell, even at a distance, the man saw himself as too important to be confined.

The enemy would be bound to wonder what he was about when they saw his prow swing away from them, but they would not shift, sure they had him trapped. A look to Vickery's tiny bastion showed he too had been active in the grey early light, for the cut bushes and branches on the front of the position, not visible to the enemy, had been refreshed. They now looked green and part of the background, not the dried appearance they'd acquired from several days of being cut.

Would the brigs do as he expected and needed? If they were content for him to blast Porto Vecchio to rubble and do nothing, he would have no choice but to engage them on their own terms. But he was seeking to draw them into water which, once *Hazard* had moved, would provide them with all the room they needed to take him on with confidence.

If they made it intact, Vickery having failed to inflict serious damage on at least one, and proved to be too well handled in both sailing and gunnery to evade, Pearce could envisage having to strike his colours: he had no intention of sacrificing his crew in a fight they couldn't win, but first the enemy would know what it was like to take on Britannia's navy.

'A course for the head of the bay, Mr Worricker. And ask the gentleman who has just come on deck to go below.' With di Borgo now looking up at him and glowering, he added, 'And if he appears reluctant, you may employ force.'

As expected, neither enemy vessel did anything different—why would they? Pearce could imagine the atmosphere on their quarterdecks, perhaps a moment of curiosity soon turning to amused bafflement. He also knew sitting up here would not aid him: they wouldn't budge until he began his bombardment, and perhaps not even then. So down a backstay he slid, finding the deck free of the pesky Corsican leader, and took a walk along the deck to address Maclehose, in charge of the forward cannon.

'I have no intention of blasting the poor inhabitants to perdition, so we must send them fleeing, and I hope they will do so when they see the guns run out. If they do not, since they have declined to go out fishing this morning—and who can blame them—we must sadly deprive them of their way of making a living, which means destroying their boats.'

This was greeted with looks from the crouching gun crews: the people in question of the same ilk as they.

'The destruction of the waterfront buildings must be selective, Mr Moberly. I would suggest you aim at what you take to be warehouses first. I will point out to you an alley which we traversed on first coming ashore. It would please me mightily if you could put a ball or two up there, without hitting anything on the way.'

'I know just who tae give the task to, sir,' Maclehose replied. 'Ma best gunner.'

'I hope by that time the inhabitants will have run for the hills, so if our two fellows have not yet entered the bay, we can set about the complete destruction of the waterfront.'

A nod sent Pearce back to his proper position on the quarterdeck, to give instructions to Livingston. 'Aloft with you, young sir, and keep an eye on those two Frenchmen. If they show any sign of making sail to enter the bay, I need to know immediately.'

There was no need to alter sail, no need to issue any more orders, and no one to retaliate. Pearce reasoned the officers and crew felt the same as he: that what they were about to do was a duty in which to take no pleasure, visiting mayhem on folk who were mostly blameless. But there was Battisti, a man who Pearce suspected would be at the forefront if people were fleeing.

'Sword and pistols, your honour,' Michael said softly in his ear, performing a duty he'd elected to cover since his friend became an officer.

'Thank you, Michael.'

The words to follow were quiet enough to be personal. ''Tis to be hoped the poor bastards don't know what's coming, John-boy, may God bless them all.'

These words induced in Pearce a strange feeling, a realisation the coming action was something he'd never done before. Despite his best efforts, an unknown number of the locals of Porto Vecchio, most of whom would be poor and had no interest in war, would become casualties: not all would or could flee. Against this, he had his own officers and men to consider, never mind di Borgo and his party. How much better to fight a known enemy on equal terms than to act the butcher?

They were closing with the shore now, the ship swinging round, the larboard ports crashing open, the guns poking out within seconds, which must induce fear in those who'd be watching the approach and wondering what it meant. Maclehose was looking at him, waiting for the order to fire, but he couldn't give it. Not even to destroy the fishing boats, reducing the people who lived here to penury, which was little better than outright slaughter.

'House the guns, Mr Maclehose, please. Mr Worricker, we will come about and make for the open sea.' Every eye was on him as he added, 'We must find another way to confound the enemy, which does not involve massacring innocents.'

As the ship came up into the wind, yards braced round, Pearce set his face in a sort of mask, not wanting to even exchange a glance with any of his officers. But behind this his thoughts were racing, not least wondering how the pair he was approaching would handle it. The sailing qualities of HMS *Hazard* he knew, and this went too for the competence of his well worked up crew. Would the French be able to match it?

And what would Vickery make of his just sailing by, when he'd been told of the plan of bombardment? The man was sharp, more so than most bullocks Pearce had met, but would he think it a move to abandon him and his redcoats? These were problems which would play out in a way he could not effect; he had to prepare for those he could depend on. All he had now was time, for they were making little headway into a stiff breeze.

'Mr Livingston,' he called aloft, 'no waving to our redcoat friends onshore. I do not want our enemies to suspect their presence. Mr Williams, it is still my intention to lure the Frenchmen into the bay, but by bearding them; for once they have got under way and begun to close with us, I cannot see them giving up the chase. At which point we will reverse our course, so please ensure we have aloft the canvas required for such a manoeuvre to be executed at maximum speed.'

Then he turned to his premier. 'Mr Worricker, I think we have time to issue a ration of grog to the crew. I must go below and explain the situation to our guests.'

Which he did, sticking to English so the majority would not comprehend what was coming. But di Borgo did, his first response being to be allowed on deck along with the head of his guard, surprisingly in a tone which lacked his previous arrogance.

'I have been a soldier, captain, and do not fear to engage in battle, and nor does the *commendatore*. We both fought under Paoli in the War of Independence.'

'*Signor*,' Pearce replied, matching the tone. 'I do not doubt your courage, but the deck of a ship is not like a battlefield—being so confined as an area of conflict, it can be the bloodiest place in creation. But I do promise, should we be at risk of being boarded, you will be called up to take part in the fighting. Now, if you tell me what weapons you would wish to employ, I will have them delivered to you.'

'Swords, Captain Pearce. What other weapon can a gentleman employ?'

A nod and he was gone, the instructions to send swords passed to Michael O'Hagan, who gave him a look which Pearce saw as curious until he said, crossing himself as he always did when he invoked any of his deities, 'Jesus, I'm glad you spared those poor fisherfolk, John-boy. There's only hell for the murder of innocents.' Then he smiled. 'Pity you couldn't nail that Battisti bastard, though.'

'Who knows, Michael,' Pearce replied, matching the smile. 'I might go after him once I've seen to those two French warships we're about to have a game with.'

Making his way back to the quarterdeck, he reflected on the fact of Michael having fetched his weapons earlier when they were not really needed. Now he understood why, only to wonder: would he be grateful when the day was done?

He came onto a deck where more canvas was being sent aloft and bent on, pleased because to those planning to give him battle, this would signal his clear intention to seek to bypass them. It would involve taking whatever damage this entailed, to then hope to outrun them in a stern chase, which would mark him, in their minds, as a man determined not to engage for a second longer than possible—the very opposite of what he now intended.

The plan, if it could be so termed, would have spread through the crew, passed on by those who'd overheard what he'd said to the master, the man he now had to talk to. He needed the information Williams had gleaned from his surveying of the bay, which, like a great deal of the Corsican coast, had shallow water running to a point well off the actual shore, with only the occasional areas of depth navigable by anything bigger than a fishing smack.

'I need you by my side, because any decisions I make must be informed by your newly acquired knowledge. It may be our friends yonder do not have charts as up to date as yours. It would be a great help to have at least one of them run aground.'

The information which followed showed the value of what Williams had been about these last days, and he spoke with an air of authority which rarely surfaced. Standing at the taffrail, and without risking too obvious gestures, he indicated in general terms where such possibilities existed, making particular reference to the upper bay from which they'd rescued di Borgo and his party.

'I recall, I told you of a delta where a river splits into twin estuaries.'

'You did.'

'There will be no chart in any locker which will give accurate depths for such a feature.'

'Silt?' Pearce asked.

'Exactly, sir. The bottom shifts with the seasons, and even then, it is variable. The silt washed down at this time of year means a central channel with deep water, but on either bank there are patches to foul our keel.'

'It's not ours I want to foul, Mr Williams.'

'Of course, but I have charted the sandbanks, in between which it remains deep water.'

'But not, I wager, enough to engage in fancy movements.'

'No.'

'Thank you, Mr Williams, and can I say I'm extremely grateful to you.'

A man who'd never really gotten over his first wholly mistaken weather prediction as HMS *Hazard* exited the Thames, Williams had always treated Pearce as if he was still under that particular cloud. Now he seemed to swell slightly, which his captain hoped had fully restored his self-esteem. On this day he needed his master confident.

'Premier sent me to say we're coming abreast of Mr Vickery's redoubt, sir.'

'Thank you, Mr Tennant.'

Pearce could not avoid looking in that direction, but he held his hands behind his back; there would be telescopes trained on the deck of *Hazard*, so the slightest sign of there being anything to remark upon off to larboard had to be avoided. All he could do was silently pray Vickery would guess what he was about when he reversed his course once more. But this would not happen till he was out of sight for a spell, a point at which the soldier was bound to have negative thoughts.

It was time for him to return to the quarterdeck, take up his telescope, and concentrate on the enemy, who had plucked their anchors but done nothing to set out any great amount of canvas. This they would do once they had a better idea of Pearce's intentions—when, he guessed, they would try to take him between two broadsides, one across his bow, the other his stern, firing high to shred his rigging while avoiding harming each other.

Having explained this to Worricker, he said, 'They will, I think, if they had done enough damage, then expect us to strike.'

'I would be very unhappy with such, sir.'

'You're not alone. Time to run out the guns again, both sides. We must make them think we intend to fight.'

It was obvious the crew were keyed up, even after their tot of rum, designed to settle them to their duty. But once the cannon were out, with the smell of slow match—placed in case the flints failed—wafting back into the Pearce nostrils, the deck went quiet and still once more.

'They're increasing sail,' he said unnecessarily.

It was plain to anyone with eyes to see.

Chapter Twenty-Nine

ON PAPER, ALL THE ADVANTAGE LAY WITH THE FRENCH: THEY HAD THE wind so could manoeuvre freely, a superior number of guns and an enemy seemingly intent on flight, which meant only one broadside to weather, while HMS *Hazard* was obliged to tack and wear into the same wind in order to make forward progress.

Pearce had his telescope on their decks now, singling out the captains, not that a long-distance sight of the pair told him much. Two men, as still as he and concentrating, no doubt brimming with confidence as to the outcome, perhaps already spending the money and relishing the moment of glory the capture of HMS *Hazard* would bring them.

They were in no rush to close, aware to do so too soon might give their enemy a chance to slip by without being exposed to their fire. They knew, once he was past, and with no knowledge of his sailing qualities, he might well be flyer enough to evade capture. The frustration for Pearce was simple: he could not discern anything much about them at present.

If it turned out they had the legs of him, and were highly capable commanders as well, he might be doomed. His hopes rested first on Vickery reducing the odds against him, and then on being able to fox the one ship still whole by leading her into waters where his knowledge was going to be far superior to theirs.

The point at which he had to come about again was a very fine calculation. Too soon and they may well decline to pursue, backing their sails to remain outside the bay. Too late and *Hazard* might suffer damage he could ill afford, given he needed everything the ship could give him for the coming battle. Yet his mind was clear and his heartbeat normal, albeit his mouth was a bit dry, as it always was with a fight in the offing.

'They've got their topmen aloft,' Worricker said. 'We'll see the sails dropped soon.'

This was part of Pearce's calculation. The sails he had set to allow him to beat up into the wind would be more than a match for anything they had aloft when he came about, which would give him an immediate advantage when it came to speed. Expecting a battle meant it was too dangerous for the Frenchmen to have too much canvas set, and certainly nothing on the lower courses. But he also knew he must not open too great a gap, for the very same reason of remaining tempting as a prize. Only once they were committed to the narrows could he begin to open the distance.

There was no need for a telescope now; he could see his opponents with the naked eye, watching what canvas they would have aloft, for this would tell him which one would seek to get slightly ahead of his consort. The obvious addition to this thought: it would also tell him who was likely to be the senior of the pair. This might mean nothing, but it could matter in terms of fighting experience. If he had to face one enemy, he wanted it to be the lesser of the two in this regard.

'Are we ready, Mr Worricker?'

'We are, sir.'

Hazard was ploughing along at no great speed while he waited for their next move: out in the narrows, which was acting like a funnel, the easterly wind slowing her markedly. He was watching for the point at which the reefs came out of those topsails and they were sheeted home, at which point, as long as he held his present course, they could close the gap rapidly.

'The fellow with the speaking trumpet.'

'I have my eye on him, Mr Worricker, never fear. But we must let them come on a bit to render them overconfident.'

Pearce saw the speaking trumpet move to the lips, the precursor to the order to loosen the topsails, which brought on a thought, he ordering on a change of course. This had *Hazard* wear right round so her starboard battery came into play, with orders to the gunners to aim high and fire on the uproll. The range was at the edge of being truly effective, but it fitted with the impression he was trying to create: that of being fearful.

On his command the cannon sent out a great blast of orange flame and smoke, this receiving an immediate reply from the enemy bow chasers, which sent up great spouts of water off the bow to match those created by *Hazard*'s broadside.

His guns were being loaded at a speed he doubted the French could match, but Pearce, using his hunter, delayed the firing half a minute. This was another piece of subterfuge, for they would place some of their calculations on the time their prey took to reload, and he wanted to surprise them later. He could almost see the increase in speed as the French topsails took the wind, just by the increase in the creaming white water on the bows.

'Who,' he asked of no one in particular, 'gives up a chase once committed to it?'

And committed they were, coming on at a lick, which Pearce was sure would get French pulses racing. Yet he waited still, watch in hand, before ordering one last broadside, one which, with the range closing, struck home on the leading enemy vessel, taking chunks of wood out of her larboard bow. Pearce then ordered the guns housed; he needed every available man to execute the next manoeuvre.

'Mr Worricker, if you please,' he said as the gunports slammed shut.

There was no need to say more; the need was known, and everyone aboard went to their place. Marlinspikes were dragged out of their holes to release the lines holding the yards; others already on the sheets, ready to haul them round to a point where the canvas began to take the wind; the rudder working to bring *Hazard* on to her new course.

There was an anxious wait to see how the Frenchmen would react, but the vessel slightly in the lead was still coming on, and so was her consort. This caused Pearce to remark he now had the senior of the pair and also, by the look of it, the one with the better ship. Again, just before Vickery's bastion came into view, he had to remind everyone to avoid any reaction.

'We must trust to our bullocks to make sense of what they see before them.'

He did hope the work had been done to change the aim of Vickery's cannon, dropping the muzzles from hitting the opposite hillside to an imagined ship sailing by at some speed. But the old guns were not set to follow the course of the vessel; they were fixed, so getting off several shots at a moving target was a hope, not a certainty.

With everything done which could be done, no one moved to quit the deck, all eyes on the pursuing enemy, barely breathing, noting the way the lead vessel was opening up the gap with its companion. The latter captain was edging fractionally to the north, so as not to take the lead ship's wind. *Hazard* had sailed through the arc of Vickery's fire, so it was a wait until the lead vessel would face a surprise.

'Don't burst now,' Pearce said under his breath, thinking that if Michael wasn't praying, he should be.

It was difficult, at an angle, to be absolutely sure when the Frenchman entered the area of danger, but the great belch of smoke which billowed up, to be blown along the shoreline on the wind, told Pearce it was now. Within seconds, two great founts of water shot up alongside the enemy bow.

'I can see no damage, sir,' said Macklin; with the cannon housed, he was now on the quarterdeck. 'I wonder what he'll do now.'

'If he's got any sense, he'll cram on sail,' Pearce replied. 'If he seeks to come about, he stays with the sweep of Vickery's guns.'

There were a couple of tense minutes while they waited to see if there'd be another salvo, and this duly came, with the same concomitant smoke. But this time the balls struck, so it was as if some great celestial hand had taken the ship and shifted it sideways—yet even then it was not possible to be sure they had wounded anything. It might just be the pressure of disturbed water.

'I'm sure Vickery's hit the sod,' said Pearce eventually, judging merely by the amount of sudden activity on the enemy deck.

He called this out as the Frenchman swung away towards the northern arm of the narrows, signals which made no sense in English shooting up the halyards, their message soon evident. The other Frenchman was being ordered to go about and stay out of the bay, at which point Pearce ordered the same for *Hazard*, who now had a chance to take them on one at a time. Vickery tried another salvo, but the balls fell astern of a target too far off. But it was close, the waterspouts, swept by the wind, flying over the taffrail to soak the enemy quarterdeck.

HMS *Hazard* came round practically in its own length, seeking to bear up once more tack upon tack, it increasingly evident the vessel they were closing with was badly hurt—indeed, she seemed to be drifting towards the northern bay in which they'd landed from the boats the day before. The whole stern of the ship was smashed, and it soon became obvious Vickery had done harm to her rudder, which could mean she would be obliged to steer with relieving tackles, never ideal when manoeuvrability would be of paramount necessity.

Getting into a position to inflict more harm was taking an age, with Pearce reckoning the longer it took, the better prepared his enemy would be. From what he could make out, wherever she'd been hit had not reduced her firepower, soon plain when, now stationary and close to the shore, she opened up with a broadside, aiming high with bar shot—as was the French way—to seek to rip through his rigging, though at a range to rob it of much of its effect.

Pearce's blood was fully up now, he planning to take the Frenchman on, yardarm to yardarm, in a gun duel and force his opponent to strike, by boarding if necessary. But first he would rely on his faster reloading rate to drive home his superiority, and he ordered the guns run out again. It was at this point Pozzo di Borgo came on deck, cautiously, to ask for an appreciation of what had happened and what was intended. His face, when Pearce outlined his aims, showed genuine concern, and he reminded Pearce what he had aboard.

'And I do not refer, captain, to myself, for whom I do not fear. But there are women and children below. Should matters go against you, it will be playing with their lives.'

Pearce then recalled the words of Nelson in the last conversation he'd had with him aboard *Minerve*. The command not to deviate from his mission, which was to get the man before him and his dependants to Elba with all speed. It was even in the orders he had in his cabin, not read since they'd been delivered. Yet he was animated by what could happen if he proceeded as intended, so giving such things due consideration did not come easily.

But be considered they must. Did he have the luxury of doing as he pleased, which was to first take this Frenchman as a prize and then go after his consort? Such actions could not be carried out without risk, and not only to the worries to which di Borgo was referring. It was all very well to be sure of his ability and that of his crew, but what he'd just witnessed stood as a stark reminder of how things could go against even the most deep-seated certainty.

The Frenchman had chased him, sure he had all he needed for victory, yet now he was damaged enough to probably be at the mercy of his opponent. But the enemy still had the ability to fight if Pearce came close, just shown in the broadside fired, which indicated no desire to meekly surrender. What if *Hazard* sustained damage as well, to rigging and possibly her masts, which could seriously jeopardise the rescue he'd been tasked to carry out? It was with a feeling of utter deflation Pearce realised he could not take the risk, much as he desired to, so he turned to the Corsican politician.

'I apologise, Your Excellency, for allowing my passion for a contest to cloud my judgement. Mr Worricker, the enemy appears to be drifting north, so we will close with the southern shore and thus be well out of range. When we get to shoal water, send boats to pick up Mr Vickery, his men, as well as any equipment they cannot leave behind. We will stay cleared for action until we have them back aboard.'

There was no doubt his officers shared his enthusiasm for the fight— probably so did most of the crew—but if there was a downside to command, this was it. Responsibility outweighed craving. If he'd been issued the orders he was given by Nelson, there were perhaps matters of which he was not aware, political considerations to which he was not privy, and there was no doubt Nelson considered saving di Borgo to be important. So he said very firmly words he doubted anyone on the ship would ever have expected to hear from a man well known for disobedience.

'Gentlemen, I have my orders, and I fear they must take precedence over whatever individual wishes we may have. Please do as I ask and hope taking our soldiers aboard will be seen as strengthening our numbers for boarding. But as soon as we have the bullocks, we will depart the bay and make all speed for Elba. Mr Williams, set us a course please.'

'The other vessel, sir?' asked Worricker.

'If he shapes to impede us, we will act accordingly, but I strongly suspect, having seen what's just occurred, he'll give *Hazard* a wide berth. He'll be more intent on seeing to the needs of his damaged superior to worry about us.'

Which proved to be the case. Vickery, being told of what was intended and knowing there was no possibility of reloading the cannon into *Hazard* before leaving the shore, had packed his old cannon with the remaining powder, jamming in every wad he possessed. He then employed all the slow match left over to set a long trail to the touchholes so when they went off, he and his men were well away. The result was obvious even to those aboard ship: the muzzles blew apart with such force they utterly destroyed everything in front, setting alight all the gathered brushwood.

This was still burning when *Hazard* made the narrows, leaving an opponent drifting into the northern bay, to find the other enemy vessel had withdrawn out to sea to a point where it was clearly not planning to engage. So the cannon were housed, all sail necessary was set, and HMS *Hazard* showed them a clean pair of heels as she headed north.

They arrived in Portoferraio to find the transports alongside the quay and already loading de Burgh's troops and equipment. The place was full of bustle, as there were masses of naval stores to either be removed or destroyed, the former being decanted into *Blanche* and *Inconstant*.

Pearce went abroad *Minerve*, happy to obey the request to ship his passengers to a transport vessel, make up his wood and water if needed, and be prepared to weigh at dawn. Once Nelson had read his report, he commended Pearce on his decisions, confirming that getting di Borgo off the island had a great deal to do with future British intentions.

'Be assured, Mr Pearce, this is a temporary departure, for I'm sure their Lordships have every intention of sending a fleet back to the Mediterranean. As for holding off from a fight, it is sometimes required. We'll seek to avoid trouble ourselves on the way home, given the responsibilities we are required to shepherd.'

It was indeed an uneventful voyage, even the weather favouring them. HMS *Hazard* was again ahead of the flotilla to look out for trouble, but this time so Nelson could take action to avoid an encounter. And naturally Cartagena was given a wide berth. It was with mixed feelings that John Pearce espied the misty tip of the Rock, but it was he who led the ships in—giving the required signal to the flagship, when he'd rather stick up two fingers towards Jervis—to anchor where instructed by the harbour master.

The first task was to send a boat ashore to collect the mail, he choosing to go with it in case there had been any developments regarding his court martial, nothing being said to indicate there were. The sack for *Hazard* was quite bulky, so none of what he collected was opened until he was back aboard and it was distributed. Then he settled down to read what was a serial reply to the many missives he'd sent home to Emily.

He wasn't settled for long: the words 'droits of the Crown' leapt off the page and had him sitting forward and cursing, likewise those from Alexander Davidson who told the same tale. The actions of Langholm, when he read what the man had been about, did nothing to calm his mood; if anything, it was made worse. As to Davidson's asking permission to pursue the case in the Admiralty court, Pearce immediately decided to grant the request.

'Damn cheek,' he said out loud. 'And when we win, I'll buy a seat in parliament and make their lives a misery.'

But the real letters he wanted to concentrate on were those from his lover, coming as they did with the smell of her scent. There was no anger in reading these: how could there be, when they were full of delightful tales of the antics of his growing son?

To be continued . . .

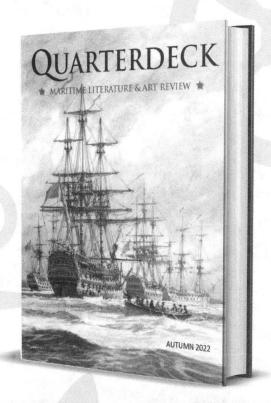